Eileen Townsend is the
novels *Of Woman Born* a
husband Colin Townsend s
personal stories of women

Born in Scotland, she s
Cumbria. She is an MA graduate in Modern History and
Political Science, and divides her time between her homes in
Scotland and the north-west of England.

By the same author

In Love and War
Of Woman Born

War Wives (with Colin Townsend)

The Love Child

EILEEN TOWNSEND

GraftonBooks
A Division of HarperCollins*Publishers*

GraftonBooks
A Division of HarperCollins*Publishers*
77–85 Fulham Palace Road,
Hammersmith, London W6 8JB

Published by GraftonBooks 1991
9 8 7 6 5 4 3 2 1

First published in Great Britain by
GraftonBooks 1990

ISBN 0–586–20891–7

Printed in Great Britain by
HarperCollinsManufacturing Glasgow

Phototypeset by Computape (Pickering) Ltd, North Yorkshire

BOOK ONE

The Valediction

───────────

If we must part,
Then let it be like this;
Not heart on heart,
Nor with the useless anguish of a kiss;
But touch mine hand and say:
'Until tomorrow or some other day.'
If we must part.

Words are so weak
When love hath been so strong:
Let silence speak:
'Life is a little while, and love is long;
A time to sow and reap,
And after harvest a long time to sleep.'
But words are weak.

Ernest Dowson

Chapter One

A small knot of passers-by clustered around the lighted window of Koehn's department store on the Unter den Linden, and the squeals of delight of the young women in the crowd were audible to the teenage girl who stood looking down on them from the apartment above. She knew exactly what was causing the commotion: the fabulous musquash coat that had pride of place was an exact replica of the one ordered by the Propaganda Minister Joseph Goebbels for his beautiful blonde wife, Magda. '*Wie schön … Wie wunderschön!*'

The exclamations from below echoed those of Goebbels himself in the memory of Martin Koehn's only daughter, Eva: the young woman gave a wry smile as she recalled her summons to the private apartment in the Reichstag the previous week to model the original of that sumptuous garment in person.

She had been called upon to model many such garments as surprise presents for ministers' wives – and, she suspected, girlfriends – over the past few months. Everyone told her what a great honour it was, not only for herself but for the whole family, that their store should be the one most favoured by those in the highest echelons of government for their personal purchases. Even their great leader Adolf Hitler had, on one memorable occasion last May, summoned her to model a selection of the latest summer dresses. It had been whispered she was the exact height and build of his longtime companion, Eva Braun, although she had never actually set eyes on the young woman in question.

But memorable though it had been, that auspicious occasion had not filled her with the joy she knew her friends would have experienced in the presence of the man they called the saviour of their nation. Her heart had not leapt as she knew it should have when those mesmeric blue eyes had looked into her own. Sometimes she felt she must be the only young woman in the whole country who had failed to respond to their Führer's legendary charm.

She closed the heavy velvet drapes with a sigh, shutting out the noise and glitter of lights from down below and glanced across at her mother who had been unusually quiet all afternoon. 'They are still at it down there – admiring Frau Goebbels' coat!'

But Margarete Koehn's thoughts were not on the proud possessor of that beautiful coat: they were far too preoccupied with the impending actions of Dr Goebbels himself. 'Something will happen this night, I can feel it in my bones.'

Her eyes were troubled as she carefully folded the embroidered teacloth and placed it back in its drawer. The *Deutschlandsender* news bulletin she had listened to on the radio earlier that day was still repeating in her head. Vom Rath, the German diplomat shot two days previously by a young Polish Jew, had died. Dr Goebbels was reportedly not amused, and firm reprisals were being called for – action that very day, in fact. The hysteria that was being whipped up against the Jews seemed to be reaching fever pitch. She shuddered visibly and gave voice to her fears. 'There will be a penalty to be paid for the death of that Nazi in Paris, and it will be paid by Jews everywhere – but especially here in Berlin.'

Eva looked startled. 'You're not still brooding about a silly radio broadcast, are you? They are always ranting about the Jews these days, it's nothing new.'

'It's more than a silly broadcast, as you put it. Much more. I tell you, Eva, the Jews in this city and all over Germany have real cause to worry over this shooting. It's just the

8

excuse the government has been looking for to crack down even harder on them.'

Eva was silent. She too had been deeply troubled by the hatred directed against the country's Jewish population. With each passing day they seemed to be subjected to even more vilification. Those that had not already emigrated to escape the contempt heaped upon them were suffering terrible degradations. To have any trace of Jewish blood at all in your family tree was considered a terrible misfortune. People were losing their homes and their jobs because of it. 'We can only thank God we had the good fortune to be born Lutheran,' she said quietly. 'At least no one can accuse us of being Jews.'

Her mother looked at her – a long, pitying look. Her daughter was eighteen years old; no longer a child, yet not quite a woman; a delicately-featured creature with wide-set gentle eyes and a nature that refused to comprehend the things that were going on all around them. Dreadful things were happening that made Margarete herself long for the security of the Germany of her own youth – the Kaiser's Germany where, despite the traumas of the Great War, you really did believe the '*Gott Mit Uns*' motto of the Prussian royal family that every German soldier carried into battle with him. But where was God now? Was He still with the German people? She looked across at her daughter. To speak of her fears to her would be to rob her of something very precious – the idealism of youth. She was at the frontier of womanhood, but had still not quite crossed over. She still believed in the ultimate goodness of human beings; perhaps that was the difference.

'What is it, *Mutti*? What's troubling you today?' Eva sat down heavily in the nearest armchair and looked across anxiously at her mother. She could not believe it was simply the news from Paris that was preying on her mind. Her mother was never one to take much notice of political rhetoric. There must be some other reason behind her troubled expression. 'It's nothing to do with *Vati*, is it? There's nothing wrong with the business?'

Margarete Koehn shook her head and attempted a reassuring smile. 'No, *Liebchen*, there's nothing wrong with *Vati* – or the business.' At least nothing I could possibly tell you, she might have added. There were some things it was impossible to speak of, even with those we loved the most – some things we wished with all our hearts that we ourselves did not know; things that lay heavy on the soul and came back to haunt us – in the small hours of the night when sleep would not come, and at moments such as this, when a news bulletin on the radio could turn a perfectly ordinary day into a time of apprehension and fear.

Her eyes travelled to the picture on the wall above the delft-tiled stove. An old man stared back down at her, an old man with dark eyes that twinkled beneath shaggy white brows, and with curling white side-whiskers and moustaches that could not disguise the proud smile on the lips beneath. Friedrich 'Fritz' Koehn had had every reason to be proud – just as she, his daughter-in-law, now had every reason to be afraid. It was true that Koehn was an old, respected Germanic name, but one only had to go back just over sixty years to find that things may not always be as they seem. The young man in his twenties who arrived on the streets of Berlin as the Aryan Friedrich Koehn had, in fact, left his native Pomerania as the Jew Efarim Cohen. Even the thought of the name sent an involuntary shiver of fear through his daughter-in-law's frame.

But at the time of his arrival in the 1870s, just after Bismarck's glorious defeat of the French at Sedan, no one in the Prussian capital was particularly interested in Jews. It was towards the Catholics that old Otto, the Chancellor, was directing his venom, so no one took much notice, or asked many questions about the young man who set up his stall alongside the others at one of the many outdoor markets that peppered the side streets off the Unter den Linden. Neither

10

did they think it remarkable that less than ten years later he had married the only daughter of one of those store owners on the Unter den Linden that he so admired. And within a generation he had changed the name proclaimed in gold above the shop door from Aldermann to *Friedrich Koehn und Sohn*.

But it was remarkable, all right. Remarkable that no one in the changed climate of Hitler's Germany had sought to investigate the family's past. The families who owned the best department stores in Berlin were a competitive breed and the faintest hint of Jewishness in one's *Stammbaum* did not usually go undetected for long. Even those who could claim a family tree dating back to Frederick the Great and beyond had been known to have whispers directed at them from behind the clinking coffee-cups of the ladies' *Kaffee-kränzchen*, or over the cognac and cigars of the smoking rooms in the best *Herrenklubs*. No one, it seemed, was above suspicion these days.

Margarete Koehn closed the dresser drawer and thought of the old lady lying upstairs in bed – her mother-in-law, Claudia Koehn, née Aldermann, Fritz's wife. It was Claudia who had confided in her less than a week ago that the family had Jewish origins: a secret that in the days since had lain heavy on Margarete's heart. Not even her husband Martin knew the truth, far less their only child, Eva, and that made it all the harder to bear. It had been a conscious decision taken by Fritz even before Claudia had given birth to Martin. What the child did not know could never hurt him, Fritz Koehn had resolved. He had buried his Jewishness in the far lands of Pomerania, along with the bodies of his own mother and father: the memory of that last pogrom had burned a wound so deep on his soul that he had vowed his own son would grow to manhood according to the laws of the Christian Bible. Adherence to the Talmud brought nothing but suffering in this world. His own child would never be subjected to the sight of a crazed mob attacking his home and massacring his parents.

11

'Be a good girl and run upstairs and see if your grandmother has finished with her coffee, Eva, *Liebchen*. I'll ring for Rosa to clear up in here.'

Eva got up soundlessly from the armchair and left the room, the strained look on her mother's face still disconcerting her. It took a lot for *Mutti* to be downhearted, but the news they had heard on the radio a few hours ago, for some reason, had depressed her more than usual. Surely the killing of a Nazi official in Paris by a young Polish Jew had little to do with them here in Berlin? Many of the Jewish families they knew had already sold up and left the city, and those that remained had stayed because they maintained they were as good Germans as any one – and who could deny that? Hadn't her friend Annaliese Goldmann's father won the Iron Cross in the Great War? And Lotte Blumenthal's family had been bankers in this city for over two hundred years. No one could accuse them of not being true patriots of the Fatherland. No one could surely imagine terrible reprisals would be meted out to the likes of them just because of an incident in Paris, of all places?

Their maid, Rosa, passed her on the stairs and the two young women exchanged tight smiles. They were almost the same age, but Eva had little time for the scrawny young woman from Gatow, who had been a keen member of the *Deutsche Jungmädel* – the League of Young German Girls – from her early teens. Rosa's proud boast was of being one of the original 'March Violets', who joined the organization at its inception on 1 March 1933, and, like most of its other founder members, she had now moved on to greater glory within its big sister organization, the *Bund Deutscher Mädel*, and the Reich Youth Leadership programme.

Their Führer's clarion call to the youth of Germany held little appeal for Eva, however, and she could raise almost no enthusiasm for the photographs Rosa brought back with her that summer from the national rally for BDM leaders held at Bamberg.

12

Even her first uniform: the white blouse, black skirt, and black scarf kept in place around her neck with its brown leather ring, had not thrilled her as it had most of her classmates at the Gymnasium. And the oath to 'promise always to do my duty to the Hitler Youth, in love and loyalty to the Führer' had stuck in her throat as she had chorused it in front of the raised flag with the others in her group. She had no love for that Austrian upstart, no matter how much he was doing to bring down unemployment and give the people back their pride after their bitter defeat in the last war. Neither had she any respect for the young thugs in Nazi or Hitler Youth uniform whom she watched from their apartment windows, marching down the Unter den Linden behind their red and black banners, or taunting the Jews that remained on the streets of their capital city.

No, she had joined the Hitler Youth because there had been little or no choice at the Empress Friedrich Gymnasium for Girls, where she had studied with Annaliese and Lotte, until her friends had been forced to leave the school – deemed not fit to take lessons alongside examples of true Aryan young womanhood such as herself and her other two best friends, Hanna Kessel and Karin Gross.

And it was just such acts that had made her a less than enthusiastic member of the BDM; in fact, she had not attended a meeting for almost two weeks now. They would be on to her soon – the Rosa Schultzes of the organization – and she would be forced to do penance in front of them all for failing to display sufficient loyalty to the Führer and Fatherland.

But enough of these depressing thoughts for one day! Her grandmother's bedroom door was slightly ajar and Eva gave three light taps on the panelled wood. 'It's me, *Oma* – Eva.'

'Come in, child!'

The room smelt of lavender from the lace-trimmed pomanders that hung from pale blue ribbons over the wooden bed-ends, and of 4711 *eau-de-cologne* from the liberal helpings of *Kölnisch Wasser* with which the old lady doused her daintily-embroidered handkerchiefs. She waved one at her approaching granddaughter. 'The door, *mein Schatz*! Close the door behind you. The draughts in this old place will be the death of me!'

A small fire flickered in the grate to the right of the bed, but it made scant impression on the chill of the room – a room that never failed to send a thrill of pleasure through Eva's slim body, no matter how often she crossed the well-waxed threshold. This bedchamber, this most sacrosanct of places, was a paean in polished wood and satin drapes to the old lady who was now *Oma* Koehn, but who as the infant Claudia Aldermann had actually been born in this very bed over eighty years before.

It was a room straight out of Imperial Berlin, with its carved and gilded furniture and plush upholstery; a room that paid no homage to the present Berlin of Adolf Hitler's Third Reich – and no more did its occupant.

An arched, gilt-framed mirror hung above the cream tiled stove and reflected the pale beam of watery November sunshine that filtered through the gap between the lace curtains of the window opposite. Plush, dusky-pink drapes of heavy satin framed the net, to fall all of four metres to skirt the polished wood surround of the floor, and the same delicate pink colour was repeated in the background to the overblown, ivory tea-roses that covered the walls. On top of the floral wallpaper hung several oil paintings of scenes of the nineteenth-century Berlin of her grandmother's childhood, and a black and white print of Dürer's praying hands hung on long cords above the ornamental headboard of the bed. Claudia Koehn's own family had been committed Lutherans and she herself never began or ended a day without addressing '*Unser Vater in dem Himmel*'.

On the carved shelves of the dressing-table, two Meissen shepherdesses, as delicate and fragile in appearance as their owner, tended their sheep alongside a collection of family

14

photographs. Pride of place, in the largest silver frame, was given to her husband, friend, and lover of almost half a century, Eva's grandfather, Fritz Koehn.

Oma herself lay in the centre of the enormous bed, a frail figure in a lacy angora bed-jacket, her cloud of white hair held back from her face to hang in two wispy plaits over her shoulders. She held out a bird-like hand to her grand-daughter. 'Eva, *Liebchen* …' She patted the cream satin of the quilt. 'Sit down and tell me what you intend doing with yourself this evening!' Her voice was still strong and vibrant, in contrast to her fragile frame.

Eva obeyed, perching with one hip on the high mattress as she clasped the proffered hand in her own; the skin felt paper-thin and cold to the touch. 'I promised I'd go round to Hannalore's, *Oma*. We're practising for the church recital on Sunday.'

Her grandmother smiled. 'You and your precious choir!' But she was pleased, nevertheless. Music had been the love of her own young life, and to see history repeat itself in the form of her granddaughter's beautiful contralto voice was one of the few real joys she had left. Then the smile faded. 'Are you sure it's wise?'

'Wise?' Eva looked puzzled. 'Hanna's expecting me. Why shouldn't it be wise?'

Her grandmother retrieved her hand and dabbed a scented handkerchief to her nose. 'It's probably only Rosa exaggerating again, but she tells me there will be trouble before the night is out. Some nonsense to do with that Nazi shot in Paris the other day … Her young man has been telling her that Goebbels ordered reprisals against the Jews if vom Rath died, and now she claims they've announced on the radio today that he's dead. Didn't you hear?'

Eva shrugged and shook her head. Rosa Schultz's young man was a Brownshirt with a face like the pig she knew him to be. Whatever he had to say she would take with a very big pinch of salt indeed. Anyway, why was everyone making such a fuss about such a trivial incident? Her grandmother wasn't making any sense. '*Mutti* did say something about it. I think she must have heard it on the news. But what has that to do with me? How will rounding up a few more of the Jewish community possibly affect me?'

There was a long pause as the old lady looked at her grandchild. The shoulder-length hair was as blonde as any true German's, only the eyes were different. While her own were as blue as summer skies over the Wannsee, her grand-daughter's were as dark a brown as those of her beloved husband, and Eva's grandfather, Fritz Koehn. Yes, Fritz had eyes that in certain lights could look as black as jet, and after his death that rich darkness lived on in his granddaughter. They were eyes that, more than any identity card, spoke of the race from which he had sprung. And it was the dark eyes of the people of the Holy Land that looked at her now from across the bed – an anxious look that expressed the confusion within. The old lady shivered, but not with cold. She feared for this child – for that was what Eva would always be to her, a beloved and much treasured child. She feared for her out there this night. There was evil in the air in this city. An evil such as she had never known in all her eight decades as a Berliner.

'*Oma* – are you all right?'

The old lady blinked and shook herself. Old age must be making her nervous. In her young days she was afraid of neither man nor beast – and would certainly not be intimi-dated by the illegitimate offspring of an Austrian *Putzfrau* and his thuggish supporters …

But Germany had come down a long, troubled road since they got rid of the Kaiser, and who could blame anyone for being apprehensive as to where it would lead? She shook her head and leaned over to pat her granddaughter's hand. 'Just take care tonight, *Liebchen*. Be careful – promise your *Oma* that. If there's any sign of trouble at all, you'll get one of Hanna's brothers to bring you straight home?'

16

'I promise.' Eva leaned over and brushed her lips lightly against the dry, wrinkled skin of her grandmother's cheek. 'Now I'd better go ... *Mutti* was asking for your cup and plate, if you've finished.'

A last morsel of *Topfkuchen* lay on the table next to the empty coffee cup, and the old lady popped it into her mouth. 'My own mother, bless her heart, used to say that rich cakes would be the death of me, but, if that's right, then I'll die happy – is that not so, *Liebchen*?'

The pale blue eyes twinkled as she handed the empty plate and cup to her granddaughter. Eva smiled in return. Claudia Koehn had already enjoyed many more years than her allotted span, and everyone knew she fully intended to go on enjoying many more yet.

Her mother was standing by the drawing-room window when Eva arrived back downstairs. She had drawn back the curtains and the window was open slightly; her curly fringe of greying hair was ruffled from the draught. Her face was turned from her daughter and concentrated on a four-columned procession of brownshirted young men marching down the middle of the road behind a red and white banner bearing a black swastika. Several late shoppers paused to applaud from the kerbside as the procession, heads held high, passed by and the traffic on either side made way for them. Their voices carried up on the breeze:

> *'Wir marschieren für Hitler*
> *durch Nacht und durch Not,*
> *für die Fahne und Freiheit,*
> *für Leben und Brot ...'*

Eva saw a shiver run through her mother's body and for the first time felt the chill of fear in her own heart, although about what she could not be quite sure.

Her eyes moved to an embroidered sampler, done by her grandmother as a child, that hung on the wall by the

17

window. It was a quote from Bismarck: '*Wir Deutschen fürchten Gott, aber sonst niemand*' ...

'We Germans fear God, but no one else,' she repeated softly. Suddenly those words had an ironic ring. Could it be that was no longer true? Could it be that Germans were now fearing other Germans themselves?

She joined her mother at the window and clasped her hand as she used to do as a small child when in need of comfort. Together they watched the column disappear into the distance in the direction of the Brandenburg Gate. 'What's happening to us, *Mutti*? What's happening to our country?'

Margarete Koehn had no answer.

Chapter Two

The November evening was clear, with a hint of frost in the air, as Eva made her way along the Unter den Linden to the corner of Friedrich Strasse, the street on which her friend Hannalore Kessel's family lived.

In the distance loomed the floodlit arch of the Brandenburg Gate, with the winged goddess of Peace, at the reins of her chariot of Victory, astride the massive centre-span. The monument was the pride of her city, but somehow it never failed to send a shudder through her. They claimed the bronze statue represented Peace, but to her the goddess symbolized all that was warlike about Berlin, this ancient Prussian capital that now dominated the whole of Germany.

Music was coming from the Café Kranzler on the corner of the two streets – the spot where the well-heeled young men about town went to be seen with their fashionable girlfriends. Eva glanced inside the lighted windows at the people sitting beneath the glittering chandeliers, and at the waitresses, dressed in black with white starched aprons, who scurried across the plush red carpet bearing trays laden with drinks. She longed for the day when she too could sip wine, or a glass of *Weisse mit Schuss* from one of the foaming goblets, and talk of the cabaret they were about to see that evening. She had been there often enough during the day with her mother or grandmother, to sip coffee from the delicate white porcelain cups, but that was not the same. That could never be the same as spending an evening in there with a young man.

She was eighteen and had never had a proper boyfriend.

She could blame her father for that. Martin Koehn was exceptionally protective where his only daughter was concerned. He had made it quite clear that any young man she had the slightest interest in must first be brought home to obtain his personal seal of approval before the friendship went any further, and up to now Eva had lacked the courage to put anyone through such an ordeal. Not that she had anyone particular in mind. The closest thing she had to a boyfriend was one of Hanna's older brothers, Kurt Kessel, and that had not gone beyond the occasional walk home after one of their musical evenings at the Kessels' apartment.

Hannalore's father, Max Kessel, ran one of Berlin's most successful cabaret and beerhalls, on the Friedrich Strasse, and the family lived above the premises. It was an occupation looked down upon by Eva's own family, who regarded such goings-on with some distaste. Not so *Oma*, however, who would recount with relish how she and *Opa*, Eva's grandfather Fritz Koehn, had visited the Moulin Rouge itself during their honeymoon in Paris over half a century earlier.

Music and laughter filled Eva's ears as she passed the open doorways of several other cabaret clubs on her way to the apartment above the Kessels' place, *Der Goldene Engel*. Hanna's father loved to claim that the nightclub in Marlene Dietrich's famous film was named after his establishment, only they changed the name to *The Blue Angel* to avoid paying him any royalties. Eva could only speculate as to the truth of such a claim, but it was typical of the man, and that was the reason she so loved these visits; the Kessels added a spice to life that was sadly lacking in her own loving but very bourgeois home.

A young man in a black evening cape, silk opera hat and cane was arguing with a fur-coated young woman on the pavement outside *Der Goldene Engel* when Eva arrived. He was obviously being overcharged for the anticipated pleasure of her company and was taking violent exception to the fact. '*Hure!*' The insult reached more than the prostitute's ears as

20

Eva hurried past and in through the side door that divided the Kessels' private quarters from the main public entrance.

The stone staircase was well-lit but had a dank, chill air to it. The bottom half of the walls was decorated with olive-green tiles, and above them Frau Kessel had hung several rather crudely executed oil paintings of her native Bavaria. 'To add a touch of class', Hanna had once informed her, and Eva had made no comment.

The door was answered immediately by Frau Kessel herself, a small, rotund woman with frizzy dark hair pulled back in a bun, and pale eyes of an indeterminate colour that blinked at you from behind thick pebble spectacles. She wore an ankle-length gown of a fine black woolcloth and several long strings of pearls bedecked the well-upholstered bosom. The bronze Mothers' Cross of Honour, awarded by the Führer for bearing her five children, was pinned to the high, frilled collar at her neck. Her face above it was flushed. 'Oh, Eva, it's only you ... Come in, child. They are all in the drawing-room. You won't mind seeing yourself through? I have had to prepare *Abendbrot* for more than a dozen tonight – and still they come!'

Eva looked puzzled. Usually there were only three or four of them at these choir practices, which were unofficial and more of an excuse for a get-together and a chat than anything else. There was no time for questions, however, as she followed Hanna's mother through the tiled hallway.

The sound of singing was coming from behind the closed drawing-room door. Male voices.

'They're all in there,' Frau Kessel said. 'Let yourself in, and I'll bring some more food. It's going to be a long night for the boys once they set out, from what I've heard.'

Eva opened the door and almost closed it again instantly. The room was full of young men in the uniform of the Hitler Youth. All were gathered round the Bechstein at the other end of the room, singing as if their lives depended on it. The song was instantly recognizable. It was less than three hours since she had stood at the window of their apartment on the Unter den Linden with her mother and heard it sung. It was the hymn of the Hitler Youth, and never had she heard it performed with more gusto:

> 'Vorwärts, vorwärts, schmettern die hellen Fanfaren
> Vorwärts, vorwärts, Jugend kennt keine Gefahren
> Deutschland wird noch fortbestehen,
> werden wir auch untergehen …'

As they sang, Eva's eyes travelled around the room. A red, black and white banner of the Hitler Youth stood furled against one wall, alongside a garishly coloured painting of the Virgin Mary and the infant Jesus – a reminder of the Bavarian Frau Kessel's Roman Catholic upbringing.

On the other side of the holy picture there leant a placard bearing a poster of the Führer. Hitler's left fist was clenched, while his right held on high a swastika banner; his mouth and jaw were grimly set, and the wind was blowing his hair against a glowering grey sky. Behind him was a sea of SA men and, above them, like the Holy Spirit descending, was a German eagle in the epicentre of a sunburst.

Eva's eyes remained riveted on their leader's face as his young followers continued to swear their allegiance in song. At the end of the fourth verse there was an almighty cheer, followed by three more for the Flag, the Führer and the Fatherland.

'Come in, Eva! Come in!' It was Hanna's voice from somewhere in the room.

Eva glanced apprehensively through the uniformed crowd to see her friend turn to say something to their classmate Karin Gross, who was seated in an easy-chair against the back wall, with her young brother Rudi perched wide-eyed on its arm beside her. The youngster often accompanied his big sister to their musical get-togethers, but from the looks on both their faces it was obvious neither was expecting such an event as this tonight.

Eva raised a hand in greeting and took a tentative step forwards from the doorway as Hanna began to push her way through the pack of young men towards her.

'You're just in time for the Dagger Words!' Hanna whispered as she took Eva's hand and led her to the corner opposite the piano where Karin and young Rudi were seated. The boy's blue eyes were wide with wonder and not a little apprehension as he watched the older members of his sex assemble for their sacred ritual.

'It'll soon be your turn,' Eva whispered to him. 'You'll be eleven just after Christmas, won't you?'

The comment brought a grimace from the child at her elbow. He was in no hurry to join this brownshirted band of brothers who seemed to spend their lives marching through the streets and singing songs, and who idolized the man most detested by his father.

'Aren't you looking forward to joining the Hitler Youth, Rudi?' Eva asked in surprise at his reaction.

'Ssh … They're about to swear …' Hanna hissed, anxious her friends should not spoil the event.

Eva and Karin exchanged glances, and Rudi shrank back further on the arm of the chair as Hanna put an admonishing finger to her lips and nodded severely in the direction of the action about to take place before them.

At that, a tall young man Eva recognized as Hanna's eldest brother Paul stepped forwards and laid his dagger on a white handkerchief on the table in front of the assembled crowd. Symbolically he laid his right hand on the hilt of the weapon, then, in unison, the young men chorused the words: 'Endurance, courage, loyalty, bearing, truth, comradeship and honour!' A rousing cheer followed, then all male arms in the room shot forwards in the Fascist salute.

Then Paul Kessel reached over and lifted his stein from the table and held it high. In a voice charged with emotion he proclaimed, *'Führer, Volk und Vaterland!'*

The salute was repeated with raised steins and a united

chorus of young male voices throughout the room, as Eva turned to Hanna. Her friend had tears of emotion in her eyes.

The ceremony was followed by an excited buzz of conversation, and the three girls, followed by young Rudi, made their way over to the damask-covered table on which was spread an array of *Butterbrote*, cakes and biscuits, and several tall flagons of *Schultheiss* beer.

'I can't remember such an excitement since the Olympics two years ago, can you?' Hanna handed her friends a plate of sliced *Sandkuchen*. 'Paul, Maxi and Karl are all taking part tonight. Only Kurt is staying at home. He says he has a cold, but Paul claims it's a diplomatic one.' Hanna made a face as she bit into the cake. 'He doesn't like to be in uniform, that's Kurt's trouble ... *Du lieber Gott!* If we girls were allowed to take part tonight I'd be thrilled to bits!'

'Take part in what?' Karin said, puzzled. 'What on earth's going on this evening?'

Hanna could not disguise her surprise. 'You mean you haven't heard?'

'Heard what?'

'About vom Rath's death, of course. They say the Führer's furious, and there are to be great demonstrations tonight all over Germany. And the biggest of all here in Berlin.' The last sentence was added with some pride.

Karin raised her eyebrows. 'That's news to me. What about you, Eva? Have you heard of this pantomime?' The Gross family were staunch Socialists but, even among friends, seldom made public their distaste for what they regarded as Nazi peacock displays.

Eva shook her head as she swallowed a mouthful of cake and accepted a glass of beer from Frau Kessel who had reappeared to make sure no one was going without. Eva took a sip of the drink, her brows furrowing. 'Just what are they supposed to be demonstrating about?' She too was genuinely puzzled. Was this what her mother was so agitated

24

about tonight? She had never even heard of vom Rath until a couple of days ago. It seemed that the diplomat's death in Paris was assuming ridiculous proportions.

'Not about,' Hanna corrected. 'Against. They're to demonstrate against the Jews. That Polish Jew – I forget his name – who murdered our man in Paris was part of a much greater conspiracy. A world conspiracy, so they say – and the Führer wants us to show them that they won't get away with it. We must show them that we know what they're up to and won't allow it. No one can murder our people and get away with it.'

Eva and Karin stared at her in incredulity. She sounded just like Frau Winkler, the physical education mistress at school, who took every opportunity to regale them with a recital of the Party's polemic against the Jews.

'You don't really believe that stuff, do you?' Eva said, aghast. 'You don't really think the Jews are a threat – not any more, surely?'

There were hardly any Jews left in Berlin – not in positions of authority anyway. Their professions, their property, their businesses – all had already been, or were in the process of being, taken away from them. They had almost nothing left – not even their dignity. Had she forgotten about Annaliese and Lotte and what had happened to them? And old Doctor Fischer who wasn't allowed to treat his Aryan patients any more, after almost fifty years of devoted service to the community? 'Are you really serious?' Eva's distaste at what she had just heard was obvious.

Hanna avoided her eyes. 'Well, I can't claim to be an expert on the cause of all the troubles in this country, but Paul swears it's true – and he knows much more about these things than I do. Than you do too, come to that.'

Eva glanced across at her friend's eldest brother. Paul Kessel was a prime example of young German manhood, with his tall, blond good looks and clear blue eyes. Hanna herself took after their mother, being below average height, plump and dark. But, more than any of her other three brothers, Paul had been the object of Hanna's adoration since childhood. Not so to Eva, however, who much preferred the gentler, younger Kurt.

'What have the others to say about it?' Karin put in.

'Maxi and Karl couldn't care less.'

'And Kurt?'

Hanna made a face at Eva's question. 'Paul tells Kurt, if he doesn't keep his mouth shut, someone will shut it for him!'

'He doesn't agree, then?'

Hanna gave a furtive glance around to make sure no one was listening, then whispered, 'Kurt reads *that Jew*!'

'*That Jew*?' Eva found herself whispering back.

'Marx – Karl Marx … The one whose books they burned.' As thirteen-year-old members of the League of Young German Girls, they had gone together to the ceremony at the Opernplatz, in May 1933, where a huge bonfire had been made of the newly forbidden literature, most of it written by Jews. 'You remember …'

'Yes, yes, I know,' Eva cut in. Karl Marx – 'the greatest Jew since Jesus Christ', her *Opa* Koehn had called him – and he himself had been as ardent a Capitalist as they came!

Karin remained silent. Her own family had enough *verboten* literature about the place to have them all locked up and the keys thrown away.

'Kurt has got an old copy of *Das Kapital* hidden under his mattress. I know because I've seen it!' Hanna continued in a shocked whisper.

Eva glanced at Karin who made no comment, but whose features had assumed a frozen expression. 'It's a crime to be a Communist now. Everyone knows that. They lock them up, you know.' Contrary to his sister's intention, Kurt Kessel was going up in Eva's estimation by the minute. Not that she knew much about Communism. Her family was too absorbed in their business to discuss the merits of another political system. The fact that Kurt had the courage to think for himself, and not swallow everything the Party told him, was enough to send his stock soaring in her eyes. 'They even lock up Social Democrats – and they're hardly the revolutionary type!' She turned to Karin. 'Your *Vati* has spent quite a bit of time in prison since Hitler came to power, hasn't he, Karin?'

Karin nodded, grim-faced, but made no comment, and Hanna looked pensive. She loved all her brothers and the thought of one of them being taken off to any of those dreaded concentration camps was a sobering notion. Her brow furrowed at such a black thought, then her attention was diverted by a commotion at the other end of the room as, banner and placard held aloft, the group began to prepare to leave.

'There's a frost out there this evening,' Eva heard Frau Kessel say to no one in particular. 'They'll be chilled to the bone in those short trousers!'

And it was true. The Hitler Youth uniform was certainly more suited to summer wear than a cold evening in late autumn, but even Eva could not deny they made an impressive sight. Most were around her own age, and only one or two were under six feet in height. Germany's future, they called them; the Führer's pride and joy.

They marched out singing the old German marching song, *'Ich hat einen Kameraden ...'*, and Eva turned to her friend Karin and whispered, 'If they'd sung that awful Hitler Youth anthem again, I think I'd have screamed!'

Karin smiled her first genuine smile since Eva's arrival, but Hanna pointedly ignored the remark. She too was caught up in the spirit of things and took exception to her friend's comment. 'You seem in a strange mood tonight, Eva. You make it sound as if you think there's something shameful in being patriotic.'

'Do I?' Eva had never really analysed her feelings on that subject properly before. It was true she had little time for all the dressing up in uniform and marching that every young German was obliged to go in for these days. Such people as

Frau Winkler at school bored her more than anything else with their constant talk of Strength through Joy, and service to the Fatherland. But did it go deeper than that? Did she really believe there was something shameful in being patriotic?

Hanna's eyes narrowed. 'It's always Kurt you've got on best with, isn't it? You wouldn't be a Communist yourself, by any chance?' The dreaded word was whispered with an expression akin to horror.

Eva laughed out loud. 'I'm not a Communist, a Socialist, or a Nazi, Hanna dear – I'm a human being. It's as simple as that!'

Her friend looked at her silently for a moment, then smiled and gave a resigned shrug. 'Come on then – *meine Menschenkinder*. We've got the piano to ourselves now. Let's make use of it!'

As Frau Kessel busied herself tidying away the food and drink, the three girls, accompanied by young Rudi, took turns to sit at the piano and play and sing all their favourite hymns, paying particular attention to '*Ein' feste Burg ist unser Gott*', and the other favourite pieces they would be singing at the church recital on Sunday.

When it came to Eva's turn to sing solo, young Rudi's bright blue eyes would grow an even more brilliant azure in hue. Apart from his sister Karin, Eva was the one female he adored more than any other.

'Isn't it unusual to have only the three of you practising – not forgetting our young gentleman here?' Frau Kessel interrupted the spirited 'Val-der-eee! Val-der-aaah! Val-der-ah-ha-ha-ha-ha-ha-ha! … Val-der-eee!' chorus of '*Mein Vater war ein Wandersmann*' to bring them a mug of hot chocolate at just after nine o'clock. 'At least Marianne, and one or two of your other classmates, usually turns up, but I think their mothers are probably anxious for them tonight. I was downstairs at the club a few moments ago and I hear tell from one of Max's "golden angels" that things are getting quite rough out there on the streets. It has probably something to do with Dr Goebbels' broadcast this evening.'

'What broadcast?' Eva asked. 'Is this something new from this afternoon's announcements?'

'Oh, yes. The minister was quite emphatic this evening. He announced, in the name of the Führer, that the German nation has undertaken to eliminate the enemies of the people. Instructions have now been given to take all male Jews into custody.'

All four young people stared at her. 'Eliminate the enemies of the people,' Hanna repeated, wide-eyed. 'Does that mean kill them?'

Frau Kessel gave a mystified shrug of the shoulders. 'Well, it sounds like it to me – doesn't it to you?'

'And arrest all male Jews?' Eva said, aghast at what she had just heard. 'Arrest them for what? Haven't they suffered enough already?'

'Don't blame me,' Frau Kessel replied impatiently, 'I'm only telling you what I heard on the *Deutschlandsender* tonight … And, like I said, that probably explains all that commotion going on in the street out there at the moment.'

The three friends glanced at one another, and Rudi looked anxiously at Frau Kessel; then Hanna ran to the window and pulled back the heavy drapes to look out. The street seemed much busier than usual, and a crowd had gathered a few hundred yards down towards the Unter den Linden. They seemed to be throwing things at one of the shops across the road.

Several members of the Hitler Youth were milling about down below, but most of the uniforms appeared to belong to the Stormtroopers, one or two of whom seemed to be doing a lot of shouting and giving orders. They were gesturing in the direction of the crowd gathered outside the shop opposite.

A bucket of white paint had been spilled on the pavement just outside the entrance to the Kessel apartment, and Hanna could just imagine what her mother was going to say when she saw it.

'Can you see anything?' It was Eva who spoke.

Hanna deliberately avoided looking down at the spilt paint and raised her eyes to the roof-tops. It was a clear, frosty night and the sky seemed to be interspersed with red glows, as if beacons had been lit across the city. Her mother joined her at the window.

'*Du lieber Gott*, what are all those fires? And what are they doing down the road at Mandel's?' Frau Kessel craned her neck to get a better look at the crowd gathering in front of the leather-goods shop across the road. 'I hope someone is keeping law and order down there tonight! Marching and demonstrations, Paul and the boys said. I hope some fools haven't let things get out of hand!'

She looked round at the two girls and young boy standing anxiously behind her. 'I'm surprised your fathers or someone hasn't come round to collect you young people yet. By the looks of it, it's not safe for any young person to be out there alone tonight.'

Eva nodded mutely, as a nervousness grew within her, but she remained seated at the piano. If there was trouble here on Friedrich Strasse, then you could be certain there would be even more on the Unter den Linden. She could not imagine why her father wasn't already hammering on the Kessels' door to take her home.

Karin reached out and gave Rudi's hand a comforting squeeze and, sensing their unease, Frau Kessel gave a reassuring smile. 'I wouldn't worry about it too much. Kurt's at home tonight. He's up there in his room nursing a cold, but he'll be glad to see you all back safely once you've had your hot chocolate.'

'*Mutti* – look at this!' Hanna almost screamed the words as she pulled her mother's arm back towards the window. 'Isn't that Herr Mandel down there!'

Frau Kessel's hand flew to her mouth as she gazed down

30

on the scene below. A crowd was dragging the elderly shopkeeper down the street; he was shoeless, and his bald head was bare; there was no sign of the little skull-cap he was never seen without.

'What are they doing?' Hanna gasped. 'The poor man! He has a bad heart, *Mutti*! He has a bad heart!'

'Yes, he has a bad heart.' Her mother's words were spoken in a whisper. Two heart attacks already. And no excitement, the doctor had said. 'A quiet life, Herr Mandel …'

As mother and daughter watched, clutching at each other now for support, their neighbour half-stumbled to the ground under the impact of a truncheon blow to the neck. His spectacles were missing and he wore no coat or jacket. His waistcoat was half torn off and hung over his one free arm which he was using in vain to fend off the blows that seemed to be coming from all directions. There could be no doubt that he had been forcibly dragged from his home. One could only imagine what had happened to his wife, his beloved Rosa …

A truncheon blow to the head felled him and he reeled back into the arms of a Stormtrooper, only to be hauled along on his knees by another. Small boys danced along around the fringes of the group chanting, *'Juden, 'raus! Juden, 'raus! Juden-Scheisse! Juden-Scheisse!'* in a sing-song chorus. For them, and for at least some of the passers-by, who applauded from the pavements, this was street theatre at its best.

'*Mutti* – we must do something!' Repelled, yet transfixed by the sight, Hanna could not tear her eyes from the scene as she spoke. 'He could die out there!'

But by this time the crowd and its hapless victim were already disappearing from view down the street. Most of those who had gathered around Herr Mandel's shop had already moved on, and for the first time they could see two large swastikas daubed in white paint on the walls. Where the windows had been were two great gaping holes on jagged glass. Leather cases and handbags from the window display lay strewn across the street.

'They said it was to be only demonstrations tonight!' Tears of bewilderment and horror welled in Hanna's eyes as she gazed almost accusingly at her mother. 'Those are not just demonstrations down there tonight. There is murder being committed on our streets, and my brothers are out there amongst those – those animals!'

Frau Kessel stood speechless beside her daughter, but had no words of comfort to offer. She turned with a helpless shrug to gaze at Eva who was still sitting on the piano stool, as if rooted to the spot. 'God help the Jews in this city tonight,' she said at last. 'May God help them, for no one else will!'

Chapter Three

'Hold my hand. Hold tight and don't let go!' Kurt Kessel reached out towards Eva as they made their way out of the street door leading from his parents' apartment to the crowded pavement beyond. He had just returned from seeing Karin and young Rudi home, and Eva had been aghast at how shaken he looked when he reappeared half an hour later to escort her back to her own home on the Unter den Linden.

From the next doorway the sound of laughter and singing came drifting up from the nightclub below, but here on the street the night air was filled with only the shouts of men. Stormtroopers were everywhere, some carrying large pots of white paint and brushes with which to daub the sign of the swastika on to Jewish property, others shouting obscenities about the Jews to whoever cared to listen.

A group marched past, led by a fat, bull-necked man Eva recognized as a local *Kreisleiter* by the name of Schleicher. His daughter had been in her class at school. Before his conversion to the Nazi cause he had been a ticket inspector on the railways; an ordinary man until, like so many others, he became mesmerized by Adolf Hitler. They were heading in the direction of the Unter den Linden and were chanting the words that had become synonymous with the Nazi regime: *'Ein Volk, ein Reich, ein Führer!'*

Kurt's grip on Eva's hand tightened and they paused, waiting for the column to pass before continuing in the same direction themselves.

The pavements were glistening with frost and slippery

underfoot, and Eva attempted to pick her way carefully past the spilt white paint that lay, still tacky, outside the street door to the Kessel apartment. Several members of the Hitler Youth came into view and she held on tighter to Kurt's hand at the sight of them. 'Shouldn't we go back in? They might be from your own group. They might see you.'

He turned to look at her. Her face was frighteningly pale in the yellowish-white light from the streetlamps, her dark eyes wide with fear. 'Let them see!' he answered through gritted teeth.

They neared Herr Mandel's leather-goods shop. Shards of broken glass sparkled alongside the frost on the road and pavement, and the smashed windows gaped open, like staring eyes, in the semi-darkness. The shop door, now smeared with a white swastika, hung grotesquely on its hinges. *'Deutsche! Wehrt euch! Kauft nicht bei Juden!'* The scrawled words exhorting Germans not to buy from Jewish shops disfigured the varnished wood. The door itself was propped open by a brass cash register, the drawer from which lay upside-down some yards away. They both glanced down at it as they passed. A few coins were scattered around it. No one had bothered to pick them up. It was not money but blood that was lusted after in this city tonight.

An open-backed, armoured truck roared past, making those in the middle of the road jump out of the way. Eva stared after it. It was driven by an armed SA man, with another riding guard in the back. The pale, drawn faces of the human cargo huddled together in the back of the truck stared back at her as the vehicle rattled over the cobbles. There were at least twenty men of varying ages and, by the look of them, all were Jews.

'Where do you think they are taking them?' Eva asked in a hoarse whisper. One of the huddled figures in the back had been only a boy; a boy with real fear in his eyes.

But Kurt could only shrug. 'Who knows?' It seemed

almost every district had its own special office for interrogating Jews these days.

The smell of burning wood was carried on the breeze in the crisp night air and all around them the sky was aglow across the city. 'They're burning the rats from their holes,' someone said, and Eva and Kurt had looked silently at one another.

Eva prayed inwardly it was only the synagogues that were ablaze, not private homes. The Jews had little enough left. Surely they couldn't deprive them of everything? Within seconds her unspoken question was answered. She stifled a horrified scream at the sight before them.

'*Um Gottes willen!*' Kurt pushed her behind him as they both gazed down, aghast, at the body of the old man sprawled on the pavement. The grizzled grey beard was saturated with blood that had oozed from the gaping wound on his forehead. It was just beginning to congeal. He had been clubbed to death.

Eva felt her legs go weak beneath her. 'I can't believe it,' she said faintly. 'Not here – not here in Berlin!' People didn't kill one another on these streets … this was what happened in uncivilized foreign countries. She stared down into the face of death, then turned her gaze to the familiar buildings of the street that she had known since childhood. Suddenly she was a stranger in her own land.

A small band of Hitler Youth passed by as they stood gazing at the prostrate body on the ground. The leader of the group aimed a kick at the dead man's foot; there was a hole in the sole of his shoe. Not all Jews were rich. His black hat was lying several feet away and they pounced on it, kicking it back and forth like a ball across the pavement.

'I'll never wear that uniform again,' Kurt vowed. And Eva believed him.

Inwardly she prayed that things might be better once they reached the Unter den Linden – that what was happening here on Friedrich Strasse was some kind of aberration. But it was not to be. As they turned the corner on to the city's most famous thoroughfare, it seemed that brown- and blackshirted soldiers were everywhere. The SS and the SA were out in force, both on foot and patrolling the street in their armoured vehicles.

A furrier's on the corner had had its windows smashed in and the windows in the apartment above were also broken. Swastikas had been daubed over the walls, and the sound of screams and raised voices could be heard from within the building itself. Eva and Kurt looked at one another, but neither made any move to investigate further. Fear had entered both their hearts. 'Thank God we're not Jews in this city tonight!' Kurt said quietly, and she silently concurred.

It seemed at times they were wading through a sea of broken glass, as they picked their way along the wide pavement, past desecrated shop fronts. 'I never knew there were so many Jewish businesses around here,' Eva said, stopping to pull a long splinter from the sole of her shoe.

'Many will be only of Jewish descent,' Kurt said. 'But the Nazis have ways of finding these things out. It doesn't pay to keep secrets from this government!'

That was certainly true. But it seemed incredible to her that the government could actually be a party to what was happening here tonight – could actually be ordering these atrocities. No matter how much she personally disliked Hitler and the young thugs he so often attracted to his cause, she found it almost impossible to believe that those entrusted with the reins of power in their country could actually encourage its people to act like savages towards their fellow citizens. There was so much she no longer understood; so much she longed to talk to Kurt about, but this was neither the time nor the place.

They continued in silence until they came within sight of the Palladian façade of the Koehn department store itself. To her horror, each of the massive stone columns was defaced with a dripping white swastika and, where the huge plate-

36

glass windows once gleamed in the lamplight, there were merely dark caverns lethally edged with jagged glass. The pavement outside the store, for at least a hundred yards, was covered in glittering shards from the shattered panes.

At first she could only stand and stare. There had to be some mistake. Some enormous mistake.

Kurt was equally astonished. 'Your family's not Jewish!' His protest was understandable, for everyone knew Koehn was an old Pomeranian name, and Eva's family one of the most respected in Berlin's business community. 'Someone will pay for this. There will be hell to pay in the morning. Some idiot – drunk most probably – will have his stripes torn off him for this.'

But even as he spoke Eva could sense a most peculiar feeling coming over her. 'Let's go inside,' she said quietly.

She had no need to search in her pockets for her key; the front door leading to the stairs to their apartment above the shop was gaping open – something that her father never allowed. Her heart was in her mouth as she pushed it open even further.

'Let me go first,' Kurt said, edging past her. 'You follow.'

Silently they ascended the wide stone steps and, as they reached the curve at the half-way point, they stopped. Eva gripped the polished yew of the banister even tighter. The sound of someone weeping – great, heartrending sobs – was coming from above. 'Do you want to go on?' Kurt whispered hoarsely, his face drained of colour. There was real fear now in his eyes too.

She nodded mutely. She had to go on. There was no choice.

The sobbing grew louder as they neared the ornate front door, and, on pushing it open and crossing the marble-tiled hall to enter the drawing-room beyond, the sobbing sound turned into a strangled scream.

Eva and Kurt stood in the open doorway and stared inside. Margarete Koehn, Eva's mother, sat up on the chaise-longue next to the stove and stared back, the scream dying on her lips. Relief flooded into her tear-stained face. It wasn't the Gestapo back. It was her daughter and the Kessel boy!

She got up and flung herself across the room into Eva's arms. *'Liebchen! Liebchen* – they've taken *Vati*! God help us – they've taken your father!' The sobs began again – great shuddering sobs that caused her whole body to shake as she clung to her only child.

Automatically Eva made soothing noises and stroked her mother's shaking shoulders as her eyes surveyed the scene around them. What had once been an elegant drawing-room was now a complete shambles. Choice pieces of Louis-Quinze furniture, passed down through generations of Aldermanns, lay overturned on the pale Chinese carpet; her grandmother's collection of fine Meissen porcelain, shattered into a thousand pieces, decorated the floor beside the open doors of the china cabinet. A small oil by Wassily Kandinsky had been torn from the wall and flung against the window opposite. It lay several feet away, half out of its frame, amidst the earth from an upturned pot plant.

The whole room looked as if a whirlwind had passed through it. But worst of all, her grandfather's, Fritz Koehn's, portrait on the wall in front of her had the word *'Jude'* slashed across it. The torn pieces of canvas hung from his face like some hideous injury. It was this, more than anything, that hurt … That and the knowledge that they had taken her father.

'When …?' It was the only word she could utter as she led her distraught mother back to the chaise-longue.

Margarete Koehn shook her head. 'Half an hour – maybe an hour ago … Who can say?' Time had ceased to have any meaning. Her world had come to an end this evening when they had confronted her husband with the truth of his paternity. He had denied it, of course. Shouted at them even. Told them he would have them thrown out of their unit for daring to insult one of Berlin's most respected citizens in such a way. Ask your mother, they had replied. Ask the one who had defiled German blood and Germany's honour by marrying a Jew.

And so he had asked …

His wife shook her head once more, tears filling her eyes at the memory. He had asked his mother all right, and when the answer came from the old lady in the bed upstairs, Margarete had been standing beside him. She would remember that look on his face till the day she died: the incredulity, the fear, the utter horror. 'A Jew … A Jew …' she repeated the words he himself had uttered in total despair such a short time ago.

Eva listened to the dreaded words from her mother's lips and struggled to comprehend what was happening to them. Until tonight Jews had been other people – people who only touched the fringe of her existence, and had nothing really to do with the close-knit Aryan family from which she believed she had sprung. Jews were the figures huddled in that truck tonight, and the bloodied corpse on the pavement in Friedrich Strasse. Jews were other people. She shuddered visibly. 'And *Oma*? How is *Oma*?'

Margarete Koehn made a despairing gesture. 'Go and see.' Her heart was bleeding for the old lady confined to the bed upstairs, who had been forced to confess the truth to her son; a truth that had brought his world – their world – crashing down around them. To live for eight decades in a city and land you loved, to have it come to this at the hands of your own people … 'Go and see her, *Liebchen* … please.'

Eva glanced across at Kurt, who had been standing silently by. He nodded. 'I'll stay with your mother, Eva. Go and see how your grandmother is.'

Kissing her mother on the cheek, she got up and walked quickly from the room and made her way to the floor above.

The salt from her mother's tears was moist on her lips as she entered her grandmother's bedroom. *Oma* Koehn was still lying in the centre of the great bed when Eva entered,

39

but there the similarity with any other visit ended. The contents of her dressing-table lay scattered across the floor; the head of the little Dresden shepherdess staring up at her from the middle of the carpet. Some objects had obviously been hurled through the window, for a hole was visible in the centre pane, causing the net in front of it to billow in the icy breeze.

Her grandmother lay propped up against the pillows like a wax doll. She made no movement when Eva entered.

'Don't be afraid, *Oma*, dear – it's only me ...' Eva ran across the room, crunching slivers of glass and porcelain underfoot, and flung herself on to the bed. She took her grandmother's hands in hers. They were as icy cold as the room itself. 'Did they harm you? Did those animals touch you?'

Oma Koehn ignored the question. Her only thought was for her son. 'Martin – they've taken Martin. Your father, Eva ... They've taken your father to the Prinz Albrecht Strasse.' Her voice shook as she uttered the address of the Gestapo headquarters.

'I know, *Oma*, I know ... But it has to be some mistake ... They were drunk, that's all – the soldiers who came here. They mistook *Vati* for someone else. They'll find out very soon their terrible mistake and let him go ...'

Oma Koehn was shaking her head. 'There's been no mistake, child. God help us, there has been no mistake.'

Eva stared at her. 'What do you mean? Of course there's been a mistake. A big mistake. We're not Jewish. How can they claim that we are Jewish?'

The old lady looked at her for a long time. For the second time this night she must divulge the secret she had carried in her heart for over half a century. She remembered the look of anguish and disbelief on her son's face, and her heart bled for what such knowledge could do to him. Her granddaughter was looking at her now with just such disbelief in her eyes. She formed the words with difficulty. 'They can claim that we are Jewish, child, because we *are* Jewish. At least your grandfather was.'

'*Opa* Koehn? You mean *Opa* Koehn was Jewish?' Her disbelief was obvious in both her voice and face. That proud, white-haired old man she remembered so well was really a *Jew*? 'I don't believe it.'

'Well, you had better believe it, child, because it's true. And I should know – I married him, remember?'

'But that makes me ...'

'A *Mischling* – Second Degree.'

Eva paled at the dreaded words. The Nazis had different categories for their *Untermenschen* – their sub-humans – as they termed them: after the full-blooded Jew came those people termed *Mischlinge* – the offspring of Aryans and Jews. *Mischlinge* themselves were now divided into different categories: *Mischling*, First Degree – anyone with two Jewish grandparents, provided the person was not of the Jewish faith or married to a Jew; and *Mischling*, Second Degree – anyone with one Jewish grandparent, provided the person was not of the Jewish faith or married to a Jew. She knew the Nuremberg Laws almost by heart. You had to these days if you did not want to be locked up for flouting the Law for the Protection of German Blood and German Honour. 'I am a *Mischling*?' The words almost stuck in her throat.

'Only "Second Degree", child,' her grandmother replied bitterly. 'Your poor father is "First Degree".'

'*Vati* ...' Eva's voice tailed off, unable even to contemplate what might be happening to him. She half-turned and stared out of the window into the dark night beyond. All she could see was the corpse of that dead Jew on Friedrich Strasse – that dead Jew, with her father's face. She buried her own face in her hands.

'Don't cry, child ... Don't cry.' Her grandmother reached out and touched her granddaughter's shaking shoulders. 'The Nazis are strong, but we must be stronger.'

She was silent for a moment. Claudia Koehn was made of

sterner stuff than her daughter-in-law downstairs. She had not wasted precious time on futile tears after the Nazi thugs made off with her son. She had lain here in this freezing room and put her mind to good use. Her body might be all but useless these days, but her mind was still as quick and active as it had been sixty years ago when she first made up her mind to marry her handsome Jew from the East, Fritz Koehn.

'I loved your grandfather, Eva. No matter what happens, I want you to remember that. To me, the fact that he had been born a Jew did not come into it.'

Her eyes softened as she remembered the young man who had stolen her heart that long, hot summer all those years ago. She took her granddaughter's hands in hers as she repeated the words of Shylock's speech from *The Merchant of Venice*: '"Hath not a Jew eyes? Hath not a Jew hands, organs, dimensions, senses, affections, passions, fed with the same food, hurt with the same weapons, subject to the same diseases, healed by the same means, warmed and cooled by the same winter and summer, as a Christian?"' Her voice broke as she came to the end. 'There is no difference between human beings, child. And there will be no true civilization in this country or any other until we stop trying to pretend that we are somehow superior to others.'

Eva looked at her, taking strength from the still bright blue eyes that were burning into hers, imparting strength and resolve to her own flagging spirits. 'I know that, *Oma*,' she said wearily. 'But *they* don't know it – the animals who took *Vati* away' – she looked round the room helplessly – 'and did this to us. What can we do, *Oma*? What can we do?'

'You see that doll over there?' Her grandmother pointed to a very old, wax-faced doll she had played with herself as a child in the Berlin of the Kaisers. 'Bring it to me.'

Eva obeyed, lifting it from its place of honour on top of a tall dresser and handing it to the old lady.

Claudia's arthritic hands pulled at the head, and eventually it came off. As Eva watched, she turned the body of the doll upside-down and shook it. A black velvet pouch fell on to the quilt beside them.

'Ah … I knew it would be there!' Her grandmother picked it up carefully and undid the braided silk tie. 'Hold out your hands, child. Both hands.'

Eva obeyed, making a cup with her upturned palms, into which her grandmother shook a collection of the finest cut diamonds that Eva had ever seen. She gazed at them, speechless.

'It's over sixty years since I've set eyes on them,' the old lady said softly. 'Over sixty years.'

'But how …? Where did they come from?'

Her grandmother reached out and took one of the jewels between her right thumb and forefinger and examined it in the light of the bedside lamp. 'Amsterdam – that's where they came from,' she said quietly, still gazing in wonder at the sparkling gem. 'My Uncle Edgar's wedding present to me and your grandfather. They were worth a small fortune in those days, so only the Good God knows what they'll be worth now.'

She dropped the stone back into Eva's hands and they both sat gazing at the jewels in silence. There were a dozen all told, in varying sizes. 'It was your grandfather's idea to keep them in there,' the old lady said, finally. 'His family had lived through generations of pogroms in the East, and he was under no illusion that such things couldn't happen again – even in Berlin … Hide them, *Liebling*, he told me. Hide them, so that no matter what they try to do to us we can still buy time.' She looked her granddaughter straight in the eyes. 'These are your "time", Eva, *Liebchen*. These few diamonds will buy you life.'

Eva's mouth went dry. 'Wh – whatever do you mean?'

'You must leave here, child. Not just Berlin. You must leave Germany. Get away from this place. It smells of death. You must go to England – London, perhaps. You must get out of reach of these murderers.'

Eva stared at her, aghast. 'But I can't leave Berlin – not just like that. I can't leave you and *Mutti* …'

Her grandmother was adamant. 'You can and you must. Don't worry about us – your mother and I – we are true Aryans, remember?' She gave a bitter smile. 'Our only crime was in marrying men tainted with sub-human blood. But even that is not yet a major crime against the state.'

'But *Vati* …?' She was playing for time as she desperately tried to collect her chaotic thoughts.

Her grandmother shook her head. 'Neither you nor I can help your father now, Eva. All we can do is to pray that no real harm comes to him.' Even as she was saying the words, she knew her voice carried no real conviction. But all was not yet lost. Hope flickered in her eyes as she forced a smile to her lips. 'I will telephone people I know in the Ministry tomorrow – high-ranking people who will bring those monsters to book for what they did to us tonight. Your father will be released soon, never fear.'

The words brought comfort. Hope was everything now. It was all they had left. 'And me? What do you want me to do?'

Her grandmother held out the velvet pouch for Eva to drop the jewels back into. 'Take off your coat.'

'What?'

'You heard. Take off your coat.'

Eva obeyed, laying the brown woollen garment across the bed.

'You will go downstairs now and make us all a cup of coffee, and while you are there I will see to it that these jewels are sewn into the hem of the coat. Over our coffee we will discuss the next move.'

Eva got up from the bed and made her way to the door. What her grandmother was saying horrified her, yet she accepted fully the wisdom of her words. Even if she herself had had a better idea, she had neither the strength nor the will to argue for it. She felt like a small child again – a hostage

44

to fate, whose life was totally beyond her own control. All she could do was to believe in the judgment of those she knew she could trust. If her grandmother was telling her she had to leave, then it must be so. Despair and anger welled within her. Who were these men who could wreck other people's lives like this? How dare that Austrian, with the silly Charlie Chaplin moustache, do this to them! They were more German than he was! This was her own city – Berlin, in 1938, not Spain in the Middle Ages.

Kurt and her mother were sitting together by the stove when she reached the drawing-room, and both looked round anxiously as she came in. Her mother appeared to have calmed down and had already made a pot of coffee, which sat on a small table in front of them. She reached over to pour her daughter a cup.

As Eva sipped the hot brown liquid she recounted to them what her grandmother had just said about her leaving. She missed out the bit about the diamonds; not because she felt she could not trust Kurt, but because it seemed needlessly dramatic.

Tears welled again in her mother's eyes as she spoke, but Margarete Koehn remained silent. She knew what was being spoken of was for the best. Those swine had decreed her daughter to be a *Mischling*, with all the threats that entailed to her safety, and there was absolutely nothing she could do to change that fact.

'You will come home with me.' Kurt said at once. 'My father will help you get to England.'

'Your father? How can he help?' It was her mother who spoke.

'Easily. He has troops of dancing girls going backwards and forwards across the Channel all the time. There are bound to be some due to leave soon. Eva can go with them.'

'But I can't dance!'

Kurt gave a patient smile and shook his head. 'That, my

dear Eva, will be the last of your worries … Anyway,' he grinned, 'neither can half the girls my father employs!'

Eva looked across at her mother. Margarete Koehn wanted with all her heart to rush to her daughter and take her in her arms – to shield her from whatever might lie ahead. But that would be shielding her from life itself, and even she did not have the power to do that.

'Well, *Mutti*, what do you think?'

Her mother gave a wistful smile. Someone once said the best thing you could do for your children was to give them the courage to leave you and live their own lives. That moment had come. It might have been forced upon them, but it had come all the same. She looked across at her daughter. The golden-haired child was turning into a woman before her very eyes. 'I think you'll make a wonderful Marlene Dietrich, my dear.'

Chapter Four

'Ich bin von Kopf bis Fuss
Auf Liebe eingestellt
Das ist doch mein' Welt
Und sonst gar nichts …'

The band was playing the ever-popular 'Falling In Love Again', and a Marlene Dietrich look-alike, in a top hat, tails and black stockings, was caressing the microphone as Kurt led the way between the tightly-packed tables of *Der Goldene Engel* and round the back of the stage.

The singer's voice could scarcely be heard above the laughter, conversation, and clink of glasses from the packed body in the huge cellar, and Eva's eyes stung from the blue haze of cigarette and cigar smoke that hung like a cloud above the tables. It was the first time she had ever been in the nightclub, but the excitement she would normally have felt on such an occasion was totally absent. The reality of what was going on outside these four walls saw to that. She was also highly apprehensive about what Kurt's father would say once he had heard their story.

But, less than five minutes later, she knew her fears were unfounded when Max Kessel looked down at her from his great height, then back at his son, and smiled. It was a smile full of sympathy; a smile that was at odds with the usual world-weary, rather cynical look his florid features had assumed over the years. Nothing surprised him any more in this life. What he had just heard came as no real shock, although no doubt it would raise quite a few eyebrows in the city that Koehn's was, in fact, a Jewish store. Everyone who was anyone in Berlin shopped there. Even the Führer was known to have had items of merchandise sent round to choose from; their huge stock of fashionable clothes and accessories was without parallel in the city.

He puffed thoughtfully on his cigar. Although he couldn't claim to have had many personal dealings with Martin Koehn, or his wife Margarete, he had always had a soft spot for their daughter, Eva, the pretty young friend of his own daughter, Hanna. And for one of his sons to come and ask for his help in her plight touched him. His watery blue eyes took in the pale blonde hair and attractive, even features of the nervous-looking young woman in front of him. 'Well, you've one thing in your favour, Eva. You don't look Jewish, I'll say that for you.'

She gave a strained smile. Was she expected to thank him for the compliment? 'That will be a help, I presume?'

Max Kessel nodded emphatically. 'Undoubtedly. And I'd keep quiet about the *Mischling* thing while you're here, if I were you. The girls are a good lot, on the whole, but not known for their discretion when they've had a drink or two.' Their customers were mainly off-duty Nazi officers and even he was more than a little apprehensive at introducing anyone with Jewish blood into his establishment, no matter how diluted.

He turned to his son. 'I'd keep quiet about it upstairs, too, if I were you, Kurt.' He had no need to explain further. All three of them were well aware of his eldest son's zeal for the Nazi cause. And his wife, Doris, wasn't exactly renowned for her ability to keep her mouth shut either.

'There are some English girls due to go home soon, then?' Kurt asked. 'Some who could take Eva as part of their group?'

His father jerked his head in the direction of a tall, red-haired young woman talking to a pretty blonde girl with pencilled eyebrows and a raucous laugh at total odds with her ladylike looks. 'Those two are from Britain and, if I remember rightly, the redhead's time's already up in the club. The blonde's supposed to leave tomorrow too, but I hear she's rather taken a fancy to an SS officer who works over in the Reichstag, so she's staying – or so she tells me. I'll introduce you.'

'Kay … Betty … Over here, please!'

Eva's heart beat faster as the two young women came to join them. They had obviously just finished their stint in one of the evening shows, for their skimpy costumes were covered in towelling robes that had seen better days, and perspiration shone through the greasepaint on their faces in the bright lights of the backstage coffee room.

To Eva all the young women around here were an exotic breed, the like of which she had never encountered at such close quarters before. None could be that much older than herself, but it was difficult to tell their exact age, for all wore very elaborate stage make-up. After their particular show – and there were four or five a night – the girls were expected to rest for half an hour, then dress and join the customers in the front of the house for a drink; and, if possible, persuade them to order a bottle of specially imported French champagne that could cost as much as an average worker's weekly wage – depending on who was buying. SS officers were a particularly favoured breed.

The two British girls smiled politely at the fair-haired young woman, standing with a slightly embarrassed air between their boss and his son.

It was Herr Kessel who spoke first. 'Betty and Kay, I'd like you to meet Eva Koehn. Eva, this is Kay Bridgewater and Betty Burke.'

'*Sehr angenehm* …' The three exchanged handshakes as Kurt's father continued, 'I have a favour to ask you girls, on behalf of Fräulein Koehn here … She has to get to London for family reasons, and I want you to take her with you when you leave for England … I'll make sure she has the relevant papers to satisfy the authorities in England, so there should be no problem on that score. As far as they are concerned, from tonight she is part of my troop.'

49

He shot Eva an encouraging smile through a puff of cigar smoke. 'I don't know what your dancing's like, young lady, but I've heard you sing often enough upstairs with my Hanna. That'll do for me. From now on you're one of my songbirds – a genuine Max Kessel "golden angel".'

Then the smile faded as he turned back to the other two young women. 'But I don't want either of you to say a word to anyone about it, understand? There's to be no gossip in this place, or out of it, if you ever want to work for me again. No one must know Eva is leaving Berlin, or where she is heading. Can I trust you to do that for me?'

Kay Bridgewater's brows furrowed quizzically as she blew a thin stream of cigarette smoke into the already hazy atmosphere. 'Cohen – that's a Jewish name, isn't it? Is Eva Jewish?'

Eva could feel her cheeks colour. It was a common enough assumption when someone had merely heard the name spoken, but this was no time for confessions. 'It's spelt K-o-e-h-n,' she said quickly to the redhead. 'It's an old Pomeranian name. My grandfather was from the East.'

There was a moment's silence. She was sure no one believed her, but they were too polite to take the matter further.

'Let's just say it is vitally important that Eva leaves Berlin very soon, and not go into the whys and wherefores,' Herr Kessel put in impatiently. 'What do you say girls? Will you look after her?'

'Of course we'll look after her,' Kay Bridgewater said with a smile in Eva's direction. 'At least I will. Betty, I think, has other plans. Haven't you, ducks?'

Betty Burke gave an embarrassed laugh. It was still a source of guilt and some confusion to her that she had fallen in love with a Nazi officer. Heaven only knew what her folks back home in Northern Ireland would make of it. 'Kay's right,' she said quietly. 'I intend staying on here as long as possible. Certainly as long as Hartmut is in Berlin.'

'Eva can share our rooms till we leave at the weekend,' Kay added. She was warming to the idea by the minute. She had always been one for lame ducks – of the animal or human variety. 'It's not exactly the Adlon,' she grinned, referring to Berlin's legendary hotel. 'But there's a sofa that pulls down into a bed of sorts.' She turned to Eva. 'You don't mind roughing it a bit for a couple of days, do you?'

'Oh, no. I'll sleep anywhere.' She had slept rough often enough with the *Bund Deutscher Mädel* over the past few years.

A roar went up from the other side of the stage curtain as Lili, one of *Der Goldene Engel*'s star attractions, finished her act to an interminable drum roll. They waited until the noise had subsided and she had rushed past them in a flurry of ostrich-feather fans, then Herr Kessel turned to Eva. 'By the way, my dear, you do speak English, don't you?' They had been speaking in German and the thought had just occurred to him. 'You'll find it pretty tough going in England otherwise.'

Eva cleared her throat. 'I speak and write it very well, thank you,' she replied in English. Studying it every day for ten years at school had seen to that.

'Excellent!' Kay clapped her hands. 'I'm sure it's far better than my German. I didn't know a word when I first came over here four years ago.'

'With your looks, *Engelchen*, you didn't need to!' Herr Kessel smiled through his cigar smoke, and Eva was sure she could detect the redhead blushing beneath the greasepaint. Did *droit de seigneur* extend to present-day Berlin nightclubs? By the look that passed between the English girl and her boss, she was convinced it almost certainly did.

'Now how about a drink to toast the new addition to our troop?' Kay looked meaningfully at Herr Kessel, who took the hint immediately and signalled to one of the waiters.

He himself declined a glass of champagne and, as soon as all three young women were served, he ground the remains of his cigar into a nearby ashtray and gave a polite bow. 'Well, now that's settled, I think Kurt and I can leave you ladies to talk things out amongst yourselves. Don't you agree, Kurt?' He looked round at his son.

Kurt had been silent throughout. The last thing he wanted to do was to leave Eva now, but he could think of no good reason to remain. What had happened during the past hour or so had left him almost too shocked to think straight. He wished with all his heart he could think of something to say – anything that might convey to her the shame he felt for what had happened out there this evening. Kay and Betty were good sorts, but even they could not shield her from the world outside these four walls. What was going to happen to her when he went back upstairs to the safety of his own home?

Sensing his inner anguish, Eva put a consoling hand on his arm. 'I'll be fine, Kurt. Honestly.' Her eyes locked with his, as if to give him a strength she herself did not possess. A deep furrow ran across his brow beneath the fall of curly brown hair. He looked so boyish – but tonight he was a boy with the eyes of an old man. 'Thank you,' she said softly. 'Thank you for – everything.'

He took hold of her right hand and raised it to his lips. He held it there much longer than necessary. 'God bless you, Eva,' he said quietly.

She smiled and leaned across and kissed his cheek. That, from Kurt, who would never admit to believing in a deity, meant a lot.

She watched him leave – a tallish, gangling figure, totally overshadowed by the much heftier bulk of his father. He looked completely out of place amongst the broad-shouldered, swaggering officer-types who frequented the club. He half-turned at the door, as if to look back. Eva made to raise her hand in response, but a bevy of dancers, complete with plumed head-dresses, spoilt the moment as they sub-merged him in the doorway on their way back on-stage.

He disappeared from sight in the crowd and, when he had gone, it was as if the last link with her old life had slipped from her grasp. She turned to her new companions and they smiled reassuringly. 'Kurt is a good kid,' Kay, the redhead, said fondly. 'Much nicer than that pain-in-the-arse older brother of his.'

Eva smiled. Her first genuine smile for hours. Someone else shared her opinion of Paul. She thought she might grow to really like these two young women, despite their garish make-up and the cloud of cheap French perfume which surrounded them.

Kay and Betty shared a small, cramped apartment of two rooms and a scullery in a block not far down Friedrich Strasse from *Der Goldene Engel*. The journey of only a few hundred yards was a nightmare. It seemed as if half the population was on the street, many obviously drunk and applauding the small contingents of soldiers who marched past, still singing their patriotic songs, while others watched in silence, their thoughts unknown.

Occasionally they passed an individual, or a couple, lugging heavy suitcases along the edge of the pavement nearest the buildings. You could almost smell the fear that surrounded them as their hunched figures slunk along in the darkest shadows. At the sight of soldiers they would shrink out of sight into the dark entrances of apartment blocks or shop doorways. 'Jews, most probably,' Kay muttered as they passed them by, deliberately trying not to notice their pathetic attempts to remain inconspicuous. Eva's heart went out to them. If they had experienced anything similar to what she had witnessed tonight, then God help them.

Die Fahne hoch, die Reihen fest geschlossen,
SA marschiert mit ruhig festem Schritt.
Kam'raden die, Rot Front and Reaktion erschossen
Marschieren im Geist in unseren Reihen mit ...'

The voices that bellowed the Nazi anthem, the Horst Wessel *Lied*, into the night air were obviously drunk. Frighteningly drunk. Each of the girls tensed as they approached, and Eva hoped the shambling figures with the suitcases they had passed were well out of sight.

'Heil Hitler!' Three of the four SA men saluted them elaborately, while the fourth went on singing. They were obviously intent on becoming better acquainted. The tunic of the one doing the singing was spattered with white paint. A few choice words from Betty sent them on their way. Eva recognized the slang for diseases that were never talked of in polite society. Even drunken soldiers, it seemed, retained enough sense to steer clear of the threat of certain things.

'Don't worry, love, we're both clean as a whistle – but it doesn't do to let them know that!'

Eva smiled. Such was the wisdom of a lifestyle she knew next to nothing about.

Another group across the street were shouting obscenities about the Jews. 'Bloody lunatics,' Kay said in English as they neared their destination at last. 'As if the poor bloody Jews haven't suffered enough already. I tell you this country's gone barmy.' She turned to Eva. 'You'll be well out of it, kid.'

The smell of stale cabbage hung in the air as they made their way up the winding stone staircase to the rooms on the third floor that had been the girls' home for the past few months.

'It's not much,' Betty said, casting a critical eye around her as Kay locked the door on the outside world. 'But it's better than some folk have at the moment.'

She gestured to the wooden-armed settee against the wall. 'That's your bed, Eva, love. If there's anything you need, just let us know. We've managed to collect quite a bit in the way of toiletries and that sort of thing one way or another since we've been here.' She smiled wryly to herself. 'So many of the customers bring us presents of soap, we're beginning to wonder if they're trying to tell us something!'

Eva sat down with a sigh on the settee that was to be her bed for her last few days in Berlin. The brown leather case she had packed with such haste earlier in the evening stood by her feet. It still bore the label from her family's trip to Baden-Baden last summer. She had an almost uncontrollable urge to cry, but knew that would only make her new room-mates feel uncomfortable. She looked up at Betty and made an attempt at a smile. 'It's very kind of you to let me stay here.'

Betty sat down on a chair opposite and kicked off her shoes, letting out a sigh of relief as she did so. 'Kindness doesn't come into it, kid. Plenty of folk have done us good turns over the years we've been in this game ...' Her eyes narrowed as she looked quizzically at Eva. 'You're not really a singer, are you?'

Eva looked embarrassed. 'I'm not anything really ... I – I just left school last summer.'

'How old are you?'

'Eighteen.'

Betty's brows shot up. 'Lord – only four years younger than me! But I left school at fourteen to go into a crummy little office just off the Falls Road in Belfast. A place I got out of just as fast as I could, I'll tell you that for nothin'!' She rubbed and wriggled the toes of each foot in turn. 'I take it your old man's got money, then? I mean he couldn't afford to let you while your time away at school otherwise, now could he?'

At the mention of her father Eva's face clouded, but she couldn't let it show. 'My family were quite well-off,' she answered slowly. Why had she used the past tense? She tried to shut the memory of the apartment on the Unter den Linden and its inhabitants from her mind.

Betty sensed her discomfort and did not pursue the subject. She knew things were happening in this city – terrible things – to ordinary people, often because their only crime was having Jewish blood.

'Herr Kessel said your boyfriend's in the SS.'

Betty nodded, her face brightening at the thought of her tall, good-looking young man from Schleswig. 'Hartmut's the most gentlemanly man I've ever met, so he is ... And, if they'd told me a few months ago I'd ever say that about a Nazi, let alone an SS officer, I'd have told them to get their heads examined!'

'It's him that should have his head examined, taking up with the likes of you, Betty Burke!' Kay grinned, as she brought three glasses of beer from the tiny kitchen beyond. 'The poor bloke doesn't know what he's let himself in for!'

'Will you marry him?' Eva surprised herself by the bluntness of her question.

'If he asks me.' The answer was equally straightforward.

'You don't mind becoming a German?'

Betty laughed. 'If a cat lives in a kipper box, it doesn't make it a kipper, does it now?'

She placed her beer glass on the table at her elbow and began to take the pins from her hair. It fell from its elaborate roll on to her shoulders, and she shook her head, running her fingers through the fair curls. 'I'll always be Irish, just as you'll always be German. And sure I wouldn't have it any other way. Would you?'

Eva opened her mouth, ready to agree, then paused. For the first time in her life she realized she could not; she could not agree to being proud to be German.

She slept little that night, but it was not the hardness of the bed that kept her awake, nor the men's shouts from the street below, beyond the drawn curtains. It was the fear of the unknown. The fear of what had become of her father this night, and what would happen to her mother and grandmother now she had gone. It had all happened so quickly. At first she had argued with her mother that she should be allowed to remain at home for a few days – just long enough to find out what had happened to her father, but Margarete

Koehn had been adamant. She must go – and go now. Already this week all Jews had been told to hand in their passports to the authorities within the next fortnight. The fact that she still had one that was not marked with the dreaded word *Mischling* was reason enough to go now, before it was taken from her forever. 'You can write to us, *Liebling*. It will be enough to know you are safe and well, and far away from this madness.'

And so she had packed her case, and donned the coat with the diamonds securely sewn into the hem by her grandmother. Her mother had pressed several hundred marks into her hand. It was all the money they had in the house. 'We can send more when you arrive in London and let us know your address,' she had said, smiling bravely as they whispered their goodbyes in the cold passage leading to the street door. Tears stung Eva's eyes in the darkness as she remembered.

So many memories came flooding back. It seemed only yesterday, yet it was already almost six years ago, that she had awoken that cold January day to hear that Hitler had been appointed Chancellor. She remembered her father had sworn at the breakfast table, something she had never heard him do before, as he read the newspaper headlines.

It had been as if a whole new era had begun, as indeed it had. Suddenly, throughout the city, swastikas decorated almost every building, waving in the chill breeze. And, as darkness had fallen that evening, she had gone down to the pavement with her parents to join the crowds watching the torchlight processions of delirious Nazi supporters who goose-stepped down the Unter den Linden to the sound of the Horst Wessel Song and other Nazi anthems that were already becoming as familiar as the old German *Lieder*.

They had followed the procession all the way down the avenue, beneath the huge lime trees, to the Presidential Palace itself, where the crowds were gathering. It seemed as if all Berlin was there, and all eyes were on the face of the old President, Field Marshal von Hindenburg, as he stood looking down from the palace balcony. He looked so tired, tired and old, and his face was pale and drawn in the torchlight as he stood next to the much smaller figure of Adolf Hitler.

But Hitler's face was not pale or drawn. In fact, she could remember the look on it to this day. There was a quiet smile there – a secret smile – as if he were already planning the grand finale to his victory over the German people. A grand finale that would rival that of the climax of *Götterdämmerung*, his favourite opera, itself.

Wagner's masterpiece was being performed that very night at the Royal Opera House on the Unter den Linden, and she had gone to see it two days later with her mother and father. They had walked hand in hand along the pavement, towards the magnificent building where huge swastika banners now hung side by side with the black, white and red flags of the old Empire.

Her father had been strangely silent when they came out, after the performance, to retrace their steps the few hundred yards back to their apartment. 'It will not be only the Twilight of the Gods, with that man at the helm of our country, Margarete,' he had said to her mother. 'It will be the end of Germany itself, mark my words.'

And Eva had remembered those words ever since. And she had particularly remembered them the day, almost two months later, on the beautiful spring morning of 21 March 1933, when in the Garrison Church in Potsdam, regarded as the shrine of the nation, next to the bodies of Frederick the Great and Prussia's other legendary kings, the banners of the ancient state were replaced by those of an Austrian corporal and his cohorts, most of whom had no links with Prussia, or its capital, Berlin.

There they had all stood, all the marshals, generals and admirals of the old Hohenzollern regime; each and every one in their Imperial uniforms; their grey heads proudly erect as they faced a new future under a man to whom only a few short years before they would not have given the time of day.

There had been one empty chair in their midst – the seat reserved for the Kaiser was empty. He was miles away across the Dutch border, at Doorn, chopping wood.

In the body of the church sat Hitler's brownshirts, and on either side the Nationalists and members of the Centre Party. Not a single Social Democrat had been present. For many that omission had served as an ominous portent of things to come.

The old order was being passed into the hands of the new, and the man who personified that old order was going with it. The aged Field Marshal and President, von Hindenburg, underwent his and Germany's final degradation that day. The victor of Tannenberg, and father of the nation, had been persuaded to take his rows of campaign medals from their étuis, and wear them on the breast of his Imperial uniform for the last time as he stood next to the man into whose hands he had passed the leadership of the German nation. The old war-horse had given the final seal of approval to Adolf Hitler and his followers.

Outside the church, Berlin had been bathed in early spring sunshine as the guns roared out their salute to the new regime and, inside, the military band played the Chorale of Leuthen. In the Empress Friedrich Gymnasium for Girls, less than a mile away, Eva had listened, along with her schoolfriends and teachers, as the ceremony was relayed over the *Reichsrundfunk* into every school, workplace and home in Germany. Their school assembly-hall had rung with their young voices as they joined in the national anthem at the end of the ceremony:

> *Deutschland, Deutschland über alles,*
> *Über alles in der Welt …'*

Suddenly those words had a meaning – a real meaning – for everyone who sang them that day. Was it a prophecy of things to come? Hitler had made no secret of his desire to make Germany the most powerful nation in the world. A shudder had run through her then, as it had run through her so many times since.

When she had got home that day she had related the ceremony to her parents. On principle, they had refused to listen. Her father had heard her out in silence as he sipped his coffee, then said quietly, 'What you have heard today, my child, was not the inauguration ceremony of a new era in the history of our country. It was the funeral service for the Germany we have known and loved.'

Eva's eyes misted in the darkness as she lay in the strange room in Friedrich Strasse. Little had she known that day just how prophetic his words would be. 'Please help him, Lord,' she whispered into the silence of the night. 'Please God, help my father …'

Then the sobs came, hot and bitter, welling from the very depths of her soul. 'God help us all this night,' she whispered.

But in her heart something had already died. Her belief in God itself.

Chapter Five

Kay and Betty slept late in the small bedroom next door, and Eva envied them the peace of mind that allowed them to do so as she struggled alone to refold the awkward contraption that was the bed settee on which she had spent the night. She had endured long hours tossing and turning on its hard mattress before sleep had finally come. Her eyes were still red and swollen from the tears that had soaked into the faded velvet cushion she had used as a pillow, and her head ached.

It was almost eight o'clock, but this was not her first time out of bed this morning. She had woken early: the marble clock on the mantelshelf above the stove had been striking five brittle chimes when she had first got out of bed to pull back the curtains at the window and gaze down into the darkness of the street below. The crowds of the night had dispersed, but some of them were still out there; for she had heard shouting: uniformed animals in the guise of human beings. But that was an insult to the animal population, for they never committed such atrocities on others of the same species as this city had witnessed throughout the night. Animals killed to live, while these brutes lived to kill. Never had she imagined she would be so ashamed of her race.

She had crept back to bed to lie shivering with a mixture of cold and fear beneath the feather-quilt. She was aware that things always seemed at their blackest in the hours before dawn, but she could not convince herself anything would be any better once daylight came.

She had thought of her father now in the hands of the Gestapo. What was happening to him? Was he still alive? To anyone who knew Martin Koehn it would seem incredible that he had been arrested as a Jew. There were few more respected members of Berlin's business community. With his tall, broad-shouldered frame, fair colouring and regular features, he looked the archetypal German. Good God – he *was* German! His forebears on his mother's side had been merchants in Berlin as far back as Frederick the Great and, for all Eva knew, his father's family in Pomerania had been there for hundreds of years as well. How far back were they determined to go in their search for Jewish blood? Were they digging into everyone's past? And who was to say that that Austrian, Adolf Hitler himself, was one hundred per cent genuine Germanic stock? He was hardly the prime specimen of Aryan manhood that Dr Goebbels waxed so lyrical about.

Such thoughts continued to tumble through her head until she could lie still no longer. At eight o'clock she had got up to struggle with the bed-settee, then wash and dress in the cramped conditions of the scullery next door.

The sour smell of bad drains hung in the air, combined with the smell of stale cigarette ash from the two overflowing ashtrays that sat on the brown oilcloth of the kitchen table. Eva emptied them on to a heap of old potato peelings and some broken egg shells in a bucket that sat under the sink, then looked around her with a sinking heart. Everything was either old, dirty, or both. She had no idea how to light the dilapidated geyser which seemed to be the only source of hot water, so she washed in cold at the stone sink.

The facilities were primitive in the extreme, and she envied the girls their ability to put up with such conditions and still remain so cheerful. A single gas ring stood on what had once been a rather fine marble-topped washstand and a meagre supply of food was lined up on the shelf above. The end of a loaf of black bread lay on a tin tray with a jar of honey next to it. It felt stale to the touch and there were mouse droppings on the wooden draining-board not far away. She replaced the bread on its shelf with a shudder of distaste. She guessed Kay and Betty ate most of their meals at the club, for there was nothing here to tempt the palate even if she had felt like eating.

She wandered back to the living-room and noticed an imposing Telefunken radio sitting on the oak dresser. It was every bit as grand as the one they had in their apartment at home and it looked totally out of place amongst the shoddy, junk-shop furniture of the room. The girls had probably hired it to listen to broadcasts from London. She curled up in the corner of the settee next to it and switched it on. A news broadcast had just begun and what she heard over the next half-hour did nothing to lessen her fears about the future.

It wasn't just in Berlin that the anti-Jewish riots had taken place last night. It seemed the whole of Germany was involved. The news reader was talking of similar outrages all over the country, only he did not refer to them as such. There was no trace whatsoever of outrage in his voice; in fact, it was devoid of emotion as he recounted the events of the night.

City by city, he informed the nation of the success of each pogrom to cleanse the nation of its pollution by Jewry. *'Judenrein'* – cleansed of Jews – seemed to be the favourite phrase of the moment. In Leipzig, where her Aunt Emmy and Uncle Franz lived, almost a hundred Jews had been killed, with more than 30,000 rounded up for deportation to the concentration camps. From Berlin itself more than 8,000 Jews had been evicted and transported. Even the sick had not escaped: patients had been taken from hospitals, children from orphanages, and the aged from old people's homes. Hundreds of synagogues and thousands of Jewish homes and businesses had been destroyed – the nightmare seemed never-ending.

Eva listened ashen-faced as the catalogue of horror mounted, then, when she could take no more, she switched it off to sit slumped and motionless in the corner of the settee. Only the sound of the ticking clock could be heard for

63

the next ten minutes until a female voice broke into her thoughts.

'Was that the radio you had on?' Kay asked from the doorway. Stifling a yawn, her new friend padded through from the bedroom, pulling on a faded blue dressing-gown against the bitter cold of the morning. Her long red hair hung in a thick plait over her right shoulder and her face was devoid of make-up. Her pale skin was covered in freckles and she looked far younger than Eva remembered from the night before. The sound of the news broadcast had roused Kay from a light sleep and she glanced from the silent radio back to Eva. 'Wasn't it worth listening to, then?'

Eva shook her head, unable to speak, as Kay continued through to the scullery, lighting a cigarette on the way. 'Can I make you a coffee?' The flame of the match was blown out with a thin jet of cigarette smoke.

'That – that would be very nice, thank you.'

The sound of water being run and things being rattled came from the scullery, then a 'Damn, we forgot to pick up fresh bread yesterday!' There was a thud as the hard heel of black bread found its way into the trashcan beneath the sink.

A few minutes later two cups of coffee were brought through and one set down beside Eva with a cheerful smile. 'Here you are, love. Get this down you.'

As Eva murmured a grateful *Danke*, Kay perched herself on the table nearby. She took a sip of the hot brown liquid, then drew deeply on her cigarette as she studied her new room-mate's face. She had obviously been crying and a wave of sympathy welled within her for this young German girl suddenly cast adrift in the madness that was Berlin – God only knew for what reason. She certainly didn't look like a Jew, but then you could never tell these days.

'I wouldn't worry, ducks, really I wouldn't. You'll like London. It's not like here. We don't feel the same about uniforms over there. We ain't impressed by them, if you know what I mean ... Them Nazis ...' She shook her head

64

and gave a bemused smile, 'God, the way that lot goose-step around would have our population in hysterics if they tried it over there!'

Eva made a watery attempt at a smile as Kay jerked her head towards the radio and continued. 'Was the news bad, then? Is that what's bothering you?'

'Terrible things happened last night – all over Germany … I can't begin to tell you.'

'Then don't,' Kay said firmly. 'Just put it out of your head. No matter what happens, you're going to be safe with us, and in a couple of days you'll be in Blighty. Have you any idea what you'll do there – in the way of work, I mean?'

Eva looked blank. Incredibly, the thought had never occurred to her. Enough was happening in the present to fill her thoughts, without dwelling on the future. She took another sip of the coffee and shook her head. 'I don't really know. I am not trained for anything … It might be difficult.'

'But you can sing, can't you? Max said so last night.'

Eva smiled. 'Only church choir stuff, I'm afraid.'

Kay wagged her cigarette at her. 'Don't just dismiss it like that, my girl. It's the voice that counts, not what you're used to singing. Even old dogs can learn new tricks if they have to – and you're hardly past the puppy stage yet. I take it you won't mind learning other songs?'

'Well, no …'

'Good – then you'll not starve.'

'You'd recommend this kind of work?'

Kay was silent for a moment as she studied her fingernails. They were long and coated in bright red varnish, much of which had chipped off. 'You've led a pretty sheltered life, haven't you, ducks? I mean, you've not had much to do with the opposite sex or anything like that yet?' She gave a sympathetic smile. 'I don't expect you've even had a boy-friend – not a proper one, I mean.'

Eva made no reply. She didn't have to, as Kay continued, 'In those circumstances, let's just say if you can land yourself what some folk would call a "respectable" job, then do it. Get yourself fixed up in some nice office somewhere. There are aspects of this work that ain't – how shall I put it? Well, they're not exactly everybody's cup of tea.'

Eva thought of the other girls in the club whom she had seen last night 'entertaining' the customers, as they persuaded them to quaff ever more champagne. How far the 'entertaining' went after they left the club she could only speculate. She looked across at Kay. Did *she* go to bed with men for money? Sitting there with her hair in that schoolgirl plait and her face devoid of make-up, she certainly didn't look like a prostitute ... But she must stop staring like this. 'Have you got another dancing job lined up yourself when you get home?'

Kay nodded as she stubbed out her cigarette in the saucer. 'Yeah – but it's in Alexandria ... That's in Egypt.'

Eva's heart sank. Somehow she had assumed she would have the comfort of knowing her new friend would still be around when she was in London. 'Egypt!'

'That's right. I've got a few days back home in London with my family, then I'm off again ... But don't look so tragic. I won't be abducted into the white slave trade or anything like that. I'm a big girl now and can take care of myself. Anyway, Alexandria's not so bad. And those Arabs!' She rolled her eyes and let out a low whistle. 'Lor, can they spend money! I reckon on coming back with at least double what's written on my contract – and most of the other girls can say the same.'

She gave a mysterious smile. 'Would you believe me if I told you I "entertained" the young King Farouk himself on my last trip out there?'

'Yes, I'd believe you.' She would have believed almost anything Kay told her right now. She had never met such a creature in her life before.

It was almost ten o'clock before Betty got out of bed. She strolled through with a cardigan pulled over her white satin nightdress just as Kay returned from a trip to the street below to buy fresh bread and liver sausage from the shop on the corner. But to their consternation their friend did not return alone.

Eva stifled a gasp of horror at the sight of the tall, black-uniformed figure of the SS officer in the doorway behind Kay.

'Hartmut!' Betty exclaimed in a mixture of delight and consternation. He mustn't see her looking like this! Leaving Eva alone to greet the imposing figure of the stranger, she dived for the bedroom to return a few seconds later with the cardigan discarded and a much more glamorous silk robe wrapped around her enviable figure.

The young man seemed to fill the small room, and Eva found herself unable to meet his direct gaze as Kay returned from depositing the shopping in the kitchen and made the obligatory introduction.

'Hartmut, this is Eva, a friend of ours from the club ...' She paused, wondering how much more to say. To give no explanation at all regarding their new flatmate would simply invite curiosity. She gave a reassuring smile in Eva's direction, and continued, 'She has landed a singing contract in London, so she's travelling back to Britain with me tomorrow.' A self-deprecating smile followed, 'I seem to have reached the Mother Hen stage of chaperoning younger chicks!'

She turned to Eva, 'Eva, dear, this is Sturmbahnführer Hartmut Schuster – Betty's boyfriend.'

'*Sehr angenehm*, Fräulein ...?' The young man gave a gap-toothed smile and bowed politely as he took Eva's hand in his. There was a pregnant pause as he waited for the name to follow.

'Schmidt!' Kay interjected quickly. She hadn't intended lying, but what she had just heard on her trip outside this morning had disturbed her. Much of the talk in the bread-shop down below had been of the arrest of the owner of

Koehn's, the exclusive department store on the Unter den Linden, and of the destruction of the shop itself during the night. It seemed the family had been masquerading as Aryans when they were in fact Jews. Koehn wasn't exactly the most common name in Berlin and, remembering Eva's embarrassed defence of her surname last night, Kay had put two and two together.

'*Sehr angenehm*, Fräulein Schmidt.' Hartmut Schuster gave a quizzical smile and emphasized Germany's most ubiquitous surname as he raised Eva's right hand to his lips. 'I can't recall seeing you at *Der Engel* before. Are you a stranger to Berlin, perhaps?'

Eva could feel a hot flush of embarrassment creep up her neck to suffuse her cheeks for all to see as she glanced nervously at Kay.

'Eva has just arrived from Hamburg, haven't you, dear?' Kay replied for her, surprising herself at how easily the lies tripped off her tongue. 'She was to begin a stint as one of Max's angels, but I've persuaded her to come back to London with me for a few days, then take Betty's place on the Egyptian job.' She gave a knowing smile in her Irish friend's direction. 'It would appear that Miss Burke here finds Berlin has too many attractions to want to leave right now.'

Betty slipped her arm into Hartmut's and murmured, 'One particular attraction, if you don't mind. My days of messing about are well and truly over. But enough about us. What brings you up here at this time of day, *Liebling*?'

Hartmut took off his cap and tossed it on the table before disentangling himself from Betty's grasp. He gave the satin material encasing her bottom a playful slap and turned her in the direction of the scullery. 'A cup of coffee, my good woman, and then I'll tell you!'

As Betty disappeared into the next room, the smile faded from his lips as he turned to Kay and Eva. 'I am here unofficially and what I have to say is to go no further than these four walls.'

He glanced round as Betty returned with a cup of coffee from the pot on the stove next door and handed it to him. '*Wunderbar!*' He took a sip and placed it on the table beside his cap. He cleared his throat and glanced across at Eva who, for the first time, met his gaze. He was obviously nervous about something, and the knowledge disturbed her. An SS man nervous?

But this SS man was not the usual hard-faced individual she had come to associate with the breed. He had gentle blue-grey eyes and there was something of the boy still visible in the roundness of his cheeks and the full, pink lips that broke easily into a smile.

He turned his gaze on Kay. 'I called into *Der Goldene Engel* just after midnight last night,' he began quietly, 'and I was told you had left for your apartment accompanied by a young woman with a suitcase.'

He paused to light a cigarette. As he handed one to Kay and Betty and lit theirs in turn, Eva could feel her stomach knot. He slipped his lighter back in his pocket and drew on the cigarette, letting the smoke out slowly through his nostrils as he continued, 'I was naturally curious and made a few enquiries.'

Eva gave an audible intake of breath and he glanced across at her before looking directly at Kay and Betty in turn. 'One of the girls recognized the young woman in question as a friend of Max Kessel's daughter Hanna. I was reliably informed the young woman who accompanied you home was the daughter of Martin Koehn, the owner of Koehn's department store, who was arrested last night as a Jew.'

There was a gasp from Betty, then silence. Kay's face was a stone mask. Eva felt physically sick and steadied herself against the dresser. She had brought this on them. She had exposed them to the danger of harbouring Jews. She looked directly into the blue-grey eyes now looking down into hers. Her face was expressionless, but her voice betrayed her fear as she said shakily, 'You are perfectly correct. I am Eva Koehn.'

'No!' Kay shouted the word. 'Be quiet, Eva! This is a nonsense! I've told Hartmut exactly who you are.'

'Don't listen to her,' Eva continued, through her friend's protests. 'Neither Kay nor Betty knew anything of my background when they kindly agreed to put me up last night. If you have any quarrel, it's with me, not them.'

Hartmut Schuster smiled and shook his head. 'Have no fear, Fräulein. I have not come to arrest you – simply to warn you that there is a warrant out for your arrest … I checked on that before I came here this morning.' To have delayed and had someone at the Kessel club report their information to the authorities would have had dire consequences for all three girls. And nothing in this world would have him risk anything happening to Betty. For her to be caught and charged with harbouring Jews would put paid to any future plans they might have to marry.

He turned to Kay. 'Is it possible for you to leave for London today instead of tomorrow?'

Kay looked flustered.

'It *is* important.'

'Well, yes, I suppose so. I officially finished at the club last night. Today was to be my day for packing up and saying goodbye.'

He looked relieved. 'In that case, I would take the first train out of Berlin – if you value your new friend's life.'

He looked uncomfortably at Eva. 'Things are happening in Germany now that make it a dangerous place if you have Jewish blood. A very dangerous place.'

Eva looked him straight in the eyes. 'Why are you telling me this, Herr Sturmbahnführer? Why not just arrest me?'

The young man in the black uniform shook his head. There was a look akin to sadness on his face. Quite apart from his concern for Betty, how could he tell them the whole truth? How could he ever admit to anyone that his own grandmother – his beloved *Oma* Petersen – was a Jew? When she had met and married his grandfather, she had submerged her Jewishness to become a typical German Hausfrau, whose only concern in life was for her *Kinder, Kirche und Küche* – the simple philosophy that provided the bedrock of all good German women. Her Jewishness was not something that had ever been talked about in the past, and was now something that must remain buried with her forever in that windswept graveyard on the western shores of the Baltic Sea.

He had joined the SS to help restore his country to its rightful place in the world, but what had taken place on these streets last night had shocked him as nothing else had done since he had so proudly donned the uniform of Hitler's élite corps. Would such deeds as he had witnessed really restore his country to its rightful place as leader of the civilized world? In his heart he already knew the answer, and it was a hard one to live with.

'Let us just say, Fräulein Koehn,' he said quietly, 'that I, like you, witnessed what happened on the streets of this city last night. And it was not only Jews they were murdering out there, but the soul of my country itself. I want you to leave Berlin today and remember that not every German believes that the path to glory for our country can only be trod over the dead bodies of its citizens, whether they be of Jewish blood or not.' He paused. 'Will you do that?'

Eva stared at him and nodded mutely. There was a heart beating beneath that black shirt, but it required more than one SS man with a conscience to save this land now. 'I will leave my country today,' she answered softly, 'and I will pray for you, Herr Sturmbahnführer Schuster. I will pray for all of you who wear a uniform with the Nazi insignia …'

She paused, fighting back the tears which welled in her eyes. 'As for Germany itself …' she shook her head as her heart cried out for the land she had once known and loved, but was now no more. 'If there is a God in heaven, then I tremble for my country if that God is just.'

71

Chapter Six

It was raining in London the day that Eva and Kay arrived off the boat train at Victoria Station. It looked a duller city than Berlin, the buildings not so ornamental, the women's dresses less stylish than those they had left behind. But there was another difference too – there was hardly a military uniform in sight.

'Well, here we are, ducks,' Kay said as they stood, bags on the pavement at their feet, and breathed in the air of England's capital city. 'I hope you'll like it here.' She had telegraphed her mother to say she would be arriving a day earlier than anticipated and would have a friend in tow. God only knew how they would squeeze one more into the cramped two-up, two-down that was their home in London's docklands, but manage they would, she had no doubt about that.

They took a taxi to the terraced house on Bellamy Street where Kay's family had lived since before the Great War. Knots of ill-clad men stood on the street corners, their hands dug deep into their pockets of their trousers. Misery was writ large on each of their faces. 'There's not much work around here these days,' Kay said by way of explanation. 'My Dad reckons he's lucky if he gets taken on three days out of five at the docks.'

That day was one of the days Alf Bridgewater was not working, but for once he did not seem to mind. His eldest daughter had come home – even if only for a few days. He stood in the narrow hallway, his pale eyes shining at the sight of his pride and joy. 'Kay, love!'

She ran into his arms and he lifted her off her feet. He was a big man – over six feet in height, with a build to match.

72

'Is Mum around?'

'She's in the back there … Ida – it's her! It's Kay back!'

Ida Bridgewater came hurrying from the back of the house, wiping her wet hands on a print, cross-over apron as she let out an exclamation of joy at seeing her eldest child again. She was a small woman with a pinched, careworn face, and short, mouse-brown hair streaked with grey. Mother and daughter embraced, then Kay turned to the figure of Eva hanging back in the open doorway. 'Mum, Dad, I'd like you to meet my friend, Eva Koehn.'

Eva put out a tentative hand which was ignored by both Bridgewaters as they hugged the young woman in turn. 'Come on in, love,' Ida Bridgewater said, half dragging her new guest over the doorstep and into the parlour, always referred to in the house as the 'front room'.

'You take the girls' cases upstairs, Alf,' she commanded her husband, 'and I'll get the kettle on.' She turned to the two young women. 'You'll be dying for a cuppa, I've no doubt.'

Eva seated herself on the edge of a tartan travelling-rug that covered the brown hide settee. Compared to their own drawing-room on the Unter den Linden, it was a small room, stuffed full of large pieces of ugly oak furniture. The ornate over-mantel above the fireplace displayed a motley assortment of family photographs on its shelves; a framed photograph of the new King George and his pretty Scottish wife, Queen Elizabeth, hung on the wall beside it. Another, much older photograph, of Queen Victoria pictured in her widow's weeds, hung on the wall opposite. The Bridgewaters were obviously a patriotic family.

Kay disappeared into the back kitchen behind her mother, but Eva was not alone for long. The figure of a gawky young girl, with the promise of budding beauty on her freckled face, appeared in the doorway. She had the same red hair as her sister Kay, inherited from their father; for Alf Bridgewater's hair had once been as thick and red as his daughters' before middle-age had put paid to most of it. The girl's slim figure was clothed in a navy gabardine raincoat, and the long, spindly legs, encased in brown woollen stockings, shifted nervously as she surveyed their visitor.

'Hello,' Eva ventured. 'You must be Trish.' Kay had told her on the journey over about her two younger sisters, the fourteen-year-old Trish, and nineteen-year-old Sally.

'Patricia,' the girl corrected. 'Patricia's me name. It's only them as don't know any better, like our Kay, calls me Trish.'

Eva suppressed a smile. 'I am so sorry – Patricia.' She too had once been fourteen and had stood on her dignity over the most ridiculous things. They were anything but ridiculous at the time, though. 'Are you still at school, Patricia?'

The girl made a face. 'Till Christmas. And I hate it. I can't wait to get left.' She sidled into the room and perched on the arm of the chair next to the door. 'Are you a dancer, too?'

Eva looked uncomfortable. 'Well, not exactly. But I do sing.'

Patricia was not impressed. 'I want to be a dancer, me. Like our Kay. She's danced before royalty – in Egypt.'

'*Ja* … So I believe.'

'You're not English, are you?' Her face wrinkled in curiosity at the funny accent.

'No, I am German, actually.' The words almost stuck in her throat as she tensed inwardly.

'Me Dad don't like Krauts. He says they were to blame for me Uncle Arthur's death. He was gassed at some place in France. Me Auntie Ethel's got a postcard he sent her just before he was killed. Real nice it was. Said he was looking forward to getting home to see the baby. It was born after 'e left, like, so 'e'd never seen it.' She looked pensive for a moment. 'He don't like that Hitler, neither, me Dad. Says he's a bloody madman. Do you know Hitler?'

Eva made an attempt at a smile and found herself lying to the youngster who was regarding her curiously from across the room. 'No, I have never met him, but I have seen him quite often. I come from Berlin, you see.'

'Me Dad says there's going to be a war. Do you think there's going to be a war?'

Eva took a deep breath. Alf Bridgewater was obviously a man of strong opinions. She had no time to answer, however, as Kay reappeared with a tea tray which she laid on the top of the sideboard. 'Well now, young lady, I hope you haven't been annoying Eva here.'

'I was telling her I'm going to be a dancer like you.'

Kay turned sharply. 'Who said that? Have you talked to Pa about it?'

'I don't have to! He let you do it, why shouldn't he let me? Anyway, I can sing every bit as well as you can. Ma says so.'

'That may well be,' Kay said impatiently as she handed Eva a cup of tea with two digestive biscuits perched precariously on the saucer beside it. 'But there's more to it than that. Anyhow, you're far too young. You needn't get any fancy ideas in your head for a good few years yet. Now scram, shrimp! Us grown-ups have got more important things to talk about.'

Patricia made a face as she tried one of her sister's scarves on for effect in the mirror of the sideboard. She turned her head first to one side then another, as she continued to admire herself, with no intention of leaving. Then she thought better of it as her sister pulled herself up to her full height and walked towards her, hands on hips. 'OK. OK. Just because you don't live here all the time, don't mean that you can boss me around!'

The door slammed behind her and Kay turned to Eva with a weary smile. 'God knows how we end up arguing with me hardly over the threshold, but I'd really hate her to join in this game.'

She saw Eva's raised eyebrows and gave a tired shrug of the shoulders. 'Oh, it's not that I don't enjoy it – sometimes. And God knows it's much better paid than anything you'll find around here, but …' She shook her head, 'Well, the kid deserves something better than flogging her guts out in some foreign flea-pit in front of hundreds of gawking men every bleeding night. She ought to be concentrating on what our Sally's doing, not me.'

'Your sister Sally … she is not a dancer?'

'God love you, no!' An amused smile lit Kay's lips at the thought of her prim, Sunday School-teacher sister taking her clothes off for any man – even her husband, if or when she ever got one. 'Sal's a clerkess with Associated Breweries … They're the reason for the smell of malt around here.' She glanced at her watch. It had just gone half-past four. 'You'll be meeting her in an hour and a half or so. She gets in just after six.'

And it was not only Sally whom Eva met at just after six, for at least a dozen sundry friends and relatives crowded into the Bridgewaters' front parlour to welcome home the traveller from abroad, as the news reached the other houses of the terrace and surrounding streets.

Once their curiosity had been satisfied over Kay's comings and goings, their attention turned to Eva. None of the womenfolk had ever met a real-live German before, and their menfolk's only contact had been during the last war, so Eva found herself being plied with questions about Hitler and the Nazis. When it became obvious that her opinion of the man and his supporters was akin to their own, she was accepted without further ado. No one suspected she could be anything other than a normal young German dancer, no different from the other foreign friends whom Kay occasionally brought home between trips abroad. Neither race nor religion was touched upon, which came as a great relief to Eva, for she had still not come to terms herself with being anything other than one hundred per cent German.

Happily, there seemed to be an unspoken decision between her and Kay that the real reason for her flight from her homeland would not be mentioned, which came as a great relief. She had little doubt that these simple, good-hearted folk would sympathize with her predicament, but

76

the traumas of that awful night were still too vivid in her mind to want to discuss such things.

Once the initial catching up with Bridgewater family news was over, it was Ted, one of Kay's young cousins, who started the sing-song, and Kay's Auntie Ada found herself seated at the piano for the knees-up to begin in earnest.

> 'Everything's free and easy,
> Do as you darn well pleasy …'

Auntie Ada sang out lustily to the assembled company, and they did just that. The carpet was rolled back and the furniture pushed out of the way as they all took to the floor to join in the Lambeth Walk.

> 'Any time you're Lambeth way,
> Any evening, any day,
> You'll find us all – doin' the
> Lambeth Walk … OI!'

The whole house reverberated to the latest dance craze and, with many of the participants being Lambeth born and bred, it was performed and sung with just as much gusto as on a Saturday night at the Hammersmith Palais. Old and young alike swaggered around the floor of the parlour and out into the lobby to finish off each verse with the jerking, thumbs-up gesture and the hand-spreading Jewish OI!

All the old songs, and many new, echoed through the house and out on to the pavement beyond until the small hours of the morning, and when the party finally broke up at a little after two only Sally had not lasted the course. She had taken herself off to bed at midnight to a cry of, 'Does yer coach turn back into a bleedin' pumpkin then, Sal?' from her cousin Harvey. Alf and Ida Bridgewater's middle daughter had given her usual quiet smile and made no comment. Rowdy family knees-ups were not her cup of tea.

Eva had watched Sally leave and envied her the freedom to go to bed when she chose. Politeness dictated that she herself stay to the end, by which time she was almost out on her feet.

When the time finally came to call it a day, she stood at the front door with the rest of the family to receive the goodbye hugs and kisses of the departing company. She could not remember half their names, but she found herself deeply touched by the strength of the affectionate embraces bestowed upon her ... So this was London family life. It was certainly different from what she had known in Berlin, but it was none the worse for that. There was an openness here that made the private life of her own small family seem very prim and bourgeois indeed.

She smiled wistfully to herself as she followed Kay upstairs to the shared bedroom. Prim and bourgeois her own family might have been, but at least it had been *hers*. No matter how fond she might get of the Bridgewaters, they were Kay's family, not her own, and her heart ached at the knowledge.

The two high oak beds all but filled the room above the parlour. The one against the wall opposite the window Kay shared with Sally, who was already asleep, snoring softly to herself at the side nearest the wall. She made a groaning sound and moved slightly as the mattress sagged in the middle when her elder sister climbed in to join her.

The other bed, beneath the window itself, Eva was to share with Patricia – a thought that she knew did not exactly delight the younger girl who was used to having it all to herself.

Eva took longer to undress than the others. She was loathe to remove all her underwear, for the room was freezing. Fearing this would be taken either as a slight to her hosts, or as a sign of a Germanic lack of hygiene, once the thick cotton nightdress was pulled over her head, she reluctantly slipped out of her brassière, knickers and vest before joining Patricia beneath the bedcovers.

The sheer weight of the heavy woollen blankets and

bedspread almost took her breath away. Did all Britons sleep with such a ton weight on them? Had they never heard of *Federbetten* over here? Her eiderdown quilt at home weighed next to nothing and was much warmer than these coarse things that made her nose itch and pinned her to the lumpy mattress.

Then she felt ashamed. How dare she criticize, even to herself, anything about this family who had opened their home and their hearts to her?

'Goodnight, Eva. Goodnight, Trish. Sleep tight.'

Kay's whisper came from the depths of the other bed, and the response was a muffled moan from her young sister and a grateful, 'Goodnight, dear Kay,' from Eva, as she turned on to her side and curled herself into as tight a ball as possible to ward off the cold. She did not even have time to reflect on the happenings of the day, for she immediately fell into the deep, dreamless sleep of exhaustion.

She did not awaken until the bustle of Sally getting ready for work, and Patricia dressing for school, roused her at around eight the next morning.

When they had disappeared downstairs for breakfast, Eva got up and wandered over to the window. A dismal drizzle was falling and people were just beginning to go about their business. A milkcart, drawn by two old shire horses, had drawn up outside the Bridgwaters' front door, and several housewives were clustered round it, waiting to fill their empty jugs from the tall grey flagons.

Most had coats pulled on over the same sort of paisley-patterned, cross-over aprons favoured by Mrs Bridgewater, and they had their heads wrapped in scarves, knotted at the front into a type of turban. A few still had their hair in metal curlers beneath the tightly wound material, and one or two of the younger ones had small children clinging to their skirts. Eva's eyes took in the pale, pinched faces and thin little legs, with their sparrows' kneecaps. The little ones, like their mothers, appeared much more undernourished than the healthy specimens she had left behind in Berlin.

She could understand better now what drove a young woman like Kay to want to get out and seek something more in life. This was an existence of grinding poverty; of living day to day and praying there would be work on the morrow; for without work you did not eat, it was as simple as that. The trouble was, in the profession her friend had chosen, the price was often more than any young woman should have to pay.

In the distance, through the mist that still clung in wraiths to the roof-tops, she could make out the tall shapes of cranes against the skyline of the docks. The Thames was little more than a stone's throw away and you could smell it on the air. Alf Bridgewater would already be down there, no doubt, praying that today he would be one of the lucky ones.

Then the house shook as the front door was banged. It was Patricia on her way out to school, closely followed by Sally. The latter was neatly clad in a fitted brown coat and matching hat and, as she watched her disappear into the morning drizzle, Eva reflected that the younger girl was every bit as attractive as her elder sister. She would have made a first class angel for Hanna's father back in Berlin, but the thought would appal her. It was funny how people differed.

Kay lay asleep in the next bed, her clothes scattered over the patchwork quilt. A deep feeling of gratitude rose within Eva for this comparative stranger who had, without any thought of reward, taken care of her and possibly saved her life.

But she couldn't rely on the kind-heartedness of the Bridgewaters forever. Today she would reimburse them from what money she had left and set about finding herself a job and a place of her own. After paying her fare, she had changed her German marks into English notes on the ferry, and had enough left to pay for the rent of a room for a week or so, until she managed to get herself a job.

She did not wait for her friend to awake, but made her own way downstairs at a little after nine. Ida Bridgewater was alone in the small kitchenette at the back of the house. She was frying a slice of bread and an egg in a pan on the stove and looked round with a smile as Eva stood awkwardly in the doorway.

'Oh, you're up, ducks! Come on in. I was just on my way up with some breakfast for you. You don't mind making do with an egg and a bit of bread, do you? I'm afraid I can't run to any bacon scraps this morning. Alf's been laid off with his back the best part of last week, and what with the clubby man to settle with and that ...'

'No. No, of course not,' Eva interrupted hastily. 'That will be lovely.'

'Sit yourself down, then. Let's be having you.' She took a plate from the rack on top of the cooker and carefully lifted the fried bread from the pan, then slithered the egg on top of it before handing it to Eva with a smile. 'Tuck in. You young uns are always hungry.'

Eva attacked the breakfast with relish. It tasted much better than it looked, and she accepted the toast and tea that followed with a grateful smile. 'I – I must see about finding a place of my own today, Mrs Bridgewater – a single room somewhere. Not too expensive.' She gave an embarrassed smile as she took a sip of tea. 'You don't know of anywhere, do you?'

Ida Bridgewater looked thoughtful as she leaned back against the draining-board of the sink. 'I can't say as I do, really. Not round here at any rate. But London's a big place, you know. There's bound to be accommodation available if you look for it. Were you planning on doing that this morning?'

Eva nodded. 'I will make a start right after breakfast. Then I must see about a job.'

'You're not going to Cairo or wherever it is with our Kay, then?'

Eva smiled. 'No, I am not. I don't really think I would be much good as a dancer.'

Mrs Bridgewater refilled her cup from the big brown earthenware pot. 'Aye, well, maybe it's just as well. I can't claim to be as happy as I make out about our Kay. It's not really what I'd have her doing, if I had my way.' She sighed. 'But young folks don't seem to take as much notice of their parents as they did in my young day. What do your parents make of you coming across here like this?'

The teacup was half-way to Eva's lips. She replaced it shakily on the saucer. Mrs Bridgewater was watching her. Somehow she could not lie to this simple woman who had taken her in and offered her hospitality without question. 'I had no choice about leaving Berlin,' she said quietly. 'You see, my father has Jewish blood. They are doing terrible things to the Jews in Germany right now, Mrs Bridgewater.'

'Good Lord! Oh, love, I'd no idea. I'm so sorry, really I am.' She had read about that awful night a few days ago in the *Daily Mirror*. *Kristallnacht*, the Germans were calling it – the Night of Broken Glass. They had killed hundreds, thousands maybe. And those that were still alive they had carted off to those awful camps they had built. 'Them Nazis are a really bad lot, ducks. You're well out of it, if you ask me. I'm sure your Mum and Dad will feel the same.'

Eva nodded and continued to eat her breakfast, but somehow her appetite had gone.

Chapter Seven

'It's a guinea a week, take it or leave it. If you don't want it, there's plenty more who will.' The speaker was a small man in his fifties, with thin, greying hair that lay heavily Brylcreemed across his balding pate. His shirt sleeves were rolled up and his thumbs hooked into the pockets of his waistcoat as he waited for Eva to make up her mind.

She gazed around her in dismay. It was the fourth place she looked at since she had left Mrs Bridgewater's this morning. It wasn't much for the money: a single room with a one-ring gas hob and a shared WC, just off the Lambeth Walk. A three-quarter size bed stood against one wall; the marble-topped washstand next to it held a chipped porcelain ewer and basin. The other furniture consisted of a small table and two chairs, a single wardrobe that reeked of mothballs, and a chest of drawers. There was a mirror on a long chain above the fireplace, which contained a two-bar gas fire. The only bright spot was a print of poppies in a vase that hung on the wall next to the window.

'A guinea,' she repeated, frowning. 'I don't understand.'

'Twenty-one bob,' the man said impatiently. Then, seeing the frown still in place, he gave an exasperated sigh. Another bloody foreigner. 'Twenty-one shillings to you … One pound, one shilling … Comprenez?'

'One pound, one shilling a week!' Eva gasped.

'And you'll understand that will be payable a month in advance, so there'll be four quid, four shillings due now, if you want the place. Four pounds, four shillings,' he repeated slowly, so there could be no mistake.

'Four pounds, four shillings!' Eva could feel her precious

money disappearing by the second. 'I cannot possibly pay so much.'

The man looked at her – at the expensive brown wool coat and matching, calf-leather shoes. Maybe he had tried it on a bit too much. Maybe she wasn't quite so well off as he first anticipated. She was Continental, by the sound of it. They weren't usually short of a bob or two, unless she was one of those refugees.

'I can give you twelve shillings a week,' Eva said firmly, surprised at her own resolve. 'Two pounds, eight shillings for the first month now – in cash – if I can move in today.'

'Twelve bob a week for a place like this in central London, or as near as dammit? You must be joking!'

'I am not joking,' Eva said, shaking her head. 'It is all I can give you. But I will pay every month; I will not be late with the money and I will keep the place clean. You will not regret it, I promise you.'

'I don't doubt it,' the man replied grudgingly. He had had more than enough of fly-by-nights who left the place looking like a doss-house. His eyes scrutinized her from across the room. She had an honest face. Good breeding too, by the looks of it. Definitely not the type to bring men friends back and make a racket when they were downstairs trying to get some sleep. He could do an awful lot worse. And the place had already sat empty the best part of a month. 'Make it fifteen and you've got a deal.'

The two looked at one another. Then Eva opened her handbag and extracted three pound notes. 'Do I get – what is it you call it – a rent book?' she asked, handing them to him.

He took the money and shoved it into his waistcoat pocket. 'I'll push it under your door tonight,' he said. 'And you'd better have this.' He lifted a heavy iron key from the windowsill and handed it to her. 'By the way, my name's Earnshaw, Harry Earnshaw.'

Eva held out her hand. 'Mine is Koehn, Eva Koehn,' she replied.

His palm was damp, and, close to, he smelt of stale sweat, but his smile was genuine enough. 'If there's anything you want, you'll find us downstairs,' he said. 'My wife, Elsie, doesn't keep too well. It's her heart, you know. But we do our best by our tenants, I'll say that.'

'Are there many other people in the house?'

Harry Earnshaw jerked his head upwards. 'There's an old boy by the name of Bright above. Retired piano teacher. An' next door to him we've got Miss Burton, who works in the haberdasher's down the road. She's a Sally-Ann, so you'll maybe hear her damned tambourine going at all hours. But she's not a bad sort.'

'A Sally-Ann?'

'She's in the Salvation Army. Don't they have them where you come from?'

'Oh – of course. And across the passage?'

'That's another old maid … The world's full of 'em, if you ask me! Miss Simpson her name is. She's a clerkess in the music shop on the corner of the High Street and Lambeth Road. Keeps herself to herself, she does, so you'll not be seeing much of her. A bit hoity-toity, if you know what I mean.' He made a sniffing noise. 'Can't grumble, I suppose. Better that than some of the riff-raff other folks take in around here. My Elsie and me – we're not like that, you see, Miss. We'd rather have the place sit empty than let it to just any old bod.'

Eva nodded and smiled. She did not quite follow everything he said, but he was obviously giving her some sort of a compliment. And what she did understand put her mind at rest. It did not seem too bad a mix. She took comfort in the fact there were two other single women in the house. 'Well, thank you, Mr Earnshaw. I will look forward to moving in later on today,' she said quite formally and extended her hand.

'Yes, well, I'll be going then.' Harry Earnshaw shook the proffered hand with a rather embarrassed cough, then backed towards the door. For a foreigner she seemed a remarkably self-possessed young lady. 'Remember now, if there's anything else you need ...'

'Thank you, I will remember.'

The door closed behind him and Eva stood looking around the room. It certainly wasn't up to much, but at least it was a place of her own. And at least she was safe here. No more would she have to stand at the window and watch those brown- and blackshirted men goose-step their way along the road. She could rest easy in her bed here. She would have nothing to fear from the knock on the door in this house.

A sound like someone trying the handle made her turn round and, thinking it was the landlord who had forgotten something, she rushed to open it.

'Oh, I am so sorry!' Instead, she found herself face to face with a white-haired, elderly woman, who looked just as startled as she did. She had been opening her own door across the narrow passage.

'Good gracious! And who might you be?'

'M – my name's Koehn, Eva Koehn,' Eva stammered. 'I have just moved in here.' She gestured with her head to the door behind her.

The woman looked surprised. 'Don't tell me he's managed to let the place at last!' She wore small, wire-framed spectacles that gave her bird-like face an even more pinched look to it. The button eyes behind them surveyed Eva with interest. 'So we're to be neighbours, are we?' She extended a gloved hand. 'My name's Simpson – Miss Winifred Simpson.' The two shook hands. 'Do you work round here, Miss Koehn?'

Eva gave an embarrassed smile. 'I – I have just arrived in London,' she said quickly. 'I hope to find work very soon.'

The small, dark eyes behind the spectacles narrowed. 'You're not English, are you?'

'No ... I am German.' There was no point in lying.

'Jewish, perhaps?' The eyes narrowed even further. 'You're

not one of those refugees?' Her boss, Isaac Levinson, was a Jew, and he had been talking of the numbers of German Jews that had moved into his own district of Golders Green over the past few months.

'Not exactly,' Eva replied, uncertainly. She could still not quite come to terms with being a *Mischling*.

The woman sniffed. What on earth was that supposed to mean? 'But you need work, you say?'

'Well, yes.'

'Are you any good at figures?'

Eva nodded. 'Arithmetic was one of my best subjects at school.'

'And you're a neat writer?'

'Oh, yes.' Her heart was beating faster in expectation.

'Good, well, that's fine then.' Miss Simpson made to disappear into her own room, leaving Eva open-mouthed in the passageway.

Amazed at her own boldness, she took hold of the older woman's sleeve. 'You – you think you may know of a job – some work for me?'

Miss Simpson looked reprovingly at the hand on her arm and, shame-faced, Eva removed it. 'Well, it's not really for me to say.'

Then, seeing the look of disappointment on the other's face, she relented. 'I'll have to speak to Mr Levinson, of course. But there just might be something in our office. Old Mr Willats retired last month and … well, we've been trying to manage without him, but it's proving difficult.'

She backed into her own room, half closing the door in Eva's face. 'It's my half-day today, so I'll not be able to find out until tomorrow … Not that I can promise anything, mind.'

'I understand,' Eva said, trying to stifle the hope in her breast. 'But you will let me know.'

'I'm not in the habit of letting people down,' Miss Simpson replied primly. 'Now, if you'll excuse me …'

The door closed and Eva leaned against the wall across from it and closed her eyes. It was almost too good to be true. A room and the hope of a job in the same day! But it was only the hope of a job, she reminded herself as she closed the door of what was now her own room behind her and made her way down the stairs and out into the street.

Out of curiosity, she headed for the corner of Lambeth High Street and Lambeth Road, where Miss Simpson had said her music shop was. It turned out to be a double-fronted place with a large sign above the door: 'Levinson and Son, Music-sellers.' One window was full of musical instruments, the other contained a range of gramophone records and sheet music artistically displayed. By the look of it they didn't go in for frequent changes of window displays, for the front covers of the music had yellowed with the sun. Hoagy Carmichael's 'Stardust', Walter Donaldson's 'My Blue Heaven', Ray Henderson's 'Bye Bye Blackbird' and 'Sonny Boy' – all lay spread out before her gaze, and her fingers itched for the gleaming Bechstein she had had to leave behind in Berlin.

It was impossible to see into the shop through the windows, so she peered through the glass panel of the door, and could just make out a long, varnished counter at which one or two customers stood. The sound of one of the American big bands was audible from a gramophone that was being demonstrated. The urge to go inside and look further was almost uncontrollable, but she resisted. It would prove too embarrassing if, by any chance, she was asked back about the job and was recognized.

She could not wait to get back to the Bridgewaters' and relate her good fortune to Kay and the others.

They were all at tea when she arrived at the house on Bellamy Street just after six, and Ida Bridgewater insisted on giving up her own seat. 'Sit you down, ducks. You look all in. It's only cabbage and hash, but I've saved some in the pot for you.'

As she disappeared into the back kitchen, her husband leaned back on his chair and voiced all their thoughts. 'Well, Eva love, have you had any luck? You've been out long enough. We were just beginning to get worried.'

Eva slipped her coat over the back of the chair and beamed. 'It has been a wonderful day. I found a room and have the possibility of a job.'

'No!' they chorused in unison.

'How did you manage that?' Mrs Bridgewater asked as she set down the plate of hot food in front of Eva. 'Neither are so easy to come by these days, you know.'

So Eva found herself recounting the events of the day, step by step, and when she had finished, it was Alf who spoke. 'Well, I'm really pleased for you, love. We all are. But I have to say that bugger deserves to be shot.'

'What?'

'That bugger of a landlord. Deserves hanging he does, taking the loan of a bit of a girl like you. Fifteen shillings a week indeed! He ought to be shot!'

Eva's face fell. 'You think that is still too much, then?' She had felt quite proud of herself managing to beat him down from twenty-one shillings.

'I'll say it's too much!' Alf Bridgewater's highly-coloured face had taken on an even more ruddy hue. 'But I'm not saying you were wrong to take the room. Far from it. Places in London are not that easy to come by these days, and if that Miss What's-'er-name can get you a job nearby ... Well then, maybe it wouldn't be such a bad deal after all. At least you'll save on bus or tube fares and that counts for something these days.'

'When do you move in?' Kay asked.

'Tonight.'

They all looked surprised, and Mrs Bridgewater protested. 'Wouldn't you rather wait till tomorrow, ducks? It seems a bit sudden like. And you're very welcome to stay on here an extra night or two.'

Eva smiled up at her. 'I know that, and I – I really …' she searched for the right word, 'I really appreciate it. I appreciate everything you have done for me. But I think the quicker I stand on my own feet, the better.'

'In that case, I'll come round with you, and then we'll go for a celebration bevy afterwards,' Kay said firmly.

Eva smiled, a forkful of cabbage half-way to her lips. 'I would like that very much,' she answered truthfully. There had been little enough to celebrate over the past few days.

Chapter Eight

'Well, Miss Koehn, I must be honest with you, we can't pay much.' Isaac Levinson shifted uncomfortably in his seat. 'To tell the truth, we didn't intend replacing Mr Willats when he retired. Things have been quite sluggish in the trade of late. But Miss Simpson tells me she can't cope much longer without help and I have to take account of that. She's a valued employee – been with the firm since I took over from my father just after the war ...' He paused, the memory still as vivid as if it had been yesterday. 'The first day of January 1919, it was. Our family liked things to be precise you see.'

His eyes moved to a large, framed, sepia photograph of a stern-looking man, with white mutton-chop whiskers, that hung on the wall opposite.

Eva's eyes followed his. Isaac Levinson Senior reminded her of a more serious version of her Grandfather Koehn, and the thought brought a stab of pain as her attention shifted back to the man behind the desk in front of her. Mr Levinson Junior was obviously in something of a dilemma, and she began to feel quite guilty for presenting herself for a job that might not exist.

He gave a polite cough and cleared his throat noisily. 'I've given it some thought since Miss Simpson mentioned it yesterday and, well, I've come to the conclusion that perhaps she's right. There is too much work for one – what with the accounts and wages and all the rest of it ...'

His voice tailed off, as if he were loathe to get round to the distasteful subject of money, then he said abruptly, 'It'll be twenty-one shillings a week to begin with – for a trial period, you might say. And we'll see how things go after that.'

'Twenty-one shillings?' Eva's face fell. That would give her only six shillings a week to live on after she'd paid the rent on her room.

Seeing her dismayed expression, Isaac Levinson did his best to reassure her. 'Yes, well, as I've said, that'll be to begin with. If business picks up and you settle down well, then no doubt we'll have second thoughts on the matter.'

Eva's mind raced. It wasn't much, there was no getting away from that. But at least it was a job. And she could always sell the diamonds her grandmother had given her. That should keep her going until the wages picked up, or she landed herself a better job. There was precious little of the other money left after she had paid Mr Earnshaw for the rent, and had left five pounds, with a note of thanks, on the mantelpiece of the Bridgewaters' parlour. She didn't have to leave that much. In fact, Ida Bridgewater had made it plain they were not looking for any reward. But their daughter had helped save her life, and that was something Eva knew no amount of money could ever make up for.

She looked up and caught Mr Levinson's eye. He was waiting for a reply. His plump fingers twiddled nervously with a propelling pencil on the blotter in front of him. He seemed a decent sort. Not the type to take advantage of her. 'I'll take the job,' Eva said in a definite voice, and was rewarded by a beaming smile.

'Excellent. When can you start?'

'Tomorrow?'

'Tomorrow will be fine … Oh, there is one other thing. We like our staff to be similarly attired. Keeps up the tone of the place, you see. Very important that, you know. Do you think you could arrange to come in tomorrow wearing a black twinset and skirt?' Then seeing her puzzled expression, he explained, 'One of those matching jumpers and cardigans – the type of thing Miss Simpson wears. You'll be called upon to serve in the front shop now and again, you see, and we like all our staff to look as business-like as possible.'

Eva nodded. 'A black twinset and skirt ... Fine.' They expected a lot for their twenty-one shillings a week.

Her new boss beamed once more as he stood up behind his desk and extended a plump hand. 'Welcome to Levinson and Son, Miss Koehn. I'm sure you'll be very happy here.'

He showed her to the door of his office, and it was the first time she had seen him standing up. He was a good half-head shorter than herself, and at least several stones heavier. In fact, Mr Levinson Junior did not look at all healthy. A gold inlay glinted in a front tooth as he smiled his goodbye, and his high collar seemed far too tight for the several chins it supported. 'Till tomorrow, Miss Koehn.'

'Till tomorrow, Mr Levinson.'

There was a dark-suited, spotty youth of about her own age, and a similarly attired elderly man serving behind the long varnished counter as she passed on her way out. They both regarded her curiously, but made no comment.

The whole place had a faintly antiquated air about it, as if nothing much had changed since the present Mr Levinson had taken over from his father all those years ago. A bust of Beethoven stood at the far end of the counter, glaring at customers as they entered, and a yellowing poster for Noël Coward's operetta *Bitter Sweet* hung on the wall next to one she recognized from home, from Leo Blech's comic opera, *Das War Ich*.

A brass bell clanged as she opened the door and found herself out on the pavement once more. She took a deep breath and turned to gaze on the shop that was now her place of work. She was glad it was a music-seller's. Music had been an abiding passion in her life for as long as she could remember. She gave a wry smile. It seemed a million light years away from *Der Goldene Engel*, or her musical evenings with Hanna in the apartment above. So much had happened in her life over the past week that it hardly seemed credible.

There was a chill breeze blowing and she turned up the collar of her coat against the light drizzle that accompanied it. She would head across the river into the city centre: Oxford Street, perhaps, where she would spend the remaining money she had left on the twinset and skirt that Mr Levinson seemed to consider so important to his business.

She had no problem obtaining the desired garments. In fact, the only problem was the price. It left her with exactly one shilling and ninepence to last her till she managed to sell the diamonds.

A glance at her watch, and the cavernous feeling in her stomach, told her it was lunchtime. She had had no breakfast that morning, for she had simply neglected to buy in any proper food for her newly-rented room. She had never had to deal with that side of life before, and she was not finding it easy, particularly in a foreign country.

The first restaurant she came to was offering soup, a sweet, and a cup of tea for ninepence, but it appeared to be full, so reluctantly she came out again. The smell of cooking was almost too much to bear. By the time she came to the next, her hunger was so bad she felt she would faint if she didn't get something inside her soon.

She looked with some trepidation at the fancy gold lettering above the door: *La Vie En Rose*. French cuisine, obviously – and probably with prices to match.

She stood uncertainly on the doorstep and was just on the point of deciding it would most certainly be out of her price range when a black-coated waiter opened the door for her and bowed. 'Madame.'

Too embarrassed to turn and flee, she found herself being ushered into the crowded dining-room and escorted to one of the few seats still available.

'I trust Madame will not mind sharing a table?'

She looked nervously at the dark-haired young man already seated there, head down, engrossed in that day's copy of *The Times*. 'No, this is fine,' she murmured, as the waiter held out his arm for her coat. She slipped it off and handed it to him, then sat down on the chair he politely pulled out for her. She gave a nod of thanks as he handed her the leather-bound menu.

Her heart sank as she looked at it. A pot of tea alone cost one shilling and sixpence. There could be no question of ordering that *and* something to eat. The void in her stomach seemed to grow even more cavernous; any minute from now it would start to rumble in protest. She could feel tears of disappointment rush to her eyes, and it was all she could do to stop herself getting up and fleeing the premises. But that would be impossible.

The waiter returned from hanging up her coat and looked expectantly at her. 'May I recommend the *filet de boeuf*, Madame? It is quite excellent today.'

She had little doubt of it. 'I – I'll just have a pot of tea, please … I – I'm not very hungry, I'm afraid.' A distinct echoing noise emanated from beneath her clothing. Her lie was finding her out.

The waiter raised his eyebrows, but made no comment other than a 'Certainly, Madame', as he wrote her order on the small pad attached to his waist.

When he had gone she glanced across at the man on the other side of the table. If he had heard either her protesting stomach, or her pathetic request for a mere pot of tea, he certainly hadn't let on. In fact, he was taking no interest in her whatsoever as he sat engrossed in his newspaper.

He was wearing a fine brown tweed sports jacket, a checked shirt, and a matching knitted tie. There was no doubt about it – *he* could certainly afford the *filet de boeuf*, or anything else on the menu, come to that, she decided glumly.

His head of thick dark hair was slightly curly and combed back from the high, wide forehead, and his almost too regular features had a faintly quizzical expression as he continued to read his newspaper. On a plate in front of him lay the most mouth-watering chocolate éclair she had seen in

95

a long time. Certainly every bit as delicious as anything the Café Kranzler served up back home in Berlin. And, incredibly, he continued to ignore it as he slowly turned the pages of the paper.

Minutes later, when she was served with her tea, she found herself still quite unable to take her eyes off it as she sipped the hot, milky brew. Her stomach was making even louder noises than before and she prayed her silent neighbour could not hear it above the background hum of conversation and the clink of plates and cutlery from the neighbouring tables.

As she continued to sip the tea, he remained totally engrossed in his newspaper. To her surprise she noticed it was not the British *Times* as she had thought at first, but the much thicker *New York Times*. He didn't quite fit into her idea of an American. He looked too staid somehow – not quite the glamorous Clark Gable type she was used to seeing in the magazines back home. But then perhaps he wasn't. Perhaps he just preferred American newspapers.

Slowly the pages continued to turn, until finally he came to the back one. Then, when every word of that too had been devoured, he rose to go.

Carefully he folded the paper and slipped it into a brown leather attaché case, which he tucked under his arm as he stood up.

Eva's heart beat faster. He really was going – and leaving that delicious cake almost untouched! She could not believe it as he acknowledged her presence for the first time, with a polite nod of the head, as he took his leave.

When he had gone she continued to stare at the éclair. The cream was oozing out beneath the thick coating of dark chocolate, and the pastry looked positively feather-light – the type that melted on the tongue. Her mouth watered. No, not even the Café Kranzler, or its rival the Café Bauer across the road, could better that piece of supreme culinary perfection.

Dare she? Her eyes grew larger as they gazed on the

exquisite object. Her mouth was watering copiously now at the thought of sinking her teeth into the soft chocolate and cream … But no, it would be unthinkable! Well-brought-up young ladies simply did not eat other people's left-overs, especially in expensive restaurants such as this.

But there it sat, tantalizing her, as her empty stomach churned within her. If she didn't do something quickly, the waiter would be back to remove it. Then it would be gone forever – tossed with other left-overs into the bucket for pig-swill, no doubt.

A hot blush crept up her neck to surge into her cheeks as she gave a furtive glance around her. No one was watching. No one.

In a split second her hand darted forward and grabbed the cake from the plate opposite. It landed on her own plate with a squelch, to lie there for all of two seconds before she took her first bite. Never had anything tasted so good. The chocolate and cream mingled on her palate to such effect that she almost groaned out loud from sheer pleasure. In three bites it was gone, leaving only the remnants of the chocolate and cream on her fingers and around her lips as she leaned back in her seat with a guilty but satisfied smile.

Then, to her utter horror, *he* appeared again, walking purposefully towards his vacant seat from the direction of the Gents' toilet.

Rigid with embarrassment, she could not move a muscle, not even to wipe the tell-tale, sticky marks from her fingers and mouth.

He gave the same polite nod as he sat down, but Eva was staring fixedly in the opposite direction. He was gazing down at his empty plate now. She wanted to disappear beneath the table.

His bemused gaze moved from the empty plate to herself, dwelling on the sticky brown and white give-away marks that clung to her lips. The ones on her fingers she had hidden from his view beneath the overhang of the tablecloth. There was a moment's silence, then he spoke. 'They make delicious éclairs here.'

Her – he was addressing her! He was mentioning it. The unthinkable was happening. What on earth should she do? She pretended she hadn't heard.

'I said, they make delicious éclairs here.' He had an amused glint in his eyes as he repeated himself.

He knew. He knew. She was going to die with embarrassment.

'I don't mind, you know. I really didn't fancy it much anyway,' he lied.

Her eyes moved slowly towards his. He had a broad grin on his face.

'You don't suit that moustache,' he said in mock seriousness as he handed her his napkin.

'I am *so* embarrassed,' she whispered. 'I have never been so embarrassed.' She avoided his eyes as she rubbed at her mouth with the napkin.

'Forget it,' he grinned, as he extended a hand across the table. 'I just hope you enjoyed it … Rutherford's my name – William J. Rutherford. Bill to my friends.'

'Koehn – Eva Koehn,' Eva replied as he clasped her right hand in his and pumped it up and down. 'And I'm so sorry, really I am.'

'Forget it! Don't keep apologizing. It was only an éclair, after all.'

He signalled to the waiter, who was clearing a nearby table. 'We'll have two more of those éclairs, Henri. And two pots of coffee.'

'Certainly, Monsieur.'

William J. Rutherford looked at her quizzically. 'You're not English, are you?'

'I'm German.'

His eyebrows rose. 'Been here long?'

'Only a few days.'

He let out a low whistle. 'You were over there when all

that stuff was going on – the *Kristallnacht*, I believe they're calling it in the German newspapers?'

She nodded, her expression darkening. 'That is the reason I left. I was in Berlin when it happened.'

He looked at her curiously, his eyes taking in the blonde hair and regular features. 'You're not Jewish yourself, though.'

Eva gave a bitter smile. 'I am what they call a *Mischling* – Second Degree. My father has the distinction of being a *Mischling* First Degree, and that is why they arrested him.'

Bill Rutherford's dark brows rose once more. 'So you are one-quarter-Jewish and he is half-Jewish.'

Eva looked at him in astonishment. 'You have read the Nuremberg Laws?'

'It's my job to,' he replied quietly. 'I'm seconded to the American Embassy over here for the time being. I'm really a scientist, but …' His voice tailed off, as if he were unsure of how much information to reveal. 'Well, let's just say that at the moment I'm specializing in German affairs.'

'I see.' It was her turn to be intrigued. 'Are you English or American?' She gave a half-smile. 'I'm afraid my English is not yet good enough to distinguish accents, but I did notice your newspaper.'

'I'm American. A Southerner originally – from Charleston, South Carolina – or just outside it, to be exact.'

'Ah,' she said with a smile, remembering her American history from school. 'You began the Civil War.'

He laughed. 'Well, I can't claim to take personal responsibility for that. But my grandfather certainly fought in it, until he was taken prisoner by General Hancock's men at Cemetery Ridge, during the Battle of Gettysburg.' He gave a rueful smile, 'It gave Grand-daddy some tales to tell for the rest of his life, I can tell you!'

She listened thoughtfully. 'Your Grand-daddy was on the wrong side, Mr Rutherford. If I had been a young man in America at that time, I most certainly would have fought on the Northern side. To have fought to uphold slavery was a terrible thing to do. I hope your Grand-daddy was ashamed of himself.'

'Hey, hang on a minute, young lady! I came in here for a quick bite to eat, not to get a lecture on the rights or wrongs of the Civil War – or even on my poor old Grand-daddy, God rest his soul!' Then, seeing the chastened look on her face, his grin returned. 'First you eat my lunch, then you lecture me …!'

His protest was interrupted by the waiter returning with his second order of coffee and éclairs.

Eva looked suitably abashed as she poured her first cup. 'I'm sorry, Mr Rutherford. It was very rude of me.' She took her first sip of the coffee. 'This is very kind of you. There really was no need.'

'There's no need to thank me. It wasn't a duty. It was a pleasure.' He lifted his pastry fork and held it above his éclair. 'Now before I dig into this and stuff my mouth with all this goo, is there anything else you'd like to beef to me about?'

She didn't quite understand the use of the word 'beef', but got the gist of his remark. He was teasing her, but her embarrassment was still too acute to join in the joke. 'Oh, Mr Rutherford, please!'

'Bill,' he corrected, taking his first mouthful of the éclair.

'Bill.' She repeated the name, as if testing it out on her tongue, then shook her head. 'In my country, we don't use a person's first name until we know them really well.'

He dabbed his mouth with the corner of his napkin. 'Well, we can soon put that to rights … Meet me here for lunch tomorrow.'

'Oh … I don't know.'

'Don't turn coy on me!'

'I – I'm not. Really I'm not. I begin a new job tomorrow and I'm not sure when lunchtime will be.'

'Really? Where about?'

She told him and watched as he scribbled the name and address into his diary.

'I'll ring tomorrow morning and find out, then I'll come and pick you up.'

'Oh, no!' The thought of what the portly Mr Levinson, or Miss Simpson and the others, would say about that brought her out in a nervous sweat. 'I don't really think you should.'

'Right then, I'll pick you up after work. What time do you finish?'

She looked at him helplessly. He was not to be deterred. But she realized that neither did she want him to be. 'I expect the shop shuts at six.'

He scribbled 6 P.M. into his diary and slipped it back into his inside jacket pocket. 'Right, fair lady. Your carriage will await you at six. Or, if I can't manage that, I'll make sure there's a taxi.'

She smiled across the table and lifted her cup of coffee to take a sip.

He returned her smile and raised his at the same time. 'Till tomorrow evening, Miss Koehn.'

'Till tomorrow evening, Mr Rutherford.'

Chapter Nine

Eva's first day at work in Levinson's shop passed much more pleasantly than she had anticipated. She was introduced to Mr Evans, the older man who worked in the front shop, and to his young assistant, Mr Bainbridge. No one seemed to go in for first names and they all appeared to keep themselves to themselves – a fact that Eva was grateful for; she had no wish to recount her reasons for being in London. Her flight from her homeland was still too recent, and the memories too painful for casual conversation over the teacups.

The back shop, where she found herself working alongside Miss Simpson, was very much the older woman's domain, and no trace remained of the Mr Willats whom she was informed had worked there for so long and whose desk she had inherited.

The room was not small but appeared so due to the bulky wooden filing-cabinets stacked around the walls. The walls themselves had been gloss painted and had turned a dingy fawn colour with age and the effects of cigarette smoke. An old *Saturday Evening Post* cover from September 1936, entitled 'The Barbershop Quartet', had been pasted to a piece of cardboard and had pride of place above the empty fireplace. 'It's by Norman Rockwell,' Miss Simpson informed Eva. 'A very talented gentleman. He does a different one every week. My sister sends them to me – four a month – never misses. She's been over there – in America that is – since the summer of '23. Royal Oak, Michigan – nice place.'

The unsolicited information touched Eva. She had not the slightest interest in American commercial artists, but the small personal disclosure meant a great deal.

Miss Simpson herself sat at a slope-fronted, oak desk next to the window, on the sill of which stood a huge spiked plant in an earthenware pot. The ceremony of the Mother-in-law's Tongue was carried out religiously at quarter-past four every day, when the dregs of the afternoon tea were poured into the plant-pot. 'It appreciates its cuppa,' Mr Evans informed her. 'Like we all do around here.' She had returned his smile and got on with her work. The British fondness for their tea-breaks was a national characteristic she was already more than grateful for. She had had the merits of a digestive over a rich tea biscuit quite seriously explained by Mr Evans as the plate was handed round, and had been offered a sticky black and white sweet called a bull's-eye by his younger colleague. She was learning the little peculiarities of English life by the hour.

Her own desk was wedged behind the door leading to the front shop, and consequently it was forever being bumped into. 'You'll have to watch you don't blot when that happens,' Miss Simpson informed her the first time it happened that morning. But it was too late: a large, blue-black stain was already spreading over the page containing the previous day's sales figures. Eva gazed at it in dismay, resolved to invest in a rubber doorstop as soon as she could afford it, then immediately had second thoughts. She had the distinct impression that innovations, however useful, would not be welcomed at Isaac Levinson's. Change was a thing to be suspicious of at all times. A few weeks ago that attitude would have annoyed her intensely, but not now. Now it brought a curious comfort after the traumatic events of the past week. Here she had a feeling of permanence and stability that nothing and no one could change. Adolf Hitler and his thugs seemed a million miles away.

Six o'clock came unexpectedly. She had not looked at her watch in over an hour and it was with some surprise that she witnessed the door opening and Mr Evans carrying the day's takings, in paper money, through to the back shop for Miss

Simpson to lock away in the big metal safe. This too appeared to have a comforting ritual to it, as he bore the metal drawer aloft and presented it to Eva's colleague as he would have done a silver salver to a king. Eva watched quietly from behind her desk as they went through the motions. It was a little ceremony that had been carried out over the years by the same people in exactly the same way, and there was a certain odd sort of beauty to it that touched her deeply.

Mr Levinson himself came through from his own office as the key was being turned in the lock of the safe. He looked tired, Eva thought, and rather harassed. 'Well then, how've we done today? Not that many folk in, if I remember rightly.'

'Just over ten pounds, Mr Levinson,' he was informed by a pleased Mr Evans. 'It was selling that tuba that made the difference.'

'Brass meks brass,' Mr Bainbridge the young assistant punned in a mock Yorkshire accent, once the boss had disappeared back into his office with a satisfied smile. 'But we'd need to sell a whole bleeding orchestra to make this place pay!'

'We'll have less of that kind of talk around here, if you don't mind, Mr Bainbridge,' Miss Simpson said sharply. 'You'll be giving Miss Koehn here entirely the wrong impression. There's nothing coming over Levinson's. We're just going through a sluggish patch, that's all. All businesses do from time to time.'

'Oh, I wouldn't worry, Miss Simpson,' Eva reassured her. 'Nothing could spoil my first day's impression of Levinson's.' Then seeing the sceptical expressions on all three faces, she added quickly. 'I like it very much – really I do. I'm sure I'll be very happy working here.' And, surprisingly, she realized she was telling the truth.

When she emerged into the early evening chill a few minutes later, her first thought was that her lunchtime companion from the previous day had forgotten his promise to meet her. However, a shout from a dark-green car parked a few yards along the road had her walking quickly in its direction.

'I didn't want to embarrass you by drawing up right outside,' Bill Rutherford explained as he leaned over and opened the passenger door for her to get in.

'I was expecting a ...'

'A carriage,' he interrupted with a grin as he drove into the traffic. 'Sorry to disappoint you. They told me the King and Queen had them all spoken for today.'

'I was going to say a "taxi",' Eva laughed. 'I didn't expect anything as grand as this.'

'She's a real beauty, isn't she? She's a Cadillac Sport Phaeton – and if you're wondering if she's mine, I have to be honest and say, No. Tough luck. She's owned by a friend of mine at the Embassy. He had her shipped over last year. Cost an arm and a leg, but he reckons it was worth it. I would too if it were mine.'

Eva made herself comfortable in the plush leather upholstery and glanced across at her companion. He had a clean-cut face – honest as opposed to dramatically good-looking – with a straight nose and strong chin: it was a decidedly masculine profile. In fact, the only unmasculine thing about him were his eyelashes, which she observed were thick, dark, and curling. They fringed a pair of eyes so light blue they appeared almost grey in certain lights. He was dressed in a grey lounge suit, and a black and white hound's-tooth overcoat was slung casually across the back seat. How old was he? Five years older than herself at the most? Perhaps not even that. But he had a quiet confidence about him that was totally at odds with her own inner turmoil. He exuded stability; she felt comfortable in his presence.

She glanced down at the few inches of black skirt showing beneath her coat as she crossed her knees. 'I – I don't mean to sound forward, Mr Rutherford, but I hope we're not going anywhere too grand. I – I've only got my working clothes on.' Then, remembering the haste with which she had packed her one small suitcase, she confessed, 'In fact, when I left Berlin I didn't bring anything with me that would be suitable for dining out.'

'I would imagine you had more on your mind than dinner at Quaglino's when you left Germany,' Bill said drily, swerving the car to avoid a cyclist. 'If those brownshirted sons-of-bitches had had their own way, you would probably be in one of their concentration camps by now ... Have you been listening to the wireless or reading the newspapers since you arrived?'

She shook her head. 'I'm afraid not. There isn't a radio in my room and they don't have one at work.' Then, remembering the stock of brand new ones in the front shop, she added, 'At least not one we can play for our own benefit ... You have been listening, though?'

He nodded as he turned the car into Westminster Bridge Road. 'It doesn't make pretty listening. Would you believe the pigs are making the Jews pay for all the glass the Nazi thugs themselves broke on *Kristallnacht*? They're imposing a fine of one billion marks on the few Jews that are left in Germany. They call it retribution for the death of vom Rath and for all the property that was destroyed last week.'

'One billion marks!' Eva drew in her breath sharply. 'But who will pay it?'

'Exactly. Who is left to pay it? From what we hear almost every Jewish male has been rounded up and thrown into prison, or into one of those camps, and by all accounts the women and children are next on the agenda.'

Eva shuddered and clasped her gloved hands tightly in her lap. She could feel tears spike her eyes and prayed she would not cry; not in front of him. He sensed the news had upset her and inwardly cursed himself for being so insensitive as to bring it up in the car. 'I hope you're hungry,' he said, diplomatically changing the subject. 'I've booked a table at a real nice little place just off Piccadilly. The pro-

106

prietor's Austrian and they do a really good Wiener schnitzel.'

He was trying to be of comfort but she grimaced all the same. The very word 'Austrian' made her blood boil these days. But that was what living under Adolf Hitler for almost six years did to you. 'It sounds delicious,' she lied.

'I thought you'd like it.' He threw a grin in her direction as he manoeuvred the Cadillac through the rush-hour traffic. It was suddenly very important to him to make her happy. For the past few months he had been studying what had been going on in her country, but somehow it had never seemed real. But now, meeting someone like her – a beautiful young girl who had experienced the horrors of the Nazi regime at first hand – made him realize just what a sheltered existence he himself had been living up till now. From home to university, from university to science lab, from science lab to a cushy little number at the American Embassy – it wasn't exactly seeing life in its true raw state, was it?

When they drew up in front of *Der Rosenkavalier* some ten minutes later, he took her arm as they walked up the steps, to be greeted by the host, Herr Winkler. The gesture touched her. It made her feel special – cherished almost – for the first time in so long.

They were shown to a table for two in a secluded alcove on the far side of the room from the three-piece band, which was playing a selection of Viennese Waltzes. Herr Winkler himself – a portly figure in brown lederhosen and a feathered hat – relieved them of their coats, before he handed Bill the menu with a polite bow and took his leave.

The room was packed, and the small dance-floor already crowded with couples. Young women in Tyrolean costume were flitting between the tables taking orders. The whole atmosphere reeked of *Gemütlichkeit* – that particular brand of cosiness and bonhomie so common to Germanic hospitality. Despite everything, Eva felt a bitter-sweet longing for home as the unashamedly sentimental music tore at her heart, and the sound of the occasional German voice from a neighbouring table brought the memories flooding back. If she closed her eyes she could even be in the Café Kranzler ...

She left Bill to do the ordering and, against all her inclinations, she actually enjoyed the huge platter of Wiener schnitzel and trimmings, and the mouth-watering strawberry cheesecake with cream that followed. The wine was a light, dry Moselle and, by her third glass, she found herself relaxing completely in his company. She had not eaten so well since leaving home, and she had never drunk so many glasses of wine at one sitting in her life. Perhaps the most exciting thing of all, though, was simply being in the company of an undeniably attractive young man. The only other male outside her own family whom she had spent any time with had been Kurt Kessel, but compared to the young man across the table from her tonight, Kurt had been a mere boy.

Throughout the meal her companion was careful to keep off the subject of Germany for fear of upsetting her, and contented himself with telling her about his own early life as a boy in a small town on the outskirts of Charleston, South Carolina.

It was a childhood far removed from Eva's own, for his parents had not been wealthy by any stretch of the imagination. His father had run a hardware store that only just paid enough to keep a minimum of food on the table for his wife and child.

Bill gave a wry smile as he thought of the borrowed Cadillac parked at the door of the restaurant. What he would have given to have been able to take his parents out for a ride in something like that. Luxuries in any shape or form simply did not exist – not in the Greensville of his childhood. Not for his small family, at any rate. In fact, often the bare essentials themselves did not exist. You simply learned at a very early age not to ask for things that other kids might take for granted. To ask was to bring a look of despair to your mother's eyes that made you feel ashamed for the rest of the day. In a family where even the basic necessities were often impossible to come by, a small child would grow up fast.

Until he reached high-school age, he wore no shoes throughout the summer holidays; that way one pair could be made to last the whole of the school year. A pair of baseball boots like those in Old Mackay's shoe-shop window were as unattainable as the moon.

His pal Jack Douglas was luckier; he had an elder brother and could be assured of most things second time around. As he grew up, he had often wondered why he himself had no brothers or sisters, until one day, from outside the open kitchen window, he overheard his mother talking to his Aunt Phoebe. To a young boy, verging on adolescence and only just acquainted with the facts of life, what he heard had both shocked and disturbed him. His parents had not slept together as man and wife since his own birth, for fear of bringing another child into the world whom they could neither feed nor clothe.

The anguish and bitterness in his mother's voice that day as she regretted their ability to raise what she referred to as a 'proper family' had lived with him. And, for the first time, he had understood something of the sadness that seemed to lie permanently behind the clear grey of her eyes.

He had remained out there on the porch for a long time that morning, dangling his bare legs over the edge of the wooden verandah, and tracing patterns in the dust of the sidewalk with a sharpened birch twig. Obadiah, an old Negro who did odd jobs for those on the street who could afford it, had passed by and commented on his unusually glum expression, and he had sworn at the old man. A fact he was still deeply ashamed about to this day.

Obadiah, who never failed to carry a buckeye in his pocket to ward off the crippling attacks of rheumatism he suffered each winter, had been the one who had taught him to fish, and had taught him a rhyme into the bargain that had remained with him ever since:

Them ez wants must choose.
Them ez has must lose.
Them ez knows won't blab.
Them ez guesses will gab.
Them ez borrows sorrows.
Them ez lends spends.
Them ez gives lives.
Them ez keeps dark is deep.
Them ez kin earn kin keep.
Them ez aims hits.
Them ez hez gits.
Them ez waits win.
Them ez will kin.

Them ez will kin … How often over the years had he repeated those words? There were losers in this life and there were winners. He had resolved to be one of those winners that day on the front porch.

Yes, there were some days in your life that remained with you. Days that, for one reason or another, etched themselves on the soul. That day, at the age of twelve, he had sworn to himself that he would never let happen to him what had happened to his father. Those that claimed there was a dignity in being poor had it wrong. There was no dignity to be found in poverty, only humiliation and despair. No matter what the difficulties, he resolved he would find a way to get out of Greensville and a future tied to the counter of Rutherford's Hardware Supplies. He would find a way to work through college and get a degree. For that was the key; even at that early age, he knew that having letters after your name was the key to unlock the door to another world far removed from selling nails by the half-pound, rakes and hoes, and his grandmother's homemade soap.

Even today, in this fashionable London restaurant, he could almost smell it – that store with its cans of turpentine and cheap paint. 'I hope I've succeeded,' he said aloud, half to himself. 'Although, I guess it's already too late.'

'Too late for what?' Eva had listened in silence as he had

talked of his past, so very different in every way from her own.

His lips twitched slightly. 'Pa's dead. He died two years ago. On the fifth of August, the day Jesse Owens won the 200 metres gold for America at the Berlin Olympics.'

Eva remained silent. She had been there in the stadium that day.

'I wanted to do something, you see. Give them both something back for what they did for me. Give them ...' his voice tailed off, as if searching for the right words. 'Well, give them life, I guess. Something they never had in all those years of living on the breadline.'

'And your mother?' she asked softly. 'Is she still alive?'

He shook his head. 'I read a poem once,' he said quietly, 'and there was one verse in it that stuck in my head. It goes:

> 'The greatest battle that ever was fought,
> Shall I tell you where and when?
> On the maps of the world you will find it not,
> It was fought by the mothers of men ...

'Ma died four months to the day after Pa ... I guess for her the battle had just been too long, too hard.' He gave a bitter half-smile. Why was he telling her all this? Why was he confessing to a virtual stranger what he had never discussed with a living soul before? Not even to Mary-Jo, his high school sweetheart, had he related the incident on the porch that day, or the effect it had had on him. And now here he was telling everything to this young German girl whom he had only just met. He took a gulp of wine, emptying his glass. If confession was good for the soul, why was he suddenly feeling so darned exposed?

They sat in silence for a moment or two, the music from the band covering the longest pause that evening as they both concentrated on their own thoughts.

Eva was both deeply touched and yet slightly troubled by what she had heard. She sensed he had probably revealed much more than he had intended about himself and his family. He was uncomfortable, she could feel it. It was important to move the conversation on to a more impersonal level. 'Why did you choose science to study?' she asked, pouring herself another coffee from the silver pot on the stand at her elbow.

He shrugged and gave a sheepish grin. 'Because it was the thing I was best at.'

It was the simple truth, but not the whole truth. But now was not the time to go into the long evenings he had sat slaving over the extra tuition set him by Ed Marlowe, his science master, who also happened to be Mary-Jo's father. The older man had taken a special interest in him and nurtured his natural curiosity about the subject. 'At first, I could only see as far as being a teacher, but I was lucky to keep getting good enough grades to go all the way.'

'And all the way was?'

'Harvard, where I got my doctorate.' It was hard to keep the pride from his voice.

'You must be a very clever scientist.' She was impressed.

'A very lucky one.'

'And what exactly were you studying?' She knew next to nothing about the world of science; it was a subject not considered suitable for the young ladies of the Empress Friedrich Gymnasium.

Bill reached across to pour himself a coffee. They were beginning to skate on perilously thin ice. The experiments they had been working on in the field of atomic research were a closed book to all but a very few, and had to remain that way. 'Far be it from me to bore you on that subject,' he said diplomatically. 'Anyway, I think it's your turn now, don't you? I've talked enough about myself for one day. I've never been to Berlin. Tell me about it.'

And so she did. Partially spurred on by his own honesty, and partially by the wine, for the next hour she found herself telling him everything about her life and family on the Unter den Linden, and about that terrible day, barely a week ago, when her world had come to an end. She even found herself telling him about the diamonds her grandmother had so carefully sewn into the hem of her coat, and of her despair the previous day when she realized she had no money for anything more than a cup of tea.

He shook his head in a mixture of sorrow and amazement. 'If only I'd known … But what about today? You won't have had time to sell the diamonds yet. What have you done for food?'

She gave an embarrassed smile. 'I had enough to buy an apple for my lunch and, apart from that, I made do with the biscuits we got with our cups of tea at work.'

'Holy Moses – you must have been starving!'

She smiled. 'Not any more.'

Still frowning, he reached inside his jacket and took out his wallet. 'Look, I'd better keep back enough to settle the bill, otherwise we'll end up in the kitchen washing dishes, but I've got at least five pounds spare on me tonight.'

He extracted a large white five-pound note from his wallet and, folding it into the palm of his hand, he slipped it discreetly across the table to her. 'For heaven's sake get yourself some decent food in that room of yours.'

She looked down at it on the tablecloth in front of her and drew back as if scalded. 'I – I couldn't. Really I couldn't.' She felt desperately ashamed for being so honest and confessing everything to him.

'Take it, please!' he insisted. 'I tell you, I won't sleep a wink until I know you've got some food in that place of yours … Now you wouldn't have a poor guy having sleepless nights, would you?'

She had to laugh. 'Oh, Mr Rutherford – to think that the first time a young man tells me he is going to have sleepless nights over me, it's all because of my empty larder!'

He grinned back, and it was his turn to look bashful. 'Given time, Miss Koehn. Given time …'

Chapter Ten

Eva could not recall a more perfect evening as she sat back in her chair and smiled her thanks as Bill emptied the last of the wine into her glass. In the mellow warmth of the restaurant the troubles of the world outside seemed a million miles away.

'You look happy.'

'I am.' She reached out for her glass, only to pause, her outstretched fingers only inches from its narrow stem. Her eyes were fixed on the far corner of the room, her brow furrowed.

'Is there something wrong?'

She shook her head as she continued to peer in the direction of the ornate coatstand. 'No ... I'm sure it's perfectly all right.' She edged further round in her seat for a better look.

'What is it, honey? Is anything wrong?'

Again she shook her head. 'I – I don't know ... It's probably nothing, but I could have sworn Herr Winkler hung my coat on that stand when we came in.'

Bill swung round in his chair and it was his turn to stare at the wrought-iron, ornamental stand in the far corner of the room. 'He did. It was hanging right next to mine. I passed it on my way to the john half an hour ago.'

They both looked at one another as Eva's face paled. There was no sign of it now. A lone checked scarf that neither had seen before hung forlornly from the peg next to Bill's coat.

'Jesus!' Bill rose from his seat, almost throwing his chair from him as he made for the stand. Eva followed in mounting panic. It couldn't be gone. It just couldn't. Not with her grandmother's diamonds still in the hem.

She could only shake her head in a mixture of disbelief and despair as the awful truth was confirmed. And she could still scarcely believe it when moments later they stood in the restaurant owner's office.

'Madame, what can I say? It is a most unfortunate thing to have happened.' Herr Winkler's florid face conveyed his dismay as he looked from Eva to Bill and back again. 'We will make recompense, of course,' continued the restaurant owner. 'Full retail value of the coat. This type of thing is, alas, not unknown on busy evenings such as this.'

Eva stared at him, white-faced. How could it end like this? It had been one of the happiest evenings of her life up to this moment. She clutched at Bill's sleeve for support. 'The diamonds …' she gasped. 'The diamonds … they were still in the hem.'

'You're absolutely sure it's missing?' her companion demanded of the embarrassed owner. 'There has been no mistake?'

Herr Winkler shook his head. 'Unfortunately no, sir. I believe two ladies' coats are missing. The brown one belonging to the young lady here, and a three-quarter-length camel one. I believe they were both on the same peg.'

Eva shook her head in disbelief. All the financial security she had in the world was in the hem of that coat and now it had vanished into thin air. Just like that. Every single one of her grandmother's precious diamonds. She felt sick at heart, as if she had somehow let her beloved *Oma* down. 'I thought it would be safer leaving them there than in my room,' she said faintly, as much to herself as to Bill. 'I never dreamt a thing like this could happen.'

They spent the next ten minutes in the owner's office, filling out details of the coat and its precious contents. Seeing the distraught condition Eva was in, Herr Winkler did not doubt her story, although he had heard some tall tales in his life as a restaurateur. 'In the circumstances,

115

madame, we will double the replacement value of the article, as an act of good faith. It is the very least we can do.'

'And exactly what would that work out at?' Bill asked grimly.

Herr Winkler shrugged his ample shoulders. 'A good class ladies' coat could be had these days for, say, five pounds. If we double that the young lady here would receive ten pounds.'

Bill stared in disbelief. 'Big deal indeed! Do you realize there could have been a thousand pounds' worth of jewels in the hem of that coat?'

Herr Winkler sighed. 'You will appreciate we only have your word for that, sir. It is not that I do not believe you and the young lady personally; but the difficulty comes in convincing our insurance company of the claim. I can tell you now they will maintain it is another fairy story.'

He made a helpless gesture with his hands. 'We get them all the time – customers claiming their jacket, or their briefcase, has been stolen, containing hundreds of pounds … This story of the diamonds in the hem of the coat,' he gave a weary shake of the head, 'they will merely put down to a claimant with a bit more imagination than most.'

'Now look here …!' Bill made as if to grab the man, but Eva kept hold of his arm. 'No, please … Let's just leave it. If he doesn't believe us, there's nothing we can do!'

Obviously embarrassed, Herr Winkler reached down and pulled open his desk drawer. He extracted a black metal petty-cash box and, unlocking it, took out two crisp ten-pound notes, which he laid on the table in front of him. There was something about this particular young couple that told him they were telling the truth, but that would not convince his insurance company. 'Here is twenty pounds,' he said, holding out the money to Eva. 'I myself will be out of pocket, but it is more important that I show my good faith in my customers.'

Eva looked at the money, then at Bill. 'Don't touch it,' he

said grimly. 'If he doesn't believe us he can keep his goddamn money. I'd rather give you the twenty pounds myself.'

'Don't be silly,' she protested. 'Why should you be out of pocket?' She let go of his arm and took the notes from Herr Winkler's outstretched hand. 'Thank you, mein Herr,' she said, as she pushed them into the zipped pocket of her handbag. 'It was not your fault. Please don't think I'm blaming you.'

The Austrian gave a weary smile. It had been one of those nights, and now he would have the owner of the camel coat to find and break the bad news to. With his luck, she would claim to have had half the Crown Jewels hidden in one of her pockets. 'Thank you, madame ... And I trust this unfortunate incident will not stop you from enjoying our hospitality again.'

Eva reached across the desk to shake his hand and Bill reluctantly followed suit. Then they made their way back through the crowded restaurant and out into the bitter cold of the night.

Bill held on tightly to her arm as they hurried across the sparkling frost of the pavement to where he had parked the car. Clad only in her black twinset and skirt, in the cold and dark she seemed even more young and vulnerable than when they first met. From that first moment yesterday, he had felt strangely protective towards her, and never more so than now. 'Don't worry, Eva,' he said quietly as he took off his own coat and slung it around her shoulders, 'I'll see that you never go short of money. You won't miss those diamonds. I promise you that.'

She looked up at him in the yellow glow of the streetlights and believed him. The Mr Rutherford and Miss Koehn had disappeared along with the diamonds in the hem of the coat. 'I know that, Bill,' she answered softly, and squeezed his arm that bit tighter.

Despite the warmth of his overcoat, her teeth were chattering by the time she seated herself beside him in the front of the car. The seats were positioned very close together and he could sense her trembling beside him, whether from shock or cold he was not quite sure. He had an almost uncontrollable urge to put his arm around her shoulders, but resisted. For a young woman of her sheltered upbringing, it might seem far too forward a thing to do. But by the time he had started the engine and pulled the car away from the kerb, he inwardly cursed himself for his faint-heartedness.

When eventually they pulled up in front of her lodgings, she made the first move as she laid an apologetic hand on his arm. 'I – I'm sorry I can't ask you in. I don't think Mr Earnshaw would approve.'

'Mr Earnshaw?'

'He's my landlord. He lives downstairs.'

He looked across at her in the dim half-light. Damn Mr Earnshaw, he felt like saying but, once again, good manners got the better of him and he resisted. Instead he lifted her hand from the sleeve of his jacket and held it to his lips. 'Till tomorrow,' he whispered.

'Till tomorrow,' she replied, as she slipped his overcoat off her shoulders and opened the car door. She did not even have to ask where or when.

That night she sat down and wrote a long letter to her family in Berlin. She addressed it to all three of them: her mother, father, and grandmother. But in her heart she knew it would be a miracle if it eventually reached the hands of even one of them. She had sent a postcard on the day of her arrival in England, but this was the first time she could trust herself to pour her thoughts on to paper with any kind of coherence. She now had a home, a job, and friends. She could not have expected more from her first week in a strange country.

She told them of the Bridgewaters, and of their kindness to her, and of her room here in the Earnshaws' lodging house, with Miss Simpson next door. She even wrote two whole pages on Levinson's, telling them all about her new colleagues, and of her work in the office alongside Miss Simpson. And, when she had finished that, she sat for a long time staring into space, wondering if she should tell them about *him*. Bill Rutherford had come into her life so suddenly and now seemed to have completely taken it over. She could think of nothing else but her next meeting with him. Even the loss of the diamonds, which she was careful not to mention in the letter, had assumed much less importance in her mind than it would have done otherwise.

It was as if she had always known him. And, more than with even Hanna or Kurt, she felt comfortable with him. He was the only person here in England to whom she had told everything, and it felt right. She could not have lied to him, nor he to her, she was sure of that. But the more she thought about it, the more she realized she could not tell her parents. They would be worrying enough about her over here without giving them something extra to fret about.

She closed the letter sending her love to all three. She had written as if they were all still together. Somehow to write about her father's arrest was to acknowledge the fact it had happened – to make it a reality – and she prayed with all her heart, to a God she no longer believed in, that this was not the case. Not a night had gone by but she had prayed that he had been returned to their home. She continued to cling desperately to the fact that he was only a *Mischling*, albeit First Degree, and not a hundred per cent Jew.

She posted the letter on her way to work next morning. There had been a hard frost again overnight and the pavements sparkled in the grey morning light. She shivered and pulled the collar of her jacket closer around her neck. She felt the lack of her winter coat and resolved to spend some of Herr Winkler's money on a new one during her lunch-break. She had been forced to put on the pale-blue tweed jacket of the only suit she had packed to bring with her, and she envied the warm winter clothing of the other women she passed hurrying to their places of work.

She told the story of the theft of her coat to Miss Simpson during their tea-break at eleven o'clock, carefully omitting the fact that it was a male friend she had been out with. The older woman was genuinely sympathetic and, to Eva's surprise, volunteered to go with her to a ladies' dress shop she recommended in the district. 'You'll get as good value there as in Oxford Street,' she informed her knowingly, 'and pay a lot less for it into the bargain.'

Two hours later, Eva was forced to admit her colleague was probably right as she stepped out into the crisp, frosty air in a brand new coat of cherry-red wool. It had a neat, fitted waist and tie-belt, and cost her all of four pounds fifteen shillings. Miss Simpson had suggested a hat and gloves to match, but Eva had not been persuaded. What little money she had was far too precious. Instead she remained hatless and made do with the black leather gloves she had brought over from Germany with her.

'You look very nice, Miss Koehn. Very nice indeed.'

'Thank you, Miss Simpson,' she had replied, hoping fervently someone else would think so too.

He was waiting for her at the same place just after six o'clock, but this time in a taxi. He got out of the black hackney cab as she approached and held the door open for her. 'Sorry I couldn't run to the Cadillac tonight,' he said with an apologetic smile, 'but Joe needed it himself.'

She wouldn't have cared if he had come on foot, she was just so happy to see him.

He took her to a little place just off Russell Square where, he informed her, many famous writers liked to eat. 'If we're lucky we might see one or two,' he murmured into her ear as they squeezed between the closely-packed tables to reach a vacant one at the back of the room.

She made an appropriate response, but knew she couldn't

care less about famous writers. She had all the company she required for a happy evening.

Her happiness was short-lived, however, for they had only just begun their first course when he dropped his bombshell.

'I'm afraid I've got bad news tonight, Eva.'

She looked up from her roast beef in curiosity, not quite comprehending. 'Bad news? About Germany, you mean? You have heard something terrible on the news today?'

He shook his head. 'No, it's not Germany this time. It's me. I've been told I'm being sent back to the States.'

Her mouth dropped open. How could this be happening? They had only just met. 'Back to the States? But when?'

'I leave tomorrow.'

She stared at him. Her mouth had gone quite dry and her words were barely audible. 'For how long?'

He shrugged his shoulders in a helpless gesture. 'I wish to God I knew.'

'You mean they won't tell you?'

'It's not as simple as that,' he said slowly, measuring his words carefully. 'I'm to relieve a colleague in the State Department who's had to go on sick leave; then I believe they have some sort of course lined up for me.'

He toyed with the handle of his knife. He had to watch his words carefully, even with her. This past month had seen a distinct shift in both the American and British Intelligences' assessment of Hitler's intentions in Europe. Reports now seemed to indicate that Hitler had received information on the inadequacies of both Britain and France's air defences, and Germany was now preparing to take the offensive in the west as well as preparing to move into south-eastern Europe. This was causing alarm in both London and Washington, with both governments taking the reports seriously. He had been asked to return to the American capital for further briefings in light of the changing circumstances in Europe. 'I was due to go on the course shortly, anyway,' he finished lamely. 'This has just speeded things up, that's all.'

Eva looked down at her dinner plate. The feeling of disappointment almost suffocated her. 'I don't want you to go,' she said softly. It was not at all what she had intended to say, but it was the truth.

He reached across the table and took her hand. 'I don't want to go, either. Not now ... Jeeezus – not now.'

'Will you come back?'

His eyes were dark grey and very serious in the lamplight as they looked into hers. 'I promise,' he replied.

And she believed him.

Chapter Eleven

It was a Sunday morning eighteen months later, on 15 August 1940, before Bill Rutherford came back into Eva's life. Eighteen months of waiting and wondering. Why hadn't he written? Was it all her imagination – that spark that had been lit between them? Or had something happened back there in the States that had changed things so drastically that he had not even bothered to write? For months these questions plagued her as she settled down to life as a Londoner.

And it was not easy settling down to life in England's capital city. Quite apart from her longing to hear from the young man from across the Atlantic again, her heart ached for news of her family back in Germany. As the weeks turned into months and still no news arrived, slowly she had to come to terms with the fact that she might never hear from them again. She had written countless letters to her parents' address during the first few months after her arrival in Britain and, when no reply came, she had written to everyone she could think of, beginning with the Kessels, to attempt to obtain some news of her family. All said the same thing: her family home in the Unter den Linden had been taken over by another family 'of true Aryan stock', and no one could tell her where the original inhabitants had gone.

The knowledge ate into her soul. But she could not give up hope. Every week she continued to write to old friends in her native city, begging them to keep on trying to obtain information for her – any detail, no matter how slight, that might lead her to the whereabouts of her mother, father, or grandmother. But no word came. And when war was declared on 3 September 1939, the letters had to cease.

It was then, amid the air-raids and deprivations of war-torn London, that her thoughts returned to the young man who had entered her life so suddenly that day in November 1938, and left it just as rapidly a few days later. Perhaps concentrating on the much lesser pain of Bill Rutherford's disappearance helped her cope with the lack of news of her family; or maybe it simply helped deflect her mind from the constant threat of bombing raids. She was never quite sure exactly why he came to dominate her thoughts so much over the succeeding months; but dominate them he did.

Thinking of him was merely a mental diversion, she told herself, not only to help her avoid thinking of her family, but also to help pass the monotonous hours she spent alone in her room after finishing work at Levinson's at six o'clock every evening.

She was now firmly established as part of Isaac Levinson's little team. He had even kept his promise of raising her wages, although not until she had been there all of six months. On May Day 1939, she had received the grand sum of thirty shillings in her weekly pay-packet.

She had also learned something of the well-known British reserve during that time. Miss Simpson continued to live across the landing from her in the Earnshaws' lodging-house, and they continued to work side by side every day; but one and half years later, she knew no more about the personal life of the older woman than she had at the very beginning.

Of the other two lodgers upstairs, Mr Bright and Miss Burton, she saw next to nothing, although she could hear the old gentleman's piano on occasions. The sound resounded through the ceiling from the room above and brought a curious comfort. Chopin appeared to be his favourite composer, and the pieces he played most frequently had also been her grandmother's favourites, played constantly on the Bechstein in the drawing-room in the days before she had been confined to bed.

It was funny how music had the power to move the soul like almost nothing else could. And it was not only the classics that could stir the emotions, popular music could be every bit as powerful. For days now a snatch of a favourite Berlin song of the 1920s had been going through her head:

> *Das gibts nur einmal*
> *Das kehrt nicht wieder*
> *Das ist zu schön, um wahr zu sein …*

'It happens only once', the songwriter had written. 'It will not come again. It was too beautiful to be true …' Such painful words wrapped up in such a pretty tune. And round and round it went in her head. And each time she saw one face before her: the face of a young American with dark curling hair and smiling, grey-blue eyes. Maybe the song was right; maybe it was just too beautiful to be true.

She thought she had seen him once, one Sunday after-noon, on her way round to visit the Bridgewaters. It was the day after war had been declared, and her thoughts were still filled with the horror of Neville Chamberlain's broadcast to the nation, informing them that they were now at war with her country. He had been walking in front of her, a tall, broadshouldered figure in a grey lounge suit. There was something about the loose-limbed gait that made her heart turn over. It was a peculiarly American style of walking. Neither the British nor the Germans walked quite like that. She followed behind him for about a hundred yards, then he stopped to buy a paper from a pavement newsvendor. She had stopped, too, and purchased a copy of the *Sunday Pictorial*, only to find that, face to face, the man looked nothing like him. The sense of disappointment had been acute and had remained with her for the rest of the day.

She still visited the Bridgewaters occasionally and always enjoyed her time spent with them. They were a happy bunch and never failed to look on the bright side of any situation.

On her last visit there they had had a new addition to the family; Alf had answered an advertisement in that week's *New Statesman*: 'Bombed-out cat, orthodox Marxist, seeks good home.' So a large, fat marmalade tom named Engels had joined the family circle.

Not to stretch the family's tight budget any further, Eva made sure she never arrived near a mealtime. Instead she would stop off at the local fish and chip shop on her way home and carry her tea back to her own flat in an exquisite-smelling newspaper parcel. The chip shop had had a new sign up on the wall on her last visit: 'Owing to Hitler, chips is littler' and some wag had added beneath: 'Owing to Hess, fish is less'.

She had still been smiling to herself over it as she left the shop that day, only to run into Kay again on one of her friend's infrequent visits home.

Instead of carrying her fish and threepence-worth back to her flat, Eva had returned to sit at a table in the shop, where she had enjoyed her meal and listened to her old friend recount, over a meat pie and mushy peas, her own experiences since they had last met.

It seemed the war had put paid to her cabaret work abroad. At first she had been able to make up for it in tours to the States and Canada, but now, with the phoney war, as they called it, well and truly over, and hostilities extending to the sea and air as well as the land, even the trips to America had had to cease. The last time they met she had been talking of obtaining a job at London's own Windmill Theatre. It was only the thought of her father's reaction to her appearing nude in her native city that was making her delay applying. She was also writing regularly to a young man in the Navy named Bill. It was a common enough name but, every time she used it, it had sent a stab of regret through Eva. If things had worked out differently, it could have been her talking about her own Bill for half the night.

But thoughts of Bill Rutherford were far from her mind

that Sunday morning in August as she lay in bed and luxuriated in the only long lie-in of the week. Every morning from Monday to Saturday she had to be in to the office before nine, but Sundays were her own.

That particular Sunday, she was lying in bed, deeply engrossed in a small red, cloth-bound book. For months now she had been working her way through the Everyman edition of Dickens, in a quest to improve her English, and she had got into the habit of reading that day's chapter aloud as she lay in bed and sipped her morning cup of tea. She had reached page 114 of *Bleak House*, and things in Dickensian London were becoming quite heated as her voice resonated in the silence of the small room:

"'Most assuredly not!' said Mr Boythorn, clapping him on the shoulder with an air of protection, that had something serious in it, though he laughed. "He will stand by the …"'

Eva broke off abruptly at the clattering sound from the direction of the window. Puzzled, she paused in her reading for a moment then continued:

"'He will stand by the low boy always. Jarndyce, you may rely upon him! But, speaking of this trespass …"

'What on earth!' she exploded, as the second clatter occurred. Then, to her amazement, as she looked across at the open window, another hail of small pebbles struck the glass.

'What on earth's going on?' She leapt from the bed determined to shout a reprimand at the small boys she was certain were up to their tricks on the pavement beneath.

Pulling a thin cotton robe over her nightdress, she ran barefoot across the linoleum to throw up the sash window even further and peer out. The sight that met her eyes made her gasp aloud in disbelief. 'I don't believe it!'

But there was no mistaking the tall figure of Bill Rutherford standing gazing up at her from the road below.

On seeing her, he raised his right hand in greeting, and swept off his hat in a single gesture. But this time, the usual grin was missing from his face. It had been replaced with a slightly apprehensive look, as if he were not quite sure what exactly his reception would be.

Eva herself was not even sure. Myriad thoughts tumbled through her head. Should she smile and wave back as if he had only just left? Or should she stand on her dignity? After all, he had been gone for a whole year and a half without a single word.

'Aren't you going to ask me up?' He more or less decided the issue for her.

'I – I'm not dressed.'

The familiar grin returned. 'I won't complain.'

She stared down at him stoney-faced for a moment, then relented as of its own accord her face broke into a smile. 'Just a minute!'

Dashing a quick look in the mirror on the wall, and running a controlling hand through her tangle of hair, she picked the outside key off the mantelpiece and returned to the window. 'You'd better come up!' she called, as quietly as possible, as she tossed the key down to him.

He caught it in one hand, and walked across to unlock the outside door as Eva slid the window fully down. Her heart was beating much too fast as she tightened the belt of the cotton robe around her slim figure. She could hear his feet on the worn linoleum treads of the stairs. She prayed inwardly that Mr Earnshaw didn't open his door downstairs to investigate. She was hardly in a fit state to receive any type of visitor, let alone a young man.

There was a soft tap at the door and she walked quickly across the room to open it. They stood looking at one another on the step.

'Hello, Eva.' He looked older and thinner-faced than she

remembered, as he stood holding his hat between his hands. But the friendly smile was still the same, if a trifle hesitant this time.

'Hello, Bill.'

'May I come in?'

She stepped aside to allow him to enter. He had on a lightweight, blue-grey sports jacket that matched the colour of his eyes. It was the first thing she noticed. 'How did you know which room was mine?'

He gave a knowing smile, then laughed. 'An old gentleman came out of the door as I neared the house. I asked him.'

She nodded. 'That would have been Mr Bright from upstairs. He has what he calls his "constitutional" every Sunday morning, and collects his Sunday paper on the way back.'

'We are all creatures of habit.'

'And some creatures are in the habit of disappearing without trace for long periods.'

'Ouch.'

She looked down at her feet in some embarrassment. 'You had every right to, of course. I hardly knew you ...'

'Or I you.'

They looked at one another across the few feet of floor-space.

'But it made no difference, did it, Eva? You felt as I did.'

His directness took her by surprise. He was looking at her intently now and she moved uncomfortably beneath his gaze. With difficulty she averted her eyes from his and looked out of the window. 'I – I really don't know what you mean ...'

He took hold of her by the shoulders. 'I shouldn't have come here today. In fact, I had no intention of coming. On my way back to England I told myself I wouldn't get in touch with you again.'

'But you did.' She turned back to face him once more.

'Yes I did. And I shouldn't have.'

'Why?' She whispered the word. 'Am I allowed to know?'

He let her go and shrugged his shoulders in a helpless gesture before reaching inside his jacket pocket for a cigarette. 'I didn't write to you from the States because I chickened out,' he said finally. 'I've got a girl back home, Eva. She's someone I've known for a long time – all my life almost …'

'And you love her – this girl?'

He looked down at her and there was real pain in his eyes. 'Yes … At least I thought I did. In fact, I was certain I did, until I met you.'

It was her turn to be silent as she weighed up his words. Her heart was still beating much too fast. Just seeing him again, being close to him, was doing something to her that she did not know quite how to handle. There was something almost tangible in the air between them – an electricity that they could both feel, and each knew for certain the other was experiencing it too. 'Why did you come, then?' she asked softly, already afraid of the answer.

He was continuing to stare down at her, as if he could not get his fill, as if he was imprinting every part of her on his memory. 'I had to know, I guess. I had to find out if what I had felt when we first met was just a flash in the pan.'

'A flash in the pan?' She repeated the words with a puzzled expression.

Just what was the equivalent in German? He couldn't think of one. He gave a sheepish grin. 'I suppose what I'm really trying to say is that I had to find out if it were purely lust – or if I had really fallen in love with you.'

'*Liebe beim ersten Blick* … Love at first sight,' she repeated slowly in both languages. 'Is there really such a thing?'

'If you'd have asked me that two years ago, I'd have said it was all romantic rubbish. I'm a trained scientist. A rational human being.'

She gave a quiet smile. All of a sudden she felt the stronger

130

of the two. Here he was, a grown man of over six feet, standing before her in a state of utter mental confusion. 'And your rationality tells you it is better to love your American girl than your German one.'

'Not better. Easier.'

She laughed. 'You are an honest man, Mr Rutherford ... Tell me about her – this American girl it is easier to love.'

His jaw tightened as he walked to the window and looked out. 'Her name is Mary-Jo Marlowe. I've known her since grade school. Her father was the one responsible for getting me accepted into Harvard.' He paused and drew deeply on his cigarette. 'He was my science teacher in high school. I owe everything to him.'

'And you must pay him back by marrying his daughter.' There was no irony or reproach in her voice; she stated it as a matter of fact.

He was silent for a moment. 'You could say that – yes.'

She put on a brave smile. 'I'll make a cup of tea.' Then she laughed. 'You see how British I have become? All the world's problems can be solved by a cup of tea!'

He followed her out to the small kitchenette on the landing and watched as she replaced the already warm kettle on the gas hob. Her mention of the world's problems had struck home. 'I – I never asked you how your family is faring over there,' he said quietly. 'Have you heard anything recently?'

She shook her head. 'I have heard nothing. Nothing at all.' Her voice shook slightly. 'It appears they have just disappeared into thin air.' Then her eyes hardened. 'No, that's not true. They just disappeared into one of those bloody camps!' It felt strange swearing in English, but no other word would do. 'No one tells me that, of course. It is politic not to see what is happening in Germany just now. Like the three wise monkeys, good Germans keep their eyes, ears and mouths closed.'

She shrugged helplessly as she emptied out the remains of her earlier tea down the sink and dropped three fresh spoonfuls of leaves into the pot. 'Anyway, this is no longer relevant. The war has changed everything. Do you know I should be locked up by now?'

He looked puzzled. 'Come again?'

'Locked up,' she repeated over the sound of the singing kettle. 'Haven't you heard? They're imprisoning all foreigners as "undesirable aliens" in such places as the Isle of Man. I should be there now – behind barbed wire, only I haven't given myself up, and luckily no one has reported me to the authorities yet.'

'Jeezus!' He stared down at her as the words sank in. He could have kicked himself. He should have thought about this – he should have been prepared. But he had only arrived back the previous night and had not had time to acquaint himself with all the conditions of wartime Britain's homefront, unless they directly affected Americans. Hell, he wasn't even sure exactly where the Isle of Man was!

She turned to smile at him as she poured the boiling water into the teapot. 'Don't worry about it,' she said lightly. 'I'm not. Whatever kind of camp the British put me into – it can't be anything like as bad as I would be in at home in Germany right now.' She gave a wistful smile. 'It seems I'm not welcome anywhere these days, doesn't it?'

But Bill Rutherford did not return her smile. A deep anger was welling within him as he looked down at this beautiful, vulnerable young woman who had already touched his heart as no other had ever done. What kind of sick world was this? What had she ever done to deserve what she was going through? Her home and family had been destroyed by her own people, and she had been forced to flee to a so-called civilized country, only to be locked up behind barbed wire like a criminal. Suddenly Charleston, South Carolina, and Mary-Jo Marlowe were as far away as the moon, and of as little consequence. 'Don't worry, Eva,' he vowed. 'Nothing is going to happen to you while I'm around. I promise you that.'

She looked up at him and their eyes met. For the first time since she had arrived on these foreign shores, she felt really safe. It was a good feeling.

Chapter Twelve

'But why should I move? I am happy here. I have no reason to go,' Eva protested. 'What do I need another room for?'

But Rutherford smiled patiently but apprehensively as he put the car into gear and moved off from the kerb. It was the reaction he had expected. He was silent for a minute or two as they drove along Lambeth Road. He had to be careful how he played it. He certainly did not want it to appear that he was bulldozing her into anything against her will but, somehow, she had to be made to see sense. It had been two days since he had last seen her and he had put them to good use. Her comments on the internment of enemy aliens, as they were termed, had shocked him, and he had done quite a bit of investigating since Sunday morning. 'There can be no question of you staying there,' he said in a quiet, determined voice. 'It can only be a matter of time before you're reported.'

She made no response, and he threw her a glance as the car rounded St George's Circus, heading in the direction of Waterloo Road. Her face was set in a frown.

'Look, Eva, I know how you feel. But quite apart from the danger to yourself, you don't want to get your neighbours or workmates into trouble for harbouring an enemy alien, do you?'

She looked across at him in surprise. She had never thought of it like that before. An imperceptible shudder ran through her. She was only too aware of what happened to people in Germany who sheltered Jews, or other enemies of the state. 'You don't really think I'm placing them in any danger, do you?'

He shrugged. 'Who can say? From what I can gather the British Government seems pretty determined to round up all foreign nationals as quickly as possible. "Collar the lot!" Churchill has said, and as far as I've been able to find out, they're doing just that … There's nothing on your passport to indicate you have any Jewish blood, is there?'

'No, nothing.'

He nodded, his face grim. It was just as he thought. 'So there's nothing at all to indicate you are anything but a hundred per cent genuine German, of true Aryan stock?'

'Nothing.'

He sighed. 'Honey, I have to inform you that you are what they term a "Category A" alien. You should already be under lock and key.'

A Category A alien. The words chilled her. Was this to be the British version of *Mischling* Second Degree? She sat in silence as the Riley sped past a large poster topped with a British crown: 'Your courage, your cheerfulness, your resolution will bring us victory' it pronounced. Since her arrival on these shores, she had never felt less courageous, less cheerful, or less resolute as she digested what she was hearing.

She herself had heard and read bits and pieces recently of what was going on regarding the rounding up and interning of foreigners, but somehow she had felt immune from the arrests. It was something that affected other people, not her. No one, either at work or anywhere else, had mentioned it and, although she knew in theory she should be regarded as one of those so-called enemy aliens, the thought that she could possibly be an enemy of the British state was just too ridiculous to contemplate. It had suddenly all taken on a faintly ludicrous quality. In her own country she would have been locked up for having Jewish blood, while over here she should be locked up for having German blood. She couldn't win either way.

As the car continued on towards the place he had told her was to be her hideaway, her eyes took in the people going about their business on the crowded pavement. A crowd of fashionably-dressed young women, with upswept Betty Grable hairstyles, stood laughing and chatting at a bus stop. None of them was going through this, she told herself wearily. The Luftwaffe's bombs notwithstanding, they would be going back to a secure home and family. She thought she had left the fear of the early morning knock on the door well behind her in Germany. Now she was beginning to feel like a hunted animal again. Was she to be safe nowhere? 'But even if you have got another room for me – what good will that do if they all still know I'm a German at work?'

Bill Rutherford's hands gripped tighter round the steering-wheel. 'I've got you another job, too.'

'What!'

He took a deep breath. He had been expecting this reaction. No one would take kindly to having to move their home *and* job suddenly overnight. Especially if the people you knew in both those places were your only real friends in the country. 'It won't be as bad as you think, Eva. I promise you. The room's real nice – and has got better facilities than you've got at the moment.'

She thought of her mean little room and the shared sink and toilet in the Earnshaws' lodging-house. That would not be hard to beat. 'And the job?'

'The job's ideal. You'll be working for the friend of a friend of mine. Arnold Kennedy's his name. He runs a small bookshop in a street adjacent to the British Museum.'

'He knows I'm German?'

Bill nodded.

'And he doesn't mind the risk?'

'He's over seventy and reckons they wouldn't exactly lock him up in the Tower at that age, even if someone did find out.'

She looked across at him suspiciously. 'And why should this man – this Arnold Kennedy – do this for me?'

Bill gave a wry smile as he lit a cigarette. 'He's been quite a guy in his time. He's a real old Irish nationalist. Spent some time in prison during the last war for his part in the Easter Rising – so he owes no favours to the British Government.'

Eva remained unconvinced. 'And the room. What about the room? Does it belong to an Irish nationalist, too?'

He laughed. 'No. It's leased by our Embassy for the use of secretarial staff. I made enquiries yesterday and discovered it's been empty for the past couple of weeks.'

'But how can I possibly use it? I'm nothing to do with the American Embassy.' When no response came, she leaned forward and glanced across at him. 'Well?'

'On that one, let's just say there are some decent human beings still around, Eva. And one of them happens to work in our accommodation office.' Then, sensing that was not going to satisfy her, he continued, 'One of the guys there is Jewish. I told him your problem. It was as simple as that.'

She slumped back in her seat. 'You seem to have done a great deal on my behalf.'

'You make that sound like an accusation.'

'I'm sorry, Bill. I should be grateful, I know.'

'But you're not and I understand why. You were perfectly happy as things were, and I come along and mess everything up. It seems like that, doesn't it?'

She nodded.

He reached across and squeezed her hand. 'Believe me, Eva, I'm not doing this for fun. I've done a lot of investigating over the past couple of days since I last saw you, and you're in real danger of being arrested and detained. In fact, you're darned lucky you've got away with it for so long. Those internment camps you mentioned are sprouting up all over the place – at Huyton, up in Liverpool, and on the Isle of Man. They're even shipping people off abroad!'

She listened as he went on to tell her something of what he had learned of the recent secret meetings of the Joint Intelligence Committee, who had met in their spacious office in Richmond Terrace on quite a few occasions since the beginning of May to decide the future of Britain's alien population.

The JIC, as it was known, operated from an elegant Georgian building that ran at right-angles from Whitehall, opposite the entrance to Downing Street. Being in American Intelligence, Bill had access, albeit often unofficial, to the decisions being taken behind its imposing façade. What he had to say did not give her much confidence as to her future in Britain.

'They're obsessed with what they are terming as Germany's "Fifth Column",' he explained. 'And they are concentrating mainly, at the moment, on the German refugee population in Britain, which they seem to regard as a hot-bed of spies.'

Eva made a feeble attempt at a smile. 'You are an Intelligence Officer yourself … Tell me, do you regard me as a potential Mata Hari?'

His face was quite serious as he glanced across at her. 'Quite frankly, Eva, I regard you as the most important person in my life at the moment. It's as simple as that.' He had not meant to speak so frankly, but the seriousness of the situation had moved beyond game-playing.

His words were to echo in her head throughout the next hour as he showed her over the two-roomed apartment, just a stone's throw from the Palladian splendour of the British Museum. It was on the third floor of a tall Georgian terraced house, and in both size and decoration it was vastly superior to her present lodgings.

'Well, what do you think?' Bill threw his arms wide as they returned to the neatly furnished sitting-room, having surveyed the bedroom, kitchenette, and bathroom.

Eva looked round once again at the cheerful, chintz-covered three-piece suite, matching curtains, and solid Edwardian furniture. 'It's very nice,' she said truthfully, 'but I couldn't possibly afford it.'

'How much do you earn at present?'

'Thirty shillings a week.'

'Old Kennedy will pay thirty-five. What's your present rent?'

'Fifteen shillings.'

'You're being robbed – that place isn't worth ten!'

She could not argue with that. 'But this place, Bill … They must be asking far too much!'

'The rent's one pound a week, so with your increase in wages you can certainly afford it … Will you do it, Eva? Will you move in? Kennedy's bookshop is just around the corner. You'll have no bus or tube fares to worry about.'

He began to walk towards her and placed his hands on her shoulders. 'This job I'm in at the moment,' he said quietly, 'it entails quite a bit of moving around. I'll be based in London, but could take off at short notice back to the States for varying periods of time. I couldn't stand the thought of leaving, knowing you might be turned in to the authorities at any time to be locked up like some common criminal.'

She looked up at him as his fingers increased their pressure on her shoulders, digging into the skin beneath her light summer blouse and cardigan. His eyes were grave as they gazed down into hers, and for the first time she noticed a jagged scar that ran from the edge of his left eyebrow to the corner of his eye. It must have been done in childhood, for it had gone white and translucent with age. She thought of that small boy sitting on the front porch of the clapboard house in Greenville, South Carolina, and wished with all her heart that she had known him then – that it had been her and not Mary-Jo Marlowe who had shared those special years with him. The fingers of her right hand reached up to gently touch the old wound.

Then, suddenly, she was in his arms. His lips found hers and, for the first time in her life, she was kissed as a fully grown woman. His hands moved through her hair as he murmured her name over and over, and she found herself trembling in his grasp as he moulded her body to his own.

Then, just as suddenly, it was over, and he unwound her arms from his neck to push her gently from him. His face was flushed. 'I'm sorry, Eva,' he said brusquely. 'I didn't mean that to happen.'

Confused, she gazed up at him. Her cheeks tingled from the roughness of the five o'clock shadow on his cheeks and chin and she could still taste the faint tobacco flavour of his kiss. Her whole being was alive with feelings she had never experienced before and she felt cheated it should be over so soon. 'Don't apologize,' she said softly. 'Not to me.'

He moved back to put some space between them, but continued to stare at her. Why her? Why did he have to feel this way about her? Why couldn't he feel like this about Mary-Jo?

Her lips were trembling, half-way between laughing and crying, and he knew the emotion he was feeling was just as real for her. He had been fighting a battle with his emotions ever since they met that day in the restaurant. The last thing he wanted was to fall in love with another woman. Mary-Jo was the girl he was going to marry; everyone in Greensville knew that. And, above all, her father knew it, and he owed everything to Ed Marlowe.

He turned abruptly and walked to the window, where he lit a cigarette and gazed out at the redbrick façade of the terrace opposite. He wasn't doing himself any favour by involving himself in her life again like this. If he were honest with himself, he had half hoped he would not be able to find her again when he came back this time. But he had found her and he knew he could not let her go. Not yet, anyway. She needed him. She had no one else. One day soon there would come a time for decisions – a time to choose between the two of them. But not now. Now he would do his best by her and let the future take care of itself. What had happened just now was a temporary slip, one which he would do his best not to repeat. It could only make things worse.

He felt a hand on his arm and half-turned. Their eyes

locked. She had tears in hers. All the jumble of emotions she had felt over the past year and a half were churning within her. She had dreamt of that moment – their first kiss – so many times as she lay alone in that narrow little bed on Lambeth Walk, and now it had happened, only to have him push her away. 'Don't turn your back on me, Bill,' she whispered. 'Please don't turn away.'

He looked down at her for a long time as the fatal battle between heart and head took place within him. The ash on the cigarette between his fingers grew into a long white column, then he stubbed it out roughly into a plant pot on the windowsill.

They were a man and a woman, both far from home, in a country at war that was not their own. And both wanted the other with a desire that neither knew how to, or even wanted to control.

She put out her hand and he took it, and together they walked the few steps to the bedroom door. She was in his arms again by the time they had crossed the threshold. He kicked it closed behind them with the heel of his shoe, then he lifted her into his arms and carried her to the waiting bed.

Chapter Thirteen

Eva moved her belongings out of her room on Lambeth Walk that same evening. She wrote a letter to the Earnshaws telling them she was leaving and pushed it through their letterbox on the way out to Bill's waiting car. She also wrote a letter of resignation to her employer, Isaac Levinson, and they drove past the shop where she had spent the past eighteen months so she could drop it through the brass flap of the letterbox for them to receive the following morning. Bill insisted she did not go back in person to tell them she was leaving. 'It would be too dangerous,' he insisted. 'The less people who know what's happened to you the better.'

She had not argued. How could she argue? She could deny him nothing now – not after what had passed between them.

Their lovemaking had been as great a surprise to him as it had been to her. Neither had anticipated it, and perhaps that was what made it so very special. Up until that moment she had never even been kissed by a man before, but she had given herself freely and wholeheartedly to him. She had known almost nothing of the art of making love, but they had come together on the soft patchwork of the quilt as if it were the most natural thing in the world. As indeed it was. She was convinced of that now. She had felt no shame, no regret. She loved him. It was as simple as that.

After it was over and she lay, at peace with herself and the world, against the smooth, damp flesh of his shoulder, he asked her if she would regret what had happened between them. She had shaken her head and, very softly, so as not to break the spell that still bound them, she recited a few lines from Schiller: *"Ich habe genossen das irdische Glück; ich habe gelebt und geliebt* …".' Those few remembered lines summed up her feelings exactly and, so there could be no mistake, she repeated them in English: '"I have experienced the greatest happiness on this earth; I have lived and loved …".'

He had kissed her again, and tried desperately to think of an equivalent few lines in English to sum up his own feelings. But words would not come. What was happening between them was almost beyond his comprehension. He had only made love once in his life before – to a girl he had met during one of his holiday jobs at Coney Island in the summer of '38. He thought back to the furtive fumbling in the back seat of the beaten-up Packard and corrected himself mentally. He had not made love before – he had had sex with a girl, that was all. There was all the difference in the world. It had meant nothing to him and, at the end of September, she had returned to Litchfield, Connecticut, and he to Harvard. He could barely remember what she looked like.

He had not even made love to Mary-Jo before. And that disturbed him perhaps more than anything else as he lay with Eva in his arms in the calm that followed their lovemaking. He had not made love to Mary-Jo before because he had never lost control of his feelings with her. Their lovemaking was confined to necking-sessions in the back of her father's car, where even a straying hand would be something that would be gently but firmly removed; and their kisses would be mostly closed-mouth affairs that left him feeling both frustrated and humiliated. That was not how it should be between them. That was not what lovemaking – real lovemaking – should be all about. But that was how it was, and that was how it would have remained for him if a young German girl had not walked into his life and laid claim to both his body and soul.

The one disturbing factor in his relationship with Eva was the unpredictability of his position at the Embassy now he was finally back in Britain. This month, secret talks had begun between American Intelligence and the British Special

143

Intelligence Service and, due to the strong Isolationist lobby in the United States and the fear of American neutrality becoming too compromised, he knew that at any time he could be recalled to Washington, should the State Department decide that they were becoming too involved in the war itself.

This month Colonel Donovan, President Roosevelt's special envoy, had arrived in London with the prime objective of assessing Britain's determination and ability to continue the war – something that was being increasingly doubted by the American Chiefs-of-Staff. It was Bill's task to brief the Colonel on various aspects of Anglo-American co-operation and pave the way for the 'Standardization of Arms' talks that were being scheduled between the two countries for the following month.

The most worrying aspect of the whole affair, on a personal level, was that if Donovan's assessment of the situation proved negative, Bill knew he could be packing his bags almost overnight. And, conversely, if the Colonel was to be too enthusiastic about military co-operation between Washington and London, he could still find himself on a plane back home, to assist in the planning stages at the State Department itself.

Returning to England this summer was something he had had many a sleepless night over. During the summer vacation in July, which he had spent with Mary-Jo in Greensville, he had taken a few days off to travel north to visit his old friend from Greensville High and Harvard, Jack Douglas, who was now part of Enrico Fermi's team of scientists at Columbia University in New York. The work that was going on there had excited him enormously. For several years he had been only too familiar with the discovery that the source of energy of the stars – the intense heat that caused light nuclei such as hydrogen to fuse – could in the process liberate incredible amounts of energy. The question now was, was it possible that the detonation of an atomic bomb on earth could create a heat comparable to that of the interior of the stars?

He had been doing work along these lines himself at Harvard before joining the Intelligence Service, and had made a point of keeping tabs on how his old colleagues, now dispersed in various physics departments around the country, were doing.

From what Jack had told him, it appeared that the focus of research in Columbia that summer, as in physics labs in other leading universities, was the construction of an atomic reactor which could sustain a nuclear chain reaction – and the search for a means of separating the substance U-235, or fissionable uranium, from U-238, or common uranium.

This was tantamount to trying to extract a needle from the proverbial haystack and, even if accomplished, the task had only just begun. While the chain reaction for a fission of U-235 had been established by the theoreticians, with chalk on a blackboard, would it actually take place in reality? The scientist's blood in him boiled to be there amongst them, finding out the answers to such problems.

Throughout his three-day stay in his friend's small apartment on Morningside Drive, high up at the top of the steep rise above the sprawling expanse of Harlem, he had fretted over his future. If he stood at the bedroom window and craned his neck to the west, he could just make out the group of buildings that was Columbia and, in their midst, the physics department in Pupin Hall. Even at night a light would be burning and someone would be in there, pushing forward the frontiers of science further than anyone would have dreamt possible a few years ago. 'We are entering a new era, Bill,' Jack had told him. 'An atomic era that will change man's conception of himself and his capabilities for ever. Why not come back and join us?'

The invitation to forsake his work in Intelligence and return to the world of the science lab had been almost irresistible. What in God's name was he doing pushing a pen behind a desk for a lot of politicians he had little time for anyway? What was stopping him returning to physics – his first love?

He knew the answer to that question only too well. Not *what* was stopping him, but *who* was stopping him. And that person was a particular young woman who had walked in off the street into his life one fine day at the tail end of 1938 and turned his world upside-down.

He had tried. Oh God, how he had tried to forget her. Even to the extent of deliberately not keeping in touch while he was back home in the States. He had read somewhere that absence was to love what wind was to fire – it extinguishes the small and inflames the great. If that was so, then there could be little doubt that what he felt for Eva Koehn was great indeed.

He had returned to Greensville for the last few days of his vacation to find a Mary-Jo who was desperately keen for him to return to academic life. One of her best friends was married to a professor in the English department at Columbia, and the thought of joining them in New York as man and wife was an exciting prospect indeed.

'But why not, Bill, for heaven's sake? It's what you're best at, after all, isn't it?' Her brow had furrowed above the candid brown eyes as she had looked at him that last evening on the back porch of her parents' house. 'You're not really so keen on this Intelligence stuff that you'd turn down a chance like this, are you?'

She had pulled at his arm to turn him to face her. He had kept her dangling long enough. Why, the whole of Greensville had been expecting a wedding announcement for months now. This would be the ideal start to married life. 'Answer me, darn you! Tell me the truth for once these days!'

He had looked at her and shaken his head. She was a good, decent human being who loved him, and she deserved better than to be kept on ice like this. He wished with all his heart he had it in him to take her in his arms and ask her to be his

146

wife. It was what she longed for more than anything in the world. Then he had lied. 'This work I'm doing at Intelligence is just as important to me, Mary-Jo. Especially now there's a war on in Europe. For all we know we'll be in it next.'

She had looked at him; a long hard look that saw beyond the bland assurances about his fondness for Intelligence work. A great chasm was opening up between them that she could no longer bridge. He was slipping away from her and there was nothing she could do about it. There was a part of him that was no longer hers, and that she couldn't bear. She had loved him for so long. He had been her beau at her Junior Prom, then at her Graduation Ball. He was part of her life, as much a part of it as the very air she breathed. 'And what if they send you back there – to London? Would you go?' Her voice was a whisper.

He was silent for a long time. 'If need be.'

'I see.'

He had watched as a stricken look had contorted the pert features of her face, but he had remained silent. Then she turned from him and walked slowly back into her parents' house and closed the door behind her.

How could he tell her what that need was? That the need he referred to was a yearning deep within him, such as he had never experienced before, for a woman only slightly younger than herself who had already gone through in her young life what Mary-Jo, secure in peacetime America, could not even dream of.

He had not seen Mary-Jo again before he returned to Washington the next day. And he had applied for a posting back to Britain immediately on his return to the capital. His request fitted in well with his superiors' plans and within a few days the clearance to return to London was through.

All this seemed a long time ago now. And, even if he wanted to, he could not share his thoughts with Eva. He could not talk of his anguish at leaving Mary-Jo like that, and neither could he talk of his fears for their own future together. That – like so much else these days – was in the lap of the gods.

It must be enough, at present, that they live for today and thank God that they had found each other again. He must try to carry on as normally as possible with her – especially now. What had occurred between them this evening had left them both in a state of shock. He had not planned it should happen like this – not yet. But he had discovered that life had a habit of springing surprises on even the most wary.

For her part, Eva was simply glad to have him back and in charge of her life again. She was not sorry to be leaving the confines of the room that had been her home for the past eighteen months; it was not a place you could become easily attached to, with its cheap saleroom furniture and peeling paint and wallpaper. The future had suddenly taken on a whole new perspective with Bill at her side.

It was with a light heart that she closed the door on her life in Lambeth for the last time.

After delivering the letters to her landlord and employer, Bill carried her cases up the stairs into the new apartment and laid them down in the middle of the sitting-room carpet.

Once the door had been closed behind them, Lambeth and the Earnshaws, Isaac Levinson, Miss Simpson and the others – the whole outside world with all its uncertainty and misery – receded. The war itself ceased to exist. They were alone once more.

'I should have bought some champagne in,' Bill said ruefully, gently pulling her towards him. 'We should be celebrating.'

'There are other ways of celebrating,' she murmured in his ear as his lips nuzzled her neck.

He looked down at her in mock surprise as the blood quickened within him. 'Miss Koehn, are you telling me you have other ideas for having a good time? You can think of something more enjoyable even than drinking champagne?'

She nodded, blushing furiously.

'You wouldn't care to enlarge on those ideas, would you? Remember I'm just a poor American boy who's not yet used to your sophisticated European ways over here!'

He was grinning from ear to ear. He knew very well it had been her first time, just as she was equally certain it had not been his. 'Do I look like a wicked lady?'

He took a step back and surveyed her critically, his eyes taking in the pale blonde hair and finely arched eyebrows above the wide-set, dark eyes. 'Do you know who you remind me of?' he said. 'Marlene Dietrich … Yes, you most definitely have a look of "The Blue Angel" herself. Did anyone ever tell you that before?'

'No,' she laughed. 'And you're a terrible flatterer. The only thing I have in common with her is that we're both Ber-liners.'

'"Falling in love again … Never wanted to …"' he grinned as he sang the lines of the actress's most famous song in a husky voice with a distinctly Germanic accent. His arms went around her waist as he swept her off her feet, and his deep baritone boomed out, '"What am I to do? … I can't help it …"'

They waltzed around the room, singing the song in unison now. Then, suddenly, he stopped. 'Come dancing with me!'

'Tonight?' She glanced at the clock on the mantelpiece. 'It's after eleven o'clock!'

'So?'

'There might be a bombing raid,' she said lamely. 'There usually is.'

'Let Goering do his worst,' he declared. 'We will be far beyond his planes this night … As far beyond them as is possible.'

His arms tightened around her. 'Nothing can touch us now – nothing and no one. We are the children of the gods … What has taken place this weekend, my love, was meant to happen. Nothing happens by chance in this life, Eva. Nothing. The more I know of you, the more I become convinced of that fact … I returned to find you here because fate decreed it. I have never been more certain of anything:

> 'Out of the nothingness of sleep,
> The slow dreams of Eternity,
> There was a thunder on the deep:
> I came because you called to me …

'And here I am! Say you'll come dancing with me, Eva! Say to hell with Goering and his Luftwaffe! We will be far beyond them, my love. Far, far beyond them. As far beyond them as is possible!' He swung her around in his arms once more as he gazed down imploringly into her upturned face.

'Did you make that up? That poem … did you make it up?' she gasped.

'Every word,' he lied, the disarming grin still in place.

They were both out of breath, but his enthusiasm was catching; it was sweeping her along in its wake. She broke free of his arms and ran to open the biggest case. It contained her only dress fit for a dance. She hauled it from the suitcase and quickly began to shed her clothes.

They did not get as far as the dance. They did not even get as far as the door.

'Come here,' he said softly, as she stood in her underwear, with one foot poised, ready to step into the dress. 'Come here … Now …'

It was morning before he left her bed. A bright sun awoke them at a little after seven. He got out from between the sheets first, to search through the kitchen cupboard for something to make a cup of tea or coffee with. A half-full jar of Maxwell House stood at the back of the shelf, next to a jar of milk powder.

He heated the water on the gas hob and took the two cups of coffee back to the bedroom. He drank his sitting on the edge of the mattress to get a better view of her. Her hair was still dishevelled from their lovemaking which had gone on until the small hours of the morning, and her skin was flushed and glowing in the early sunlight. 'I'll take you round to Arnold's before I head on to the Embassy,' he said, lighting up a cigarette. 'Then I'll pick you up at lunchtime for a bite to eat.'

She nodded her acquiescence. He was taking over her life completely and she had never been happier.

Once she had washed in the small, blue-tiled bathroom, she realized with a sense of delight and liberation that she did not have to dress in the funereal black skirt and jumper that they demanded at Levinson's. Instead she donned a white cotton blouse, pale blue cardigan and blue floral dirndl skirt.

'How do I look?' she asked, blatantly fishing for a compliment as she returned to the sitting-room to stand before him.

He had already been out for a morning paper and was sitting reading it by the window. 'Hunky-dory!'

'I beg your pardon?'

'*Wunderbar!*' he declared. 'You'll knock old Arnold for six!'

She regarded him sceptically and smiled quietly to herself. There was only one man she wanted to knock for six, or for any other number, come to that, and he was sitting less than six feet from her. 'I'm ready when you are!'

He got up, folding his newspaper and stuffing it into his jacket pocket. 'It's only a short walk to the bookshop, but we'll take the car. I'll head on to the Embassy once I've seen you safely delivered.'

It took less than five minutes to reach The Shamrock, Arnold Kennedy's full-to-overflowing bookshop, which was squeezed between a curio shop and a shop selling old prints and maps. The owner himself was in the act of opening up for the day as the Riley slid to a full stop on the pavement alongside.

He was a small leprechaun of a man with stooped shoulders and twinkling brown eyes that smiled into Eva's own as he extended a welcoming hand on Bill's introduction. 'Very pleased to meet you, my dear. It's high time I had some proper help around this place.'

She followed him into the dusty interior and gazed in awe at the overflowing shelves. She had never seen so many books in one small space before.

'You read a lot yourself, then?' her new employer asked. She nodded, and he gave a satisfied smile. 'Well, there's plenty here for you to choose from. You must feel free to borrow them as you will. There'll be no need for Boot's lending library and the like now.'

He lifted a tooled-leather volume from the top of his desk and fondled the binding lovingly before handing it across to her. 'Here's one you'll enjoy. It's a special edition of Rupert Brooke's poems I came by just the other day.'

Eva accepted it with a smile and looked up to catch Bill's eye. What on earth was he grinning at her like that for?

'Mr Kennedy, sir,' he said, in mock seriousness. 'I think you have just shattered a beautiful illusion about my poetical abilities. From now on I will no longer be regarded as the Bard of Bloomsbury as far as this young lady is concerned!' He winked at the old Irishman on his way out of the door, then turned to blow a kiss to Eva. 'Till lunchtime!'

Arnold Kennedy watched with a bemused expression on his gnarled features. 'A nice young man that, my dear. Very nice.'

'I quite agree with you, Mr Kennedy.' She smiled and glanced down at the slim volume in her hand. 'Even if this little book proves he isn't quite the marvellous poet he would have me believe him to be!'

Chapter Fourteen

Breathless, we flung us on the windy hill,
Laughed in the sun and kissed the lovely grass.
You said, 'Through glory and ecstasy we pass;
Wind, sun, and earth remain, the birds sing still,
When we are old, are old ...' 'And when we die
All's over that is ours; and life burns on
Through other lovers, other lips,' said I,
'Heart of my heart, our heaven is now, is won!'

'We are Earth's best, that learnt her lesson here.
Life is our cry. We have kept faith!' we said;
'We shall go down with unreluctant tread
Rose-crowned into the darkness!' ... Proud we were,
And laughed, that had such brave true things to say.
– And then you suddenly cried, and turned away.

Eva pensively closed the slim volume of poems that had been Bill's gift to her and sat staring into the gathering gloom of her bedroom. The tea in the cup on the small table beside the bed lay cold and untouched, a milky skin gathering on its surface.

She replaced the book on the tabletop beside the cup and saucer and slid down on her pillow, beneath the sheet and single blanket that covered her. It was exactly thirty summers ago that Rupert Brooke wrote that poem, but it could never have been more relevant to another human being than it was to her today.

She lay quite still and closed her eyes; once more she was on that hilltop, and joy and pain in equal measure flooded through her.

Bill had picked her up in the Riley at ten in the morning; the weather had been perfect – warm and balmy, with just the hint of a breeze wafting like a warm breath through her newly-washed hair as she stood at the edge of the pavement and waited for the car to come to a stop outside her front door. His eyes had smiled into hers as he threw open the passenger door for her to slide in beside him. He had raised her hand to his lips and kissed it, before slipping the car into gear and setting off in the direction of Russell Square and the main roads south out of the city.

A wicker picnic-hamper lay on the back seat on top of a tartan travelling-rug. It was impossible to avoid seeing it and excitement had tingled through her. It reminded her of those golden days long ago when her father would take them for surprise outings in his beloved Mercedes-Benz SSK if the weather were fine. The sight of the maid, red-faced and perspiring, as she carried the heavy hamper in front of her down the stone staircase and out to the waiting car used to thrill her beyond measure. Even today, although she had left childhood far behind, wicker picnic-hampers still had that effect. The promise was still there in their golden weave and securely fastened leather straps.

'Where are we going?' she had asked Bill excitedly, snuggling down into the bucket seat next to his.

He had smiled a knowing smile. 'Where the fancy takes us! Who wants to stay in the city on a day like this and breathe the same air as several million other folks when we can just take off and head for the open road? The countryside's our oyster, Eva honey – for a few hours at least!'

And so they had set off south, heading for the Sussex Downs. It was her first real encounter with the British countryside outside London, and as Bill had seen almost nothing of life outside the capital, the sense of adventure was real in them both as the car left the city streets behind and headed for the county of gently rolling hills and pebbled beaches.

They crossed the Sussex border just after midday and were not disappointed with what they found. The countryside around them, with its meadows fragrant with wild flowers and bordered by tall hedgerows, seemed more green than they had ever imagined. They had the car windows open and the heady sights, sounds and smells of late summer wafted in on them, reminding them that life in war-torn Britain was not all bomb-shelters and the drab uniformity of city life.

It had seemed an enchanted land as the car sped along the quiet lanes almost devoid of traffic. Save for the occasional farm cart, or herd of cows being trundled from one field to another, they seemed to have the world to themselves. It was a land she had always imagined as essentially English, with its small farmsteads and cottages with thatched roofs and whitewashed walls. The neatly-kept gardens were edged with hedges of old-fashioned roses, and spires of hollyhocks stood tall and stately behind beds of sweet-scented pinks and asters. Their colours dazzled the eyes and their fragrances dizzied the senses as Bill slowed the car to almost walking pace through the roadside villages.

In many of the fields beyond, the harvest was already being gathered in, and amongst the bronzed, weather-beaten faces of the older men, now long past the age of call-up, Land Girls worked, bare-armed and glowing with exertion as they pitchforked and bound the golden corn into sheaves. Occasionally snatches of their songs would reach them as the car drove past and Bill would honk his horn and wave a friendly arm out of the window. There was a camaraderie about life in wartime that affected everyone.

The summer sun was high in the cloudless sky when they eventually arrived at the little village of Clayton, with its ancient medieval church, clinging, like the stone cottages themselves, to the foot of the green Down. 'Feel like stretching your legs?' Bill had asked, and she had jumped at the chance to get out of the car and breathe in the clean, sweet air.

Above them, on the crest of the hill, standing guard over the little community down below, stood two old windmills.

An elderly man, pushing an even older bicycle, passed by and saw them admiring Clayton's beloved sentinels. 'They're called Jack and Jill,' he informed them. 'It's a grand walk up there if you've the legs for it.'

'Are you game?' Bill asked her. And she did not need a second invitation.

They left the picnic-hamper in the car at the foot of the hill and set off in high spirits to view Jack, the black tower mill, and Jill, his smaller, white post companion.

Everything about the day seemed peculiarly heightened as they made their way up through the long grass alive with chirping crickets towards the grassy summit. It was as if they had just awakened from a long sleep. But maybe living in a huge grey city like London had that effect upon you, Eva decided. It made you almost oblivious to the changing seasons. In London they seemed to merge into each other with little to distinguish the difference between them. But out there on the Downs, away from the madding crowd of humanity, you could see it in the colours all around you and almost taste it on the very air you breathed.

She knew Bill must be experiencing the same sensations as they climbed ever upwards, as if into the heavens themselves. Every now and again she would steal a glance at his face and the sheer exhilaration on it thrilled her. He seemed to come alive out there in the wide open spaces and she wondered if it reminded him of his home in South Carolina: she would dearly love to have asked. Natural shyness had always prevented her from prying into his life back home in the States, but it did not stop her imagination from working. And out there with the breeze blowing freely through his hair and whipping the colour into his cheeks, she had the distinct feeling he was not a city person at heart. 'Happy?' he had asked, and she had made no reply – there was no need; she had simply squeezed his hand that bit tighter as they slowly made their way upwards towards the top of the hill.

There was a special magic about this time of year that had

156

always appealed to her. Soon it would be Keats's season of 'mists and mellow fruitfulness', for in the distance they could see the fields of wheat, glowing gold in the summer sun, and bejewelled with crimson from the few late-blooming poppies that had still to cast their remaining petals to the wind. In the air above them a skylark soared and dipped. It was a day to be alive and to thank God for it.

On the summit itself they found they were not alone, for they could see a young couple with rucksacks coming up the path towards them. This was obviously a popular spot. 'Fancy carrying on and finding somewhere a bit less public?' Bill had asked, and she agreed. This was not a day to be sharing him with the world.

'You'd never guess there was a war on, would you?' Bill had murmured on the way down, and it was true. And, for the briefest of moments, a fleeting pain stabbed her heart. If only her parents, and grandmother, could be here to experience it – to share these enchanted hours with them. What right had she to be so lucky when they were …? She could not even bear to imagine what fate had befallen them and she had gripped Bill's hand even tighter as they strolled back down to their waiting car.

About three miles to the west, in the lap of the rolling green hills around the Devil's Dyke, lay the little village of Poynings, its houses strung out along a leafy avenue of trees. It seemed as nice a place as any to have their lunch.

They parked the car in the vicinity of the ancient, square-towered church and took the picnic-hamper from the back seat. Bill slung the tartan travelling-rug over one shoulder and, taking a handle of the basket apiece, they set off to climb one of the nearby hills in search of a private place in which to enjoy their meal.

It took almost half an hour to reach the summit and both were red-faced and glowing with exertion as they let down the basket with a clatter of dishes and spread out the rug beside it, beneath the branches of the tallest and widest sycamore tree that Eva had ever seen. Its leaves were as wide as the plates on which they laid out their fare, and Bill told her of the sycamore tree that had grown in his own backyard when he was a small boy. It had had branches that would shade him every summer, and in the winter they would wave to him from beyond his bedroom window like wide white arms, protecting him from all ills. He had read, he had told her, of how in Ancient Rome men had honoured the sycamore by watering its roots with wine, and Xerxes had halted his whole army for days in order that he might contemplate the beauty of a single sycamore.

'And thank God for this one today,' he sighed, as he lay back on the warm dry grass and closed his eyes against the brilliance of the light. 'Don't anyone ever tell me the British don't have hot summers! This can stand comparison with back home any day!'

Eva had agreed as she passed the wine for him to open and remembered the summers of her own youth, spent mainly on the Wannsee in Berlin. The lake had been the coolest place to be beneath a scorching summer sun, and she wondered at the strangeness of a fate that had brought her a thousand miles from her home to this English hillside to eat a lunch of brown bread and cheese and drink a bottle of French wine with a handsome young American.

She so much wanted to know all there was to know about him. 'Tell me about America, Bill,' she begged as she lay back, her hands beneath her head, and gazed up into the azure blue of the sky. 'Tell me about your country.' What was it really like, she wondered, that land he called home, thousands of miles away across the Atlantic Ocean? Surely he could spare a few details?

He raised a quizzical eyebrow. 'You really want to know?'

'I really want to know.'

'That's a tall order.' He lay down on the soft grass beside her and closed his eyes. 'America, Eva, can never be summed up in a few words … Not by me anyway. I guess, most of all,

158

to me it's a land where people can breathe free ... Our forefathers fought and died for that freedom, and it is not something we will ever give up while there is one of us still alive to defend it.'

The passion of his reply took her by surprise, and she wished with all her heart that she had not been robbed of that same faith in her own land. It was as if a part of her very heart had been cut away and there was nothing to replace it with. 'If America came into the war then, you would fight?'

'Darned right I would.'

She frowned, unsure if his answer pleased or worried her. 'It's not like the Old World, is it, Bill? Your New World has no Hitlers or Stalins to terrorize its people. There you still have that freedom you talk about ... Freedom ...' She repeated the word softly to herself. It was something she had not known for so long: freedom to hold her head up and say with pride, 'My name is Eva Koehn, I am German and part-Jewish'. To do so would risk death in her native Germany and imprisonment here in England. 'I'm sure America must be a wonderful place,' she sighed wistfully, wishing with all her heart she too could be there and breathing free.

He had made no reply and his silence had cut deep.

She had sat up and set about dividing out the food, although her own appetite had suddenly vanished.

After making a half-hearted attempt at a sandwich, she had lain back on the soft wool of the rug. It was silly to brood about something that was outside her control. For all she knew Bill was in no position right now to make plans for their future. America must remain a pipe-dream, for her at least, until this crazy war was over.

She could not remain despondent in a place like that for long, however. This was a day to cherish; a day to make you glad to be alive, despite the terrible things that were happening elsewhere in the world. The war seemed a million miles away from them lying there in the soft grass of an English hilltop. Nothing and no one could touch them in that enchanted spot. Now and again they glimpsed the silver glint of an aeroplane's wings high in the blue of the heavens, but the air battles that had been taking place over the Channel during the past few weeks seemed part of another world that had nothing to do with them any more.

Eventually he had lain down beside her and begun to stroke her hair. He knew what was on her mind. She craved assurances he could not give. She wanted him to tell her that today could go on for ever, that their love could go on for ever. But he could not bring himself to make promises he might never be able to keep. Who knew what tomorrow might bring, let alone next week, or next year?

Eventually they had made love, slowly and tenderly, beneath the brilliant blue canopy of the sky. It seemed the most natural thing in the world. No words passed between them to break the ethereal silence and, when it was over, she had rested her head in the crook of his arm and smoothed back the dark curling hair from his brow. The time for silence was past. She was no longer able to contain her fears, 'What will become of us, Bill?' she had whispered. 'When this war is over and sanity returns to the world, what will happen to you and to me?'

She was not sure what answer she was expecting, but his reaction left her with a cold, hollow feeling in her heart, as he sat up and half-turned from her to light a cigarette and gaze in silence over the endless grasslands of the Downs.

For a moment he had been hers. For a golden, enchanted moment – and now he was slipping away. She could feel it, like sand through her fingers, and there was nothing she could do about it. She thought of Goethe's Faust who risked everything if he succumbed and cried to the moment, the *Augenblick*: '*Verweile doch!*' ... 'Last forever!' This moment – their time in this enchanted spot – could not end like this, with a chasm opening up between them that she could not bridge.

She had reached out to touch his arm, but had drawn back, her fingers poised in mid-air. She could not see his face, but she could tell from the hunch of his shoulders, and from the way he held his cigarette in the hollow of his palm, that his mind was no longer on the intimacy they had shared such a few moments ago. A nerve was flickering beneath the white scar tissue at the corner of his left eye, and the muscles of his jaw were taut as he dragged deeply on the white smoke. He had gone from her in soul, if not in body. Something was on his mind; something he could not speak of; something he could not share with her. Was he thinking of *her* – that girl in South Carolina? The very thought ate into her soul.

And so they had come home, back to London and reality. He had dropped her off at the door of her flat at a little after six, but declined to come in for a cup of tea or coffee. 'I'd better get back to the office,' he had said. 'I'm expecting a dispatch from Washington today that will have to be dealt with right away.'

On a Sunday, she had thought, as he bent to kiss her? He was expecting an urgent dispatch on a Sunday? Then she had dismissed her doubts as a sign of her own insecurity. Of course he could have urgent business awaiting him on a Sunday. They were living in a country at war, after all, and although America itself was not at war, it was no secret where her sympathies lay. His work in Intelligence was a twenty-four-hour-a-day, seven-days-a-week job, and she should be grateful for the hours she had already managed to share with him over the past month since he walked back into her life.

Since his return she had seen him almost every day; sometimes for only a few minutes, sometimes for a whole evening and night. The fact that they loved each other was never in doubt, although talking of their feelings was not something that came easily to either of them. He seemed to prefer to show his love in other ways. When she attempted to give Mr Kennedy back his volume of Rupert Brooke's poems, she was informed that there was no need, Bill had already bought it for her.

And now she lay with it on the pillow beside her tonight, while her thoughts remained firmly entrenched on that Sussex hillside. Perhaps it was understandable that she should be so insecure after all she had gone through over the past eighteen months. The whole world was in a state of flux, so why should their lives be any different?

Bill talked little about his work at the Embassy, but that was understandable, and she made it easy for him by asking no questions. They seemed to be living in a vacuum; only the present existed. The past, for her at least, was too painful a place to dwell in, and the future was beyond their ken. No one knew how this war would end. There could be no doubting the might of the German Army; France had already fallen beneath its jackboot, and now the Luftwaffe was engaged with the RAF in a fight to the death for superiority of the skies. For weeks now, London had been waiting for the bombing raids that were sure to come before the summer was over and, when that happened, there might be no future for any of them.

But at least her days now were as happy as most of her nights. Mr Kennedy, her employer, was a dear little man with a wry sense of humour, much given to quoting the poets of the Easter Rising: Patrick Pearse, W.B. Yeats, Joseph Plunkett et al. He not only knew all their poetry by heart, but he had known them all personally, and the memories of those dear, dead days of 1916 lived with him still.

As befitted a one-time Irish rebel, he seemed to have no particular love of the English, but had a definite soft spot for Americans. He always referred to Bill as 'Your Yankee-Doodle Dandy', a title that, as a Southerner, did not exactly endear itself to the young American; but he bore it with the same disarming smile he always wore whenever he picked Eva up from work at the shop.

Arnold Kennedy was to be out of town the following day. 'I'm going up to Hatfield to a booksale on Monday, m'dear,' he had said, as they prepared to lock up on the Saturday night. 'If there's nothing much doing that afternoon, you needn't sit around here gathering dust along with the books. You're welcome to shut up shop a bit earlier if you like.'

The suggestion had cheered her and she had mentioned it this afternoon to Bill, on their way back from Sussex, hoping he would say that he too might manage an hour or so off on Monday afternoon. But it had not happened. He had received the news in silence, then said, 'That's real decent of him. You could do with a bit of time to yourself.'

Didn't he realize that she did not want more time to herself? Every minute spent apart from him was a minute wasted. All she lived for was the time they were together, but those precious moments had been getting fewer over the past week. That there was something brewing regarding his job she did not doubt – but what? Perhaps he would tell her tomorrow night when he picked her up from the shop.

The following day passed more slowly than usual. She did not particularly enjoy being alone in the shop and, although her English was excellent, she did not feel competent enough to deal with the specialist queries that often arose. But luckily they had very few customers. Apart from the usual trickle of browsers, an old man came in to offer a first edition of Tennyson's *Poetical Works* for sale, and a young woman arrived just before she was due to pull down the shutters at six o'clock to enquire if they had a second-hand copy of *Gone With The Wind*. She had to disappoint them both by telling the old gentleman to call back when Mr Kennedy was in himself as she did not feel up to settling a price for his offering, and informing the young woman that perhaps Margaret Mitchell's American Civil War epic was rather too recent a publication to find its way on to the second-hand market, but she would keep her eyes open for it.

She had not intended remaining at her post until six

o'clock, but was reluctant to leave on the off-chance that Bill might call by early. They had made no definite plans for the evening, but he seldom missed picking her up from work. As the grandfather clock on the back wall of the shop ticked its way round to six o'clock, she comforted herself with the thought that he had probably forgotten she had had the opportunity of getting away early, and would pick her up at around five past as usual.

At twenty past six she was still seated behind the desk waiting.

With the shutters down, the interior of the shop looked as gloomy as she felt, she thought ruefully to herself, as she took a last despairing glance at the clock and reached for her jacket. It was obviously a waste of time waiting any longer; with a bit of luck he would call round later to her flat.

The heavy iron key was stiff to turn in the lock of the outside door, and it was with a heavy heart that she dropped it into her handbag and took a last glance up and down the street. There were cars a-plenty, their drivers relieved to be on their way home after the day's work, but no sign of the Riley.

All evening she waited, but to no avail. Neither did he call the next day. Nor the next.

Finally, on Thursday 15 August, she took her courage in both hands and called the Embassy, asking to be put through to Dr William Rutherford.

The switchboard operator's voice was brisk and business-like: 'I'm very sorry, ma'am, Dr Rutherford is no longer in this country.'

Eva's heart turned over. 'Not – not in this country?'

'That is correct, ma'am.'

A long silence followed as she fought with her emotions. At last she spoke: 'Can you tell me where he has gone please – or when he will be back?'

'I'm very sorry, ma'am, we are not allowed to give out information regarding the whereabouts of our personnel.'

The reply, so calmly and clinically delivered, stung her. There was a silence on the other end of the line. A curtain had come down. They were not allowed to give out any information. She should have known. Orders were orders. It would be no use pleading. A numbness came over her. 'Thank you ...' The words were barely audible as Eva replaced the handpiece in the receiver and stared down at it. The woman's voice echoed in her head: 'Dr Rutherford is no longer in this country ...' He had gone. He had gone without a single word.

She pushed open the heavy glass door of the telephone box and emerged into the early evening sunshine. Tears stung her eyes. The sun had no right to be shining like this, or those children to be laughing as they kicked that ball around on the pavement before her. Didn't they know her world had come to an end?

She stumbled on the edge of the kerb, ripping a hole in her stocking and grazing her knee before picking herself up and running blindly in the direction of her flat.

> ... Proud we were,
> And laughed, that had such brave true things to say.
> – And then you suddenly cried, and turned away.

The poet's words resonated in her brain as she ran on along the outer edge of the pavement. He knew. He knew up there on that Sussex hillside that this might happen. She had no evidence, but she knew it was the truth. He knew it, and yet he did not tell her. The knowledge tore at her insides as her heart fought with her head. Perhaps he could not tell her. It was not unknown for him suddenly to be posted off somewhere without word. Things were like that when you worked for a government. And, after all, he had warned her he was awaiting an important dispatch from Washington. The knowledge did little to lessen the pain. It was as if the sun had gone out of her life.

165

'Please, dear God, bring him back to me soon … Please bring him back to me soon …' She prayed to a deity she had not believed in since that awful November night in 1938 when Hitler's henchmen had smashed her world, along with the windows of Jewish Berlin.

From behind the closed door of the flat below her the sound of voices and laughter reached her as she passed by on her way upstairs to her own apartment. It seemed as if the whole world had someone to call their own.

She turned the key in the lock of her door and entered the cool silence of her own small home. It had never seemed more empty.

Chapter Fifteen

Eva did not go to a doctor to find out what was wrong with her. To do so was to risk being found out and being sent to one of those awful camps she feared so much. Instead she read her way through all the medical books Arnold had in the shop and came to an unmistakable conclusion: she was pregnant. There could be no doubt about it, and the knowledge filled her with a mixture of horror and delight.

Her child would be a bastard in the eyes of the world, but not to her. Despite the fact that she had not set eyes on its father since that Sunday he disappeared from her life in mid-August, she knew that this child would be special. This would be a child born out of wedlock, it was true, but it would be a child conceived in love. Beneath her heart she was carrying the love child of Eva Margarete Koehn and William J. Rutherford. How could it be any other than a very special human being?

Slowly, very slowly, over the months, she had become accustomed to the fact that she would probably never see Bill again. She could not pretend it did not hurt, for sometimes the agony of missing him was almost too much to bear. But she had her pride, and when, in the first few weeks of his absence, Mr Kennedy asked if she had had any word from him, she had lied and replied lightly that they corresponded from time to time. But it was just one of those things, she assured him; one of those summertime romances that was fun while it lasted, but could not survive the chill blasts of winter.

And it *was* a chill winter they endured that year. Not only the weather chilled the bone, but the heart itself was chilled by the constant bombing raids, and the news from the war-front which was not always as heartening as the beleaguered civilian population might have hoped. Arnold Kennedy had installed a second-hand Pye radio in the shop so they could keep track of the latest developments. But it brought little comfort: 1940 had not been a good year by any stretch of the imagination, and no one could pretend otherwise.

The old year ended with the most horrifying blitz yet on the City of London, on 29 December, and the population looked forward with trepidation to what the coming year of 1941 would bring.

For Eva it had been a lonely Christmas. She had cherished the secret hope that the festive season might bring a Christmas card from America. A friendly line would have sufficed, just to say that he was still around and thought of her occasionally. But nothing came, she had to accept the fact that she would probably never hear from him again, and life went on as usual.

The only thing that really changed in her life was her shape, which she would examine with growing apprehension every night in the dressing-table mirror. How she was managing to keep it a secret from her boss she could not imagine. Loose clothing helped, of course, and from five months she had taken to wearing a baggy overall to work, which she assured Mr Kennedy would work wonders in keeping her good clothes clean. The old man had remarked on the good sense of the idea and she had breathed easily once more.

It was on Friday 14 February – St Valentine's Day – that her secret was almost revealed, but not to the old man for whom she worked. He had closed early for the day to make an attempt at some stock-taking, and had said to Eva she would not be needed. 'It's better I make a start at this myself, m'dear. Then maybe, if I can get some kind of order into things, you can give me a wee hand later on.'

168

It was a beautiful day, with a late winter sun shining from out of a silver-grey sky as she bade him goodbye and left the shop. It was too nice to go straight home, so she resolved to head for that part of the city into which she seldom ventured. Harrods would be her first stop.

She had got no further than the main door of the exclusive department store when a delighted exclamation made her turn round.

'Eva! Why, Eva Koehn – as I live and die!'

She was looking straight into the amazed face of Kay Bridgewater.

Her old friend stood in the marble-tiled doorway, clutching an armful of expensive-looking packages and bags. She was dressed in a sleek fox-fur cape and matching turban. 'I don't believe it,' she declared, shaking her head. 'I'd no idea you would still be around. When we didn't hear from you, or see you again, we just presumed you had been rounded up and sent off to the Isle of Man or somewhere.' She made a face at the very idea of the internment camps as she took Eva by the arm and led her into the shop. 'How come you're still here?'

Eva knew there could be little point in lying to her old friend, and there was something distasteful about the thought of being less than truthful to someone who had helped save her life. 'It's a long story.'

'All the better! I've got a full hour before I meet Charlie.'

'Charlie?'

A secretive, almost smug smile lit the redhead's beautifully made-up face. 'I'll tell you all about him in good time. In the meantime, I want to hear all about what's been happening to you, over a nice cup of tea … Or would you prefer something stronger?'

Eva assured her that a cup of tea would be perfect, so ten minutes later found them seated opposite one another in the elegant, pillared tearoom. And over the delicate porcelain cups of best Ceylon tea she found herself opening her heart

169

as she described that first meeting with Bill on her arrival in London, then his return into her life the previous summer, and his insistence that she 'go underground' to avoid internment. She told it all – everything. Everything except the fact they had slept together. But her friend was no fool.

Kay sat listening in wide-eyed amazement. 'He must have been quite a bloke – I can see why you fell for him. Did you ever talk about marriage before he disappeared?' She felt immediately embarrassed at the directness of her question, and attempted to qualify it, 'What I mean is, some men are like that – to get a girl to sleep with them, they promise them the moon – gold wedding band included.'

Eva's cheeks coloured as she shook her head. How could she possibly explain? How could you expect another human being to understand what there had been between Bill and her? How could you say, it had never come into it, the thought of marriage; that what they had together went far deeper than society's conventions. She had given herself to Bill because she loved him more deeply than she had ever loved another human being. There had been no qualifications to her love. It was as simple as that.

'He didn't mention marriage, then, I take it?' Kay gave an 'I might have known it' look, as she replaced her cup in its saucer. 'And when it was all over he just upped and hot-footed it back to America?'

'Something like that.' The words stuck in her throat.

'Hmm.' Kay stirred another lump of sugar into her tea and frowned. She had never been one for chasing after a man once he had obviously lost interest, so she could understand her friend's predicament. 'He's been the only man in your life, hasn't he, love?'

Eva nodded and lowered her eyes. She was still not comfortable being questioned on the subject.

Kay sighed. 'That makes it all the worse. Now me, for instance, I'd never get that involved. Especially with one of those Embassy blokes. Intelligence, you say he was attached to. Did that mean he was one of them Secret Service spy type of fellas?'

'I – I expect so. He never really talked about his work.'

'That doesn't surprise me; those Bulldog Drummond types are all the same. *Boy's Own Paper* heroes most of 'em. What they know about how to treat a lady I could write on the nail of my pinky!' She wiggled the crimson tip of her little finger to emphasize the point as she raised the teacup to her lips. 'What you need is a bloke like my Charlie ... Now there's someone who knows how to treat a lady!'

'Charlie?'

'The Honourable Charles Bartholemew, to give him his full title.'

'But what happened to *your* Bill – the one in the Navy?'

Kay's fingers tightened around the delicate handle of the cup as she forced her lips into the semblance of a smile. 'Your lot, love – the bloody Germans. That's what happened to him. His ship was torpedoed by them last June.' A shudder ran through her. 'It was his twenty-third birthday that week. We were going to be married on his next leave.'

Eva reached across to press her hand. 'Oh Kay, I'm so sorry. Really I am.'

'Not half as sorry as I am, love.' She smiled with her mouth once more, but not with her eyes. 'Anyway, now I've got Charlie ... I don't love him, he knows that. But, in a way, that makes it easier for him. He doesn't have to worry about asking me to marry him and shocking all those blue-blooded relatives of his.'

She toyed with the sugar tongs in the bowl. 'Let's just say it's worked out quite nicely for both of us. He gets what he wants and I get ...' she glanced down at the red fox-fur slung casually on the seat beside her. 'Well, I get certain advantages too.'

They sat in silence for a moment, each lost in her own thoughts of the men they had both loved and lost in very different ways. Then Kay glanced at her watch. 'Crikey, look

171

at the time! If I don't get a move on, Charlie'll be wailing louder than old Wailing Winnie herself,' she exclaimed, referring to the air-raid siren that was now part and parcel of city life.

She got up from her seat, grabbing her fox-fur and draping it around her shoulders as she took a final gulp of tea. 'Look, love, I'll have to dash, but now that we've run into each other like this, you'll not lose touch again, will you?'

'I'll keep in touch, Kay. Really I will.' But even as she said it, Eva knew that it was a promise she might not keep. Quite apart from her wish to remain as anonymous as possible for fear of what the authorities might do if she were reported, her rapidly swelling stomach was reason enough to avoid as many social contacts as possible for the next few months. But she could not regret having run into Kay again. It was good to know she was still around and keeping a cheerful outlook on life. But then, her friend was never one for letting things get her down. Londoners were a lot like Berliners in that regard; even under the direst circumstances, their natural good humour kept breaking through.

'Good luck then, kid.'

'You too, Kay.'

With a rustle of silk petticoat and swish of fox-fur she was gone. Eva watched her disappear through the swing doors of the dining-room and smiled wistfully to herself. Despite the brave front they had each put on for the benefit of the other, both would need every ounce of luck they could lay their hands on this coming year.

She sighed deeply as she poured the remains of the tea from the silver pot into her cup. As she did so, the baby within her moved quite violently, as if to say she mustn't forget it. He or she would need Lady Luck smiling down every bit as much as they would in the months to come.

As winter gave way to spring and the British Seventh Army dug in for a long confrontation with Rommel's troops in

172

North Africa, and the population at home came to terms with rationing, and 'dug for victory' to the extent of planting cabbages in the public parks, Eva found herself becoming less and less concerned with the problems of the outside world, and more and more apprehensive over her rapidly approaching confinement.

On the days when her energy flagged and her breasts seemed more tender than usual and the weight beneath her heart even heavier, she wondered at the wisdom of not seeing a doctor. Then the thought of having her baby behind barbed wire would convince her she had made the correct decision. Her child would not be born in captivity; he or she would be born a free person – a valued human being, not a second-class citizen to be locked away from their fellow human beings. She had escaped Hitler's Germany to avoid being locked up in a concentration camp, and she was more determined than ever that if she had managed to escape incarceration by the Nazis, then she would certainly do so again by the British.

She still listened avidly to all the news broadcasts, drawing comfort from Winston Churchill's rally cries to the nation. Propaganda, she knew, was part of the price one paid for keeping up the nation's morale in wartime, so she could never be quite certain if the things she heard of conditions in her homeland were accurate. And because of her decision to go it alone and avoid the internment camps, she did not even have the evidence of other refugees to go by. Very little was written in British newspapers about the concentration camps the Germans had set up throughout Europe, but it seemed certain that the few Jews who remained alive on the Continent were now imprisoned behind their barbed wire. She could only hope with all her heart that they really were the work camps the German authorities claimed them to be, and that her family would return to their own home once this terrible war was over.

There was one particular broadcast on the evening of

27 April which moved her more than any other, for in it Churchill had ended by entreating the beleaguered nation to cast their eyes to the west, to America, for strength in their darkest hours:

> 'For while the tired waves, vainly breaking,
> Seem here no painful inch to gain,
> Far back, through creeks and inlets making,
> Comes silent, flooding in, the main.
>
> And not by eastern windows only,
> When daylight comes, comes in the light;
> In front the sun climbs slow, how slowly.
> But westward, look, the land is bright!'

She was looking westward all right. She had never failed to look westward in the vain hope that the father of her unborn child would return. She was not entirely certain when the baby was actually due, but had worked it out to be sometime around the first week of May. The thought of having it alone, with Bill knowing nothing of its birth, weighed heavy on her heart. In the early months it hadn't seemed to matter quite so much, for the birth seemed a lifetime away. Now, however, she found herself looking at things quite differently, and her apprehension at what lay ahead grew with each passing day.

To add to her worries, on the morning of Monday 5 May, a letter came through her door; an official-looking letter that made her fingers tremble as she opened it before leaving for work. Inside, the white vellum bore the crest of the American Embassy, and the information it imparted was precise and to the point. The apartment was required by the Embassy for a member of its staff. Would she be kind enough to find herself alternative accommodation by the end of the month? She read and re-read the words with a sense of mounting panic. Somehow she had felt herself inviolate here; she had almost come to believe the flat was hers for as long as she required it. And now they wanted her out.

She replaced the letter in its envelope and slipped it into her bag. It was something else to worry about in the days to come. Was there to be no respite for her? Where was she to go? And who would take her with a new baby in her arms? Spare rooms, let alone whole flats, were like gold here in London. With so much bomb damage it seemed that half the population was in search of somewhere to stay. What hope had she, a single mother-to-be, of getting another place?

The problem preyed on her mind for the rest of the week, but she had neither the time nor the energy to do more than scour the local newspaper and glance in the newsagent's window as she passed by on her way to work. But there was nothing new to be seen next to the grubby, fly-blown postcards advertising the charms of the local ladies-of-the-night, and pleas for homes for abandoned dogs and cats.

Perhaps she could let Mr Kennedy know of her predicament? But something inside her balked at the thought. She had deliberately avoided discussing her personal life with her boss, although the little Irishman had made several attempts to bring their conversation round to a more personal level.

He was, she knew, concerned about her lack of friends of her own age, and had often brought up the subject of boyfriends or, in her case, the lack of them. He had even resurrected the subject of Bill once or twice recently, but it had been a remark he had made over their morning cup of tea one day at the end of March that had chilled her to the bone. 'Sure and when you think about it, it was a good thing, was it not, that yon American lad got posted back home?'

Her fingers had gripped the handle of the cup that bit tighter as she tried to remain casual in her reply. 'Really? And why is that, Mr Kennedy?'

He had squinted at her over the top of his glasses as he added another spoon of precious sugar to his tea. 'Well now, you think about it, m'dear. Just think about it for a minute. You're a German, born and bred, are you not?'

'Yes,' she had answered uncertainly.

'With nothing on your passport to state you're a Jew.'

She had nodded mutely, her apprehension growing as he sighed and lifted his cup.

'And he was in Intelligence at the American Embassy, if I remember rightly.'

Again she nodded.

'Well now, sure and you'd have to be a right eejit not to know that consorting with a Jerry wouldn't have done his career one bit of good if it had become known, now would it? In fact, it could have brought him no end of trouble, and that's a fact.'

She had stared at him as the words sank in.

'Aye, it was probably a good thing, right enough, that they sent him home, or wherever. You wouldn't have wanted to have blighted the lad's career before it had hardly begun, now would you, Eva m'girl?'

'No, Mr Kennedy.'

No, Mr Kennedy … No, Mr Kennedy … A thousand times no, Mr Kennedy. And that was why, despite her growing nervousness at the impending birth, she had resisted the temptation to get in touch with the American Embassy again for news, or even to attempt to write to him care of them. The last thing on earth she wanted to do was to blight Bill Rutherford's career.

And so she had continued to keep her secret from the world, and from the father of her child, as that child continued to grow beneath her heart – a heavy weight on her body and soul, but a weight that was born of love. She would love this child as she had loved its father, and she would bear it with pride. It would be *their* child: a child born of their love. There would never be a child more special than this.

By the morning of Friday 9 May, she knew her time was due. She had even more difficulty than usual in dragging her heavy body from bed in the morning and dressing for work.

Old Arnold Kennedy was in a particularly cheerful mood

when she appeared at her usual time of five minutes to nine. He had come across a rare first edition of Thomas Moore's *Poetical Works* in a pile of penny dreadfuls he had picked up at a house sale in Richmond, and he insisted on keeping her amused throughout the morning by reading excerpts from the most unlikely of poems: lines from *Thoughts on Tar-Barrels* was followed by *The Fly and the Bullock*, and *Louis Fourteenth's Wig*.

'Sure an' they don't write poetry like that any more, Eva my girl,' he declared, rubbing at the soft calf-leather of the bindings with an old duster. 'It's all tripe they're writing nowadays, so it is ... Would ye be reading much poetry yourself these days?'

'Now and again, Mr Kennedy.'

He looked pleased. 'That young man of yours – the Yankee-Doodle Dandy fella – he gave you a copy of Rupert Brooke, if I remember rightly.'

Eva nodded and half-turned her head so he should not see the change of expression on her face.

But Arnold Kennedy was concentrating on the polishing of his latest acquisition. 'A right eejit yon young fella was and no mistake – the Brooke fella, I mean. "Now, God be thanked Who has matched us with His hour",' he quoted, with a shake of his grey head. 'Now who in their right mind would write such a thing about being called to fight in the Great War? Cannon fodder, that's all they were to be, Eva m'girl. Cannon fodder in an Imperialist war. It would have been the end of the Capitalist system if the working man had joined hands with his brothers in Germany – but what happened? They tugged the forelock to their so-called betters, that's what happened. Instead of the workers of the world uniting, they listened to the vested interests of the upper classes and pointed a gun at each other instead.'

But Eva was no longer listening as she gripped the top rung of the library steps for support. Her insides were being squeezed in a vice, so painfully that she had to bite her teeth into her lower lip to stop herself from moaning out loud.

'We could have shown them all up, you know. We Irish had the chance and threw it away. We could have shown them that time in 1916 that …' his voice tailed off. 'Are you all right, my dear?'

She nodded mutely, afraid to speak, as her face turned ashen and a cold film of perspiration appeared on her brow. 'It – it's nothing – really,' she said at last. 'A touch of indigestion, that's all … It must have been that powdered egg I had at breakfast.'

Arnold Kennedy was already carrying across a chair for her to sit down. 'More than likely,' he nodded in agreement as he helped her on to the rush-seat. 'If you ask me, that stuff's never been near a hen.' He looked down at her in concern. 'You don't look too good to me, m'girl.'

Her first inclination was to insist she would be all right but, as the pain began to subside, she feared it would be only a matter of minutes until it began again. She was going into labour. There was no doubt about it.

'You're going home.'

She opened her mouth to feign a protest, but he held his hand up to stifle any attempt at dissent. 'There's to be no argument! You'll be no good to man nor beast in the state you're in!'

His brow wrinkled as he looked down at her. 'A taxi's what you'll be needing. You'll never be able to walk back home in a state like that. Sure and you'll be fainting all over the place, and then where would we be?'

She was in no fit state to argue so, ten minutes later, she found herself seated in the back of a black hackney cab on its way along Montague Street, towards her apartment. Her boss had paid the taxi-driver in advance, and for the whole of the journey she lived in apprehension of another contraction starting.

Her fears were unfounded, for it was almost two hours

before her lower abdomen was gripped in another seizure. She was convinced that this one was even worse; but she was to go on believing that each one was more painful than the last for the next twenty-four hours, as the pains followed each other at irregular intervals until, by six o'clock the following evening, her waters had broken and the contractions were only ten minutes apart.

She found she got most relief by walking around the room, and standing gripping on to the back of the settee when the pains started. They were like nothing she had ever known before. Surely this could not be normal? Surely other women did not go through this same agony? If they did, she was convinced the population of the world would come to a full stop.

By eleven o'clock they were only a few minutes apart and she had an uncontrollable urge to push downwards with each one. The pain was so bad she was sure she was going to faint and could not stop herself groaning out loud in agony as she rolled around on the floor in front of the single bar of the gas fire. She was too afraid to lie on the bed for fear of ruining a mattress that was not her own, and then being asked to pay for it.

Then the sirens went. Their long, screaming drone filled the whole flat. The Luftwaffe was on its way back. London was in for yet another night of death and destruction. But this time there could be no question of making her way downstairs and along the street to the nearest air-raid shelter, or the local tube station at Russell Square. Tonight she had other things than the might of Hitler's Luftwaffe to contend with.

She could hear them going over the roof of the building; their ominous droning never failed to send a chill of fear shivering its way through her body. A rumble in the distance told her some poor devils had got it, not too far away.

She managed to stagger to the window and draw back the blackout material far enough to see a group of bombers picked out in the beam of the anti-aircraft searchlights. It looked as though they were heading in the direction of Westminster, perhaps even Parliament itself.

A great fire was raging in the next street. Orange tongues of flame were licking heavenwards and white smoke was billowing in huge clouds around the area of Russell Street. Had they hit the British Museum? She craned her neck in a vain attempt to verify her suspicions, then she doubled up and fell to her knees, clutching her stomach.

It was coming. Dear Lord, it was coming …

The deep rumble then ear-splitting crash of exploding bombs and incendiaries, coupled with the incessant noise of the ack-ack from the nearby anti-aircraft battery, only went some way to muffling her screams as she writhed in agony on the rumpled towels laid out on the fireside rug. Despite her pain, she was aware of trying desperately not to roll off them on to the carpet. At all costs she must not stain it; her meagre finances could not pay for a replacement.

In a momentary lull in the bombing, she could hear shouting from the street below. 'They've got Westminster Abbey!' she heard a man's voice cry from the pavement below her window. 'The buggers have got the Abbey – and St Paul's!'

Then all went silent again, save for the incessant noise of the battle being fought above her, between the planes of her own Fatherland and the defences of this land that was now her home.

She stared up at the ceiling, her eyes blinded by tears as, despite her agonies, her thoughts flew back to her home on the Unter den Linden. The faces of her mother and father and her beloved *Oma* swam before her. Would she ever see them again? Would they ever see this child now fighting to enter a world not fit to bring any innocent infant into?

Then another face floated before her, and she screamed his name aloud: 'Bill …!' Where was he now – now that she needed him so much?

She had never felt more alone. Outside these four walls, her own people were wreaking death and destruction all around her as she lay here writhing on the floor. The whole world had gone crazy. And all the time the new life within her tore her apart on its agonizing journey into the hell that was London this night.

'Aaaahhhhh…!'

Then, suddenly, it was born.

She struggled to sit up and clutch at the slithering scrap of humanity that lay in a pool between her legs. The tears continued to stream down her face as she picked it up and pressed it to her breast. It let out a strangled squawk. To Eva it was the most beautiful sound in the world.

'My daughter … My daughter …'

Tenderly she stroked the damp tendrils of hair on the infant's brow as it opened its eyes. They looked straight into hers and, at that moment, a great love welled within her for this tiny creature she had brought into the world. Her daughter – her own daughter. She gazed down at the red, upturned face, as the tears continued to stream down her cheeks. What was going to become of them? A child without a father, but born of love … A love child born to a woman with no past she could ever speak of, a fearful present, and an uncertain future …

Her tears tasted salt on her lips and splashed on to the red wrinkled brow of the child in her arms as she whispered, 'What will become of you, my *Liebchen*? What will become of you and me?'

Chapter Sixteen

On the morning of Sunday 11 May 1941, the elderly Irishman stared in a mixture of horror and disbelief at the pile of rubble that had been the home of his young German assistant. There was practically nothing left of it, and what little there was had been almost completely destroyed by the ensuing fire that had raged into the small hours of the morning, despite the gallant efforts of the Fire Service and volunteers. The whole top half of the street had been cordoned off, but a sympathetic Air-raid Warden had let him through to verify his worst fears.

Last night had been one of the worst nights of the Blitz. Many of the city's best known buildings had been hit: Westminster Abbey and Hall, St Paul's Cathedral, the British Museum, the House of Commons, even Big Ben itself ... the list went on and on.

But it was not the great landmarks of the city that concerned Arnold Kennedy this Sunday morning. It was the fate of the young German girl he had grown so fond of over the past ten months as she had worked alongside him in his shop.

A policeman stood guard over the smoking remains of the Georgian terrace that had been Eva's home. He turned to look curiously at the small, bent figure of the Irishman. 'You from round here, Guv?'

The old man shook his head. 'I was lucky,' he jerked his head in the direction of Montague Street. 'I live a quarter of a mile or so away, not far from the Museum. My flat missed the worst of it, although my shop was hit ... But my assistant lived here ...'

His eyes, already red-rimmed, stared into the pile of

smoking rubble. Only one or two interior walls remained standing, with parts of floors and ceilings hanging precariously from the few joists that remained suspended above the heaps of debris. It looked as if at least four houses in the terrace had got it, with the house sixth from the end of the row receiving a direct hit. From what he could make out, Eva's flat had been one or two down from it.

His eyes smarting from the smoke, he gazed up at what was once her front window; most of the window-panes had been blown out by the heat, and a tattered piece of burnt curtain fluttered in the breeze through a hole in one of them. On a part of the floor that was still intact, the remains of a sideboard perched precariously above a huge, gaping cavity.

'Lucky most of 'em were in the shelter,' the policeman said shaking his head. 'Only a couple of 'em copped it from this lot. A young lad who'd gone back for his dog, and a young woman who lived in the middle flat. Bloody unlucky, really. If they'd made it to the shelter with the others, they'd have survived.'

The officer turned to survey the carnage once more, then lifted his helmet and scratched his greying hair beneath. 'There was one piece of luck, though. They found an infant still alive in the wreckage. Bloody miracle, if you ask me ...'

But Arnold Kennedy was not interested in infants. Beneath the straggling white brows, his eyes were still smarting, and not only from the grey and black smoke that still drifted up from the ruins of what had once been family homes. 'The – the young woman,' he heard himself say, 'the one who didn't make it – she wasn't German, by any chance?'

The policeman gave a hollow laugh. Trust an Irishman to come out with a daft question like that! 'I'm afraid you've got hold of the wrong end of the stick, guv,' he grinned wryly. 'The Jerries were the ones up there dropping the bleeding bombs, not the ones down 'ere copping it, remember!'

The old man looked up at him, uncomprehending for a moment, then nodded slowly. 'Of course ... Aye, you're right enough there, so you are.' There was no point in disclosing poor Eva's secret to him or anyone else now. She had gone and nothing could touch her any more. Not Hitler, nor the authorities who wanted to intern her, not anybody …

He had not cried since that day on 12 May 1916, when the British had tied the wounded body of the Irish rebel leader James Connelly like a dog to a chair and shot him in Kilmainham jail for his part in the Easter Rising. But he cried like a baby as he turned and walked away from all that remained of Eva Koehn's young life.

BOOK TWO

The Lost Lilies

———————

'What if one heaven by sin forfeited?'
(Thus in my wilful bitterness I spake)
'More loves remain, though one young love be dead:
Shall all my life be void, for a dream's sake?
– Let me arise! Beauty yet awaits, I wis,
Red blooms more passionate than these wan lilies!'

So, after desolate questing through the years,
At length I won to this dim languorous place,
Fragrant with night and roses. All my tears
Fade from me, bending to hide my weary face
Deep in this drowsy gloom of fragrances,
And drown remembrance of my lost lilies.

Ah! surely here at length oblivion
Shall drown my wandering, and this dim perfume
Cover away remembrance of things gone,
In scented groves and passionate warm gloom!
Surely more sweet the roses' purple kiss,
Than the pale sorrow of my lost lilies!

Yet sometimes, in a still twilight, it may be,
Even these roses scentless grow and stale;
Joy for a time seems but Satiety;
The warm spells of the subtle darkness fail;
Till the sick heart's memorial litanies
Sigh for the pure grace of my lost lilies.

And all the murmur and scent of sun-setting
Awake the passionate old dreams; and I
Sit weary-eyed in silent sorrowing,
And nurse the old regrets that will not die,
Remembering where the perfect beauty is,
The immortal pallor of my lost lilies.

Rupert Brooke

Chapter Seventeen

The young woman stood looking up at the new council tower block, her dark eyes squinting against the brightness of the afternoon sun. Her pale blonde hair hung long and loose over the shoulders of her blue cotton mini-dress; her arms and legs were bare, slim and tanned, and her face wore an expression of apprehension rarely seen on it. Anna Lloyd-Jones was nervous, and the knowledge disturbed her. How could someone undaunted at taking on the Prime Minister himself in an argument be in a state of anxiety at the thought of meeting a middle-aged housewife?

She glanced down again at the letter in her hand. How many times had she read it since its arrival last week? She had lost count and already knew it off by heart. It was written in the painstaking hand of someone not usually given to letter-writing. It read:

Dear Miss Lloyd-Jones,
    In answer to your request in our local newspaper for information regarding anyone who knew an Eva Koehn who lived in London in the early part of the war, I think I may be of some help to you. I knew Eva quite well and last saw her at the beginning of 1941, I think it was. Should you want to know more, you can contact me at the following address …

And now Anna stood across the road looking up at that address – a council block in Canning Town. She could feel a dampness in her armpits and the palms of her hands that had nothing to do with the heat of the midsummer sun. She was about to find out the answers to questions that had plagued her for the past thirteen years – ever since that fateful night before she left home for her first term at boarding school. That was the night her parents had decided it was the appropriate time to reveal to her she was adopted.

The knowledge had come as a bombshell. At twelve years old you do not question how a petite, plump English woman, with sea-green eyes and red hair, and a short, stocky, dark-haired Welsh doctor could produce a tall, willowy daughter with pale blonde hair and dark, walnut-brown eyes. Never for one moment had Anna dreamt that Owen and Peggy Lloyd-Jones were not her real parents. The secret kept for twelve long years, and revealed with hugs and kisses, and assurances she was extra special because she was their *chosen* one, came as a revelation of devastating proportions: something to brood about alone in her bed at night for years to come.

She had never even heard the word 'adopted' before that day. Was she the only one in the world to be adopted? Certainly, when she arrived at her new school and got to know the other girls, none of them seemed to have mothers and fathers who were not their own. She had shared her secret with no one. It was not the done thing to be different. Yet different she was, and it was a heavy cross for a young girl to bear.

The knowledge had had a marked effect on her, particularly after hearing her father's story of the day he first set eyes on the baby that he was to grow to love as his own.

Owen Lloyd-Jones had been a young houseman at St Thomas's Hospital when the air-raid victims were brought in on the night of the Blitz of 11 May 1941. Her real mother had been brought in mortally wounded, clutching her newborn baby in her arms.

'You were nothing but a pathetic little scrap of humanity, Anna love,' Owen Lloyd-Jones had told her. 'You never even cried that first night. To tell you the truth, we had our doubts about *your* survival, too … As for your real mother – well, it was a miracle she even survived long enough to reach the hospital. With those injuries …' He had shaken his head. 'To be honest with you, I felt then, and I still feel today that she clung on to life just long enough to make sure *you* were safe.'

And it was true. Eva Koehn had lived only long enough to know that her baby daughter was in good hands, and to say a few words to the earnest-faced young doctor who tended her.

His heart had gone out to the badly-injured young woman that night. She looked little more than a child herself. From the little she said in reply to his questions on her injuries, and on the baby's birth, she was obviously not English. A refugee from the fighting in Europe, perhaps. She had even managed to spell out her surname for him, and nod weakly when he asked if it was a German name.

Who were her next of kin, he wondered? Where was her husband? He should be informed immediately. He was convinced she would not last the night.

'Your husband … The baby's father?' he had asked. 'Where is the baby's father?'

The young woman had smiled wanly at him and shaken her head on the pillow.

'Is he here? Can we contact him?' Owen Lloyd-Jones had persevered, bending over the bed so he should not miss her reply.

Again she shook her head. It was not the earnest face of the young Welshman that was swimming before her closed eyes. Tears oozed between the damp lashes. 'He's in America … America …' The words were barely audible. She had lost a lot of blood and was fading fast, despite the life-giving drip in her arm.

'He's an American?'

Her lips formed the word, '*Ja*', then her eyes closed, never to open again.

From the day she heard that story at twelve years old, its effect on Anna had been profound. She had hated that unknown American with a passion that ate into her very soul.

What kind of a man was he to run out on them both like that? She had not the slightest doubt that, had he not deserted her, her mother would be alive today. And now, hopefully, she was to find out exactly who he was and who exactly the young woman with the German name was who had given birth to her that awful night during the Blitz.

What had made her wait so long in placing that letter requesting information in the local newspaper, she really did not know. Perhaps it was a combination of things: concern for her adoptive parents, the sheer fullness of life itself, plus the apprehension of what she might find out. And it was perhaps the last of the three that had taken the most conquering. As Anna Lloyd-Jones, the daughter of an eminently respectable, middle-class British couple, her place in the scheme of things had been secure; but who was this young woman with the German name who had given birth to her, and who exactly was the American who had fathered her and run out on them both?

These questions had plagued her throughout her young life, from the day she first set out with that secret of her origins weighing more heavily on her than any of the suitcases containing her worldly goods, as she waved goodbye to her mother and father on the steps of her new school.

Boarding school in Sussex had led on to a place at university, and when she came down from Oxford with a First Class Honours in Politics, Philosophy and Economics, there was her Ph.D. to study for. Her thesis on 'The Politics of Food in the Third World' still lay unfinished in a desk drawer at home, awaiting the day she would have the time to devote to it that it deserved. Life, over the past few years, had taken precedence over scholarship. Student politics at university had led on to an active involvement in the Campaign for Nuclear Disarmament, and membership of so many radical political groups she had often begun to lose count.

She had been a mere seventeen years old when the first meeting of CND took place in London on 17 February 1958, and she had gone along with her parents and several of their medical friends to the Central Hall in Westminster, which had been booked for the occasion.

It had been a day to remember. Over 5,000 people had turned up to register their concern over nuclear weapons, and four overflow halls had to be used to accommodate them all. And what speakers she had heard that day ... Even now, all these years later, she still thrilled to the memory of listening to the likes of the philosopher, Bertrand Russell, J.B. Priestley, one of her best-loved authors, and her favourite historian, A.J.P. Taylor. A.J.P. had graphically described the effects of an H-bomb explosion and asked whether anyone present would want to inflict that on another human being. There had been a total silence in the hall. 'Then why are we making the damned thing?' he had demanded. The applause had been deafening, and no one had applauded louder than she had.

Afterwards, several hundred of the people, including her mother and father and a few of their friends, had marched on to Downing Street. They had been a good-humoured crowd, still filled to overflowing with a surfeit of the milk of human kindness that the speeches had instilled in them all. But then the police had arrived with dogs and had begun arresting people. Incredibly, her mother, who had never even dropped a sweet paper in her life, let alone broken any real law, was amongst those hauled off into one of the Black Marias. She had been kept in prison overnight, then appeared in court next day to be fined £10 for 'causing an obstruction'.

From that day on Anna had stopped regarding the police, or any branch of the Establishment, as her automatic ally. On the contrary, they were increasingly to become objects of the greatest suspicion. And as her suspicions grew, so her opinions hardened politically. Gradually, from that day in

February 1958 forward, from being merely an impression-able apolitical teenager with an abhorrence of nuclear weapons, she became a politically motivated and totally committed young woman. And the most recent manifestation of that commitment was her appointment as a political journalist of London's latest radical journal, *The Vital Spark*.

But neither as a journalist nor at university had she written anything that had caused her so much heart-searching as her letter to the local rag last week, requesting information regarding the young woman by the name of Eva Koehn.

If her mother and father had still been alive, she would probably never have done it, out of respect for them. But both Owen and Peggy Lloyd-Jones had been dead for over a year now – killed in a car crash on 29 March 1967 in France, on the same day de Gaulle launched that country's first nuclear submarine.

Their deaths had been a terrible blow. They had been good people; people with a conscience, who if they saw an injustice had at least made an attempt to put it right. Those ideals, far more precious than any worldly wealth, they had passed down to Anna, and their untimely deaths had left an aching void in her life. Perhaps that was why she had at last written that letter to the newspaper. Perhaps in seeking out her past she was trying to compensate for being robbed of the two most important people in the present.

At any rate, whatever the reason, she had not expected a reply. The war had been over for twenty-one years, after all.

But it had come – the small, cheap envelope with its matching sheet of lined notepaper inside. Her hands had shaken as she read it, and they were shaking now as she stuffed the well-thumbed letter back into her handbag and pulled her sunglasses down from her hair. Taking a last glance up at the concrete tower block in front of her, she set off across the road in the direction of the address of her correspondent.

Number 21 turned out to be on the third floor. The lift

was out of action, despite the fact the block had only been up for a year, and the concrete stairwell was disfigured with graffiti so obscene that she averted her eyes as she climbed the three flights of steps. The name Hallam on the door corresponded with the one at the foot of her letter, all right. She stared down at the white plastic nameplate before taking a deep breath and pressing her finger on the bell.

Three times she pressed it and still no answer, and she was on the point of turning to go when she heard footsteps behind the door. There was the rattling sound of a chain being pulled back. Then a woman's face peered through the narrow gap at her.

'Yes? What do you want?'

'Are you Mrs Hallam? Mrs K. Hallam?'

'Yes.' The woman continued to eye her suspiciously through the chink in the door.

Anna cleared her throat. 'My name's Anna Lloyd-Jones … You – you wrote me a letter informing me you knew my mother. Her name was Koehn. Eva Koehn.'

There was a moment's silence, then the voice said, incredulously, 'You're Eva's kid?'

There was another rattle as the chain was pulled out and the door opened further to allow for a better look. The woman was around fifty, fairly tall and well-built, although her ample figure was now running to seed. Her hair was done up in an elaborate bouffant and bright titian in colour. Judging by her age, it was obviously dyed. Her eyebrows were over-plucked and pencilled in again in two arched, brown lines reminiscent of a Thirties filmstar. The face had once been pretty, but the years had not been kind. It was the face of a woman to whom life had dealt out the blows, but there was something about the look in her eyes that said she had taken them on the chin and come back for more. She removed the cigarette from her mouth and gestured to Anna to enter the narrow hallway. 'You'd better come in.'

Anna followed her into a brightly furnished sitting-room.

A print of Van Gogh's *Sunflowers* hung above the electric, coal-effect fire in the grate, and on the wooden mantelpiece sat a collection of china animals. To the side of the fire, a display cabinet held a collection of dolls in national costume; a small plastic one of a Red Indian head-dress caught Anna's eye. Had she been to the States? A Billie Holiday album was playing on the ageing radiogram against the far wall, its sultry tones filling the room with a soulful blues number that seemed curiously appropriate.

The woman walked over and lifted the needle from the record, leaving the turntable to revolve in silence as she turned back to Anna who was standing awkwardly in the middle of the room. 'Sit down, love.' She gestured to where a fat tabby cat lay curled in the middle of a black vinyl settee. She shooed it off. 'We're not allowed to have pets in this place,' she said, giving a half-hearted wipe at the remaining cat hairs on the cushion. 'But what they don't know won't harm 'em, that's what I say.'

Anna smiled as she made herself comfortable, and the animal clambered back up beside her. 'I do hope you don't mind me just dropping in on you like this. I would have phoned, only you weren't on the ...'

'Do you think I've got the money to put a phone in in the likes of this place?' the woman interrupted with a forced laugh. 'I'll tell you this, love, it takes me all the time to pay the bloomin' rent! We may have a Labour Government in power, but it's doing damn all for the likes of us.'

She walked to a formica bar in the corner of the room. 'Would you care for a cup of tea, or would you prefer something stronger?'

Anna noticed a half-full glass of whisky sitting on the curved top of the bar, and deduced that tea might be something of a bother. 'Something stronger would be fine. I'll have a vodka and lemonade, if you have it.'

'One vodka and lemonade coming up.' She poured the mixture deftly into a tumbler and brought it across. 'Eva's your mother, you say?' She looked at Anna curiously. 'I can believe that. You look just like her.'

A shiver ran through Anna at the words. She had had no inkling of what her mother had looked like until this moment. It was not something she had thought to ask her father about. 'Really?'

Her hostess nodded. 'She was pretty, too – and had fair hair just like yours. And them dark eyes.'

Anna's heart beat faster. This was going better than she could ever have hoped. 'You knew her in the war, you said in your letter.'

The woman walked to the window and gazed down at the road below as she sipped her drink. 'I first met Eva in Berlin in 1938,' she said slowly. 'November '38. *Kristallnacht*, the Germans called it. It was the night they turned Berlin's pavements into a sea of glass.'

Anna shifted nervously to the edge of the settee. Her mother was a Berliner? 'You knew her family then?'

The woman shook her head, her eyes clouding as she tapped the ash from her cigarette into an ashtray and cast her mind back to that awful night of 9 November 1938. 'I was dancing at a nightclub owned by the father of a friend of Eva's,' she said, her brow furrowing as she tried in vain to recall its name. '… No, it's gone. But the family's name was Kessel, who owned the club. I remember that because they opened another one in West Berlin after the war and I did one further stint there before I gave it up completely.' She tapped a false tooth with a red-lacquered nail. 'It was something like The Blue Angel, but it wasn't that.' She watched Anna scribble the information into a notebook. 'Anyhow, Eva was brought to us to escape the pogrom.'

'She was Jewish?' Anna asked in amazement.

Kay Hallam, née Bridgewater, shrugged. 'A *Mischling*, I think was the technical term for her. Mixed blood, you see. As far as I remember, her family had owned a big department store on the Unter den Linden and lived above it – at least they did until that awful night in '38.'

Anna could hardly believe her ears. She was hearing about relatives – family – she never knew existed. A Jewish family, of all things; it had never crossed her mind before. 'And her family – what happened to them?'

Kay Hallam shrugged as she took another sip of her drink. 'Auschwitz, Belsen, Buchenwald … take your pick … I really don't know, to be perfectly honest with you, ducks. But I expect they all ended up in one of them camps. Almost all the European Jews did, didn't they? Unless they were lucky enough to make it over here, that is.'

She placed her whisky glass on the windowsill and lit a fresh cigarette from the remains of her old one, drawing deeply on the smoke as she looked down at Anna. 'But I expect you know as much about that period as I do. I'm just a bloody historical relic who was lucky enough to live through it all and come out the other side. I mean it's all written down now in the history books, isn't it – the Holocaust and all that.'

Anna nodded, grave-faced. Her thoughts were in turmoil. She had accepted the fact that her mother might be of German descent, because of her name, but she had never expected this. Not for one moment had she imagined she could have Jewish blood. 'My mother – she escaped then, I take it? She came to Britain?'

'That's right, love. She came back with me. Stayed with us at my Mum's, she did, until she got a place of her own. Got a small room round Lambeth way, and managed to find work in a music-seller's … Owned by some Jewish feller, it was, and bombed out in the Blitz, if I remember rightly.'

She tapped thoughtfully on the end of her cigarette as she tried to put dates to the memories that came flooding back … Eva was only part of so many memories of those days. She could see a face in her mind's eye – a face that she had seen so often in dreams, waking and sleeping, over the years – Bill,

196

her fiancé … Then the grinning countenance of old Good-time Charlie Bartholemew …

'But my mother, she wasn't in the shop when it was bombed?'

Anna's question roused Kay from her reverie. 'Oh – Eva … No, love, she had gone by then. I remember going round and asking them at the shop if they knew what had happened to her. But they were as clueless as I was. She disappeared around the time they were rounding up all the foreigners in the country to shove them off to the Isle of Man and places like that, you see. We knew they'd either taken her, or she'd gone underground.' She sighed. 'So many folks just disappeared during them years, it was a part of life. You just accepted that's how things were in those days.'

'You never saw her again, then?'

Kay Hallam's face lightened. 'Oh, yes, I did. Once – now I come to think about it. It was a funny thing. I ran into her in Harrods. Around the beginning of '41 I think it was. I remember I was real surprised to find she was still around. We were convinced she'd been locked up in one of them camps, like I said.' Something akin to a wistful smile came to her lips. 'I remember she told me about a bloke she'd been seeing a lot of. He'd walked out on her and she was pretty cut up about it. Didn't say a word against him, mind – I'll say that for her.'

Anna sat grim-faced, balancing her notepad on her knees, her pen poised above it. 'He wouldn't have been an American by any chance – that guy who walked out on her?'

Kay Hallam looked down at her in surprise. 'You know about him, then?'

'Not really. But I'd be grateful for anything you can remember. His name, for example, or where he worked.' She held her breath. It was too much to hope for.

'Oh, I remember his name all right, love. It was Bill – the same name as my own young man who'd just been lost in that bloody war. And his other name was Rutherford … It's funny how some things stick in your mind, isn't it? Without really thinking about them, I mean. They just stay with you, somehow … I went to school with a Rutherford – Elsie her name was. Best of friends we were. Maybe that's why it stuck … Yes, Bill Rutherford his name was, and he worked for the American Embassy. Some sort of spy, if I remember rightly … Eva's "Bulldog Drummond", I remember I told my folks when I next saw them. He worked for their Intelligence section, at any rate, and you can make of that what you will.'

Anna had sat holding her breath as the information came spilling forth, and she let out a great sigh at the end of it. Bill Rutherford. Bill Rutherford was her father. It had too familiar – too English – a ring to it to be an apt name for the man she had hated so much for all these years … But American Intelligence, yes, she could buy that.

'Do you know what became of him?'

'Lord no! I never even met the bloke. He went back to America, I presume. Came from that place they named the dance after, if I remember rightly.'

'Lambeth?'

'No – the American place … Charleston, so Eva said. I remember she corrected me for calling him a Yank. Said he didn't take kindly to it – his grandfather having fought in the Civil War and all that. Yanks only come from New York, you see.'

Anna nodded and sat back on the vinyl cushion. She took a gulp of her drink. Bill Rutherford, from Charleston, South Carolina, working in Intelligence at the US Embassy. She smiled grimly as she sipped her vodka once more. This was more than she could have hoped for. 'What was she like – my mother – Mrs Hallam? Was she happy here in England?'

Kay Hallam walked to the bar to top up her drink from the bottle of Bell's, then seated herself on the arm of the chair next to the fire. She thought about the question for a minute or so before answering. 'She was a nice girl. A really nice girl … And I'm not just saying that 'cause it's you sitting there.

Didn't talk much about herself, mind. Not at first. To be honest, I think the whole Jewish thing came as a real shock to her. She didn't know she was Jewish, you see. Not till the Nazis found out. And once *Kristallnacht* occurred ... Well, her whole world must have fallen in.'

'Do you know if I have any relatives still in Berlin?'

'That I wouldn't know, love. All I can tell you is that Eva came over here alone. Only a teenager she was, as I remember. And, to be perfectly honest with you, until I met you, I had no idea she'd even had a kid. You've no idea yourself what happened to her after the war – whether she went back to Berlin, or anything like that?'

'My mother died the night I was born, Mrs Hallam. I was adopted by the doctor who attended her in the hospital that night.'

Kay Hallam's jaw dropped open. 'Oh, love, I'm so sorry.'

'Not half as sorry as I am.'

'You'll be anxious to get in touch with your real father, then.'

Anna's lips tightened. She was anxious to get in touch with her real father all right. But not to throw her arms around him as a long-lost daughter. She was anxious to get in touch with her father to get even; to let him know exactly what he did a quarter of a century ago. He destroyed the life of a young girl who loved him and, but for the grace of God, could have destroyed their child's life, too. Bill Rutherford, wherever he was now, should not get away with that fact. He had killed her mother just as surely as if he had taken a gun to her head.

'You've been an invaluable help, Mrs Hallam,' she said quietly, rising from the settee. 'I should certainly be able to get in touch with my real father now, thanks to you.'

The older woman beamed through a cloud of cigarette smoke and picked a speck of tobacco off her tongue. 'I'm glad to have been of some help, love. I hope for your sake he turns out to be a nice bloke ... Not like the one I landed myself with after the war was over.' The skin between her pencilled brows furrowed as she remembered the young sailor she had married within a month of their first meeting, after Charlie Bartholemew let her down. Harry Hallam had loved the bottle more than he had ever loved her. Booze had been his life, and it had been the death of him, too.

She walked Anna to the door, and looked at her intently as they shook hands. 'Yes, you're the spitting image of her, ducks. You're Eva to a T ...'

She put out a beringed hand and clasped Anna's arm. 'I haven't been much help, I'm afraid. And I'm really sorry to hear about her death. I didn't expect that ... Poor Eva, she deserved better than an end like that. To escape the Nazis to finish up being killed by the bombs of her own people over here. It don't seem right, somehow, does it?'

Anna gave a tight smile. 'No, Mrs Hallam. It doesn't seem right.'

Chapter Eighteen

'Up the revolution!' Two teenage boys, with Beatles haircuts and wide grins, gave Anna a clenched salute as she approached the door of *The Vital Spark*'s office on Charing Cross Road.

She made a facial grimace that might have passed for a smile and half-heartedly raised her own fist in salute. It was expected of her. That was what came of being a known face of the Left. A giggle caused her to glance behind her; one was giving her the V sign behind her back. That was the problem – you never knew if they were taking the mickey or not. This time they were. 'Morons,' she muttered under her breath.

She glanced into the window of the New Left bookshop beneath *The Vital Spark* office and found her own face staring back at her. A copy of her latest book, *Conversations*, compiled from a succession of interviews with the rich and powerful over the past year, had been placed in the centre. The publishers had insisted on featuring her own face on the cover and she cringed inwardly every time she saw it. Peering with a pair of panda-black eyes through the fringe of long blonde hair, and with that ridiculously pouting mouth, she looked more like one of Carnaby Street's dolly birds than a serious journalist.

She had never been happy about her appearance, and had tried scraping her long hair back into a bun for a while, believing that would somehow give her a more serious air; but having to fiddle with loose strands and constantly dropping hairpins had made that a short-lived phase.

'If you've got it – use it, kid!' her last editor had told her. 'How the hell do you think you get granted so many interviews with those guys, anyway? Do you honestly think they'd all be so ready to accept lunches from you if you looked like the back of a bus?'

She had been appalled at this confirmation of what she already suspected. If you were a woman and expected to be taken seriously – forget it, at least until you were well over forty. It had been a chilling realization, until the day she had come to terms with it and decided her boss was right. If you couldn't join them, then you darned well beat them at their own game. If men – particularly men in positions of power – found her attractive, then she would exploit that fact for all it was worth, if it got her the stories she wanted.

And that was exactly what she had done over the past two years. Her weekly column was now syndicated to over a dozen major left-wing newspapers throughout the world, and she had Tory and Socialist politicians alike queuing up to be interviewed by her. In fact, to most of the new arrivals at Westminster, to be taken apart by her in newsprint was now regarded as the final confirmation that they had actually 'arrived' on the political scene.

It was an old adage but a true one that there was no such thing as a free lunch, particularly in the media, and she had few scruples left when it came to what she regarded as the legitimate pursuit of truth and justice. After all, they were using her every bit as she was using them. As far as she was concerned, the end almost always justified the means, and she was not particular in which direction her literary venom was aimed – the Left were every bit as fair game as the Right in her book. Often more so.

A young woman from *L'Humanité* passed her on the way down as she climbed the stone stairs to the second floor of the old Georgian building. They exchanged smiles.

A glance at her watch told her it was just after two o'clock; she had been with Kay Hallam less than half an hour, but already what had passed between her and the middle-aged housewife in that council flat had blotted out the early part of the day in her mind. The buzz of voices and intermittent laughter from above made her realize she had no appetite at all for dealing with what lay beyond the half-open door she was now approaching. Intense political polemic she could do without right now. Most of them were pains in the neck, anyhow.

As she expected, the office was packed with people, as it always was on the day following a major political demonstration. People, particularly intellectuals, loved post-mortems. Several were out on bail from arrest during the previous day's anti-Vietnam War rally outside the American Embassy in Grosvenor Square, and she recognized one or two of the others as correspondents from sister papers of the New Left on the Continent and in the States, who had been in London covering the demonstration. All had been in some way involved in the previous day's events and they were now allowing themselves the final indulgence of summing up its success or otherwise amongst kindred spirits before heading for Heathrow and home.

It had become traditional for *The Spark*'s office to be put to such a use: its position on Charing Cross Road was within easy reach of most people, and it was well-known for a never-ending supply of Nescafé, as well as the very latest information on the state of political radicalism at home and abroad.

'Heard the latest from Bucharest, Anna?' her sub-editor Neville Howland called above the din. 'The Warsaw Pact has offered to send volunteers to North Vietnam if Hanoi wants them.'

'They won't.' She slung her handbag on to her desk and slumped down in her chair. For the past couple of hours the agonies of South-East Asia had receded in her mind, giving way to those of pre-war Berlin and the London Blitz, and it was difficult to drag herself back to the realities of the present.

She lifted two plastic coffee-cups that had been used as

ashtrays from the desk in front of her, wrinkling her nose at the smell as she dropped them into a nearby waste-basket. Someone had spilt coffee on the first draft of an article she had been doing on George Brown, Labour's new Foreign Secretary. She crumpled the page up and it joined the plastic cups in the bin. She would have had to redraft it anyway. It was positively libellous as it stood.

That accomplished, she lit a cigarette, adding to the already thick blue haze in the room, as she leaned back in her chair and surveyed the mêlée. The noise of raised voices, as people vied with one another to have their opinions heard, vibrated in her head. Why couldn't they all just clear out and leave her to her own thoughts for a while?

'Hey, Anna, thank God you're back!' It was her editor, the bearded Tony Barnes, yelling at her from across the room. He squeezed his way through a knot of bodies to perch on the edge of her desk. 'Where the hell have you been? I was beginning to think you'd buggered off on a whole day's assignment.' He helped himself to one of her cigarettes, lit it, and tossed the used match into the waste-basket. 'The fact is, I need your help.'

'How come?' She groaned inwardly and eyed him suspiciously through a puff of cigarette smoke.

'I've got myself double-booked,' he confessed. 'Bloody inconvenient because they're both liable to be good copy. I'm due to meet a founder member of L.B.J.'s "Great Society" – a real hawk of a Democratic senator – at the same time as a West German geezer – three o'clock this afternoon. You can't deal with one of them for me, can you?' Seeing the pained look on her face, he added quickly, 'If you can't I'll have to send Camilla, there's nobody else available.'

'I'll do it.' Camilla Haydon-Hartley was keen but useless. The only thing that kept her on *The Spark* was the fact that she was in possession of a gilt-edged private income from her father, so they could get away with paying her a mere pittance of a salary.

'Great. Which one would you prefer? The American's an old Texan buddy of L.B.J.'s from way back, but sees himself as a bit of an Anglophile. Not quite so anti-Wilson as his master. Was over here in the war or something and still sees the old place through a rose-tinted whisky glass …'

'And the German?'

'He's a part-time journalist and a lecturer at the Free University in West Berlin. Very keen on head-hunting old Nazis in high places – that type of thing.'

'Say no more. I'll take the German.' Middle-aged American males who had been over here in the war were not exactly her favourite copy material at the moment, and she had no wish to give this Senator Whatever-his-name-was a hard time just because of a rat called Bill Rutherford.

'That's fine by me. He's called Karl Brandt, by the way – the Kraut.'

Anna raised her eyebrows. 'Any relation to Willy?' The German Social Democrat leader was one of her favourite politicians.

Tony Barnes grinned and shrugged his shoulders. 'Could be his favourite son for all I know. You'd better ask him yourself. You're doing the interview now, remember.'

And it was the first question on her lips after shaking hands with the tall, shaggy-bearded German less than an hour later in a small bistro just off Leicester Square.

With his dark, reddish-brown beard and flowing, shoulder-length hair, he was not exactly the archetypal Teutonic male she had envisaged, but he seemed pleasant enough as he gave an apologetic smile in answer to her question.

'I am sorry to disappoint you, Miss Lloyd-Jones, but we have no politicians in our family.'

'The Free University, my brief says – you're a Berliner, then?'

'Only by adoption. My family were originally from East Prussia, although my mother moved to Berlin during the war to be near my father, so I was born there. She now lives in Kiel.'

'And your father?'

The smile faded. 'My father is dead.'

'I'm sorry.'

'I'm not.'

Anna balked. Such honesty could be uncomfortable for the recipient.

'My father was a Nazi, Miss Lloyd-Jones.'

'So were thousands of others.'

He shook his head impatiently. 'An important Nazi ... At least the judges at Nuremberg thought so.'

She looked across at him in surprise and growing interest. 'He was in the dock at the Nuremberg Trials?'

'In the dock and sentenced ... To death.'

She took a deep breath and continued to stare at him in a mixture of horror and fascination. Did she say she was sorry, or what? For once words failed her. 'I – I don't know what to say – and, believe me, I'm not often lost for words.'

Karl Brandt gave a shrug of his shoulders. He had a thin, rather intense face, and had a disconcerting way of looking straight into your eyes when he spoke. 'Why should you? The legacy of the Third Reich is our problem, not yours ... We are Hitler's children, Miss Lloyd-Jones – not you. We, who first saw the light of day as your bombs were falling on us, are the ones who must now carry the burden of guilt for those years.'

Anna raised her eyebrows but said nothing.

'You have nothing to say on the matter?'

'You're carrying around a pretty heavy cross there ... I just hope your back's strong enough to bear it, that's all.'

His lips twisted into a sardonic smile as he looked at her quizzically. 'Oh, don't you worry about that ... How old are you, may I ask?'

'Twenty-five.'

He nodded. 'We are the same age. But I can't really expect

you to understand what it is like for us over there. You are much too concerned in fighting against the Vietnam War to bother yourself about a war that was over twenty years ago. But, for some of us, Miss Lloyd-Jones, that war still goes on.'

He shifted in his seat, as if unsure how deeply to get into a subject obviously very dear to his heart, but which might be of no interest to his companion.

'Go on.'

He sighed, but looked relieved, as he dug into his jacket pocket and extracted a much-used Meerschaum pipe. 'Over here you grew up in the warm glow of knowing that in the war – the Second World War – your parents had justice on their side ... *Gott Mit Uns* – and all that ...' He gave a mirthless smile. 'In the First World War our soldiers went into battle with that emblazoned on their helmets and their hearts, Miss Lloyd-Jones. In the Second that was no longer possible. In that war Germany allied with the devil himself – and that is something it is no easy matter to come to terms with. Especially when it is your own flesh and blood who made that pact with the devil.'

He paused as he opened his leather tobacco pouch, extracted a small wad, and pressed it into the bowl of the pipe. Anna watched in silence as he struck a match and puffed the contents into life before continuing, 'It is not only in the Bible that the sins of the fathers are visited on the succeeding generation. It is happening to us in Germany now.'

There was a moment's silence as his words hung in the air between them. Then he gave an apologetic smile. 'But why should this concern you here in London?'

Anna felt a coldness within her. A few short hours ago she might have agreed with him. It really would have been no concern of hers how the German younger generation coped with their parents' guilt. But not now. Not now that Eva Koehn had become a real person; not now she knew for certain she was herself half-German. 'My mother was a

Berliner,' she said quietly. 'A Berliner and a *Mischling* who escaped the concentration camps to die right here in London beneath the Luftwaffe's bombs.'

It was his turn to look surprised, and he was on the point of saying so when a white-jacketed waiter appeared at the table. Two espresso coffees and two strawberry ice-cream gateaux were ordered. 'And your father?' he asked, once they were left alone again.

Anna's lips tightened. 'My adopted father was a doctor – a very nice Welshman by the name of Owen Lloyd-Jones. My real father was an American.'

'Was? He too is dead?'

'That I have yet to find out.'

Then, incredibly for someone who hated talking about her personal life, she found herself telling him of what she had learned that morning, and of her growing determination to find her real father. He listened, nodding quietly to himself as he puffed thoughtfully on his ancient Meerschaum.

Their order was delivered in the middle of her story, and Karl Brandt continued to listen quietly as he sipped his coffee and cleaned every last bit of ice-cream from his plate. What he was hearing both surprised and fascinated him. He had come here to interview and in return be interviewed by a self-possessed young woman commonly regarded as the high priestess of International Socialism, but he was sitting here listening to a patently insecure girl who had just received a major shock to her system. When she had finished talking there was no coffee left in either cup, and he pushed his aside to relight his pipe before saying in a quietly determined voice, 'I can help you.'

'To find out more about my mother?'

'*Ja*. And your father, most probably … He worked for American Intelligence, you say?'

'Yes, right here in London – at least at the beginning of the war.'

'And his name was Rutherford.'

'Bill Rutherford.'

He nodded, writing it down in his diary so there could be no mistake. 'It shouldn't be a problem. The Amis have always kept good files.'

'But how can you get access to them?' She was genuinely interested. It was something they at *The Vital Spark* would give their right arms to have.

'Miss Lloyd-Jones – or may I call you Anna now? Would I presume to ask *you* to divulge your sources?'

She smiled ruefully. 'You're right, I should know better than to ask. But I can't deny I'm curious.'

He slipped the diary back into the inside pocket of his jacket and smiled. 'You are supposed to be interviewing me on the state of radical student politics in Berlin, while I am gathering information for an article on the effectiveness of the Left in London right now ... It seems to me we have spoken a great deal about the past during the last hour, but very little about the present or the future – the very things we are supposed to be discussing. What do you say we remedy that tonight?'

'Tonight?'

'Why not?' His hazel eyes narrowed. 'Unless your boyfriend would not approve.'

'I don't have a boyfriend.'

'I know.'

It was her turn to regard him quizzically. 'What do you mean, you know?'

He laughed, showing a row of white teeth beneath the red-brown hair of his beard. 'Modesty becomes you! You are quite a celebrity, Anna – not only in your own country – or have you forgotten that? We have seen your interviews relayed on German television with Harold Wilson, Edward Heath and Co. And, of course, the one last year in America with Martin Luther King ... Most impressive for ...'

'For a woman?' she interjected, with a raised right

eyebrow. If that was not what he was going to say, it was certainly what he was thinking.

He looked shocked and shook his head. 'I was about to say – for someone so young.'

She gave a sceptical laugh. 'I've been on this planet a quarter of a century – quite time enough to handle any politician – male or otherwise.'

He made no comment, but a half-smile flickered at the corners of his mouth. 'And it has to be said that you write about them very well. Will we one day soon see a book on those who are in power at the moment, and have had the fortune – or misfortune – to have been interviewed by you?'

It was Anna's turn to smile, but she deliberately made no mention of the book at that moment in bookshop windows throughout the country. 'You mean, "Men I Have Known And Not Loved" – that type of thing?'

He took a pound and a ten-shilling note from his wallet and laid them on the table next to the bill, although he had been her guest. 'It would make very interesting reading,' he said, as they stood up in unison and headed for the door.

She turned to him on the pavement outside, remembering the personal information in the brief on him in her handbag. 'Tell me about your own latest book. I believe it's on the dialectic in post-war Marxism. Will it be out soon?'

He regarded her seriously for a moment, then shook his head. 'I am writing for posterity, Miss Lloyd-Jones.' Then he grinned. 'That's what you write for after being turned down by every publisher in the country!'

'I don't believe it!'

'Would I lie to you?'

She gave a quizzical smile as she held out her hand to be shaken. 'That I have yet to find out, Herr Brandt!'

'Shall we begin right here at eight o'clock tonight?'

'Why not?'

Chapter Nineteen

'What would you say if I told you that your father was not only one of the world's leading nuclear physicists, but was also the guy leading America's nuclear defence programme?'

Anna gasped aloud. 'You're kidding!'

Karl Brandt shook his head. 'No, I'm not.'

Anna pushed back her chair, as if she were about to get up and flee the restaurant. 'You've got to be kidding!'

'Would you prefer it if I were?'

'Damned right I would!' She slumped back in her chair, feeling as if all the breath had been knocked from her. It was like some sick joke. Here she was spending her life fighting against wars, particularly nuclear wars, and her own father – that swine who was responsible for her mother's death – was spending his time figuring how to wipe out half the planet.

'Aren't you going to ask me how I found out?'

She nodded dumbly.

Karl grinned. 'Well, I'm not going to tell you.' He tapped the end of his nose. 'Sources, Miss Lloyd-Jones … you understand. But it's quite true, you can rest assured of that. The William J. Rutherford who worked for American Intelligence in their London Embassy for a short period during the war is the same guy who is now leading their nuclear defence programme. As far as big shots go, he is the biggest, believe me!'

Anna sat dumbstruck. 'But I've never even heard of the guy.'

'You will. You will.' Karl took a gulp of his wine and refilled both their glasses from the bottle on the table at his elbow. 'It seems he just took over the top job this month, although he has been the leading authority in nuclear physics over there for decades. One of the Oppenheimer originals from the wartime Manhattan Project, so I'm told.'

'God!'

'Next thing to it!' he joked.

It wasn't appreciated. Anna reached inside her bag for another cigarette and held it to his match with shaking fingers.

'Do you fancy meeting him?'

'Wh – what do you mean?'

'He's due in Berlin this week for a meeting of NATO Defence Chiefs. You could kill two birds with one stone. I could help you dig out your mother's past and you could meet old Daddy into the bargain.'

'Good God ...' Anna could only shake her head as the words sank in. These past twenty-four hours had been too much – first her mother, and now this ... Her own father the brains behind the nuclear bomb ... 'The bastard, the absolute bastard ...' She might have known he'd be involved in something like that.

'Will you come then?'

'Come?'

'Back to Berlin – with me. I'm leaving tomorrow. We could fly back together.'

Anna stared across at him. He was smiling back at her. Did he know – had he any idea what effect his words had just had on her?

'You *can* come, can't you? It seems far too good an opportunity to pass up.'

Oh, it was that all right. She nodded slowly, then lifted the wine glass to her lips, downing its contents in one. 'To us – in Berlin,' she said softly.

They clinked glasses. He had kind hazel eyes and they were smiling directly into hers. 'To us, Anna.'

He finished the contents of his glass and looked across at her once more, his eyes serious. 'It seems we have more in common than we realized. Our fathers were both bastards.'

She nodded grimly. 'Correction, Karl … Wrong tense. My father *is still* a bastard. He's still alive, remember? Although that's more than you'll be able to say for half the planet if he has his way.'

'Then we'll have to stop him.'

She looked at him in surprise. 'Is that possible?'

He looked thoughtful. 'Anything is possible in this life, Anna – providing you are prepared to pay the cost. It all depends on how much you really hate this man for what he did to you.'

'Not so much for what he did to me,' she interrupted bitterly. 'I hate him for what he did to my mother by walking out on her like that. He knew better than anyone how terrible it must have been for her – a young girl, pregnant by him, and alone in a foreign country like that.'

To her embarrassment, she could feel her eyes misting over as she thought of her mother struggling to keep her pregnancy a secret, then braving the bombs alone as she gave birth to her that awful night during the Blitz. It was almost a sick joke to think that he had left her mother to give birth, alone, and to die under the bombs, while he went back to America to design even bigger bombs. And to think that he was still at it … 'Whatever happens, Karl,' she asked softly, 'will you be there? Will you be behind me?'

He reached out and took her hand across the table. 'I'll be there, Anna,' he promised quietly. Just what he was letting himself in for, he hadn't a clue. But then neither, he suspected, had she.

The weather was hot and sultry, but there was a fresh breeze blowing when they arrived in Berlin the following afternoon. Karl had left his car, a battered Volkswagen, at the airport, and Anna squeezed into the front passenger seat next to him as he took the wheel and headed out of the car park towards his small apartment in the district of Charlottenburg.

It was her first time in Berlin, and she felt strangely

apprehensive knowing she was now in the home city of her mother. Luckily she spoke good German, having studied it to university level, and she was curious to discover if she felt any real affinity with her new surroundings as the car sped into the Western heart of the old German capital.

Certainly the young people they passed seemed every bit as fashionably dressed as those she had left back in London and, apart from the very obvious pockets of bomb damage that remained, the city had a cheerful, colourful air that surprised her. It was not all the grim last bastion of Capitalism that she had envisaged.

As they joined the stream of traffic on the broad avenue of the Strasse des 17 Juni, and approached a vast circle named the *Grosser Stern*, she looked out on a huge stone column, rising at least 200 feet in the air and surmounted by the gilded figure of Victory. 'That's the *Siegessäule*,' she heard Karl remark, at her elbow. 'It was raised in 1873 to commemorate Bismarck's victory in the Franco-Prussian War. It originally stood in front of the Reichstag.'

The Reichstag … Even the name sent a shiver through her. 'Impressive.'

'Your mother lived on the Unter den Linden, you said.'

'That's right.'

'You realize that's now in the East?'

She hadn't. 'Oh, really? We can still visit it, though, can't we?'

'Oh, sure. No problem. But first you'll have a chance to see, if not meet, your "illustrious" father. I understand there's a press conference arranged for tomorrow morning, and he's bound to be featured – he being their prize "big nuclear fish" and all that.'

Anna glanced across at him. 'Are you sure about that? You never mentioned it on the flight.'

'Didn't want to spoil a pleasant journey,' he smiled. 'William J. Rutherford is not exactly your favourite person, after all.'

'You're dead right there.' Anna's stomach churned. This time yesterday morning all she had known of her past was that her mother had been a young German girl called Eva Koehn, and her father an unknown American. Now here she was, only a day later, in her mother's home city, with the chance of meeting her own father face to face. It was almost too much to take in.

Before turning into Kant Strasse, Karl drove round the busy square, the Breitscheidplatz, pointing out the black-ened stump of the Kaiser Wilhelm Gedächtniskirche, the bombed-out ruin of what had once been a beautiful neo-Romanesque church. Next to it loomed the twenty-two-storey, newly-constructed Europa-Center. 'You name it, we've got it in there,' Karl commented with obvious pride. 'Whole streets of shops, restaurants, a casino, an ice-rink, a planetarium – there's even a swimming pool on the roof, if you fancy a dip amongst the clouds!'

Anna wound down the window beside her and let the cool breeze fan through her hair. 'Don't tempt me,' she murmured. 'It's even hotter here than back home.'

Karl had two rooms in a modern apartment block on Kant Strasse. The furniture was modern, of the latest Scandinavian design, and the living-room she walked into behind him was surprisingly tidy. A long, low, wooden-armed settee stood along one wall, facing a wall of over-filled bookshelves opposite. Behind the settee hung a row of prints from *Der Blaue Reiter* school of early German modern art, and a Piet Mondrian print which she immediately recognized, but could not name. He obviously knew what he liked, Anna noted mentally. There was no sign of Andy Warhol or any other currently fashionable artists around here. Two low, black leather armchairs with matching footstools sat facing a small portable television set at the far end of the room, next to a hi-fi system. There seemed to be almost as many records stacked neatly around it as there were books on the wall opposite.

'Nice … Very nice.'

Karl looked pleased by her comment as he slung their two cases on to the settee. 'I'm very lucky: good places are like gold here in Berlin. Particularly after the Wall went up. This belonged to a colleague of mine at the University. He couldn't stand it after the city was divided permanently like that – too claustrophobic, he said; so after three years he gave up and went back to Hamburg.'

'You've stayed, though.'

He gave her a surprised glance as he headed for the kitchen to pour two beers. 'It's my hometown.'

'*Ich bin ein Berliner* …' Anna murmured.

'I beg your pardon?'

She gave a wry smile as she walked through to join him. 'I was quoting Jack Kennedy.'

He grinned as he handed her a beer. '*Ach, ja*, the "I am a Berliner" bit! That raised quite a few smiles around here, I can tell you. Did you know what he really said was, "I am a doughnut"?'

'You're joking!'

'Hand on my heart!' He made the appropriate gesture. 'He *should* have said, "*Ich bin Berliner*". Sticking the "*ein*" in like that turned it into one of our favourite types of confection.'

Anna's grin was as wide as his as she took her first sip of the beer. That piece of useless information really appealed to her.

'Come on, I'll show you the rest of the flat.'

They left the small, well-fitted kitchen to cross the living-room and enter the minute bathroom, with its blue-tiled walls and perspex shower screen along the side of the bath. On the wall above the toilet hung a large oil painting of Marilyn Monroe in her infamous nude calendar pose. It was a far cry from the *Blaue Reiter* prints in the other room. Seeing her glance at it, Anna noticed that Karl had the good grace to blush beneath his beard.

'It was a birthday present,' he said quickly. 'From an artist friend of mine.'

'You prefer blondes?'

'Most gentlemen do, so I'm told.'

They were both smiling as they re-entered the living-room and Karl gestured with his head towards the one remaining door. 'There's only one bedroom, I'm afraid. Would you like to see it?'

'Of course.'

She followed him into a room almost as big as the one they had just left. It was dominated by a huge, low bed, only about a foot off the floor. It was covered in a black and white striped duvet, with matching pillows, of the huge, square German type she had always wished you could buy in Britain. Along one wall were fitted pine wardrobes, and a matching, fitted dressing-table and bookshelves ran along the wall opposite the bed.

She walked over to the dressing-table and picked up a bottle of *Je Reviens* that stood alongside the normal collection of male toiletries. 'I will return,' she murmured, translating the name of the popular French perfume, half to herself. 'I hope this is not to be taken literally – at least not while I'm here. It could be rather embarrassing.'

Karl made no comment, and she continued, 'Does she stay here often?'

He shrugged, but was colouring again beneath the beard. 'Now and again.'

'Are you in love with her?'

'No.' He surprised himself with the emphatic response. But suddenly he knew it was the truth. Irmgard Müller no longer held any fascination for him. In fact, he had never given her a second thought over the past twenty-four hours. And the reason for that was standing in front of him right now smiling back at him.

She half-turned from him and, to his embarrassment, lifted a copy of *Playboy* from one of the bookshelves.

217

'Interesting choice of bedtime reading ... As a woman, opening one of these, I get some idea of what a Jew must have felt like reading a Nazi manual! Did your artist friend give you this, too?'

She was teasing him, but he was in no mood for jokes. What the hell could she think of him? 'I get them from another friend of mine,' he said gruffly. 'One of the Amis ... he ...'

Anna tossed the magazine back down on the shelf. 'You don't have to explain,' she said lightly. 'Not to me.'

She glanced round at him and the expression in his eyes made her catch her breath. The atmosphere in the room had changed. The sexual chemistry that had been there from the beginning had caught light. She felt suddenly very vulnerable. The bedroom door had swung closed of its own volition and the room was bathed in the soft afternoon light that filtered through the half-closed blinds. Only the bed stood between them.

Her heart was beating much too fast beneath the cool cotton of her dress. It wasn't as if she had never made love to a man before; she had had several lovers at University. Who hadn't? But, in the main, they had been short-lived affairs – nothing to lose sleep over once all passion had been spent. Even her most serious romance with a Canadian journalist the previous year was now little more than a bitter-sweet memory.

'I can sleep on the settee next door tonight, if necessary.' His voice was huskily low.

She walked round to his side of the bed to stand between him and the door. 'If necessary,' she said softly, before walking back into the brighter light of the living-room.

They went out almost immediately. What was happening between them made staying in and making small talk an impossibility. He took her to a restaurant on the Kurfürsten-damm where the waiters wore red waistcoats and tight black trousers and balanced their silver trays on three fingers and a thumb as they darted between the tightly packed tables. In the corner a four-piece band played the latest Beatles' numbers in the sentimentally melodic way only German bands could.

They talked of their respective childhoods in London and Berlin, and she listened in silence as he told of how his safe world of childhood had crumbled about him that day in 1950 when a schoolfriend had told him his father had not died in the war, but had been hanged as a war criminal at Nuremberg. He had beaten the boy almost unconscious and had been sent home from school in disgrace, only to be told by his mother that it was indeed the truth.

'Can you imagine what that did to a child, Anna, to learn that your father – your own father – was directly responsible for the death of thousands, if not millions, of innocent people?'

She was silent for a moment, then nodded slowly. 'Yes, Karl, I can imagine … Until yesterday I knew only that my own father was responsible for my mother's death, but now, thanks to you, I have learnt that not only was he directly responsible for all those thousands of horrific deaths in Hiroshima and Nagasaki, but that he is still at it.' She shook her head in a mixture of incredulity and despair, then her eyes hardened. 'You say he is giving a press conference at his hotel tomorrow on the proposed talks?'

'So I've heard.'

'I'm going to be there.'

'Then I'll be with you.'

She shook her head. 'No. If you don't mind, this is something I'd rather face alone.'

When William J. Rutherford came face to face with his daughter, she wanted no other distractions. Something inside her told her it would be a momentous occasion for them both.

Chapter Twenty

Anna awoke to a Berlin morning awash with midsummer sunshine, which filtered through the slats of the blind to paint a horizontal pattern on the face and naked upper torso of the young man in the bed beside her. Karl Brandt had good reason to sleep; last night they had made love until the early hours of the morning. It wasn't something that she had intended to happen, but neither could she deny they had both known it was inevitable from the moment he invited her to accompany him back to Berlin.

She looked down curiously at the face on the pillow beside her, and studied the pale, lean cheeks with their thick growth of reddish-brown hair. Above the beard his skin was faintly pitted and the lashes of his closed eyes were thick and dark, like those of a girl. There had been nothing girlish, however, about his lovemaking last night. In fact, she had found it difficult to reconcile the rather shy young man whose company she had kept over the past twenty-four hours with the person who closed the bedroom door behind them last night. And now, in the clear light of another day, the memory of that passion disconcerted her. An affair of the body was one thing, but the last thing she needed right now was to involve herself in an affair of the heart, and she had more than a passing suspicion that as far as Karl was concerned this was already far more than a one- or two-night stand.

She had slept with only three other men in her life before – two of them students like herself during her time at Oxford, and the third a Canadian journalist by the name of Guy McKenzie, whom she had actually believed herself to be in love with until he went back to Toronto, and his wife, the week before Christmas.

They had met on a visit to Hanoi the previous summer – staying in the same old French colonial hotel overlooking Halong Bay. She had not meant to fall in love with a married man, but it had happened to her that evening in North Vietnam, as it had never happened to her before, and probably never would again.

She looked down at the figure asleep on the bed beside her. Last night had been the first time in her life she had gone to bed with a man so soon after their first meeting. With all three of her previous lovers, lovemaking had been the natural extension of an already established relationship. With Karl, however, it was something else entirely, and it was that intenseness about his feelings towards her that she found slightly unnerving. But now was not the time to be pondering over a love affair. There was a far more pressing matter on her mind this morning.

Leaving him still sleeping peacefully on the crumpled sheet, she slid out of bed and headed for the shower.

Awoken by the sound of running water, Karl was sitting up in bed smoking a cigarette when she returned to the bedroom, damp and glowing, several minutes later. He had a still sleepy, satisfied smile on his face and he reached out an arm in her direction. 'Come here, *Liebchen*.'

She backed away, throwing a glance at the bedside clock as she did so. 'It's after eight. The press conference is at nine!'

'So? I'll drive you. It's only five minutes from here.' He reached across the bed and made to grab her around the waist, but she avoided his grasp.

'I've got an important assignment this morning, remember!'

'How could I forget!' He flopped back on the bed, admitting defeat with a petulant frown as she proceeded to dress. His masculine pride was hurt but he was determined not to show it.

She chose her clothes carefully, donning a business-like Mary Quant sleeveless mini-dress in navy-blue, with dark-

221

blue leather, sling-back shoes to match. She then sat down at the dressing-table to do her make-up.

'Why do you wear that stuff? British and American girls seem to use far more of it than German ones.'

'I like it.' She spat delicately on to the small block of solid black mascara and rubbed the brush in it. Then each eye was carefully made up in turn. 'Dorothy Parker was quite wrong, you know … It's not girls in glasses who men don't make passes at – it's those with Sunday-school teacher clean faces.'

He smiled quizzically at her. 'It matters to you – that men make passes at you?'

She shrugged as she blotted her lipstick on a tissue and examined the result in the mirror. 'I don't like to be ignored, if that's what you mean.'

His eyes grew serious. 'That you will never be, Anna. You are one of the beautiful people, *Liebchen*. One of life's winners. But there are one hell of a lot of losers in this world.'

She turned to face him. What a time to get serious. 'Don't you think I know that? Why do you think I paid that visit to North Vietnam last year? And why do I flog my guts out trying to get that damned war stopped? Why do I spend my life exposing injustices wherever they are to be found, rather than accept some cushy number peddling politics to a lot of spotty kids in a university somewhere?'

She made a despairing gesture with her hands before dropping her make-up pouch into her handbag, which she slung on to her shoulder with an air of irritation. 'God only knows if what I'm doing will have any results, but I've got to do it, Karl, can't you see that?'

She walked over to the edge of the bed and took a cigarette from the packet on the side-table and lit it from his. She exhaled the smoke slowly, watching it drift lazily to the ceiling through the slatted bars of sunlight. 'It was a curious feeling coming back to Britain after that visit to Vietnam last year,' she said quietly. 'It reminded me of a passage in Orwell's *Homage to Catalonia*. Have you ever read it?'

He shook his head. A translation of George Orwell's famous work on his personal Spanish Civil War experiences had stood on his bookshelf shamefully unread for some years now.

'Well, there's a part in that where he writes of returning to England after witnessing the tragedy of Spain at first hand. The effect of returning to a land where the milk is still delivered to the doorstep every morning and the *New Statesman* drops through the letterbox as regular as clockwork every week, while so much suffering is still going on elsewhere in the world, is a shattering experience. It was for him and it was for me too … But I don't have to tell you that – you feel things just as deeply as I do. You are every bit as much a crusader as I am. Don't you spend most of your time fighting to rid Germany of the last vestiges of Nazism? And who gives you any thanks for that? Precious few, I've no doubt! Quite the contrary: no one thanks you for digging up the past and attempting to exorcise its ghosts.'

He gave a bitter smile. 'My trouble is I am fighting the ghosts of a past war, Anna *Liebchen*, while you are fighting something much more tangible – one taking place right now …'

'And, God help us, the one to come – the big nuclear bonanza – which, if William J. Rutherford and his like in the Soviet Union have their way, will see the end of us all on this crazy planet.'

Karl glanced at his watch. 'Speaking of "Darling Daddy", isn't it time we were moving?'

Luckily the morning rush was over by the time they set off and the traffic did not hold them up too much. He pulled the old Volkswagen up in front of the Conference centre with five minutes to spare.

There seemed to be police everywhere, including military police with their red caps and blancoed white belts and spats. Anna fished her Press badge out of her bag and fixed it to the bodice of her dress. 'It looks as if I'll need this even to set foot on the pavement! ... Wish me luck,' she smiled, leaning across to peck his cheek.

'Are you sure you don't want me with you?'

'Positive.'

He smiled bravely in defeat. 'Well, I'll be working from the apartment all day. You know where to find me.'

She watched the small car disappear back into the morning traffic and joined the steady stream of people heading into the main door of the building. After having her credentials checked, she was allowed through into the room where the press conference was to take place.

It was one of the smaller auditoriums in the hotel and held, she guessed, around 200 people. It was already about three-quarters full. Spotting a free seat right at the front, she headed for it, just beating a young man with a *Der Spiegel* badge. He gave her a chilling smile and headed for the row behind.

The conference opened with the usual speeches emphasizing America's military commitment to Europe, and in particular to ensuring the continuance of a free West Berlin. Then the main speaker, a tall, thin-faced man in his thirties with a distinct clipped-vowel, Boston accent threw the discussion open to question. Immediately much wider issues were raised, with questions encompassing the Vietnam War, and nuclear weapons themselves.

At this point, the chairman stood up and announced, 'Ladies and gentlemen, I feel this is as good a point as any to bring in our distinguished guest, who I understand has just arrived.'

He glanced behind him into the wings of the stage. 'We are honoured indeed to have with us one of our country's leading physicists, and now Chief of our Nuclear Defence Programme: William J. Rutherford.'

An expectant buzz went round the room and Anna felt her stomach turn over as a man walked forward from the wings of the stage. He was tall and well-built, with a head of dark, wavy hair streaked with grey at the temples. His face was deeply tanned, as if he had just returned from holiday, and two deep furrows ran across his brow above the shaggy eyebrows. He was soberly dressed in a clerical grey suit and matching tie. Only his shoes were out of place; they were brown suede and looked as if they had seen better days. He took a pair of horn-rimmed glasses from his breast pocket and gripped both edges of the lectern with his hands as he surveyed his audience.

He cleared his throat. 'Well, I understand my colleagues have briefed you pretty well on the purpose of our meeting here in Berlin this week, so I won't waste time by going over old ground. Suffice to say, we are all glad to be here in the free half of this great city, and you can be sure we will do our best to make sure it remains that way ... Now who's got a question for me?' He looked around the members of the press corps seated below him.

Anna sat frozen in her seat as she stared up at him. His voice was still echoing in her head. It was authoritative all right, but there was a distinct edginess to it, as if he did not relish this degree of public exposure as much as others might.

His gaze had fallen on a bespectacled young man about three rows behind her, who proceeded to regale him with a flow of invective about American involvement in Vietnam. Bill Rutherford demolished his argument in less than half the time he took to put the questions. 'Now who else has a question?'

He looked down at the sea of faces before him. One or two hands were raised in the body of the room but in the front row a young woman was standing up. She looked familiar – disturbingly familiar. His eyes narrowed as they stared at the figure before him in the dark-blue mini dress. Then an involuntary shiver ran through him and he found himself clinging even more tightly to the lectern. The whole audience seemed to fuse into one mass of humanity and only one face was visible. In God's name what was he seeing? *Who* was he seeing? Was he in some sort of time-warp? He was no longer in the Husum hotel in Berlin in the summer of 1966, but had been transported back a quarter of a century to another European capital – London. He was in pre-war London ... 'Eva ...' Of their own volition his lips soundlessly formed her name.

'Mr Rutherford, I would like to bring you back, if I may, to what I believe to be the major issue facing mankind today. To those of us with a conscience, the war in Vietnam is an abomination of which history will be the judge. My concern today is not with the ethics of your military policy, but with a much wider issue – how can you as an intelligent human being justify the spending of billions of dollars, the main purpose of which is to bring death and destruction to mankind, when more than half the human race is living in abject poverty?'

Bill Rutherford's mouth was dry and his voice, when he spoke, had a much harsher ring than he intended. 'Young lady, I am not here to discuss moral issues with you, or anyone else for that matter.'

'You would agree, though, would you not, that the reason for US involvement in Vietnam is to hold back the spread of Communism and thereby preserve the American way of life and its values?'

He cleared his throat once more. 'I wouldn't argue with that.' God, even after all these years, he could still remember her voice, and it was speaking to him now ... Dammit, this young troublemaker even sounded like Eva. She had that same slightly breathless way of talking that totally belied the strength of character beneath.

'In that case, would you not also agree that he who wants to end wars on this planet must also end mass poverty. For surely morally it makes no difference whether a human being is killed by one of your bombers or condemned to death through your indifference. You, more than anyone, must be aware of the terrible danger to world stability caused by the arms race, particularly with the danger of nuclear weapons getting into the hands of more volatile nations; would it not make more sense, therefore, to spend your surplus billions of dollars putting food into the mouths of the hungry, rather than blowing innocent people to smithereens? We are all familiar with the old adage that revolutions are never made on full stomachs! Surely the people of South-East Asia, and the Third World in general, would be much more amenable to putting their trust in Uncle Sam and hitching their wagon to the American Stars and Stripes if that were the case, and you proved yourself to be their saviour rather than their destroyer?'

There was a moment's silence after Anna sat down and she could detect a bead of perspiration on the brow of the man on the podium in front of her. Bill Rutherford stared down at her and met her eyes for the first time. He knew what she had just said had a valid moral basis, but for the life of him he could not recall the content of her questions.

'You have no answer to that?'

He took a sip of water from the glass in front of him. 'On the contrary, I have several answers to the points you raised so eloquently, but I do not think this is the time or the place to be discussing such general moral issues. I have come here today to answer questions specifically on America's commitment to the Western Alliance in general, and to our future nuclear strategy in particular. As for your more general moral issues ... Some other time maybe.' Very deliberately he averted his gaze to the other side of the room. 'Now another question, please ... More relevant to the subject under discussion, if you don't mind, ladies and gentlemen.'

Slipping her notepad back into her bag, Anna got up and walked from the room. The patronizing swine! More relevant to the subject under discussion indeed! What could be more relevant than the survival of this planet and the people on it?

She could feel the eyes of the others on her as she marched

down the centre gangway, heading for the door. And she was well aware that the man in centre stage had not missed her exit either.

'What do you make of him, then – their latest nuclear "big cheese"?' It was Ted McKenna, an ex-*New Statesman* colleague, who was standing just outside the conference room door.

'As far as "big cheeses" go, he takes the biscuit!' Anna grimaced.

'Very punny, old girl!' Ted grinned.

Anna did not return his smile. 'No humour intended.'

'That bad, eh?'

She shrugged and accepted a cigarette. 'He got the better of me in there, Ted … A real put-down it was.'

'Then pay him back – in print. If you can't do it, God knows who can!'

Anna accepted a light and looked at him steadily as the words sank in. He was right, of course. Only he had no idea just how right. She would pay William J. Rutherford back, all right, but not just for a dismissive remark from the stage this morning. Oh no, she would pay him back for much more than that …

Chapter Twenty-One

Bill Rutherford gathered his notes together and with a polite 'Thank you' and nod to his audience he left the stage to a scattering of polite applause.

Instead of joining the assembled official personnel seated at the back of the platform awaiting the closing speeches, he walked quickly off into the wings.

'Join us upstairs for a drink, sir?' A captain in the USAF who had been officiating amongst the delegates approached him tentatively. 'We'll all be gathering up there shortly.'

'Sure ... Sure. In a minute or so. I need a breath of fresh air, that's all.'

He continued out towards the front of the building. His face was set, and had there been anyone there who knew him really well, they could have seen that he was still visibly shaken. He had seen a ghost back there in the conference room; the ghost of a woman long dead, but who had continued to haunt him down the years.

A fresh breeze greeted him on the front steps of the hotel, where he paused to light a cigarette and stare out into the chaotic mid-morning traffic.

'Good morning again, General. That is your official title now, isn't it?'

Good God, it was her again! He had the greatest difficulty meeting her steady, slightly sceptical gaze, so he averted his eyes streetwards once more. 'You're perfectly right, ma'am. It's a courtesy title I now use for official business.'

'And this is very official business here in Berlin.'

'Berlin is a very important city.'

'And you are a very important man.'

'Look, Miss ...'

'Lloyd-Jones. Anna Lloyd-Jones.' She held out her hand and he took it a trifle uncertainly, although his handshake was firm.

'You sound English,' he said, for want of something better to say.

'I am.'

Her educated English voice had come as a surprise to him earlier; he had half-expected to hear his own language spoken with a distinct Berlin accent. To have met Eva's double a quarter of a century on, in her own native city, but speaking with an English accent didn't seem right somehow. He shifted uneasily on the stone step. 'Well, it's always a pleasure to talk to a member of the British press corps. That "special alliance" between our two countries that they like to talk about means a great deal to me personally.'

Anna winced inwardly. 'I believe you spent some time in London during the war.'

He looked surprised. 'You do your homework, I see. Yes, I did, as a matter of fact. I was with Military Intelligence in our Embassy over there for a while ...' He gave a wry grin. 'And you don't have to tell me that's a contradiction in terms, I've had that said to me often enough, believe me.'

'I try to avoid the old clichés where possible. But there are quite a few other points I would like to put to you, General.'

'Such as?'

'Well, for example, how would you personally react to the statement that the basic problems facing the world today are not susceptible to a military solution?'

'Bullshit.'

'Interesting. It was a direct quote from your late President, J.F.K. himself.'

Bill Rutherford drew deeply on his cigarette, his eyes narrowing as he turned to face her. He had met young smarty-pants females like her almost everywhere he'd gone over the past few weeks. Usually he did not waste breath on them, they would end up writing what they darned well liked about him anyway, no matter what answers he gave to their questions. This one was different, though. There was antagonism there on her part, he could feel it. But something inside him wanted to prolong the conversation. Just looking at her was like recapturing a part of the past that he thought had gone forever all those years ago.

'Perhaps you didn't agree with much that Jack Kennedy had to say,' she went on. 'Maybe you were a Nixon man yourself.'

'Like hell.'

She smiled. 'Would you care to enlarge on that and give me some idea of your political stance?'

'No.'

Anna tried another tack. 'I understand you were a colleague of Oppenheimer's at Los Alamos during the war. Did you personally regard him as a covert Red?'

'Young lady, that's none of your darned business. But, if you must know, then no, I most certainly did not. Oppie was as true an American as they come.'

Anna was poised to press him further on his relationship with the father of the atomic bomb, when out of the corner of her eye she could see someone else was vying for his attention. The young captain who had spoken to him earlier was approaching from the doorway. They obviously wanted his company inside.

'It looks like your presence is required elsewhere.'

Bill Rutherford turned his head in the direction of the approaching young officer. To his surprise the interruption annoyed him intensely. This young woman might get under his skin politically, but in a perverse way he was enjoying her company. Even the way she tilted her head when she asked a question was unnervingly like Eva. And that direct way of looking at him out of those dark brown eyes … He held out his hand. 'Yes … Well, it's been intere…' He cut himself short, still holding on to her hand. 'Look, Miss – Lloyd-Jones, wasn't it …? Why don't we … I'm sure you'd like a proper interview for your paper …' Dear God, he was fumbling for words like some still-wet-behind-the-ears kid.

'Sure. Say when.' She withdrew her hand and wiped a stray lock of fair hair from her eyes.

He glanced behind him at the captain who was fidgeting a few feet away. 'In the foyer here at ten tomorrow morning. Would that suit?'

'I'll be there.'

He gave an embarrassed half-smile. 'Yes, well – till tomorrow morning, then. It's been nice talking to you.'

She watched him walk back up the steps into the building. He was a tall man and still had the spring of youth in his step. Outwardly he gave the impression of a force to be reckoned with and she was sure he was held in awe by younger colleagues such as the captain who brought up his wake as they re-entered the building. Then she smiled quietly to herself as she remembered his fumbling for the right words as they parted. The big shot General wasn't quite so big when it came to face-to-face encounters with members of the opposite sex, and the knowledge both surprised and intrigued her.

She couldn't wait to get back to tell Karl. Maybe the confrontation in the conference room hadn't gone quite as she had hoped, but she had been given another bite of the cherry the following day, and she would certainly make use of it, she promised herself.

Karl was on the phone when she arrived back by taxi half an hour later. He waved to her to fix herself a coffee and she made her way through to the kitchen to make two mugs, which she carried back through to the living-room just as he replaced the receiver in its cradle.

He took the proffered drink with a murmur of thanks, a pensive look on his face.

'Bad news?'

He took a sip of the coffee and shook his head. 'No, not bad news …'

'Anything I can help with, then?'

'God, no!'

She looked surprised. 'Well, that was definite enough! What on earth are you planning – a mass break-out over the Wall?'

'What made you say that?' His tone was surprisingly sharp.

'It was only a joke!' She made a mock hands-up gesture as she sat down on the settee and retrieved her coffee mug from the side-table. She took a sip of the drink and looked at him quizzically. 'I didn't hit the nail on the head, by any chance?'

'*Bitte?*'

'You're not really planning something like that – an escape over the Wall?'

He looked at her steadily for a long time, then said quietly, 'It's a very dangerous business getting people out from the East.'

'You can say that again – they shoot them if they catch them, don't they?'

He nodded pensively. 'That *verdammt* Wall ... Unless you are a German you cannot know what it has done to our country. You know what they call it here, Anna? *Die Schandmauer*, that's what – the Wall of Shame ... May they rot in hell, the swine who ordered it to be built through the heart of this country. Why should people have to risk their lives because of that damned thing? People have died, Anna – good people – some of them friends of mine, trying to help others to freedom.'

They sat in silence for a moment or two, then Anna leaned forward on the settee and said quietly. 'Look, you don't have to tell me anything you don't want to, but if you are involved in anything like that and I can be of help, then for God's sake say so. There must be a place for a foreigner like me in any plan. I mean, who would suspect me of smuggling someone across the border?' Then seeing he was not responding as she hoped, she added, 'Or surely there could be a job for me as a courier? You know I intend making a few trips into the East of the city while I'm here, anyway; I want to find my mother's old home, and you yourself said the Unter den Linden is now in the Eastern Sector.'

He nodded slowly as he sipped his coffee. 'Leave it with me, Anna *Liebchen*,' he said quietly. 'Just let it rest.'

She took his advice and said no more about it for the time being.

They lunched together on beer and a salami salad at a crowded *Kneipe* not far from the apartment. He had promised to pay a visit to some former students of his in the afternoon, but was concerned she should not be lonely.

'I can call it off, you know — if you'd rather I stayed here with you.'

'Good God, no. I'm quite capable of amusing myself for an afternoon.'

So they went their separate ways: he to visit his friends on the Bismarck Strasse, and Anna to wander off in the direction of the Wall.

The nearer she got to the East Berlin boundary the more curiosity got the better of her. What if she could find that family that Kay Hallam, her mother's old friend, had told her about: the Kessels, wasn't it? She *did* say that Herr Kessel had still been running a nightclub after the war. But surely that must have been in the West of the city?

She made for the nearest phone box and began to search through the telephone business directory. There seemed to be dozens of nightclubs in West Berlin. Then her eyes lighted on one called the *Der Gefallene Engel*. 'The Fallen Angel', she said softly. Could that be it? Could that be Herr Kessel's new nightclub? Kay Hallam had said that the original one before the war had been called something to do with angels, hadn't she? Her pulse raced. It was a long shot, but worth following up.

She took a taxi to the address on the Kurfürstendamm it gave in the directory and stood on the pavement outside looking up at the black-painted sign with an illuminated devil alongside it.

The foyer was full of photographs of beautiful, nubile young women in various stages of undress. A bored-looking but equally pretty young woman in an abbreviated costume reminiscent of a drum majorette sat doing her nails in a kiosk just inside the front door. Anna went up to her and asked very tentatively in German if the owner was by any chance a Herr Kessel.

The young woman shook her head. '*Nein. Überhaupt nicht.*'

Anna's heart sank, and she was on the point of turning away when the drum majorette spoke again, and said in badly-accented English, 'The owner is Frau Graubaum. Herr Kessel was her father.'

Anna's heart leapt. 'Would it be possible to speak to Frau Graubaum?'

The young woman shrugged, then reached for the telephone at her elbow. '*Einen Moment, bitte.*'

Anna stood nervously by the open front of the kiosk while the girl had a short conversation with someone on the other end of the line. Then, in response to a beckoning wave of the arm from the young woman, she moved forward. 'Frau Graubaum is very busy this afternoon. She asks what is the nature of your business?'

Anna hesitated, then taking her courage in both hands she said truthfully. 'I am here in Berlin searching for my mother's family. Her name was Eva Koehn. I believe Frau Graubaum may have known her as a young woman.'

The girl behind the desk relayed the information down the line as Anna stood nervously by. Then the young woman began to nod. '*Ja. Ja. Gewiss, Frau Graubaum. Gewiss.*'

She replaced the telephone and looked at Anna. 'Frau Graubaum will see you for a few minutes.' She pointed to a door on the left at the back of the foyer. 'That is her office.'

'*Danke … Danke schön, Fräulein.*' Anna gripped her

shoulder bag tightly to her, her whole body suddenly tense, as she made her way in the direction indicated.

There was nothing on the door to indicate whose office it was, and she knocked tentatively on the white painted wood.

'*Herein!*'

She entered a large airy room to find an expensively dressed, rather plump middle-aged woman sitting behind a glass-topped desk. Her hair, which was dyed the colour of bright corn, was done up in an elaborate bouffant, with just the faintest trace of dark roots showing. A pair of blue-shadowed eyes regarded Anna curiously from behind elaborately-winged, diamanté spectacles. She stood up as Anna entered and offered a beringed hand to be shaken.

'It's very good of you to see me, Frau Graubaum,' Anna said quickly. 'My name is Lloyd-Jones. Anna Lloyd-Jones.'

The woman gestured for Anna to take a seat on one of the modern, white leather chairs in front of the desk. 'Did I understand Elsa properly?' she said in accented English. '*You* are Eva's daughter?' She leaned back in her chair and continued to regard Anna curiously from behind the huge expanse of desk.

Anna nodded. 'My mother came from Berlin and her name was Eva Koehn. I understand from someone who knew her during the war that she was helped to escape by a family called Kessel who had a nightclub here at that time.'

The woman was silent for a long time, then she nodded slowly. 'That is correct.'

Anna's heart leapt. 'Then you knew her – you knew my mother?'

Again the woman nodded. '*Ja … Ja …* I knew your mother. Eva Koehn was one of my best friends. It came as a shock to discover she was also a Jew.'

An awkward silence fell, with the word 'Jew' hanging in the air between them.

It was Anna who broke the silence. 'Did that matter to you – that she was a Jew?'

236

Hanna Graubaum, née Kessel, shrugged. 'It made no difference to my life. Eva had disappeared by the time I found out.'

'Who told you, then?'

Hanna's brows furrowed behind the diamanté frames. 'I think it was Kurt ... Yes, I'm sure it was Kurt.'

'Kurt?'

'He is one of my brothers. The only one to remain alive.' Her chin tilted perceptibly higher and a hushed reverence came into her voice. 'The others died for the Fatherland.'

'I'm sorry.'

'*Danke* ... The Good God moves in mysterious ways over who he chooses should die and who should live.'

'Kurt survived the war, though?'

The other's mouth tightened. 'Kurt did not fight for the Fatherland, Miss Lloyd-Jones. So he survived the war.'

There could be only one explanation. 'In a concentration camp?'

The question was ignored. 'He is really the one you should talk to. He was with Eva when she went home that terrible night of *Kristallnacht*. They were very close ...' She paused, her lips pursing once more. 'He never quite got over what happened to the Koehns, or the fact that he might never see her again.'

'Is he still in Berlin? May I see him – speak to him?'

Hanna Graubaum's eyes hardened. 'Kurt is still in Berlin. But not in the real Berlin – he has chosen to remain in that Red prison behind the Wall of Shame.' There was no disguising the bitterness in her voice.

'Kurt is a Communist?'

'Phhh!' Hanna made a dismissive gesture with her right hand. 'An imbecile would be a better word for him! ... But, yes, yes, he is a Communist. The only one in our family to remain on the Friedrich Strasse after they built that terrible "thing" through the heart of our city.'

'But you have his address?'

The other sighed. 'Oh, I have his address, all right. He is still living in one of the rooms of our old apartment over there. I believe the rest of it has been taken over by the piece of trashy Communistic filth of a journal he helps edit.'

'May I have it – his address?'

Hanna sighed once more and reached for a nearby pad. She scribbled something down on it, ripped off the page and handed it to Anna. 'You will find him there. And he will be able to tell you much more than I can about your mother's last days in Berlin.'

She rose from behind the desk and held out her hand. 'I'm sorry I can't really spare any more time right now. I'm already late for another appointment.'

'You – you've been very kind seeing me at such short notice.' She followed behind as the much shorter, older woman walked towards the door and opened it.

Hanna Graubaum extended her hand once more. 'You're very like her, you know. You are so like Eva, it is quite uncanny. I thought for one moment I was seeing a ghost when you walked in through the door.'

Anna gave a wry smile. It wasn't the first time that had been said to her. 'Did you never keep in touch after she left for England?'

The smile on the well made-up mouth opposite her faded and a certain tenseness etched itself on the other's features. 'I – I did write once or twice, but I couldn't be of any real help to her. She wanted information about her family, you see, and there wasn't any to be had. Anyway, I got married not long after Eva left. It would have been too …' she searched for the right word. 'Too difficult to remain in contact after that.'

'He was a Nazi – your husband?' The question had come from nowhere, but even before the reply came, Anna knew it was the truth.

'My husband was a sincere patriot – and still is.'

Anna dropped her eyes, unable to hold the other's defiant

238

gaze. She opened her bag and slipped the piece of paper into it. 'Yes, well, thank you, Frau Graubaum. You've been a great help.'

'It has been a pleasure making your acquaintance, Miss Lloyd-Jones.'

Anna gave a strained smile, but somehow could not bring herself to return the compliment.

Chapter Twenty-Two

The office smelt of stale cigarette ash and bitter coffee dregs, and was cluttered with back numbers of the newspaper that emanated from it twice weekly. They lay in untidy piles on shelves, next to rows of old box files with indecipherable labels. A bust of Karl Marx glowered down from the middle of the shelf directly behind the desk from which Kurt Kessel rose awkwardly to greet his visitor. The small hairs at the back of his neck stiffened as he came forward, with a distinct limp, to greet Anna. 'So *you* are Eva's daughter.'

His once handsome face was now deeply lined beneath the balding, greying hairline, but his handshake was warm, as was his smile. Anna nodded her confirmation eagerly. 'It was good of you to see me at such short notice, Herr Kessel.'

'Kurt – *bitte*. And, on the contrary ...' he shook his head. How could she possibly know? How could she have any idea what this visit meant to him? The very sight of her brought it all back; she was so like her mother. It could have been yesterday – *Kristallnacht*, 1938 ...

'You said on the phone that my sister sent you.' His voice, already husky from a lifetime of nicotine abuse, betrayed his nervousness as he gestured for her to take a seat and made his way back to his own chair. He lowered himself into it with some difficulty. 'So you've seen Hanna?'

'Yes. I've just come from there.'

'*Der Gefallene Engel*,' he mused bitterly. 'The most exclusive whorehouse in the West. My sister does a good job. My father would have been proud of her.'

He opened the lid of a small tobacco tin and began to roll himself a cigarette. For the first time she noticed that the fingers of both hands had no nails and were badly mutilated at the tips. 'Don't get me wrong – in some ways I admire what my sister did in taking on the business when Father died. Paul, Maxi and Karl, my brothers, they were all killed in the war, you see. She was the only one left when the old man died in '55.'

'There was you.'

He gave a bitter smile as he lit the thin roll of tobacco. 'Yes, there was me ...'

'She said you were a Communist – a Marxist.'

The smile returned. 'Hanna always loved labels. Did she also tell you she and Peter-Klaus, her dear husband, are both Nazis?'

'But, surely, no one admits to being a Nazi any more?'

'*Natürlich!*' he waved the hand with the cigarette. 'No one admits – in public at least – to still holding Nazi sympathies, but those beliefs did not automatically die with the Third Reich, my dear Anna. They simply went underground. Hanna was always mesmerized, even as a young girl, by that *verdammt* uniform. Our eldest brother Paul was her idol before she met her husband, who was even more of a rabid Nazi than Paul was.'

He studied the burning tip of his cigarette. 'Peter-Klaus Graubaum was one of Hitler's closest aides by the end of the war. He was also the man who had me arrested and transported to that hellish camp.'

'Your own brother-in-law betrayed you?'

'For sure.' He confirmed her question almost light-heartedly. 'And why should I be any different from the thousands of others he personally sent to their deaths?'

His eyes took on a faraway look. 'Arresting the opposition was all part of the fun, you see, Anna. They even had a special tariff, you know, for their daily beating of political prisoners: simple membership of the Social Democratic Party merited thirty blows with a rubber truncheon on the naked body; membership of the Communist Party forty blows. To be a Party official or trade union official merited extra blows in accordance with your status. And, of course, to be a Jew into the bargain gained you fifty lashes of the whip on top of that!'

Anna could only shake her head. To be sitting here listening to someone who had actually been through that terror was a humbling experience.

'I was with Eva, you know, the night they took your grandfather away.'

'Tell me what would have happened to him, please.' Suddenly she had to know. She had to know everything.

He shook his head. 'I can only tell how it was for me personally. But I doubt if it was any different for Martin Koehn, or any of the others ...'

He drew deeply on the cigarette between his fingers as his mind went back to that day in January 1940. He had been hauled like an animal from his hiding place in the basement of a friend's house in the Berlin suburb of Mariendorf, and taken to Gestapo headquarters on Burgstrasse for interrogation, then from there to their prison on the Alexanderplatz.

'After your arrest – was there a proper trial?' Anna asked. 'Did they give those they arrested any proper means of defending themselves?'

'Oh, there was a "trial", all right ...' The word stuck in his throat. 'I can see it now ... The "judge" – the highest ranking Gestapo officer available at the time – sat behind a table, the stars on his brown shirt signifying that he now had the power of life and death over the poor devils brought before him. That bastard had the power to play God himself.'

He reached forward and poured two glasses of schnapps from a bottle on the table in front of him and handed one to Anna, before downing his own drink in one and pouring himself another with shaking fingers. He could see it now. Even after all these years, the scene was imprinted on his very soul. 'Daggers and bayonets were stuck into the wood of the table he sat behind, and there were candles flickering at each end. Imagine it, Anna – the prisoner is pushed forward and the brown-shirted hyenas cluster around him. When he answers, they hit him. If he attempts to declare his innocence, they kick him and beat him further. The prisoner then hears the source of the denunciation which brought about his arrest. For one beautiful moment he imagines he can immediately disprove the charge and he attempts to speak. The blows become more severe. He doubles up in pain and is hauled to his feet once more. They demand addresses. They believe they can break him by telling him his comrades of the Left have betrayed their brothers. The prisoner refuses to utter a word. The blows draw blood and more blood, but still he remains silent.'

Kurt Kessel's voice was growing fainter, but harsher. It was only possible to tell his story in the third person: to personalize it was to bring back the pain, the unbearable pain … 'He is losing consciousness by now and is dragged off to the cellars. In the semi-darkness the torture benches are waiting. His head is pushed into a bucket of cold water to revive him. This itself is one of the worst tortures in his half-comatose state. Half-drowned, he splutters back to life and retches at the smell of the dried blood, vomit and sweat that envelops him. He is forced face down on to one of the benches where steel rods hammer down on to his back. Four of the animals in brown shirts then take it in turns to cut the raw flesh to pieces.'

He paused, the sweat standing out in beads on the furrowed forehead as he poured himself yet another drink. 'You want me to go on?'

She nodded mutely, only too aware what it was costing him.

He took a rasping breath and nodded in understanding. It was right the young should know, no matter what the cost to the old. 'Eventually he is dragged out into what they called the "waiting-room", to be thrown on to a pile of bloodied straw beside other victims. They are told they are to be shot the following morning. The pain is such that it comes as a relief to many. It is now night. The torture has lasted for over six hours. Outside in the corridor, a guard leans against the door and sings: "Dawn, dawn, you light my way to early death …"

'But dawn found it already too late for some, Anna. The old man beside him is already dead, as is a young boy in the far corner. He himself is left for days with the threat of death hanging over him. He hears the repeated beatings from the next room and occasionally he too is dragged out once more to be "tried" over again …'

His voice tailed off as he studied the glowing tip of the cigarette between his mutilated fingers. His face had taken on a haunted look as the ghosts of the past enveloped him once more, and the ever-present pain in his body seemed to grow more intense by the minute. 'It is curious,' he said at last, 'how I can only speak of that time in such an impersonal way. It is as if I must still after all these years attempt to distance myself from it in order to survive.'

'But you did survive, thank God,' Anna said softly. Her cheeks were wet with tears.

'God had very little to do with it, Anna … But, yes, you are quite right, I did survive. At least part of me did. Bits and pieces did not.' He smiled grimly as he glanced down at his disfigured hands, one of which he slapped on to his left thigh. 'This leg here is made from the finest Linden tree on the Unter den Linden itself. Carved for me by a friend who also survived our little holiday camp of Bergen-Belsen.' His lips twitched as he stubbed out the remains of the cigarette. 'It was one of the trees that Eva could see from her bedroom window … It went, along with her whole block, at the beginning of '45.'

Anna caught her breath as disappointment stabbed home. 'There's nothing left there to see, then? No sign of her old home?'

Kurt Kessel shook his head sadly. 'Nothing.'

'And of her family?'

Again he shook his head. 'I heard the old lady – her grandmother – died of a heart attack shortly after Eva left. But what exactly became of her mother and father during the war I cannot say. I suspect Martin Koehn, her father, did not survive the camps. Few did of his age, you know.'

'And her mother?'

'Ah – Margarete ...' He gave a helpless shrug. 'A nice woman ... She just disappeared. Either left the city or was killed by the Allied bombing. Who can say?'

'You did try to find out, you said?'

'Oh, sure. Once the war was over and the camps were emptied, I came back to Berlin.' He shook his head. 'No one can imagine what the city was like then ... Hardly a whole building left standing and refugees pouring in from the East in their thousands. Everyone was looking for someone ...'

'You were a good friend of my mother. What was she like? Tell me what you remember of her.'

He was silent for a moment or two. 'You said when you phoned your mother died when you were born.'

'That's right.'

'You have never even seen a photograph of her.'

Anna shook her head. 'Nothing. I understand her belongings were all destroyed by the same bomb that fatally injured her.'

Kurt Kessel sat quite still for a moment, as if struggling with his conscience over something. Then he reached into the inside pocket of his jacket which was hanging on the back of his chair. He extracted a brown leather wallet held together by an elastic band. As Anna watched, he flicked through the wad of papers inside to gently extract a well-thumbed, faded photograph of a young girl. 'You'd better have this, then.'

Anna leaned across the desk and took the picture. She gazed down at it, cradling it in the palm of her left hand, as if it might shatter into pieces before her very eyes. A young girl in her late teens smiled back at her. A young girl in a summer dress, standing beneath a cherry tree in full blossom. She held a large straw hat, bedecked with a long ribbon, in her hand, and her blonde hair was blowing freely in the breeze. The waters of a lake sparkled in the distance and the remnants of a picnic lay on the grass at her feet.

'I took that,' Kurt said quietly. 'The summer of '38, it must have been. We were on a family picnic to the Wannsee. Hanna asked Eva to come along. They were like sisters then.'

Her mother! This was her mother! Anna's fingers shook as she held up the card to examine it in more detail, but the blur of tears in her eyes made a closer inspection impossible.

'Take it. It's yours,' Kurt said. 'I've carried it around with me for a quarter of a century. But you have laid her to rest for me today. I know now that bloody war killed her too – just as it killed my country and my city, by dividing them into two ... Take it, Anna. It's what Eva would have wanted.'

She shook her head as she slipped the precious picture into her bag. Thanks were totally inadequate, and she knew he knew it too. He had loved her, really loved her. She could sense it, and tried to imagine the once handsome, idealistic young boy behind the worn-out shell of the middle-aged man who sat before her ... Then her thoughts moved on to another man who had also once loved the young woman called Eva Koehn, and as the painful memory of Bill Rutherford clouded her eyes, Kurt Kessel asked the question:

'Just tell me one thing, Anna. Who was your father?'

The tears dried in her eyes as she looked across at him and thought of the man who had sired her. And then she found herself telling him all about her discovery that very week. How she had found out that her real father was himself in Berlin that very week. The man who had left her mother to die under the Luftwaffe's bombs was the father of the West's nuclear defence programme.

Kurt Kessel listened in silence, a curious mixture of emotions churning within him as he studied the intense face of the young woman before her. She should have been *his* daughter – his and Eva's. Not the child of this American he already hated with all his heart. Throughout all those long years in the camps, and in the years that followed, he had carried the memory of Eva Koehn locked deep in his heart. No other man could have loved her as he did. No other man had the right to father her child. To hear now, after all these years, that someone had used her like that, then walked out on her, leaving her a helpless young woman in a foreign land …

The anger welled within him as Anna related the story; an anger that became mixed with a curious excitement. Less than half an hour before she arrived he had been reading a secret file on this man, Rutherford – a file given to him by one of his oldest friends who, as well as being one of East Berlin's most talented journalists, was also a diligent *apparatchik* for the KGB. He could just imagine Rudolf Gross's reaction when he met him with this news in their local *Kneipe* tonight. What he had here could be the opportunity of a lifetime to do something tangible for his beleaguered country and the Soviet Union itself. But perhaps just as importantly, it would be a chance for a very personal revenge on the man he now knew to be responsible for the death of the woman he loved. It was difficult to keep his voice steady as he said quietly, 'You hate him very much, don't you – this William Rutherford?'

'I hate him so much it hurts,' Anna said simply. 'I hate him for what he did to my mother in his personal life, and I hate him for what he's doing to the future of the human race in his professional life.'

Kurt Kessel's grey brows furrowed as his mind raced ahead. He had to be careful how he worded this: 'Do you hate him enough to want to destroy him professionally?'

Anna gave a strained smile. 'To destroy his professional career might go a little way to compensating for my mother's death. But I hardly think I'm high-powered enough to do that.'

'There is a way.'

'What do you mean?'

He shifted awkwardly in his chair as the idea took shape in his mind, and his mutilated fingers toyed nervously with a ballpoint pen on the blotter in front of him. 'You look incredibly like her, Anna. Even my own heart stood still when you entered this room today. It was as if Eva Koehn had been reborn ...' He shook his head, 'I cannot believe it was not the same for William Rutherford when you met this morning ... He too is a human being – a human being who was once in love.'

He looked pensive, as his fingers clicked the retractable point of the pen backwards and forwards, and the plan formed in his mind. 'You are to meet again tomorrow, you said.'

'Yes, that's right.' Her heart was beating much too fast. What was going on behind that furrowed brow? 'At ten in the morning.'

'Make him fall in love with you.'

'What?'

'Make him fall in love with you. It will be easy. You are your mother incarnated.'

'But that's obscene!'

Kurt leaned forward in his seat, his voice insistent: 'He must not know you are his daughter, of course. The plan would not work otherwise ... No, you must make him fall in love with you for just long enough to get the evidence you will need.'

'I will need?'

'To ruin him.'

Anna could feel a nervous sweat break out on her body. 'I still don't understand.'

But Kurt's brain was working overtime. It was incredible; as well as the chance to revenge Eva's death, he had the power to remove one of the West's best nuclear brains from his post. The professional future of the head of America's nuclear research programme was in the palm of his hand. Revenge would not only taste sweet to his own tongue for all those wasted years spent dreaming of the young woman he now knew to have been destroyed by this man, but, *Du lieber Gott*, what this could mean to the East …

A cold sweat broke out on his brow. Yes, sweet revenge would also be wreaked on the West itself. It would be paying them back with a vengeance for all those scientists they had lured across the border before the Wall went up to stop the rot. Now fate would be enacting its own divine retribution for that scientific rape of his country in the form of his beloved Eva's only child. 'Photographs, that's what's required, Anna. Photographic evidence of the two of you in – how do you put it in English – in "a compromising situation".'

'But that would be incest,' Anna said, appalled.

Kurt gave a fatherly smile and shook his head. 'Use your imagination, Anna. You arrange for someone to take the photographs before it can go too far – but just far enough to put paid to the career of the man responsible for your mother's death *and* the West's nuclear defences. Just think of the headlines: 'America's Defence Chief in bed with Red! … Of course it need not ever find its way into the newspapers – to reach the eyes of the CIA will be sufficient.'

She gazed across at him in a mixture of horror and mounting excitement.

'Have you someone – a friend in the West of the city who can help?'

She immediately thought of Karl and nodded. 'Do you really think it would work?'

'I have no doubt of it.' He smiled wryly. 'You did not have to explain to me on the telephone this morning that you were a left-wing journalist, you know. Your fame has long since spread as far as East Berlin. Have you any doubt they will not have heard of you also at the CIA? If these photographs were to get into their hands …' His smile grew broader. 'Well, you can imagine the result. Our friend William J. Rutherford will no longer be a threat to world peace. They will do to him what they did to his old colleague Robert Oppenheimer – only more so. He will be dropped from the nuclear programme faster than you can say World War Three!'

Anna sat open-mouthed. He made it all sound so plausible – so incredibly easy. Then a doubt crept in. What if the plan *did* work? She still had her professional reputation to think about. 'You don't really think they would make it public, do you?'

Sensing her apprehension, Kurt said quickly, 'No, of course not. No nation likes to see its sacred cows slaughtered in public, and the Americans are no exception. They will move heaven and earth to see it is hushed up. The damage will be purely internal, Anna, I can assure you of that.'

She sat silently for a moment as they gazed at each other across the top of the desk. Then he said softly, 'Will you do it, Anna? Will you do it for the death of your mother and for the future peace of the world?'

She found herself nodding automatically as the excitement mounted within her. This man had loved her mother and had been made to suffer by his own country, just as she had in that awful war. A great wave of sympathy, of love almost, welled within her, and she reached across and clasped his hand in hers. It was a gesture that brought a glint of moisture to the eyes of the East German that owed nothing to the thick fug of pipe-smoke in the room. 'Yes, I'll do it,' she said in a voice that betrayed the emotion she too was feeling at that moment.

'You are a brave woman, Anna. You are your mother's daughter.'

Chapter Twenty-Three

It was late evening before Anna returned to the West. Kurt had taken her for a tour round what was left of the old landmarks on the Eastern side of the Wall that were once familiar to her mother; even pointing out what was left of her old school. The broken remnants of the four Palladian columns that had adorned the Empress Friedrich's front entrance were the only things identifiable on what looked like a vast building site. 'There's talk of rebuilding it about half a mile east of here,' Kurt informed her, 'and changing its name to the Krupskaya Gymnasium for Girls, after Lenin's wife.'

Anna had made no comment. Like so much else in the East, the past had been buried, but the present existed only in the future. Life had become a series of promises that might never be carried out.

She was struck with the bleakness of that half of the city in comparison with the colourful Western Sector. What had happened, or, to be more accurate, what had not happened to the Empress Friedrich Gymnasium seemed symbolic of so much of East Berlin. Even the old Alexanderplatz – the pre-war city's most famous square and favourite meeting place – had now been rebuilt into a vast concrete wasteland, as was so much of the surrounding area. And although Kurt proudly showed her the new homes that were going up, most looked like impersonal multi-storey prisons. There had been no visible attempt to recreate any of the charm and elegance of the old Berlin that had disappeared beneath the Allied bombs. Even the people had a depressed air about them.

She had made a comment to that effect to Kurt, then

immediately regretted it. To insult his beloved Berlin, or its people, was to twist a knife in his heart, and he had leapt to its defence. Was it any wonder that East Berlin was not so prosperous? Did she not know that the West had lured all the East's most skilled citizens with its promises of more money and material goods? Had she any idea of the amount of American dollars that had been poured into that part of the city on the other side of the Wall? West Berlin had become the whore of Capitalism, that was all – the whore of Capitalism.

She had been tempted to suggest that if that were so then, by the same token, East Berlin must surely be the whore of Communism; for, even worse than selling its body for material goods, it had sold its soul to an ideology imposed on it from its powerful ally in the East.

But then, appalled at her own reasoning which flew in the face of all she had believed in over the years, she had remained silent. Instead, she had listened quietly and made sympathetic noises as he rallied to the defence of his beloved home.

By the end of the evening Anna was both surprised and dismayed at how dispirited she felt. There had been almost nothing to see of the old Berlin that her mother must have known and loved. What remained of the Unter den Linden seemed a shabby travesty of what it must once have been. Near the Brandenburg Gate some linden trees had survived the bombing. They had been planted by the Nazis before the war to replace several aged ones and they were now over thirty feet tall, but they appeared to be the only genuine reminders of how it must have been then. Even the adjoining Friedrich Strasse had a peculiarly depressing air about it, and by no stretch of the imagination could she visualize the gay café society that had once flourished there, in Berlin's two most celebrated pre-war streets.

The Karl Marx Allee, one of the East's showpiece thoroughfares, she found grandiose but dowdy. Half-way down, they passed a Soviet revolutionary art exhibition, but although free, it had no viewers. She found herself deliberately avoiding looking at the portraits of Marx and Lenin that seemed to abound everywhere. Their red and black likenesses, and the banners that fluttered alongside them entreating the workers to greater glory for the state, somehow smacked of other red and black banners that had bedecked these selfsame streets a generation ago. Then the god had been a crazed Austrian by the name of Adolf Hitler, whose ideology and dreams of world dominance had been destroyed, along with much of Germany itself, to be replaced here behind the Wall by another ideology even more powerful.

For the first time in her twenty-five years, as Anna walked the grey pavements of the part of their city always referred to by the West Berliners as 'Over There', and observed the joylessness that was present in the faces of the inhabitants, she began to experience creeping doubts about the wisdom of imposing any totalitarian system on an unwilling people. The experience, and the responses it evoked within her, she found desperately unsettling. It was something she would have to ponder on at greater length, but right now, with Kurt at her side, it was neither the time nor the place.

At a little after nine o'clock, as the shadows of evening began to lengthen into twilight, they said their goodbyes with genuine affection at the control post, with a promise from Anna to return as soon as possible. Under the eyes of the green-uniformed *Volkspolizei*, he had kissed her on both cheeks, then she had turned to wave before disappearing through the wooden barrier for the first passport check.

Then, despite all Kurt's explanations for his half of the city's shortcomings, it was with a sense of enormous relief that she found herself back in the decadent, materialistic West and heading for Karl's apartment on Kant Strasse.

He was delighted to see her and had been keeping a curry warm, awaiting her arrival, for the past few hours. They ate in the kitchen, washing the Calcutta Special down with a bottle of hock he had bought specially for the meal. And afterwards they retired to the living-room, where she promised to give him a full account of her day.

He lay back in his chair, his feet on the glass and chrome coffee-table in front of him, and listened, interrupting only with an occasional low whistle as she recounted word for word her conversation in Kurt's dingy office that afternoon.

He was particularly interested in the East Berliner's remarks about Hanna Graubaum and her husband Peter-Klaus, and he scribbled their names on to a pad on the table in front of him. Any details on Nazi sympathizers still in prominent positions were worth following up: doing a little 'ground work' in *Der Gefallene Engel* itself should be something to look forward to. The Kurfürstendamm's most exclusive nightclub was not a place he could regularly afford to frequent, but this would not be purely for pleasure. He might even take Anna before she headed back to London.

When her story moved on to the subject of her father, however, his feet came down from the coffee-table and he found himself reaching for his pipe. He lit it and clenched the stem even more firmly than usual in his teeth as the plan that had been put to her unfolded. He leaned forward in his seat as the full impact of what she was saying became clear to him. This was even more exciting stuff than smuggling people across the Wall!

She could sense she had gripped him with the idea and was eager to know his reaction. 'Well, what do you think? Do you believe it would work?'

He took a long drink of his beer and nodded slowly. 'Oh, it could work all right. But you realize the plan has much deeper implications than merely moral blackmail?'

'Meaning?'

'In some eyes it could be regarded as treason. You realize you'd be giving the Soviets' own nuclear programme a major boost by getting rid of Rutherford.'

Anna gave an impatient shrug and reached for the bottle of Coke on the table in front of her. 'Don't tell me they don't have a whole lab full of physicists in the West every bit as good as my father who'd be only too willing to step into his shoes should he be forced to resign!'

Replacing the bottle, she reached forward and took a handful of peanuts from a brass dish beside her. 'Anyway, what's with this moral indignation stuff all of a sudden? I thought you were every bit as much against the nuclear arms race as I am?'

'I am. I was only pointing out how it might look to others if it ever became public.'

'But it won't, will it? I told you – Kurt said divulging the photos and details of the so-called "affair" to the CIA would be all that's required. Good God, it's hardly in their interests to splash it all over the front page of the *Washington Post* now, is it?'

'They have some bloody good news-journalists on the *Washington Post* who have rather a good reputation for sniffing out such stories.'

'Dear God – what is this? I expected you to be at least as excited I am at the idea. Kurt Kessel's a godsend, Karl, for heaven's sake! You can bet your boots he's got lots more information on Nazi sympathizers that he could let you have – and here he is handing me a way to get back at that murdering so-and-so on a plate, and all you can do is pour cold water on it!' She slumped back in her chair and glared across the coffee-table at him.

He puffed thoughtfully on his pipe as a slow smile lit his face. 'You look even prettier when you're angry.'

'Jesus!' She threw a handful of peanuts across at him. One landed in his beer. 'Don't be so bloody patronizing! I'm being serious, Karl, for heaven's sake!'

He fished the nut from his drink, the smile still on his face. 'So am I, *Liebchen*, so am I … I'm not pouring cold water on anything, believe me. I think it's a brilliant idea.'

'Then you'd be willing to help?'

'To take the photos, you mean?'

'Of course.'

'Yes, if that's what you really want.'

Anna let out a sigh of relief, but his initial reaction had puzzled her. And his last comment had her reaching for her cigarettes. It *was* what she really wanted, wasn't it? She was being given the ideal opportunity to get even with the man she now knew to be her father – who could blame her for being over the moon? It both annoyed and disappointed her that Karl should have seemed so lukewarm about the idea at first. 'What would you do – in my place?'

'You mean if it were my father?' He gave a half-laugh. 'If it were my old man, Anna *Liebchen*, it wouldn't just be a camera that would be aiming at him, I can tell you that! Shooting with a .45 automatic – not a Canon or Rolleiflex – would have been too good for that bastard after the thousands of innocent people he sent to their deaths.'

She smiled, but her fingers drummed on the wooden arm of the chair. Why was she suddenly so nervous about the whole thing? After all, her father had already been partially responsible for the deaths of tens of thousands in Hiroshima and Nagasaki, and could be instrumental in the destruction of the planet itself. It made what Karl's father had done seem very small beer indeed.

'You're not getting cold feet, are you?'

She glanced up and met his eyes. 'Of course not. I suppose I just feel rather guilty involving you, that's all.' He was quite right – some people could see it as akin to treason. Perhaps she had been presumptuous in assuming he would automatically be as enthusiastic as she herself was about the idea. 'If you do help me, Karl,' she said quietly, 'then you must let me do something in return for you … You want to get someone across the border, don't you?'

He nodded, but made no comment.

'I promised Kurt I'd keep him informed on the plan, which will mean more visits over the Wall. On my last visit I could accidentally "lose" my passport. Presumably there's at least one East German girl with my colouring?'

He scratched his beard as he glanced across at her long blonde hair. 'One or two.'

'Right, I'll lie low until she's well through the Wall, then report it stolen.'

His face was still deadpan.

'Look, it beats tying someone underneath the chassis of a car and stunts like that, you must admit!'

He nodded reluctantly.

'Right. Have we got a deal?'

'You're quite a girl.'

'Woman,' she corrected. 'I'm a woman, Karl — remember …?'

He grinned and placed his pipe in the ashtray. 'How could I forget …?'

The dawn came early, creeping over the house-tops in silver-grey fingers that probed through the half-open blinds and fell on the rumpled foot of the duvet, before the sun rose to bathe the bedroom in its golden glow.

Anna lay quite still on the plump pillows and stared silently at the coming day. Beside her she could hear Karl's even breathing and she envied him his peace of mind. They had made love until, exhausted, they had fallen asleep in each other's arms. But while he had remained asleep, she had woken again shortly afterwards to stare with unseeing eyes into the darkness of the room and listen to the faint, whistling sound of his breathing as he lay face to the ceiling on the bed beside her.

Once awake she found it impossible to get to sleep again. Too many things were going through her mind. And occasionally, as the night wore on, she even wished she had not made this trip to Berlin – this journey back into the past. It was akin to opening a Pandora's box full of conflicting emotions in her mind.

But most of all she thought of those two very different men she had met for the first time yesterday – the two men who had loved her mother – Kurt Kessel and Bill Rutherford.

The difference between them and their circumstances could not have been greater: one a mutilated victim of Nazism, now a committed Marxist and defender of the Communist state; the other a charismatic American, and one of the most powerful men of the Capitalist West.

Which one would her mother prefer if she were still alive? The question haunted her and she yearned to know better that young woman the world had known as Eva Koehn. Would she have been like her in more than just looks? Would she too have shared this passionate urge to champion the underdog, or would she have been seduced by the type of lifestyle Bill Rutherford could provide?

Had she lived, would she have returned, like Kurt Kessel, to that part of the city that had once been her home – East Berlin – and opted for a much harder lifestyle lived for a political ideal, or would she have chosen the softer option and remained in the Capitalist West?

Anna did not find it a comfortable question. She remembered the feeling of desolation that had pervaded her own spirit on the other side of the Wall, and the sense of relief on her return to the Western Sector. That experience, so unexpected, had struck at the very core of all her political beliefs. Could it be that at heart she was that creature she professed to abhor more than all others – an armchair revolutionary? The very idea was too appalling to contemplate. Her whole existence was geared to fighting for World Socialism; she had even given up her academic career to do something more tangible in that regard. Could it be that that commitment was only skin-deep – that if the crunch came she would not be able to swap the freedoms she enjoyed as a matter of right in the West for the benefits promised by Marx's 'Brotherhood of Man'?

She gazed down at the face of the man who was now her lover. Had he ever experienced such doubts too? Did Karl, sleeping here so peacefully beside her, ever stop to wonder at the paradox of risking his life to help people escape from a political system that he himself ostensibly both approved of and supported, although choosing to live in the West himself?

She had not done herself any favours coming here to Berlin. It was as if coming face to face with the two great political systems of the twentieth century she was coming face to face with her own conscience. It was not a comfortable experience.

Chapter Twenty-Four

Bill Rutherford got there first. He stood just inside the main doors of the Husum Hotel and gazed out at the morning traffic as he smoked his cigarette. He was dressed casually, in a light grey summer-weight suit, but there was a set look to his features that betrayed his inner turmoil. What the hell was he doing making this appointment?

He dragged deeply on his cigarette and frowned into the glass panel of the door. It was the first time in months he had dreamt about Eva – if it were Eva in his dream last night. He could be sure about nothing any more. And the experience had left him drained and surprisingly on edge. So much so that he almost got one of his aides to come down here to cancel this appointment. Any excuse would have done … 'General Rutherford has been called away to another meeting.' She would have been none the wiser.

But he had not done it, and, as he stood here awaiting her arrival, he was not at all sure it was the right decision to turn up in person.

Anna was four minutes late and that in itself seemed to him to give her the edge. Here he was, perhaps the most important man in the city right now, standing around waiting for a bit of a girl in a mini-dress.

'General – it was good of you to wait!' Anna ran up the steps and held out her hand.

He shook it and commented on the continuing good weather. An inane subject, he knew, but she seemed to have that effect on him. She was looking particularly attractive, in a pale yellow, sleeveless dress, with a white scarf tied Alice-style around her hair. He commented on the fact.

'I must admit to feeling a bit like Alice-in-Wonderland

amongst all you high-powered types,' she smiled, aware it would do no harm at all to play the helpless female.

He gave an embarrassed half-smile in return and made a gesture in the direction of the downstairs restaurant. 'Fancy a cup of coffee – or something stronger if they have it?'

'A coffee will do fine.'

He held her lightly by the elbow as they made their way across the tiled mosaic floor of the foyer. It was a curiously proprietorial gesture by a virtual stranger and she was immediately aware of how her mother must have reacted to such a man. He exuded an air of capability and strength such as Anna herself had not encountered in any of the men she had known before – surely an irresistible combination for a young refugee girl in a foreign country all those years ago.

Her lateness this morning was not intentional. She had endeavoured to phone her editor, Tony Barnes, at the office before leaving Karl's apartment, and had had difficulty getting through. When eventually she succeeded and informed him she might be a day or so longer in Berlin than she had originally intended, the groan that came over the phone was ear-shattering – until she gave the reason. Then his attitude changed abruptly. 'Go for it, Anna. Take as long as you need. An exclusive with that bastard Rutherford will be quite a coup.' Everyone who did not fit in with Tony's own quite militant Trotskyite views was deemed to be a bastard, but Anna had given a satisfied smile as she replaced the phone. She knew he would be pleased, to put it mildly, at her pulling this off. If only he knew the whole story …

The restaurant was done out in shades of grey, and had sepia-coloured prints of the nineteenth-century North Sea fishing port of Husum – the great German novelist Theodor Storm's 'grey town by the grey sea' – adorning its walls. Even at this time in the morning it was over half-full and exuded an air of culinary opulence, with its solicitous waiters and trollies laden with cream cakes and gâteaux of every description. The smell of rich roasted coffee filled their nostrils as they entered.

A black-coated waiter attempted to usher them to a table in the centre of the room, but Bill Rutherford politely shook his head and instead, ignoring the man, made for one well away from the door and half-hidden behind a large potted palm. 'Life's enough of a goldfish bowl as it is,' he commented beneath his breath as she made herself comfortable on the carved mahogany chair opposite him.

'Would sir and madam care for the sweet trolley?'

'Two portions of *Schwarzwälder-Kirschtorte* will be fine, thanks. And a pot of coffee for two – medium roast.'

'Thank you, sir.' The young man wrote the order on his pad and bowed his head politely before taking his leave.

'You do like Black Forest gâteau, I take it?'

'And if I didn't?'

He had the good grace to look slightly abashed. He was so used to dining out with Mary-Jo and taking charge of things, it had come as second nature.

'Black Forest gâteau is one of my favourites,' she assured him. What a strange mixture this man who had fathered her was – half the 'big shot', well used to taking charge of things in every walk of life, and half the surprisingly gauche young man still buried inside the greying, middle-aged exterior. She had the distinct impression that despite his very obvious charisma he was not totally at ease entertaining attractive young women.

The order was delivered before she even had a chance to look around at the decor. 'Typical German efficiency,' she commented as she dug her fork into the dark moist cake for the first mouthful.

She glanced across the table as he followed suit and she noticed for the first time that he wore a gold signet ring on the third finger of his left hand. He was married. She shouldn't have been in the least surprised with a man of his age, but the knowledge jarred somehow. Had his wife been the proverbial 'girl back home' all the time he was making love to her mother? She could feel her features begin to harden and had to fight to keep a relaxed air. 'Nice cake,' she murmured, forcing an appreciative smile to her lips as she took her second forkful.

'Not bad, not bad at all. Although I must admit the best Black Forest gâteau I've ever had came from a little delicatessen I know back in New York.'

'Ah, New York … One either loves it or hates it, isn't that so, General?'

He raised his eyebrows quizzically and glanced across at her before piercing a cherry with his fork and swirling it in the thick cream.

> 'Vulgar of manner, overfed,
> Overdressed and underbred;
> Heartless, Godless, hell's delight,
> Rude by day and lewd by night …
> Crazed with avarice, lust and rum,
> New York, thy name's Delirium!'

'I take it you don't like it?' she smiled.

'On the contrary, I love the place – warts and all, as they say. Some of the happiest times of my life were spent there.'

'At Columbia?' she said, showing she had done her homework.

'And watching the Yankees.'

'You look like you were quite a sportsman yourself in your day.'

'In my day?' He affected a look of mock horror. 'Every guy, like every dog, has his day – is that it, Anna – and mine is past?'

She had the good grace to blush as she reached for her coffee. 'Oh, I really didn't mean to insinuate that you were past it!'

'Past "it"? And what might the "it" be you have in mind, I

263

wonder?' He stressed the two-letter word meaningfully as he suppressed a grin.

Her cheeks were flushed as she avoided his eyes and toyed with the cake on her plate. 'This conversation is taking us down a path I didn't quite envisage at the moment.'

He took a sip of his coffee and felt half inclined to enquire exactly when she would be willing to go down that particular path, but he thought better of it; she was obviously uncomfortable, so rather than tease her further he diplomatically changed the subject. 'Have you been to Germany before?'

'Mm hmm,' she nodded, dabbing some cream off her chin with the napkin. 'Quite often. But not to Berlin. How about you? This can't have been your first visit.'

He picked up his fork and dug it into the cake, his fingers tightening slightly around the silver plate handle. 'No … I came here first just after the war.'

'Business or pleasure?'

A nerve flickered at the corner of his jaw. This was not the path he would have chosen for this particular part of the conversation. 'Neither really … But that's a long time ago now. I thought we were here to talk about the present.'

He was aware of sounding unnecessarily sharp in his retort, but he certainly wasn't going to go into the details of that visit with her. It still lay, an unhealed sore, deep within him. A visit to London just after the war had almost proved to him that Eva had been killed in the May Blitz of 1941. Almost proved … Nothing short of finding her grave could settle the torment in his mind, and that he had been unable to do. That first visit to Berlin shortly afterwards had been a futile attempt to lay the ghost of his past love once and for all. By the end of that week twenty years ago, however, he had known there was no hope of ever finding any trace of Eva or her family – the war had seen to that. The pain of that knowledge had made him almost physically ill, even though he was by then a married man …

Anna sensed his unease immediately and did not pursue the matter. There was going to be a lot of thin ice in this conversation, and she had to be prepared to skate around it as best she could if she were ever to see him again socially. She had also to put out of her mind totally the fact that he was her father, or the whole thing became impossible to contemplate. For the meantime she would steer clear of the personal angle and attempt to put him at his ease by sticking to physics. 'Tell me, General, is there now, or has there ever been, any conflict in your mind about what you're doing?'

He took a sip of his coffee. 'You mean about our nuclear defence programme? None at all.'

His answer was quite unequivocal and took her by surprise. Somehow she had expected a chink in the armour which she could have probed with a telling follow-up question.

'I can see I've disappointed you. You wanted me to have great moral doubts about my profession.'

'Tiny little ones would have done.'

He smiled as he ate his gâteau. 'I love my subject, Miss Lloyd-Jones – more than I love anything on this earth, apart from my family. I was sixteen when I first decided to make science my goal, and as soon as I entered Harvard and discovered the world of nuclear physics … Well, let's just say I knew immediately that that was where my future lay.'

'And it was a deliberate choice to channel your career into nuclear weapons?'

His mind went back to the day in late 1942 that he was told he had the chance of working with J. Robert Oppenheimer himself. 'Yes, you could say it was a deliberate choice. If I'd opted to do anything else I'd have found myself on the scientific gravy-train with a second-class ticket, there's no doubt about that. Los Alamos was where it was all going to be happening, and I wanted to be in on the act. It was as simple as that.'

'They say Oppenheimer was very sympathetic to the

265

Communist cause back in the Thirties. It never attracted you, I take it?'

He sighed, as if he'd had this question fired at him more times than he cared to remember. 'Communism, Anna, is the opiate of the intellectuals in the West – it was in the Thirties and it still is today in the Sixties. I may be a scientist by profession but I would never claim to be an intellectual.'

'That's exceedingly modest of you.'

'Not modest – honest. To me as a young man in the Thirties, Communism was like Prohibition – a great idea, but it would never work.'

'It never crossed your mind they might have a point?'

'Oh sure, they had a point all right. It seemed to me every one of them I ever met had a point: they had nothing themselves and were hellbent on sharing it with the world.'

'You're a cynic, General.'

'I'm a realist, Miss Lloyd-Jones.'

They both smiled, then it was his turn to ask the questions. 'Tell me, then, since you were so keen to know if I ever considered Communism as a political philosophy – being British, have you ever considered the virtues of your Conservative Party?'

She had her mouth full and pressed the napkin to her lips as she suppressed a derisive snort of laughter. 'That last phrase was a contradiction in terms as far as I'm concerned. Believe me, General, to be a Tory today is to be engaged on one of man's oldest philosophic quests – that is to find a moral justification for selfishness. He – or she – is someone whose whole *raison d'être* is to demand a square deal for the rich, and most haven't the good grace to blush into the bargain!'

He raised one eyebrow quizzically. 'I'm surprised so many people vote for them, if that's the case.'

'So am I.' Then realizing she was in danger of appearing far too much of a left-wing zealot, she mellowed into a rather embarrassed smile. 'As a journalist I admit I may have rather a jaded view of politics. It's an occupational hazard, I'm afraid.'

'Politicians are not exactly your favourite people, I take it?'

'Oh, some of them are all right, I suppose. I expect your lot are not quite as hidebound as ours because there's less to choose between the parties. And what's more they get away with far less because your political correspondents in Washington aren't half the toadies ours are in Britain. In fact, to be honest, I wouldn't mind working there as a political journalist myself – on a temporary basis, of course. I'd want to come back here to Europe eventually, though.'

Her companion gave a wry smile. 'Anna honey, believe me, there's nothing so permanent as a temporary job in Washington … I know that to my cost.'

She waited for him to continue, but to her disappointment he didn't. Instead he reached over and topped up both their coffee cups from the silver-plated pot on the stand in front of them. Dozens of questions spun in her head – questions about both his private and his professional life that she would dearly have loved to have had the answers to. But her companion seemed to have said as much as he intended to about himself for the present.

For the next five minutes she attempted to make innocuous small talk about the purpose of NATO, as the ornamental clock on the wall opposite ticked on. Despite his reservations, she knew she had to get more personal. Time was running out. She knew he would not have all morning to spend on her. 'Tell me, General, how do you like to spend your spare time?'

'What spare time?' He grinned as he pushed the empty cake plate from him and reached for his coffee cup.

'You mean you don't get any time off at all – not even while you're here in Berlin?'

'These trips are no joy-ride. We're not here that long, you know – another couple of days, that's all. Tomorrow evening's the only few hours they've given me to myself before we get the show on the road again and head for SHAPE headquarters, just outside Paris. But I'm not complaining. It's time enough for a swim. I find that's the best relaxation of all these days.'

Anna's disappointment was obvious in her face. He would be in France within forty-eight hours. 'I understand the hotel's got a first-class pool.'

'It may well have, but I won't be using it.'

She raised her eyebrows.

'Can you blame me?' he asked, as Anna pushed her own empty dessert plate aside and accepted one of his cigarettes. 'I'm surrounded by these guys almost twenty-four hours a day … No, on my precious few hours off I'll head out to the Wannsee and commune with nature.'

'Alone?' Her dark eyes narrowed quizzically as they met his through a puff of cigarette smoke.

'Unless you've got a better idea.' What the hell was he saying?

Anna's heart raced.

'You do swim, I take it?' Despite himself he was pursuing the idea. She tossed her hair back in a gesture so reminiscent of Eva that his grip on his own cigarette involuntarily tightened and snapped the thin white paper tube. 'Damn …' He discarded it into the ashtray and lit another as he repeated the question, more insistently this time. 'You do like swimming?'

She nodded. 'But I've never been to the Wannsee.'

'That makes two of us.'

She dropped her eyes to the table and toyed with her teaspoon.

'Well …?'

'Was that an invitation?'

'It was the best you're liable to get,' he grinned almost shyly.

She raised her coffee cup in a salutation gesture. 'I'll bring a picnic.'

'Better still.' He let out an audible sigh and leaned back in his chair as he drew deeply on his cigarette. Dear God, had he taken leave of his senses? He was aware of smiling across the table at her through the cigarette smoke and there was not a darned thing he could do about it. Every nerve-end in his body was alive; it was as if he were living life on a more heightened plane when he was around her. He thought of Mary-Jo back home in Washington, but strangely felt no guilt. In fact, he didn't give a damn.

Anna leaned across the table and poured the remains of the coffee into their cups. He found himself asking her about her life in London and genuinely listening to the answers. He wanted to know about her – all about her. But Anna, for her part, was not enjoying the experience. She realized she had to be more than careful to gauge her replies to what she felt was acceptable to a man in his position. As she answered his questions one by one, her left-wing sympathies meta-morphosed into a passionate care for the environment and the Third World. She was careful to make no mention of *The Vital Spark* or anything else that might alienate him, and merely described herself as a freelance journalist still working for her doctorate on World Hunger.

'So that's why you're so against the so-called "arms race": you reckon that the money can be better spent feeding the Third World.' He sounded almost relieved.

'More arms do not make mankind safer, General – only poorer. It seems to me that every nation defends its partici-pation in the arms race as essential to defend its national security, but this is self-delusion. All they're doing is buying even more insecurity at ever-increasing costs.'

Bill Rutherford gave an indulgent smile. 'The trouble with you journalists, Anna, is that you're full of fine phrases but usually pretty thin on facts.'

'I'm willing to listen. That's what I'm here for, remember?' She glanced down at the unopened notepad by her empty coffee cup.

Bill Rutherford looked at it too. The fact that she had not opened it seemed indicative to him that this was no ordinary interview for her either. The strange excitement he felt whenever he was around her was growing within him. Could it be – could it just possibly be that she was enjoying this meeting as much as he was? Oh sure, he was a hell of a lot older than her, but maybe that was part of the attraction. After all, they did say that it was power and not looks that many women found attractive in a man, didn't they?

He gave a rueful smile to himself as he stubbed out the remains of his cigarette and glanced at his watch. It could just be he was selling himself short. She had accepted that invitation to the Wannsee after all. Maybe he wasn't that bad looking, come to think of it, and, thank God, he could still cut a pretty mean figure in a pair of bathing trunks.

'I've taken up far too much of your time, I can see that.' She had caught the sneaked glance at his watch.

'Yes, you have.' He had a broad smile on his face.

'And you don't mind?'

'Does it look like it?'

She opened her bag and slipped the unused notepad into it. 'I'm highly flattered.' She pushed her chair back and looked across at him quizzically. 'Tell me, do all female journalists who request an interview get this sort of treatment?' She was genuinely curious.

He stood up and signalled for the bill. When he looked back in her direction his eyes were unusually serious. 'No. No, Anna, they don't.'

He took his leave of her just inside the main door of the hotel, promising to meet her at the same place the following day at around seven. His hand held on to hers just that bit longer than was necessary and she was conscious of his eyes following her as she ran lightly down the front steps to disappear quickly from view amongst the morning shoppers.

Then almost immediately his doubts began. Had he taken leave of his senses? What in heaven's name was he doing arranging to see her again like this? She was half his age and he was a married man.

A married man. He thought once more of his wife, Mary-Jo, and this time there *was* guilt. There was guilt because he knew he was attracted to this young woman more than he had been attracted to anyone since Eva. And the knowledge both disturbed and excited him more than anything had done in years.

Chapter Twenty-Five

'*Phantastisch!* How did you manage it?' Karl Brandt could not conceal his surprise or his admiration as Anna told him of the proposed trip to the Wannsee. He was standing by the kitchen sink, a dark-blue striped butcher's apron wrapped around his open-necked shirt and blue jeans as he chopped the mushrooms to adorn the pizza already in the oven.

Anna tossed her handbag on to the worktop and pushed a hand through her hair, pulling off the white scarf in the process. 'Believe it or not it was surprisingly easy. I asked him if he ever got any time off and that was it – I'm going swimming with him tomorrow evening.'

'He fancies you – like all men.'

'Shut up, Karl!' She turned abruptly from him and stared out of the window into the backyard of the adjoining apartments. That kind of talk made her blood run cold. Good God, he was her father after all … The very thought brought a sick feeling to the pit of her stomach. 'I wish it was over.'

Karl gave a grunt as he concentrated on the mushrooms. 'Don't worry – it sounds like it soon will be! From what you say about him leaving for Paris, it'll have to be tomorrow evening, after the swim, won't it? You'll have to bring him back here.'

She tensed inwardly and the skin of her arms turned to gooseflesh at the prospect. A grey and white tabby cat was scrabbling in one of the dustbins in the concrete yard down below and she stared at it, yet saw nothing of its antics; her thoughts were fixed firmly on the following evening.

'You still want to go through with it, don't you?'

She nodded grimly, her teeth chewing into her bottom lip. 'Yes. Yes, I do.'

'Right then, we have to decide on our plan of action.' He tipped the prepared mushrooms into a pan of melted butter already heating on the cooker and stirred them thoughtfully with a wooden spoon. 'There's not a lot to prepare really. You tell me approximately what time you'll be bringing him back and I'll be ready with the necessary.'

'You mean with the camera?'

'What did you think I meant – with a gun?'

'Don't joke about it, please.' Her voice was as tight as her lips. Bill Rutherford's face swam before her. He was smiling that slightly embarrassed smile she already knew so well. They might as well be killing him. This would well and truly finish his career.

Karl turned to face her, his eyes serious. 'Look, Anna, if you're having second thoughts about this whole thing, tell me now. You're not getting fond of the guy, are you?'

'Good God, no!' She sounded genuinely horrified, then she sighed deeply and walked over to the cooker to take the wooden spoon from him. 'Fix me a drink, would you, Karl? I don't mind what it is as long as it's good and strong.'

He gave her a searching look and disappeared into the living-room to return with two large whiskies. 'Want some ice?'

She shook her head as she took a glass from him and downed half of her drink in one. 'If I can persuade him to come back to the apartment with me – and it's a very big "if" – where will you be when we get here?'

He gave a helpless shrug of his shoulders as he gazed around him. 'I don't really have much choice, do I? It's not exactly a huge place. I'll have to stay here in the kitchen with the camera. But for God's sake don't let him come through when you arrive. Get him into the bedroom as soon as possible, then while he's undressing make some excuse to slip out. Say you're going to the bathroom, then get down to your underwear as fast as you can and give me the signal. I'll give you a minute or so to get him on to the bed then I'll do the needful.'

'There's no way you can take the photos without him knowing. I mean there'll be the flash going off for a start.'

'Correct.'

'There could be one hell of a scene after it. He could attack you.' Her voice had dropped to a whisper.

'Don't you think I haven't thought of that?' He came across to where she was standing and switched off the cooker.

Anna moved aside as, picking up a tea-towel to protect his hands, he opened the oven door and removed the pizza.

'The way I see it, he's not going to be able to get very far in his underpants, now is he? I'll rely on you to do your best to prevent him coming after me for a few seconds at least. But even if he does make a grab for me, I can be out of the apartment a lot faster than he can, and I'll lock the front door behind me. I'll be off in my car before he's even got his trousers back on.'

'You make it sound so simple.'

'It can be – if we keep our heads.'

He divided the pizza into two and slipped a half on each plate before pouring a generous helping of mushrooms on each one. 'Here.' He handed her one of the plates and they made their way back through to the living-room.

They sat facing one another across the coffee-table as they began to eat in silence.

'I feel so guilty involving you like this.'

'There's no need to,' Karl assured her through a mouthful of pizza. 'Look, *Liebling*, we're both suffering from the same debilitating disease – fathers who were bastards. The state saw to it that mine paid his debt to society, but if it hadn't, then, by God, one way or another *I* would have made damned sure he did. Even if Rutherford hadn't been responsible for your mother's death, the work he's been involved in for the past quarter of a century makes him Public Enemy Number One in my book, for a start.'

Anna sighed and toyed with a mushroom on her plate. 'You're right. I know you're right.'

'But you still feel bad about it?'

She nodded, not trusting herself to speak.

'I could get someone else to stand in for you if you really feel so squeamish about it.'

'What good would that do? The whole idea is that the CIA would be horrified at him having a so-called affair with such a well-known Red. You can hardly just pick up some little nonentity of a left-wing student and get her to stand in for me instead.'

Karl opened a bottle of beer and took a swig. 'I guess you're right,' he admitted ruefully, wiping the froth from the hair around his lips. 'There's nothing else for it, then.'

'It'll have to be me.'

They stared at one another across the table. All of a sudden what had simply been little more than a pipe-dream had become a chilling reality. 'You realize you'll have to leave Berlin immediately,' Karl said quietly.

'But I can't! I promised to help you get someone through the Wall.'

'To hell with the Wall! Your safety is far more important. You can come back as soon as this dies down and Rutherford is on his way back to the States.' He took another drink of the beer. 'Hell, Anna, do you think I want you to go? I'll go crazy here on my own with you back in London.'

She looked across at him and knew he was speaking the truth. He was in love with her. She was certain of it.

She pushed her plate with the half-eaten pizza aside and sank back in her chair. 'I wish I'd been born stupid!' she said bitterly. 'I wish I'd been born so bloody stupid that all I was bothered about was if I could afford to buy the latest Beatles' hit record, or the latest shade of eye-shadow. It's a curse caring about things, Karl. A bloody curse!'

Tears rushed unbidden to her eyes as she continued. 'I wish to God I didn't give a damn about the bomb, or how many people were suffering through hunger and violence in the world today. Sweet Jesus, I wish I were a moron!'

She got up and pulled a cigarette from an open packet lying on the coffee-table. Her fingers were shaking as she lit it with an impatient flick of the table-lighter. She drew the smoke deep into her lungs as, grim-faced, she walked to the window and stared out through the blinds. Her eyes were swimming and she closed them tightly to prevent the tears spilling down her cheeks.

Karl watched helplessly from his seat, his appetite for the remaining piece of pizza completely gone. The last few words of her outburst repeated in his head and he remembered a piece of an English nonsense rhyme someone had once taught him:

> 'See the happy moron,
> He doesn't give a damn.
> I wish I were a moron –
> My God, perhaps I am!'

But instead of raising a smile, he could only look on in dismay as before he had even got to the end, Anna had turned and rushed blindly from the room.

He sat staring at the closed bedroom door through the deepening gloom of the evening. The blinds were already half-closed, but somehow he hadn't the heart to get up and turn on the lights. Neither did he have the courage it required to go through and comfort her in her misery.

He would never understand women. Her outburst had come as a complete surprise. Until tonight he would have sworn that she felt every bit as bitter about her father as he did about his. As far as he was concerned all that stuff about the sins of the fathers visiting themselves on the succeeding generations was too true to be good. The knowledge that his

276

own father had been one of Hitler's staunchest henchmen had blighted his life, but how much more bitter he would have felt if he had discovered, as Anna had done, that the man who had sired him had also been morally responsible for his mother's death. What on earth had happened to make her go soft all of a sudden?

He was still puzzling over the abrupt change in her mood when the bedroom door opened.

'I'm going out for a little while, Karl. I need some fresh air.' She had on a light cotton jacket over her dress and a scarf knotted gypsy-style round her hair. Her face looked pale and drawn and she avoided his eyes as she made for the door.

He leapt from his chair at the sight of her. 'I'll come with you.'

She held up a restraining hand. 'No – please don't do that. I need some time to think, that's all. I'll be better on my own. Please.'

'If you're sure.'

'I'm sure.'

He reached inside the pocket of his jeans. 'Then take the car. I don't like the idea of you walking around on your own at this time in the evening.'

She gave a wry smile as she dropped them into her jacket pocket. It was only seven-thirty.

She had not really intended heading for East Berlin, and almost turned back from the queue of traffic waiting to cross into the Communist half of the city at Checkpoint Charlie. Something inside her made her go on, however, and at just after eight she found herself driving down the Unter den Linden in the direction of Friedrich Strasse.

She did not expect to find anyone in the premises that housed Kurt Kessel's newspaper but, to her surprise, lights were burning at several of the windows. She pulled the car up outside the main door and decided to chance her luck. Maybe talking to him again would give her the resolve she required to go through with the plan the following night.

He was still in the building, although preparing to go home for the night. His delight at seeing her again so soon was genuine. 'Anna – how wonderful! How did you know I was just about to telephone you?'

She succumbed to his warm embrace and kisses on both cheeks. 'I didn't know,' she confessed. 'I just came over on the off-chance you might be here.'

'That is quite incredible,' he said, pulling out a chair for her to sit down, 'because I have had the most astonishing telephone conversation this evening.'

'Really?'

He limped round to the other side of his desk and picked up a piece of paper. 'Can you imagine whose address this is?'

'How could I?'

'It will surprise you – just as it surprised me.'

Anna shook her head, uncomprehending. 'I really have no idea what you're talking about.'

'It's your grandmother's, Anna – it's Margarete Koehn's!'

Anna jumped to her feet as if stung. 'You're joking!'

Kurt Kessel shook his head. 'Would I joke about a thing like that? No, it's true, Anna – I swear on my mother's grave.'

'But how …?' She shook her head, completely at a loss for words.

'How did I get such a thing?' He eased himself into his chair as Anna sat back down in hers. 'I can only say the gods must have been smiling on us this day. I was enjoying a beer with a journalist friend of mine, Rudolf Gross, in the *Kneipe* not far from here this lunchtime, when I happened to mention your visit, and that you were Eva Koehn's daughter … He too knew Eva, you see, before the war.'

'And?' The excitement was mounting within her.

Kurt took out his pipe and began to fill it, pushing the tobacco into the briar bowl with the stump of an index finger. 'It is quite strange how life works out, Anna, is it not? Although, as I said, Rudi too knew your mother, throughout these years since the war I have never discussed

278

with him my … my … feelings for Eva.' His voice dropped so she had to strain to hear. Her mother was still quite obviously a painful subject for him. 'What one feels most deeply one does not broadcast, you understand.'

She nodded, willing him to continue, as he paused to puff the tobacco into life.

'Well, today there was little choice. Because I mentioned your visit, I had to explain to him who you were. Can you imagine my feelings when he replied, "What a coincidence. Her grandmother lives in the same apartment block as me!" … I can tell you, Anna, I almost fell off my wooden leg!' His seamed face broke into a wide smile as he leaned back in his chair and beamed across at her.

Anna was speechless. This was more, much more, than she could ever have hoped for.

'You have nothing to say?'

'She – she's still alive? You're telling me my grandmother is still alive?'

'I was talking to her myself this evening on this very telephone.'

'You – you told her about me?'

Her companion was silent for a moment, then said quietly, 'Not exactly, Anna. Rudolf warned me the old lady has not been well. It's her heart, I understand. She suffered greatly in the war … Ravensbrück …'

Anna blanched. 'That was the women's concentration camp, wasn't it?'

Kurt Kessel nodded grimly as he clenched the stem of his pipe between what was left of his teeth. 'It was about ninety kilometres from here. Margarete remained in the vicinity of it, working on a farm, for several years after the war – that's why I couldn't trace her. She said she couldn't bear to come back to what was left of Berlin, with all its bitter memories … She only returned here two years ago when her health began to break down completely … I did not think it was wise to break such news to her – that she had a granddaughter – over

279

the telephone. Instead I simply said I had a friend of Eva's over here from England who would like to see her ... You *would* like to see her, I trust?'

'Would I?' she breathed. 'There's nothing in this world I'd like more. How soon can we go?'

'How about tomorrow morning? Frau Koehn said any morning around ten o'clock would suit her.' He glanced at his watch. It was not yet nine o'clock. With a bit of luck she should still be up. 'I can telephone her right now and confirm it, if that's what you want.'

Anna took a deep breath. 'That's what I want,' she said softly. 'That's what I want more than anything in the world.'

Chapter Twenty-Six

Karl was already asleep when Anna returned to the apartment just after eleven o'clock. An empty Johnny Walker bottle lay on the carpet at his side of the bed, where it had slipped from his outstretched arm. The last few drops of its contents had spilled on to the carpet and the whole room stank of whisky. She grimaced as she bent to pick it up. It had been three-quarters full when she left.

She slept little that night and was first out of bed in the morning. Even at seven o'clock the street outside was already busy with traffic and people hurrying to work as she opened the blinds in the living-room and allowed the early morning sun to stream in through the slats. The room smelt of stale cigarette ash and she carried the two brimming ashtrays with her through to the kitchen and emptied their contents into the bin beneath the sink before putting on a pot of coffee.

There was something magical about this time in the morning, with the promise of a brand-new day ahead. And what a day it could turn out to be. She waited impatiently for Karl to awake, desperate to share the good news about her grandmother. It was forty minutes later before he finally wandered through to the kitchen to avail himself of what was left of the coffee she had prepared.

'God, I feel awful!'

'You look it.' She cast a critical eye over his dishevelled hair and the dark shadows that circled his eyes as he scratched his beard and sank down on the chair opposite hers at the small kitchen table. 'Do you want something for your head?'

He made a face as he took his first sip of coffee. 'A guillotine's about the only thing that could get rid of this headache.'

'Well, I can't quite run to one of those, so this will have to do instead.' She tossed a packet of aspirin she had on stand-by across the table at him. 'Serves you right. At your age you should know that Johnny Walker's bad company when you're on your own.'

'He was the only *verdammt* company I had last night!'

She took it as the criticism that was intended and her face softened. 'I know and I'm sorry, Karl. Really I am. I just had to get away on my own to do some thinking. But as it happened, it turned out to be just about the most exciting evening of my life.'

She was rewarded with a sceptical glance as he popped two of the aspirins on to his tongue and drank them down with a mouthful of coffee. 'What happened? Did you hear you've been nominated for the Nobel Peace Prize for planning to get rid of Rutherford?'

Anna ignored the jibe. 'I've found my grandmother, Karl. At least, Kurt has found her for me.' It was impossible to keep the excitement from her voice. 'Isn't that wonderful?'

He looked across at her through sleep-swollen eyes and reached into the pocket of his dressing-gown for his cigarettes. 'If you say so.'

His reaction was like a douche of cold water. 'I tell you I've traced my grandmother and that's all you can say?'

'Goddammit, Anna, what's the big deal? So you found the old lady – I'm happy for you. Honest to God, I'm happy for you.' He scowled into his coffee cup, avoiding her accusing gaze. Her hang-ups with her damned relatives were becoming a pain in the neck. When would she devote some time and energy to *their* relationship?

'Well, thank you for that, Karl, I must say. Thank you for being so happy and enthusiastic for me.' She got up from the table and emptied the last of her coffee down the sink, then rinsed the cup under the tap.

He sighed inwardly. She was annoyed, he could see it. He got up from the table and stubbed out his newly-lit cigarette before padding barefoot over to the sink to put his arms around her. His face nuzzled into the hair at the back of her neck. 'To hell with everyone, Anna. To hell with the whole damned world – let's go back to bed.'

'I can't. I'm going out.' She turned far enough round in his arms to push him gently from her. 'I'm going back into East Berlin this morning to see …'

'Jesus Christ!'

'No, my grandmother,' she continued patiently. 'I told you, Karl, Kurt has found her for me and he's taking me to see her this morning.' She reached for the teacloth and carefully dried her cup before hanging it back up on the rack.

'Why him? Why can't you go with me? Why do you have to go with that damned old Commie?'

Anger flared in her eyes. 'Oh, so he's a damned old Commie now, is he? Well, let me tell you something, Karl Brandt – he's twice the man you'll ever be!'

'Meaning?'

She threw up her hands in a helpless gesture. 'Oh God, this is a stupid conversation!'

He got hold of her by the wrist. 'You said he was twice the man I'll ever be … Meaning, Anna? Just what the hell did you mean by that? Just what were you up to with that slimy Red bastard last night?'

Anna wrenched herself free. 'Dear God, I don't believe this conversation. I *do not* believe it!' She headed for the door. 'I'm getting dressed and getting out of here before this conversation gets any crazier than it already is!'

He barred the way, standing arms akimbo between the door-posts. 'We've got to talk.'

She pushed against the curling dark hair of his chest. 'What about – my "affair" with Kurt Kessel?'

'No, *Liebling*,' he replied softly. 'Your affair with your father.'

Anna drew back with a sharp intake of breath. 'You

bastard! You really know how to hit below the belt, don't you?'

Karl groaned and shoved a hand through his hair. 'I'm sorry, Anna. I'm sorry ... Jesus, I think I'd better go back to bed and get up again. This day is getting off to one hell of a start!'

She had never seen him look so dejected. Despite her irritation, her heart went out to him. He was feeling neglected, that was all. 'Truce?' She held out a conciliatory hand.

'Truce.' He took it, but instead of shaking it he held it to his lips. 'Forgive me, Anna *Liebling*. I'm crazy about you, that's what's at the bottom of it ... But I – I get the feeling sometimes you don't really think about our relationship in the same way I do. It's not what's most important to you right now.'

She reached up to place a light peck on his cheek. 'Bear with me, please. After tonight things will be different, I promise.'

He looked down at her and forced a smile to his lips. That was just what he was afraid of.

Despite his inclinations, they did not make love before Anna left for the East. Instead they sat and talked, over a fresh pot of coffee, and laid their plans for the evening. But the forthcoming scenario with her father had taken second place in Anna's mind to the meeting with her grandmother. No longer was Bill Rutherford her only living relative – she was about to meet her mother's mother. The prospect filled her with undiluted joy.

As prearranged the night before, she arrived outside Kurt Kessel's office at nine-thirty. The contrast between the two halves of the city struck her quite forcibly once more as she set out on the long walk from the checkpoint to the part of Friedrich Strasse that had once been the Kessel family home and nightclub. There were far fewer cars than on the other side of the Wall, and already several shops had long queues outside for basic supplies. Shortages were a way of life here.

Kurt had told her he would be waiting outside his office for her, but she could see no sign of him as she approached the heavy wooden door. Instead, a black Skoda car was parked at the kerbside and, as Anna approached, a man got out from behind the wheel and walked towards her.

'Miss Lloyd-Jones?' He was not much taller than herself, late thirties perhaps, with short fair hair and an easy smile that crinkled the skin around his eyes which were a quite startling colour of blue. He was dressed rather formally in a grey lounge suit, white shirt and red tie; the figure beneath appeared quite muscular, and from that and his tanned skin he looked as if he were no stranger to outdoor sports. 'My name is Rudolf Gross – I'm an old friend of Kurt's.'

She took his proffered hand, a perplexed look on her face. 'Is – isn't Kurt here? He's not ill, is he?'

'No, he's not ill. He's been called away on an assignment, that's all. He's asked me to stand in for him – with his apologies.'

Her disappointment was obvious, then her expression changed as she looked at him curiously. 'You're not the one he was telling me about – my grandmother's neighbour?'

'I am.'

Her spirits began to rise once more. 'Then you also knew my mother.'

Rudolf Gross's smile grew a trifle sheepish. 'Eva Koehn was the love of my young life,' he confessed. 'She was in the same class as my elder sister Karin, and by far the most beautiful of all her schoolfriends. They used to practise singing together at Kurt's parents' apartment in this very building.' He gestured up at the windows above. 'Sometimes, as a special treat, Karin would take me with her, and sometimes they would even come round to my parents' place for a sing-song. But, I must admit that, being at least five years younger, although Eva was very sweet to me, as a prospective suitor I didn't warrant as much as a second glance!'

285

Anna returned his smile as her excitement grew. Simply to be amongst people who knew her mother meant so much. 'Do you also work here, Herr Gross – in this building?'

'Rudi – please. And no, I don't work with Kurt, although I am a journalist too by profession. I work mainly for the national broadcasting service, as well as doing freelance journalism – foreign assignments for *Neues Deutschland* and that sort of thing.'

'I'm impressed.' If he contributed regularly to East Germany's main daily newspaper, he was nobody's fool. She followed him round the front of the car and murmured her thanks as he opened the front passenger door for her to enter.

He got in beside her. 'May I call you Anna?'

'Please do.'

'And you must call me Rudi,' he said, as he started the car and pulled out into the traffic. 'Well, Anna, I must warn you your grandmother's health is not good. In fact, she has had two bad heart-attacks in the past year or so.'

Anna's face was grave. Kurt had already warned her of that. 'You know her quite well?'

Rudi Gross nodded. 'I have had several conversations with her since she returned to Berlin. To tell you the truth, I am surprised that she came back at all. This city is not a place of happy memories for her. Her world fell apart here on *Kristallnacht* in 1938 and, like so many people after the war, she never managed to put the pieces together again.'

'Does she – does she know my mother was killed in the war?'

'That I do not know. She has never spoken to me of Eva in any context except before *Kristallnacht*.' His voice softened as he glanced across at her, 'She loves to reminisce about those years before '38, but it is as if a dark curtain came down that November night when they burned the synagogues and arrested her husband. She never saw him

286

again, you know – your grandfather – she never even found out what happened to him until after the war.'

'It's very difficult for those of us who never lived through that experience to comprehend what it must have been like.'

'Even for those of us who did live through it, Anna, it seems hardly credible now. I was just a boy when war broke out, but I had already seen the brutality and repression of the Nazi regime at first hand. My father was a Social Democrat and was arrested in 1933, shortly after Hitler came to power. I was still in kindergarten when he was imprisoned, and already a young man when he was released by the Allies in 1945. But by then it was already too late; he was a broken man. He died within six months.'

Grim stories of the past seemed to be the norm for everyone she met in this city. 'And what about you? It must have been terrible having to outwardly support a system that had done that to your own family.'

He swung the car off into a narrow side street and nodded grimly. 'I was barely seventeen when the war ended, but already I had been forced to leave school and join in the defence of the Fatherland.'

His hand left the steering-wheel to point to his right ear. The bottom of the lobe was missing and a faded scar ran up into the hair behind it. 'You see that – that was the result of too close an encounter with a piece of Russian shrapnel in the siege of Berlin, in the spring of '45.' He gave a bitter laugh and shook his head at the remembered folly of it all. 'There I was with a gun in my hands when I should still have been in school studying for my *Abitur*; instead I was being forced to fight the people I regarded as my country's saviours.'

They had left the narrow street to emerge into what seemed to be a grey wasteland of rubble and half-built multi-storey blocks of flats. He drew the car to a stop in front of a large apartment building that appeared to have been up for some time, judging by the state of the concrete which was already discolouring in places.

'We're here,' Rudi informed her, switching off the ignition and pulling on the handbrake. 'Frau Koehn lives on the second floor. In the apartment directly beneath my own, to be exact.'

Anna stared out of the windscreen as a great sense of sadness overwhelmed her. The old lady had come back from the country – to this. It must be a very far cry from life on the farm, and an even further one from her previous home on the Unter den Linden.

'She's very lucky,' she heard Rudi's voice continue in her ear. 'Not many people have the good fortune to have a whole apartment to themselves – even if it is only two rooms.'

'Do *you* have to share?' Anna asked.

'Happily, no.'

'You're not married, then?'

'Only to the Party. Body and soul.'

She looked at him quizzically across the small space between them. 'You've *never* been married?' For a man as undeniably attractive as he was she found that hard to believe.

'I didn't say that.' The blue eyes were smiling directly into hers. 'And I most certainly have been in love … Look, I'll show you.'

He reached into his inside jacket pocket and took out a brown leather wallet which he proceeded to open. He extracted a small photograph and handed it to her. Three teenage girls, their arms around each other, were smiling into the camera, and a small blond boy, bare-kneed and smiling shyly, was clinging to the skirts of the girl on the left of the picture.

Anna stared down at it. 'I take it the gorgeous little kid is you?'

He gave a modest grin. 'Guilty, I'm afraid … But it's the females who are the important ones. And I freely admit I was passionately in love with the one in the middle.'

Anna continued to gaze down at the photograph in her hands. The girl in the centre looked instantly familiar and was certainly the prettiest of the three.

Rudi gave a theatrical sigh. 'But as I told you earlier, she was much too old for me … Wouldn't look at me, in fact. She was much more interested in that old warrior Kurt Kessel, if I remember rightly.'

She knew now why he was smiling as she continued to gaze down at the picture of her mother. 'It's her, isn't it?'

'Yes, it's her. I thought you'd like to see it. So I looked it out specially and brought it with me.'

She was touched by his thoughtfulness as she studied the smiling faces of the three friends. They looked so young, so carefree; little could they know of what was to lie ahead. 'Who are the other two?' she asked softly.

'The one on the left with the long blonde plaits is my sister Karin; the small, darker, plumpish one on the right is Hanna Kessel. I believe you've already met her.'

Anna nodded as she handed back the photo. It was difficult to relate that overweight, dark-haired teenager to the glamorous bottle-blonde who now ran *Der Gefallene Engel*. 'Does your sister Karin still live in Berlin?'

Rudi shook his head. 'She moved to Leipzig after she married. She's now a children's doctor in a Polyklinik there.'

Anna nodded but said nothing as she watched him replace the picture in his wallet. Who could have imagined when that happy photograph was taken the fate that would befall each of those young girls? It would most certainly have been beyond even their own vivid young imaginations.

Rudi reached out and unexpectedly squeezed her hand. 'But enough of the past, Anna. This is Berlin 1966, and you are about to meet someone much more important to you than Eva's friends. Behind that lace curtain and the potted geranium up there is an old lady who is about to get the surprise of her life.'

Anna followed his gaze up to the small, white-painted window as her stomach turned over. Dear God, let it be a good one for her, she prayed inwardly. Let it be good for both of us …

Chapter Twenty-Seven

Anna followed Rudi up the two flights of concrete stairs and along a cream-tiled corridor, to pause in front of a door with the name 'Koehn' handwritten on a piece of paper stuck behind a small plastic plate.

They glanced at one another. 'Nervous?' he asked.

'A little.'

He gave an encouraging smile, then rapped sharply three times on the metal knocker before trying the handle. It opened. She was in. Anna held her breath as he put his head round the door to shout, 'Frau Koehn – it's Rudi Gross here. May I come in?'

From where she was standing, Anna could not make out the reply from within, but the smile on Rudi's face told her the answer had been in the affirmative. 'I usually just call and walk in,' he explained. 'The old lady has trouble walking and it saves her coming to the door … I know it's Kurt Kessel she's expecting, not me, but I'll explain what's happened – and at least she knows me well enough.'

Anna nodded but said nothing, wondering if the nervousness she felt inside was obvious on her face as she followed Rudi into a narrow hallway. It was devoid of furniture, but a metal coat-rack was fixed to one wall. A single dark-blue cloth coat hung there alongside a black umbrella. The two items looked strangely forlorn against the blank, whitewashed wall.

She could feel her heart pounding as he reached the living-room door and opened it. Rather than follow him in, she remained in the hallway and listened nervously as he explained that it was he and not Kurt Kessel who had brought the visitor from England to meet her.

'*Ach so* …' They were the first words she heard her grandmother utter. Then Rudi beckoned to her to join him in the living-room.

The old lady was sitting in a chair by the window – a smallish woman with thinning grey hair wound in a sparse plait around her head. Her skin was curiously unlined but there was a look of infinite sadness about her features, and her pale eyes had a misty quality to them, as if tears were never far from the surface. Her knotted hands were clasping a piece of knitting in her lap, which she immediately laid aside at the sight of her English visitor.

Rudi walked over to clasp her right hand in his and kiss her on both cheeks, then stood aside as he turned to introduce Anna. She stood awkwardly in the middle of the square of carpet, gazing down at the woman who had given birth to her own mother. Her eyes searched desperately for some flicker of recognition in the other's, but the old lady merely smiled politely as she waited for the introductions.

For her part, Margarete Koehn was perplexed. First she had expected Kurt Kessel, and she was looking forward to that. She had not set eyes on the Kessel boy since that awful night in November 1938 when he brought Eva safely home from singing practice with his sister Hanna. She had always had a soft spot for the Kessels' youngest son and felt bitterly disappointed at being deprived of the promised visit by him. Instead she was faced with her neighbour, Rudi Gross, who had appeared with this young stranger. From what Kurt had said she had presumed he was bringing a friend of Eva's from England, but this young woman was far too young to have been any friend of her daughter's.

Rudi was aware of the look of disappointment on her face as he sank down on one knee and clasped one of Margarete's hands in his. 'Frau Koehn,' he began hesitantly, 'this is not quite the visit you were expecting, but it is a very special one for you. You see this young lady here is no ordinary visitor …'

Anna held her breath as the old lady looked up at her, a puzzled frown etched across the pale skin of her forehead. 'Really?' her grandmother replied hesitantly.

'Yes, really, Frau Koehn … This young lady here is no ordinary friend of Eva's …'

Anna took a step forwards in response to a gesture from Rudi, and she too knelt down beside the old lady as he continued, 'You see, dear Frau Koehn, this is Anna – Eva's own daughter, and your granddaughter …'

Margarete Koehn drew in her breath sharply and shook her head. This was going too far. Much too far. 'No, no!' She made to extract her hand from Rudi's as she looked askance from one to the other. 'My daughter is dead. Eva is dead. She had no daughter.' Her voice was stridently defensive, almost harsh.

'It is true Eva is dead.' It was Anna herself who spoke, her voice shaking slightly from the emotion welling within her. 'She died in London during the bombing one night in May 1941,' she continued softly. 'She died in the bombs the same night she gave birth to me.'

The old lady gasped – a harsh strangled sound – and her hand flew to her throat as she looked from one to the other again, then back to Anna. Her weak eyes searched the stranger's face. What was she saying? What were they telling her? Why had they come to torture her like this? Was this some kind of terrible joke? She moved back in her chair, as if to distance herself from her tormentors.

But they would not let up. 'It's true,' Anna's voice was continuing in her ears. 'I am your granddaughter, Frau Koehn …' She wanted to say more but the words would not come as her throat closed up and her eyes began to swim. A single tear trickled down her cheek and the old lady reached out her hand to touch it. Whoever she was, this child was practising no joke. She was experiencing genuine emotion as she gazed back at her and whispered softly, 'You are my grandmother, Frau Koehn. You are my *Oma*.'

Margarete glanced at Rudi who was also experiencing the emotion of the moment, and his eyes were full of compassion for the feelings that were overwhelming them both. He nodded, as if to verify the truth of what she had just heard.

'You – you are my Eva's daughter?' The old lady's voice was barely audible as her eyes took in the long blonde hair and earnest expression on the young woman's face at her knee. She could be any pretty young woman on the streets of Berlin today – except for one thing ... Except for the eyes. No one else could have those eyes. They were her husband Martin's eyes, and Eva's eyes looking back into hers; dark and fathomless, the like of which she had never thought to see again. She let out a sob and flung her arms around her granddaughter's shoulders. 'Eva's child. You are Eva's child ...'

Rudi got up and walked to the window to look out into the cloudless blue of the summer sky as grandmother and grandchild embraced for the first time. Both were sobbing softly now as each endeavoured to comfort the other. He felt an intruder in this most personal moment in both their lives. 'If you will excuse me for a short time, I have a couple of important phone-calls I must make.'

He gave an encouraging smile to Anna behind the old lady's back and said quietly, 'I'll be downstairs in my apartment. Perhaps you'd like to come down and join me in half an hour or so, Anna?'

'Of – of course.' She got up from her knees and pulled a nearby chair close to the one on which her grandmother was seated, then once more clasped the arthritic hands in hers. 'Tell me about her,' she said softly. 'Tell me about my mother. Please ...'

And so for the next half-hour she listened as Margarete told Anna of Eva's young life in the Unter den Linden before the war, and of that terrible night in November 1938 when their world came to an end.

'We thought it was only for a short time, Anna ... Only for

293

a short time, you understand. *Oma* and I – we thought Martin would be released and it would all blow over, then we could send to London for Eva … It would be safe again and life would go on as normal.' She shook her head in remembered despair. 'But it didn't happen, you see … He never came back. It never blew over. Not for almost seven long years.'

She paused to take a deep erratic breath that rattled in her chest. 'The shock, it killed *Oma* soon afterwards, so very soon, and I had to leave our home. Jews were no longer allowed to own property or businesses, you see.'

Even after all these years she could still not fully understand. It was still some sort of terrible nightmare from which she had never quite woken up. 'I tried to tell them,' she continued softly. 'I tried to tell them *I* wasn't Jewish. I tried to tell them that I was *evangelisch*, like most of them had once been. But it didn't matter. I had contaminated myself by marrying a half-Jew – a *Mischling*.'

She began to sob softly once again: dry, tearless sobs that seemed to come from the very depths of her being. 'He was a good man, Anna. A good, good man.' She shook her head. It had all been so stupid, so tragically stupid. 'He didn't even know he was Jewish until the day they came to take him away. He kept telling them it was all some silly mistake. But they told him to ask his mother …'

Her fingers fiddled nervously with a small cameo brooch at her neck as she relived the horror of that moment in *Oma*'s bedroom. 'She had never told him, you see … She had never told him …'

She stared out of the window, past Anna's head. She was trembling now as she remembered those moments alone in the old lady's bedroom after they had taken him away. *Oma*, the strong one, the rock of their family, had wept for the first time since the death of her beloved Fritz, Martin's father. 'She kept repeating, "I am responsible. I should have told him years ago when that madman Hitler first came to power." But she couldn't, you see. It was Fritz's own wish that no one should know. He had witnessed the pogroms in the East and had been determined to put all that behind him. He loved his country and wanted to be a true German – nothing else.'

They looked at one another as the bitter irony of the old man's dearest wish sank in.

'And – and what happened to you?' Anna asked, hesitating at first, lest the opening of so many old wounds proved too painful to bear. The last thing she wanted to do was to add to her pain. 'During the war and after. What happened to you, *Oma*?'

The old lady's lips twisted into the semblance of a smile as she shook her head. 'There was a little poem going the rounds at the time,' she said, frowning slightly as she cast her mind back, remembering the words:

> *Lieber Gott mach mich stumm*
> *Dass ich nicht nach Dachau kumm.*
> *Lieber Gott mach mich taub*
> *Dass ich nicht am Radio schraub.*
> *Lieber Gott mach mich blind*
> *Dass ich alles herrlich find.*
> *Bin ich taub und stumm und blind*
> *Bin ich Adolfs liebstes Kind!'*

Her grandmother gave a small sigh of pleasure at remembering the nonsense verse after all those years. 'Did you understand?'

Anna smiled:

> 'Dear God make me dumb
> So I don't to Dachau come.
> Dear God make me deaf
> So I don't sit glued to the radio.
> Dear God make me blind
> So I everything wonderful find.
> If I'm deaf and dumb and blind
> Then I'm Adolf's favourite child!'

The old lady clapped her hands. She had never heard it in English before. 'That would have been the only way to be, you see, Anna, *mein Kind*. Only a blind, deaf, mute could have failed to see what was going on, could have failed to protest; and I was none of those things. They told me when he was arrested that I should be a good German and divorce him, but I couldn't do that. I loved him, you see, Anna. I tried to tell them, but they couldn't understand. They wouldn't understand. They kept talking about the blood – I had contaminated the blood. But I wasn't alone – oh no, I wasn't alone.' There was a defiance in her voice as she raised her chin and said quietly, 'There were others like me, you know. Many others – Aryan women who had married Jews, and not all of them agreed to divorce their husbands and be "good Germans" either. There was a protest – a real protest by them, did you know that?'

Her granddaughter shook her head, ashamed of how very little she knew about that period in her family's past.

'Oh, yes, there was a protest, all right, by over six thousand of us. Think of that, Anna – over six thousand Aryan women whose Jewish husbands had been arrested got up in arms and created such a stir that even the SS thugs were impressed. We all gathered that day, many pushing infants in prams, with toddlers hanging on to their coat tails, outside Number 2 Rosenstrasse – that was one of the Berlin centres for Jewish transportation to the camps – and we made such a fuss, I can't tell you.'

'Did it do any good?'

Her grandmother sighed. 'Not for me, alas. But a few whose husbands had only recently been arrested got them back. That protest must have been around 1943, for Martin had already been gone several years.'

'And you never saw him again.'

Her faded eyes gazed out into the blue of the sky beyond the window of the small apartment, and her voice faltered. 'I – I met a young man once, long after the war, who had been on the same transport out of Berlin as Martin. He came to the farm where I worked after the war to deliver goods. A seed salesman, he was. He told me they had been taken to the same assembly point, at 26 Grosse Hamburger Strasse, it was. Hans, the young seedsman, remembered the address: it had once been an old people's home, you see. His grandfather had died there, and he wondered why on earth they were being taken to an old folk's home.' She gave a bitter smile. 'It didn't take him long to find out! From there they were taken to the Putlitzstrasse goods yards where they were loaded into open cattle trucks for the long journey to the East. Hundreds of miles in freezing conditions. First Theresienstadt, then Auschwitz, he said. Martin died in Auschwitz in the spring of 1941.'

A shiver ran through Anna. It was the same season that had seen the death of his daughter and the birth of his granddaughter. 'And they put you in a camp, too.'

Her grandmother nodded wearily. 'It had to happen sooner or later. I wouldn't do what they asked. I had no idea Martin was dead. I wouldn't consider divorcing him and I wouldn't be quiet. After the protest in 1943 I became even more active. I had seen other women get their men back, you see, so I kept making a noise – asking people, writing to officials, newspapers, anything and anybody I could think of to find out what had happened to him. He was all I had left, Anna – with *Oma* dead and Eva gone. But they didn't like that. They didn't like that at all. They asked me if I'd like to join him – be resettled in the East as he had been. They told me at Gestapo headquarters that he had been sent to Poland – resettled there, they said – and I could join him if I wanted to. They were sending transports out there every day.' Her eyes searched Anna's. 'What would you have done, *mein Kind*? They told me we could be together again.'

'But they didn't send you to Poland, did they?' Anna said softly.

'They sent me to Ravensbrück. And I never saw him again … I never saw anyone again, any of my loved ones …'

Her voice tailed off and she sank back against the cushion of her chair. Never, never in the past twenty-one years had she spoken at such length about that terrible time. The energy seemed to have drained from her. 'Forgive me, child,' she whispered. 'Forgive me.'

Anna knew words were inadequate for the thoughts that were going through both their minds at that moment. She could only stroke the work-worn hand in hers as she gazed at the crumpled figure of her grandmother. The years had weighed heavily on her, and reliving the worst of them had taken a lot out of her – too much. 'Now it's my turn,' she said softly. 'Now it's my turn …'

And so she began to tell what little she knew of Eva's life after she left Berlin for London. The details were pitifully few but the old lady devoured them eagerly, shaking her head every so often as she gazed at the young woman beside her. How could she have failed to recognize her? It could be Eva to the life sitting here beside her. 'It is a miracle, child. A miracle to have found you.'

Anna clasped the swollen hands even more tightly. 'I can't let you go again,' she whispered. 'I mustn't lose you. You must come back to London to live with me.'

But the old lady shook her head. 'No, child – Berlin is my home. I was born here and I will die here. Here I stay, I can do no other.'

Anna recognized the final sentence; it came from Martin Luther. He too refused to be forced to flee in the face of oppression. But she was disappointed nevertheless, and it was obvious in her voice. 'Here in the East? But life could be so much more comfortable in the West!'

'Comfort? What is comfort?' The old lady gave a disparaging laugh, and touched Anna's head as one would do to a small child not yet old enough to understand the complexities of the adult world. '*Kristallnacht* taught me one thing,

Anna *mein Kind* – it taught me that material possessions count for nothing. Political systems count for nothing. They come and go. It is people who are important. The people on that farm, they were good to me. What did it matter to them if it was Ulbricht or Adenauer who was governing them?'

She gave a weary smile, 'If we could survive Hitler, we can survive anyone! No, I came back to settle here because this is the part of Berlin I know best. Why should I move elsewhere just because they build a stupid wall?'

'It doesn't bother you then, the Wall?'

'I survived the barbed wire and electrified fences of the camps, didn't I? What can bother me now?'

Anna knew she was right. Her grandmother had survived the terrors of the Third Reich to find a kind of peace here in this forlorn little flat two storeys above the wasteland that was now East Berlin. But it was her home. Anna had no right to expect her to leave it.

It was an emotional leave-taking, with Anna promising to visit again as soon as possible. As she closed the door of the small apartment behind her, she found her legs could barely carry her downstairs. The meeting had drained her emotionally and physically, but had been worth every second.

Chapter Twenty-Eight

Anna was relieved Karl was not at home when she got back to the apartment at a little after three. She could not have faced him. The effect of the meeting with her grandmother had left her feeling drained and distinctly on edge.

She had not felt like calling in on Rudi Gross in the apartment downstairs so soon after that emotional encounter with her grandmother, but she knew he would be waiting, and, after all, it would have been impolite not to thank him properly, for he had been responsible for the visit in the first place.

He seemed genuinely pleased to have acted as go-between and she felt strangely comforted knowing that the old lady would have someone like him close at hand, once she had returned to London. They had chatted for over an hour and she was surprised how well informed he was about life in the West, and was even more surprised when he suggested he might visit her in London. 'I thought it was almost impossible for East German citizens to get through the Wall,' she had said, recalling how Karl and his friends regularly risked their lives getting people to the other side. But he had merely rewarded her with an enigmatic smile, before saying quietly, 'You don't believe everything you read in your newspapers, do you, Anna?' She had had no answer, but resolved not to be in the least surprised if he did turn up in London. He seemed to be a man who meant what he said.

Rudi had driven her back to the checkpoint after making a careful note of her address and telephone number in London. They had spoken little in the car. By nature he seemed to be a man of few words and she was still wrapped in thoughts of her grandmother. Over coffee in his apartment, he had recalled one or two more anecdotes about her mother as a young girl and she could already feel herself becoming more a part of the young woman who had given birth to her during that horrific night in the Blitz.

For the first time, the sight of the armed guards at the border had brought a feeling of anger mixed with apprehension to her as they approached in the black Skoda. She had found part of her family there in the East and those people with their green uniforms and loaded guns, with their watchtowers and barbed wire, were creating enemies where they did not exist. 'Is there really a need for all this?' she had asked Rudi, as they pulled up just in front of the checkpoint. 'Will this awful Wall ever come down?'

His eyes had darkened. 'Not in my lifetime or yours, Anna, of that I am sure. The Party needs it to protect the people.'

'The Party needs it to protect itself!' she said, finding it impossible to keep the bitterness from her voice.

He had leaned over and opened the car door for her to get out. 'They are waiting to check your papers. We can continue this discussion at another time – in another place – in London, perhaps?'

She had held out her hand to be shaken. 'Till our meeting in London, then.'

And so she had left East Berlin behind and returned to the Kant Strasse apartment to ponder on the turn of events of the past day. Things were happening so fast, she could barely put her chaotic thoughts in order. But apart from the emotional upheaval of meeting her grandmother, when her thoughts returned to the man she now knew to be her father, most of all she was aware of an enormous sense of guilt overwhelming her. Here she was living in Karl's apartment, knowing he had already fallen in love with her, and allowing him to assist her in her plan to sabotage her father's career, when, in her own heart, she knew she did not love him. No matter how she tried to rationalize it, she could not escape

301

the feeling she was using him, and it was not a thought that rested easy on her mind.

It was almost five o'clock before Karl returned and he sensed an unease within her which he put down to the imminent meeting with her father. 'Don't worry about it,' he said, with more bravado than he felt, as he threw his jacket down on the nearest chair. 'It'll all be over in a few hours. What time do you expect to be bringing him back here, anyway?'

She froze at the thought. 'Oh, between nine and ten I would imagine. He may suggest we go for a bite to eat after our swim.'

'If you suggest you eat here it will get it over with more quickly.'

She grimaced. 'You make it sound like an execution.' The words hung in the air between them.

He decided a change of subject would be a good idea. 'By the way, did you hear the news? Brigitte Bardot has married some German by the name of Sachs.'

'She must have good taste.' She was trying to be conciliatory to make up for the morning.

'It could be catching.'

'I beg your pardon?'

'Her good taste – it could be catching.'

She wrinkled her brow, not quite catching the allusion, as she redid her lipstick in the mirror.

But he was persistent. 'Marriage to a German, Anna ...'

She could feel him coming up behind her, until his face was just behind her left shoulder in the mirror. His arms went around her waist, as he studied her face in the glass. 'You know what I'm saying?'

Her heart sank. 'I – I think so,' she answered hesitantly. Don't let it be, she thought desperately. Please, don't let it be. Not today of all days, she couldn't bear it.

'Do I have to spell it out? Do you want me to go down on bended knee?' The look in his eyes in the mirror told her it was no joke.

'Please, Karl ...' She attempted a laugh but it died on her lips as he sank to one knee at her side, his hands clutching at hers. The lipstick went rolling over the carpet.

'Leave it!' he commanded. 'Goddamn it, Anna, I'm serious!' He jumped to his feet, his face beneath the beard colouring at the spectacle he knew he was making of himself. 'I'm asking you to marry me and all you can do is scrabble after a goddam lipstick!'

She retrieved the small gilt tube from beneath the coffee table where it had rolled and stuffed it into her handbag. Her face was flushed and she was aware of deliberately avoiding his eyes.

'Look at me, damn you!'

She obeyed and his voice softened as he came across and put his arms around her. 'You might not believe this, but this is the first time I have ever asked anyone this question. And I'm asking you now. Marry me, Anna. Be my wife.'

She gazed up at him in a mixture of disbelief and mounting panic. 'But – but you hardly know me.'

He relaxed his hold of her to say impatiently, 'What else is there to know? I know all your opinions – God knows I have read enough of them over the past few years. I know more about your background than almost anyone, I should imagine. And I enjoy making love with you more than with any woman I've ever known ... What else is there? That is more than enough to convince me I don't just want small bits of you, Anna. I want all of you. I want all of you – forever.'

'I'm not a thing you can own, Karl.'

He let go of her to make an impatient gesture with his hands. 'Hell, I know that. And you know what I'm trying to say. I may not be expressing myself all that well, but the fact remains I'm asking you to be my wife.'

'I don't know what to say.'

'Then say yes.'

She made no reply, but bent and took two cigarettes from an open packet lying on the coffee table. She lit them both

303

from the table lighter and handed him one. He took it grudgingly, his eyes following her every move. At last she spoke. 'I – I'll have to think about it. I need time.'

'How long?'

'A day or so – I don't really know.' She knew nothing in the world could persuade her to accept him and her heart went out to him, but now was not the time for true confessions; she could not afford to alienate him at this late stage in her plans. 'I'll let you know tonight.'

'Tonight you could be back on a plane to England. It certainly won't be safe for you to stay here.'

She knew he was speaking the truth. 'All right, I promise I'll let you know tonight before I leave this apartment – whatever happens.'

He sighed. He knew it was the best he was going to get out of her right now.

'Will I fix you something to eat before I go out?' she asked, heading for the kitchen. Go out – she was making it sound like she was just popping round to the butchers.

'Thanks, but no thanks.' His appetite had completely gone. There was something about her demeanour since he got back today that told him she would not be marrying him, not now, not ever, and the knowledge tore at his heart.

He walked through to the bedroom and flopped down on the bed, staring at the ceiling as he smoked the remains of his cigarette. He had chanced his hand proposing out of the blue like that. He should have waited – until they were making love, perhaps – a time like that. But time had all but run out for them making love – at least here in Berlin. He knew her stay in the city was drawing to a close. It just wouldn't be safe for her to hang around after tonight. He stared at the ceiling then closed his eyes, as if to shut out the reality of the situation. He wanted her. He wanted her badly – right now – but he was damned if he was going to go crawling back through there to face yet another rejection.

His legs were crossed and Anna could see the soles of his

shoes resting on the cotton duvet cover through the half-open door. At any other time she would have been tempted to go through and console him, despite what it might lead to. But not now, not tonight. Her mind was too full of the past and the immediate future to spend time worrying about the present.

She walked over to the television and switched it on. It was the end of a news programme and the announcer was relaying the main points once more. The lead stories were on the Social Democrats' recent success in the North Rhine-Westphalia state elections, and the continuing success of West Germany's economic miracle, particularly where their own city of West Berlin was concerned. The newsreader went on to stress, that this success was underpinned by the secure knowledge that West Berlin security, like that of West Germany itself, was assured by the presence of a strong NATO alliance, led by the United States.

Then, as Anna watched, a photograph of her father flashed up on the screen, surrounded by the other leading participants at the conference presently being held less than a mile from where she now stood. The young man went on to give a brief outline of the morning's defence talks in the city, then another shot of the smiling delegates shaking hands appeared, and she hurriedly reached across to switch off the set.

Seeing him there surrounded by all those other military men was too much. And talking to her grandmother this morning had reinforced in her mind just what a heel he must have been to have walked out on her mother like that. No, she decided, she felt no guilt at what she had resolved to do. Men like William J. Rutherford used other people. Her mother had merely been used to satisfy his sexual appetite during his wartime stay in Britain, in the same way the people of Hiroshima and Nagasaki had been used to demonstrate the power of his invention. And now *she* would use *him*. Her face was set as firmly as her resolve as she headed for

305

the bathroom to finish her preparations for the evening ahead.

Karl only reappeared a few minutes before she was due to leave for her appointment outside the Husum Hotel. His face was devoid of expression as he poured himself a coffee from the lukewarm remains in the pot and took it through to the living-room to drink. 'You're all prepared then – to go through with it.'

She nodded. 'And you?'

'I got the new spool this afternoon on my way home.'

Nerves clutched at her stomach as she stole a last look at herself in the mirror. Her face looked pale and drawn, not at all the picture of someone just off to enjoy herself at Berlin's favourite holiday spot.

She lifted the nylon sports bag containing her swimming things and the food and drink off the coffee table. She had bought some cold chicken legs and fruit from the delicatessen on the corner, and, not having a swimsuit with her, she had indulged in a shocking-pink bikini from a shop in the *Europa Center*. Its brevity had taken her aback when she tried it on, on returning to the apartment that afternoon, but she consoled herself with the thought that that was all the better for her purposes.

Karl came to the door with her as she prepared to leave. 'You're sure you don't want a lift?'

'No thanks. I can't risk it.'

He moved awkwardly from one foot to the other, as if uncertain whether to embrace her or not. She solved the problem for him by leaning across to place a light peck on his lips. 'Good luck, then.' His voice was gruff.

'Thanks, Karl.'

He watched her disappear down the stairs, his gloom deepening along with his apprehension. He had wanted to go through with this for her. It was a task he could do that he knew she could call on very few others, if anyone, to perform; a very personal favour that he had felt would somehow bind them together. But that was not the case now. She had been slipping away from him, he could feel it. But maybe she had never really been that close in the first place. Maybe it had been all in his imagination. Maybe their lovemaking had merely been a way of showing how grateful she was for what he was doing for her. Maybe … Maybe … So many maybes …

He sighed deeply as he turned and walked back into the empty apartment to face yet another evening alone …

Anna could see him as she turned the corner fifty yards away. He was standing in the early evening sunshine by one of the stone pillars that added a touch of palladian grandeur to the late Fifties hotel. He was dressed casually in light-grey canvas trousers and a pale-blue, short-sleeved shirt. A towel roll, no doubt holding his swimming trunks, was under one arm. He was looking down the street in the opposite direction, one canvas beachshoe tapping nervously on the concrete step. She was almost upon him before he turned and set eyes on her for the first time.

'You came.'

'Didn't you expect me to?'

Bill Rutherford gave a strained smile. He had been so darned worked up about this meeting that he had already had two double whiskies in the bar; a practice he did not usually indulge in before six in the evening. 'I've hired a car,' he said, ignoring the question and pointing towards the hotel carpark. 'It's over there. You stay put and I'll get it.'

She obeyed his command, perching on the wall and dangling her bare legs like a child, as she watched him walk quickly in the direction of the two-year-old Mercedes convertible. He was nervous, she could sense it. But then so was she, for a very different reason.

He drew the car up at the foot of the steps and she ran down to join him, sliding into the plush leather upholstery of the front passenger seat and closing the door behind her. 'Impressive!'

'It's hired,' he replied, stating the obvious, and thinking ruefully of the four-year-old Lincoln in the garage back home. He doubted if it would elicit such a compliment from her.

'I've been looking forward to this,' she lied, as he pulled the car out from the kerb into the early evening traffic. 'Have *you*?'

He grinned. 'Yes and no.'

'Meaning?'

'Meaning I don't know what the hell I'm doing here, but I'm sure as hell enjoying it.' It was as near the truth as he could get.

She sank back in the seat with a satisfied smile. 'Tell me, General,' she said, deliberately using his official title. 'Have you ever been unfaithful before?'

The limousine swerved dangerously close to the kerb as he threw her a startled glance. 'You don't pull any punches, I'll give you that! Do you want an honest answer?'

'That's the only kind that interests me.'

He could feel the palms of his hands grow moist and he gripped the steering-wheel that bit tighter. He felt distinctly unnerved as he thought for a moment, then said quietly, 'Only once. Geneva 1955, to be precise.'

'The Atoms for Peace Conference.'

'Good God, what are you – a walking encyclopaedia?'

'No, just a journalist with a good memory. I wrote a piece about it for my school newspaper. It was my first time in print, and no one ever forgets that.' She could have added that Owen Lloyd-Jones, the father who had given her his unreserved love and affection for over twenty years, had framed it and hung it in his study, where it had remained until his death a few years ago. But instead she said nothing of that and asked another question, 'Was she very beautiful?'

'Not as beautiful as you.' He was speaking the truth.

'Compliments get you everywhere, General.'

A thin film of sweat broke out on his brow and his upper lip. That was exactly what he had been dreaming of, yet half dreading, from the moment they met.

Chapter Twenty-Nine

The Mercedes was doing over 100 mph as it swept along the Avus, the superhighway that cuts through the Grunewald, on the way to the Wannsee. Bill had put the top down once they had left the vicinity of the hotel, and, despite her basic feelings about the situation, Anna could not ignore the sense of sheer exhilaration she experienced as the warm wind whipped her hair back behind her head and brought tears streaming from her eyes. The sensation was not to last, however, for on the last mile of the six to Berlin's favourite lake the limousine was forced to slow to crawling pace amid the nose-to-tail traffic.

'Poor so-and-sos,' she murmured, as she glanced across at the occupants of the other cars sweltering in the early evening sun. 'A convertible is the only way to travel in this weather!'

She was almost sorry when eventually they reached the Wannsee and joined the queue of cars nosing their way along the already crowded lakeside. It was with the greatest difficulty they found a space to park, just next to the place where they hired out the sailboats.

The golden sands that bordered the lake were already crowded as they made their way from the car to the beach. He bought her an ice-cream from a van doing a roaring trade with the hoards of bronzed sun-worshippers. It seemed as if most of the population of the western half of the city was here to enjoy what was left of the day.

Above them was a sky of flawless blue, save for the vapour trails of jet-fighters that criss-crossed it constantly. 'Soviets,' Bill said, as he saw her looking up. 'But I bet those boys would give their eye-teeth to be down here with us right now!' She had no doubt he was right.

As they wandered down the sandy path leading to the beach, Anna envied the lucky ones sheltered from the direct heat of the sun as they lay in the shade of the gaily-coloured beach huts that edged the shore.

The latest Motown hit blared from a nearby transistor radio and from somewhere in the midst of the surrounding crowd she heard a male voice, quite obviously from south of the Mason-Dixon line, calling to a child. It was probably one of the servicemen from the American sector, but who was to say there would not be others from the NATO delegation attempting to escape the heat of the city in the same way? She turned to Bill. 'What if someone was to recognize you – to see you with me – one of your men, say? What would they say?'

Her companion gave a fatalistic shrug as he bit into the end of his cone. 'Lucky swine, most probably. Knowing the guys I work with.'

The answer both pleased and surprised her. 'They're all quite human, then – all that sober-sided retinue we see surrounding you on television and in the newspapers?'

'Too human sometimes,' he said, avoiding a small child on a bicycle. 'That's what keeps the KGB in business.'

The child, a boy, toppled off and sprawled in the grassy verge just ahead of them, and Bill bent to help him to his feet and right the bike before turning back to Anna, with a touch of irony in his voice, 'The weakness of the flesh is something no government can legislate against.'

'From the President down,' she added, remembering the reputation the late Jack Kennedy had enjoyed as a ladies' man.

'They're men like the rest of us. Why should those in power be any less human than the guy next door?'

'So you think L.B.J. is quite likely to be at it as well?'

He laughed. 'You'll have to ask him that question!'

I just might at that, she thought. An interview with the American President would be quite a coup – and to get his thoughts on adultery would guarantee international syndication for any article.

'Have you had much to do with him – L.B.J., I mean?'

'Uh huh … More so recently.'

'What do you make of him?'

'As a man or as a President?'

'As President will do for starters. Do you think he'll settle for some sort of compromise over Vietnam or is he hell-bent on victory at all costs?' The journalist in her could not resist the question.

'Lord, that's a tough one for a hot day!' He swatted a fly from his face and thought for a moment. 'On the one hand he's fond of describing his strategy over there as one of seduction rather than rape …'

'What the heck is that supposed to mean?'

He gave a slow smile as he rested his arm around her shoulders. 'It means a slow moving into North Vietnam, always being prepared to draw back if China slaps us down,' he explained patiently. 'But on the other hand he said to me himself just last month that some sort of modus vivendi might be reached if someone – meaning one of us – can come up with an OK solution to suit both sides.'

Anna raised her eyebrows. 'The guy talks in riddles. What on earth does he mean by an "OK solution"?'

'That's exactly what I asked him and he countered the question by asking me if I'd any idea of where the expression "OK" came from.'

'And did you?'

'Nope,' he shook his head emphatically. 'So he went on to explain how it originated with the Choctaw Indians. Seemingly it means, "We can agree on a solution now, providing you aren't so all-fired set on perfection." "That just about sums it up, Bill," he said. "It's over to you guys now."'

Anna looked sceptical. 'And *can* you come up with an "OK solution"?'

He gave a weary grin. 'Honey, that's the sixty-five-thousand-dollar question – and I don't intend finding an answer to it today! ... Let's just say right this minute I've got certain other things on my mind than solving the world's problems!'

She looked up at him and caught his eye. 'Such as, for instance?' There was a deliberately coquettish air to her question.

But he wasn't going to get caught out. 'Oh, I don't know ... Getting a tan, I guess.'

She glanced across at his already bronzed skin. 'I would say that's a pretty superfluous ambition. You look like you've just come back from a fortnight in the sun.'

'Actually so I have. I took the family on holiday down to Florida before flying out here.'

Anna looked away and wished she had never mentioned it. Just who exactly did this 'family' consist of? One part of her was desperately curious to find out and the other part equally keen not to know. The less she discovered about the personal life of this man who had sired her, the easier her task would be.

The crowds were now much greater as they skirted the edge of the sand and the conversation lapsed for a minute or so as they picked their way between the sprawled bodies to pause about fifty yards from the water's edge and look about them.

There was a multitude of small craft out on the lake itself: canoes, rowing-boats, racing sculls and speedboats; but it was the yachts which provided the best spectacle with their colourful sails contrasting brilliantly with the azure blue of the water and the sky overhead. Nearer to the shore young and old alike lay sprawled on airbeds listlessly paddling in the warmth of the shallows.

'Jeez!' A giant beachball caught Bill in the back of the head and a young woman ran up to apologize profusely in German, while her young family stood around stifling giggles in the background.

'*Bitte! Bitte!* OK. OK. Forget it! *Macht nichts!* I'll live!' Bill assured her, before turning to Anna. 'Let's make for somewhere a bit quieter,' he muttered, echoing her own thoughts as he took her arm. 'How about those trees over there?'

She allowed herself to be ushered to the small copse of pines a hundred feet or so back from the water. Their aromatic branches offered a welcome, verdant shade from the warmth of the sun and they were far enough back from the sand to escape the attention of the ball-throwers and other sun-worshippers on the beach.

'This'll do just fine,' he said as he let go her arm to discard his shirt, then throw his towel on to the grass and sink down on top of it. He stretched out, his arms behind his head and gave a comfortable sigh as he watched her spread out the two towels she had brought beside him, one for herself to lie on, and one for the picnic.

'Looks good,' he commented, as she unpacked the cold chicken and fruit and handed him the bottle of wine to uncork.

As she watched him struggle with the bottle-opener, she noticed for the first time the faint silver streaks of faded scars that cut across the lower part of his chest, to disappear beneath the blue stretch nylon of his bathing trunks. What were they: old operation scars, or long-faded battle wounds? She had no way of telling, but whatever their origin there was no denying he had been in a pretty bad way at one time.

He had trouble with the opener, then the cork exploded from the neck of the bottle with a loud pop and the clear liquid fizzed out in a gush covering his hand and arm. 'Mmm, old and fairly dry – just like myself,' he grinned, as he licked it from his soaking fingers, and his eyes scanned the label on the wine.

'You're not so old.' She searched her bag for some paper tissues and handed them across to him.

'Old enough to know better, as they say,' he commented wryly, as he mopped up the remaining spillage, then reached

314

for two glasses. He was very conscious of the disparity in their ages and could not resist the next question. 'How old are *you*, Anna? Or is that an ungentlemanly thing to ask?'

'Old enough,' she answered softly.

Their eyes met and he smiled, but could not hold her gaze. 'What made you agree to come out here with me today?'

'I like you.'

'Is that all?'

'Isn't that reason enough?'

He shook his head. It was something he had thought a lot about over the past few hours. He just couldn't figure what was in it for her, why she should be bothering with a much older man like him. There must be dozens of younger guys queuing up to date her. 'I'm a lot older than you,' he said, sitting back down on the bed of dry grass beside her. 'Twenty years, at least. And you must know I'm married.'

'Must I?'

'Well, I'm wearing a ring, and you're a pretty sharp young lady, if you don't mind me saying so.'

She accepted one of the glasses of wine he had poured and raised it to her lips. 'What attracts any young woman to an older man?'

'You tell me.' He was genuinely curious.

She gave a slow smile and sat up on the towel as she tapped her lower lip thoughtfully with the glass. 'Don't they say power is the ultimate aphrodisiac? Maybe it's your four-star uniform that turns me on.'

He gave a hollow laugh and averted his eyes once more as he took a gulp of his own drink. 'In that case I'm sorry that I left it back at the hotel!' Then his smile faded slightly. 'So you think I'm pretty powerful, is that it?'

'Aren't you?'

He studied the glass in his hand, then fixed his eyes on some distant spot on the lake. 'I was once – very powerful,' he answered with some hesitancy. 'In fact, the decisions I was once party to changed the whole world ...

315

> When the white flame in us is gone,
> And we that lost the world's delight
> Stiffen in darkness, left alone
> To crumble in our separate night ...'

His voice tailed off as he sat lost in his own thoughts for a moment. Then he gave an embarrassed half-laugh. 'Rupert Brooke,' he said. 'Always one of my favourites. It's from a poem called "Dust". Pretty appropriate for my life once.'

'You mean at Los Alamos, when you were working on the first atomic bomb?'

He nodded, no longer surprised by her knowledge of his background. 'Los Alamos and the guys who worked there – they were something special. It was a time apart. A time for crossing frontiers that no one in the realms of science had ever dreamt existed a generation before. We held the power of the universe in our hands – for good or ill – we had created it. We had split the atom and harnessed its energy. To be alive then – to be part of it ...' he shook his head, 'that was something, Anna. That was really something ... It's different now. The decisions that really count are all political. The scientists are no longer more powerful than the politicians or the military. If we ever were.'

'But you are part of the military – a very major part of it.'

'That's true. And I'm proud to be in the position I am. I'm proud to be leading the West's fight to keep Communism at bay.'

'You have no doubts about your political role?'

'I have a framed motto on my desk in Washington, Anna; it comes from *Measure for Measure* and it reads:

> Our doubts are traitors,
> And make us lose the good oft we might win,
> By fearing to attempt.

It was a new one on her, but very apt. 'So you had no doubts in 1945 and you have no doubts now.'

'None whatsoever.'

'You're a very lucky man, General.'

He was lying stretched out, resting on one elbow now, and studying her closely over the top of his wine glass. 'And you, Anna, what do you believe in?'

She hesitated. 'Are we still talking politics?'

'If you like.'

'British Socialism,' she answered finally.

'Isn't that a contradiction in terms?'

She laughed. 'That's usually my line!'

'No, I'm serious.' He pulled a long reed of dry grass from a clump beside his elbow and chewed on it thoughtfully before continuing, 'This is 1966, Anna. We're more than halfway through the twentieth century. Don't you think it's high time all the "isms" in this world became "wasms"? Don't you think it's time we began putting the freedom of the individual before the power of the state? Why do you think I'm still bustin' a gut at my age building up our nuclear arsenal, and am so determined to keep it the most powerful in the world?'

He looked across at her, challenging her to answer. She said nothing.

'Because I care dearly for the values we have in the West, that's why. My country fought a revolution to build a land based on justice and freedom for all and I aim to keep it that way.' He gave a half-hearted attempt at a smile and lapsed into an embarrassed silence after what had turned out to be much more of a speech than he intended.

'Next you'll be telling me you grew up in a log cabin and shoes were for Sunday.'

'That wouldn't be too far removed from the truth.'

She sat up and wound her arms around her knees as she looked at him sceptically. 'Oh come now, General. Are you or are you not the epitome of the Ivy League WASP?'

'Well, I can't deny I'm white, of basically Anglo-Saxon descent, and Protestant – and yes, I did go to an Ivy League university, as you put it, but I certainly didn't start life with any of the advantages you imply by that remark. There was barely a tin spoon, let alone a silver one, in this mouth, I can assure you.'

'Tell me about it – that log cabin,' she said with ill-disguised irony, as she refilled both their glasses. 'I don't suppose for a minute poor white folks like you could afford such luxuries as this wine, for example.'

He chose to disregard her cynicism and his eyes softened perceptibly as he shook his head. 'No, but we had something far better. My Grandma made the finest elderberry wine in the whole of the Carolinas!' He laughed. 'How's that for a totally unbiased remark!'

She looked at him through narrowed eyes. 'But you believe it.'

'Sure I do. My Grandma Ryan was a real mountain woman and I remember spending my summers up there at Hunter's Creek, with her and Grandpa before they both passed on. We'd watch the elders come into bloom in July, then, just before I was due to leave for home in September, when the berries had turned to that beautiful purple-black and were bursting with juice, I'd be sent to pick them. I tell you that elderberry wine was like nothing you ever tasted. And that wasn't all she did. She also made all the soap that my folks would sell in their hardware store throughout the rest of the year.'

'She made her own soap?'

'Sure she did. Made it the real way too, with pure hickory ash straight from the fireplace. None of that trashy oak ash stuff for her! She'd put it in a hopper and strain water through it to make the lye, then she'd boil it up with all the grease and cracklin' and other bits and pieces from the old hogs that Grandpa had slaughtered for meat. Funny thing was, the mixture could only be made by the light of the moon, or she swore it would never firm or turn white, and it could only be stirred with a sassafras stick. I never did find out why …'

He fell silent and Anna shifted uneasily on her towel. She felt small for having mocked at what she did not comprehend. 'It – it must have been marvellous for a small boy experiencing that kind of a life … I mean, it must have all but gone by now.'

He nodded and gave a wry smile. 'Gone – like them.'

'Did you ever go back – afterwards, I mean: when you were grown up?'

Again he nodded, but the smile was gone. 'I did once, but it was a mistake. There was nothing there anymore. Hunter's Creek had all but disappeared. The old horse and buggy road to their home was overgrown with weeds, and the cabin itself …' He shook his head as he remembered the roof, each one of the oak shingles hewn with his grandfather's axe, and now with great gaping holes. No chickens scratched around the porch anymore, and in an outbuilding he had found the hoe on which his grandmother had baked all those delicious hoe-cakes amidst the glowing embers of the hearth. Billy-cakes, she had called them, because he had loved them so. A peculiar smell had seemed to linger about the old place; just what he could not quite distinguish. The smell of a lost childhood, perhaps? For never again were there to be golden days like those. Never again after his sixth summer had he experienced such joy, for the following winter had seen his grandparents follow each other into those shallow hillside graves within a period of two weeks over Christmas. Pneumonia, the doctor had said. It was the first time he had heard the word; it sounded a fearsome thing. The Blue Mountains could be cruel to those who loved them. Just as people could be.

Being torn from them – the two people he had loved most dearly – without the chance to say a proper goodbye had remained an open wound long into adulthood. And maybe that was what made him feel so much sympathy at the very beginning when he first met Eva. He too knew what it was like to lose those he loved.

He swallowed the remains of his wine in one gulp and reached for the bottle, pausing with it halfway to his glass, as, noticing the one opposite was also empty, he asked politely, 'More wine, Eva?'

He could not understand the frozen look that came over Anna's face, or the reason for her getting up from the grass so quickly.

The effect of hearing her mother's name from his lips was electric and she had difficulty in curbing the biting retort that sprang to her tongue. To have responded in such a way would have been to give herself away completely. That, she could not afford to do at this late stage. 'It's far too hot,' she called, already running in the direction of the water. 'I'm going in for a swim!'

She cast off her clothes as she ran and by the time he joined her she had already been in the water for some minutes. She regretted her action in running off like that almost immediately. She had to curb her feelings and do or say nothing that would give him any grounds for suspicion at all.

He was content to sit beneath the trees and watch her at first, and enjoy another glass of wine along with his chicken leg. She was a strange girl. Like quicksilver. But the more she surprised him by her actions or remarks, the more intrigued he became.

She was beckoning to him to join her and, after wiping the chicken-grease from his fingers, he undressed quickly down to his swimming trunks. He was aware of her watching him as he ran down the beach and into the water, and was thankful for those two weeks in Florida that had bronzed the normally pale skin of his body. He ran on until the water was lapping around his waist, then dived in and broke into a powerful crawl to join her where she was doing a leisurely side-stroke several yards further out.

'I thought you were never coming.' She flopped backwards in the water to lie floating on her back, her eyes closed against the brightness of the sun. Despite her closed eyes, she

320

could sense him looking at her as he circled her lazily, his eyes taking in the litheness of her young body and the halo of pale blonde hair that floated around her head.

They remained in the water for over half an hour, sometimes having half-hearted races to the shore, but more often just lazily floating in the sunspeckled blue, their faces turned to the dazzling brightness of the heavens.

Out there a hundred yards from shore, the noise on the beach had receded to a distant hum and the still blistering heat was counteracted by the blissful coolness of the water. Anna even found herself forgetting occasionally the reason for her being there, then she would catch a glimpse of him watching her, out of the corner of her eye, and she would be brought back immediately to the chilling reality of the situation.

'I'll race you for the shore again – this time right back to the picnic,' he called eventually, as a fresh breeze blew up and the sun began to dip in the cloudless heavens. 'Last to get there pays a forfeit!'

Before she could agree or disagree he had broken into one of his powerful crawls and was heading for the beach, leaving her yards behind. He reached the spot beneath the trees about a minute ahead of her and was already towelling himself down, a broad grin on his face, as she came panting up the sand.

'General, you're no gentleman!' she laughed as she threw herself down on to her towel.

'I never claimed to be – not where you're concerned at any rate!'

Their eyes met and Anna flinched inside. From the way he was looking at her there could be no question what was uppermost in his mind, and the thought of it was almost more than she could bear. If they stayed there much longer in this state of undress he was going to make a pass at her, she had no doubt about it. And that she couldn't cope with. Not now. 'About that forfeit,' she began. 'I have an idea ...'

'Really? Let's hear it then. But I'm warning you, it'll have to be a good one – and better than mine!'

She rolled over on to her back and raised one shapely leg to gently towel it dry. He was watching her every move. It was now or never. She couldn't fail now. She dropped the towel to turn on to her side, so that she was facing him and could look him straight in the eyes. Her head bent to one side as she looked him up and down slowly. 'I'm glad you won,' she said softly. 'I told you, General, powerful men turn me on … Power is the greatest aphrodisiac in the world.'

'What are we going to do about it, then?' he asked huskily. He was towering above her, his eyes burning into hers. There was no disguising it, he was quite obviously aroused and past the stage of playing games.

She tossed a long strand of wet hair back behind her bare shoulder and glanced around her very deliberately. Despite the imminent setting of the sun, the beach was still crowded with people enjoying the last of the evening sunshine. 'This is much too public for what I have in mind,' she murmured. 'How long will it take to get back to my place?'

He didn't even need to look at his watch. 'No time at all, honey,' he said softly. 'No time at all.'

Chapter Thirty

'No, please … Not yet …' Anna wriggled from the embrace that almost pinned her to the front door of the apartment. 'Let's get inside first.'

Bill Rutherford ran a frustrated hand through his still damp hair. Every minute in the car heading back here had been sheer torture. Now all he wanted to do was to get it over with – the guilt could come later.

· She closed the door behind them and led the way into the living-room. There wasn't a thing out of place. Karl had obviously done quite a bit of tidying up after she left.

'Yours?' he asked, glancing around him.

'It – it belongs to a friend of mine,' she said, squeezing her way between the coffee table and a chair. 'She's out of town right now.' Her eyes scanned the room for any tell-tale signs of its male owner that would give the lie to her remark. There were none obvious and she breathed a silent sigh of relief as she headed for the bedroom door.

'Nice. Beats hotel living any day,' he commented politely, his eyes moving from a general glance around the room to her bare legs as she crossed the floor ahead of him. There was still sand clinging to her calves, and the cotton mini-dress clung like a second skin to her slim figure. She had on her wet bikini beneath it. The dress dissolved before his eyes and he could visualize those two minute strips of shocking pink right now. It had left little to the imagination, but even that was too much. She was saying something about the view from the window, and he was aware of making an appropriate reply, but it was impossible to concentrate on small-talk as the desire within him became more unbearable by the second.

Anna was aware of his eyes on her as she glanced nervously

at the closed kitchen door and prayed that Karl was in there with his camera at the ready. All she wanted was to get it over with. She felt almost physically sick with apprehension at what lay ahead.

The bedroom door loomed ominously close. She paused in front of it for a second, then took a deep breath and threw it open with a flourish.

The whole room was awash with the golden glow from the setting sun. Karl had the blinds pulled up to ensure maximum light should his flash equipment fail. Nothing could be left to chance; there would not be another.

In front of them, dominating the room, was the double bed and Anna could hear the breath catch in the throat of her companion as he stood in the open doorway just behind her. She deftly avoided his reaching hand as she moved lightly aside to allow him to enter. Despite the effects of the sun, she could see his face was flushed and a film of perspiration glowed on his brow and upper lip as his eyes moved from her face to the waiting bed and back again.

He made another rather clumsy move towards her, knocking his shin on the end of the bed.

'Patience, General!' she admonished softly, moving out of his reach back towards the door.

'*Now*, Anna … I want you *now*.' His voice was hoarse and he almost hissed the words at her. Why was she torturing him like this?

'Can you wait two minutes?' she pleaded, putting on her best Shirley Temple expression. 'If it's amply rewarded?'

'Not even two seconds!'

'I must go to the bathroom,' she insisted, her fingers now clasping the door-handle. 'I promise you, I'll be back in two minutes flat – and it'll be well worth the wait. If you promise me one thing, that is.'

'Name it.'

'You'll be ready and waiting for me,' she whispered. Her eyes were locked on his as she walked slowly back towards the double bed. She stood silently beside it for a moment, then bent down and threw back the quilt. She smoothed an imaginary wrinkle from the sheet, her eyes never leaving his face. 'Sans clothes, sans swimming trunks, sans inhibitions, sans everything …'

'Jeezus God …' he blasphemed softly beneath his breath as he looked from the waiting bed to her and back again.

'Well?'

'I promise,' he swore huskily. 'I promise … Only for Chrissake hurry!'

She did not need a second telling as she made for the door and closed it quickly behind her. She almost ran to the kitchen.

Karl was sitting, white-faced, at the small table smoking a cigarette. He stubbed it out roughly at the sight of her.

'He's in there now,' she hissed, jerking her head in the direction of the bedroom. 'He's undressing.' Her eyes took in the camera sitting on the table at his elbow. 'Is everything ready?'

'*Jawohl* … As ready as it will ever be.'

She gave a strained smile. 'I'm going into the bathroom to undress. Leave it only a few seconds once I go back into the bedroom, then come in.' Any longer and the situation could become grotesque.

He nodded, but said nothing.

She turned to go.

'Good luck.'

'Thanks.'

She walked swiftly in the direction of the bathroom, pulling down the zip at the back of her dress as she crossed the living-room carpet. She was half out of it as she entered the small tiled room and caught sight of herself in the mirror. Her face had a haunted expression to it that she did not recognize.

She stepped out of her dress and left it lying in a heap on the floor as she kicked off her shoes and undid the top of her bikini. She cast it aside also and stood looking at herself in the mirror. She had caught the sun and her breasts looked startlingly white against the rest of her skin.

Her fingers reached for the G-string bottom of her bikini, then froze. Something inside her would not allow her to go any further. Whatever photos were taken, her half-naked body would have to do.

She reached for one of Karl's brushes that sat on a glass shelf over the sink, and pulled it hastily through her hair. It had dried an even lighter blonde with the effects of the sun and water and it puffed out like a golden cloud around her bare shoulders as she made for the door.

She felt physically drained as she recrossed the living-room carpet and she cursed the demon within her that had brought this torture about. She had wanted to get even, yes, but until that meeting with Kurt Kessel the other day she had never imagined a situation like this.

Out of the corner of her eye she could see the kitchen door open a fraction as Karl made sure of her movements. Her hand reached for her left breast and she could feel her heart pounding within as she grasped the handle of the bedroom door.

Bill Rutherford was lying on the bed, his clothes discarded carelessly in a heap on the carpet beside him. He had kept only part of the bargain for he had not removed his swimming trunks, she noticed. He half sat up on the pillows and let out a low groan at the sight of her. His hand reached out towards her. 'Come here …'

She hesitated a second, then walked slowly towards the bed. She attempted a smile, but her lips stuck to her teeth and she knew it was nearer a grimace than the real thing.

'You promised me, Anna,' he was saying softly. 'You promised me it would be worth waiting for …'

Then she was on the bed beside him and he had pulled her on top of him, only to roll over immediately so that she was the one resting on the pillows beneath. He was murmuring endearments into the soft, sunburnt flesh of the hollow of

326

her neck as, over his right shoulder, she saw the door open and Kurt manoeuvre for position to take his first photograph.

She found herself holding her breath as first one was taken and then another. The two flashes momentarily lit the bedroom, but, incredibly, Bill Rutherford's eyes were closed, his face buried in the soft skin of her shoulder. He was far too engrossed in what was taking place on the bed to be aware of what else was now happening in the room.

Then, as the sun-bronzed body on top of her groaned and moved position slightly, Karl moved silently round to the side of the bed. He had to get one of his face – that was all-important. The head of America's nuclear defence programme had to be recognizable in bed with a Red.

Bill Rutherford's hands were moving down her body now in the direction of her bikini bottom as she threw back her head and arched her breasts, as if in the throes of desire. She had to get him to raise his head so Karl could get a proper view of his face.

The sudden movement succeeded. He was breathing erratically now and sweating profusely; oblivious of all but the two of them and of the burning physical need within him. For a split second his eyes met Anna's before out of the corner of his eye he saw a movement by the side of the bed.

'What ...?' Leaning all his weight on one elbow, he glanced around him in confusion as first one further picture was taken and then another.

'Holy Jesus – what's happening?' His features distorted as he glanced down at Anna, then back in horror at the camera pointing at him. He attempted to make a lunge off the bed in the direction of the now retreating figure of Karl, but Anna had him held fast.

'Let go! For Chrissake, let me go!' He was pulling against her as she clung steadfastly to his right arm.

She was half off the bed and being dragged along the floor, still clinging on to him when she heard the front door slam.

He had gone! He had got out! She breathed an enormous sigh of relief and let go.

Bill Rutherford heard it too and whirled round, to stand, wild-eyed, staring down at her half-naked figure at his feet. 'What the hell's going on here?'

She remained silent, averting her eyes from his as she rubbed the shin she had banged on the edge of the bed.

'Answer me, damn you! Answer me!' He bent down and hauled her to her feet, half shaking her arm from its socket as he yelled the question at her once more. 'What the hell's going on, Anna? Just who the hell *are* you?'

Still she remained silent and he threw her back down on the bed and looked around the room in mounting panic. 'A set-up! This was a goddam set-up! Jeezuz …!'

He began to throw things off the dressing-table top, as if in some desperate search for evidence to bear out his worst fears. A magazine lay face down on the glass top, next to a bottle of Old Spice. He grabbed at it. '*Playboy.*' He threw it from him in disgust. There had to be something here – something to prove what a fool he had been to fall for the oldest trick in the book.

Anna watched him from the bed in a state akin to shock. She felt totally numb and could not have uttered a word, even if she had wanted to. Her whole mind and body was frozen.

Finding nothing of consequence in the room he turned to her once more as he pulled on his trousers. 'You're a goddam Red bitch, aren't you? That's what you are – a goddam Red bitch! A common Commie whore!'

Still receiving no reply, he grabbed her by the arm and hauled her from the bed. 'Why, Anna – if that's your name – why?'

She shook her head defiantly, determined to give him no satisfaction.

'Answer me!' The slap rang out, causing an instant red weal on her left cheek. It was the first time he had ever hit a woman. Then, realizing he was getting nowhere with her, he cast her aside and made for the living-room. There had to be something, something somewhere that would give him some clue as to what was happening here.

She followed him, grabbing Karl's shower-robe from the back of the bedroom door, and pulling it around her just in time to see him reach for her handbag. 'No – don't! That's mine!'

But she was too late, he was rifling through it, determined to find what he was looking for. First her British passport was pulled out. 'Anna Lloyd-Jones. Writer.' At least she was who she purported to be.

There were two slips of paper inside it with two names and addresses in East Berlin. Kurt Kessel and Rudolf Gross. A look akin to triumph transformed his face. 'Which one is the Commie agent?' he asked, fluttering them in her face. 'Or is it both? Do both of the sons-of-bitches work for the KGB?'

Anna's lips tightened as she attempted to make a grab for the precious addresses.

'You lied to me, didn't you, you little bitch? You're no supporter of the British Labour Party – you're nothing but a little Commie whore! How much are they paying you for this – a hundred marks – a thousand? Or do you do it for the love of it? Is blackmail one of the ways you get your kicks?'

He stuffed the two sheets of notepaper into his trouser pocket, an expression of sheer disgust on his face as he looked across at her. 'Your kind makes me sick,' he said quietly. 'You're lower than vermin. In destroying me it's your own country you're sabotaging as well, you know that don't you? You'd do that for a few goddammed pieces of silver?'

'Not for money, General,' she answered quietly. 'I'm destroying you for a cause. Partly for personal reasons and partly for – I can assure you – deeply held political and philosophic beliefs. Quite simply I abhor everything you stand for. You stand for Death in my eyes, General Rutherford. Death. And if by destroying you I can guarantee the future of mankind for at least a few precious years more, then my life on this doomed planet will have been worth living.'

'You're talking crap – a load of leftwing bullshit that every college student has grown out of by the time he's got the vote. You and your kind are always mouthing off about the good of mankind and all that hogwash, but has it ever dawned on you it's the likes of me who have guaranteed you little birdbrains the right to protest as much as you do? Just try some of your precious marches and protests in Red Square and see where it gets you – into Lubianka, that's where!'

The contempt in his face and voice was obvious as he turned his attention back to her handbag and tipped the remaining contents out on to the top of the coffee table. Lying uppermost, on top of her make-up bag, was a photograph of a young woman.

Anna watched in horror as his gaze fixed on it. He picked it up and his fingers froze along with his whole body as he continued to stare at the object in his hands. It was a photograph taken a long time ago of a young woman who was almost the double of the one he had just attempted to make love to. He stared from the photograph in his hands to Anna, then back again as the blood drained from his face. It was not her in the photograph. It was Eva. Eva Koehn. There could be no mistake. That face was burned forever on his soul.

'Who are you?' he breathed, his nightmare deepening. 'Just who the hell are you?'

Anna's mouth went dry. She hadn't bargained for this. She had never meant it to turn out this way. But now he knew, he might as well know it all.

'I'm Eva's daughter,' she said, with a defiant tilt to her chin. 'I'm Eva Koehn's daughter.'

He gaped at her, as if unable, or unwilling, to believe his ears. 'You – you're Eva's kid? ... But she died. Eva died in the war. I saw the place. I saw the crater where ...' he shook his head, unable to finish the sentence.

'You found the place where you left her to die under the

Luftwaffe's bombs – is that it, General? You found the spot that you picked out for her that turned out to be my mother's graveyard?'

He felt sick to the pit of his stomach. He was here because she had reminded him so much of her – of Eva. It was as if in the last couple of days the past had been re-created especially for him here in Berlin, her hometown. It wasn't as if he was even being unfaithful to Mary-Jo because he would have been making love to a memory here tonight – a memory of a woman he once loved with all his heart, and who died a quarter of a century ago. 'How old are you?' he asked at last. His voice was foreign to him and barely audible.

'Twenty-five,' she replied. 'I was twenty-five in May of this year. I was born on the very day she died.' She gave a bitter laugh. 'How was that for timing?'

But he was already counting back. 'Are you trying to tell me Eva got pregnant in the summer of 1940?'

'I'm not trying to tell you, I'm stating a fact.' She walked round the edge of the coffee table to confront him face on. 'Does it ring a bell for you, General Rutherford? You don't happen to know of a young Intelligence officer who was working in the American Embassy in London at about this time – a young Intelligence officer that Eva just happened to be in love with? A young Intelligence officer who left her, pregnant, to die in the Blitz of the following year.'

A strangled sound was emitted from his throat, as Anna continued chillingly, 'Does any of that ring any bells – Daddy …?'

He backed away from her and half-slumped against the hi-fi unit, shaking his head. 'No, no …'

'Yes, General, yes.'

'You are Eva's child.'

'And *your* child, General William J. Rutherford – murderer of thousands at Hiroshima and Nagasaki. Murderer of my mother.'

Chapter Thirty-One

Anna stood slumped against the window-ledge watching the hired Mercedes disappear at high speed into the stream of traffic down below. He had gone. He had gone. She was shaking from head to foot.

Her legs would barely support her as she walked the few steps to the settee and collapsed on to the leather cushions. She lay back and closed her eyes. All she could see was his face. She had never seen an expression like it as he had stared at her in mounting horror as realization dawned.

She had spared him nothing. She had told him all she knew of her mother's suffering and death. The look of sheer pain on his face as he listened was a soothing balm to the hurt she had nursed within her own heart for so long.

'Can you imagine it, General?' She had aimed her words like daggers to his heart. 'Can you imagine the agony of a young woman – a stranger in a foreign country – who had already lost everyone and everything she had known and loved, who found she was carrying the child of the man she loved with all her heart, only to have that man walk out on her for ever? Can you imagine the prolonged agony of those nine months beneath the bombs? And can you imagine the unimaginable – giving birth to that child, alone in the middle of a bombing raid? Can you? Can you? You killed my mother, General Rutherford, just as surely as if you had taken a gun to her head, make no mistake about that.'

His face had contorted grotesquely, and suddenly he had looked old, very old. It was as if he were crumbling before her very eyes. A sound akin to a sob had formed in his throat, and then he had made for the bathroom to retch violently into the sink.

When he emerged he stood looking at her for a moment; father and daughter divided by a few feet of carpet. It could as well have been the Atlantic Ocean.

His right hand had moved slightly as if to reach out to her, but she had turned her head abruptly and he had aborted the gesture. There was nothing he could say; nothing that could make up for what had happened. Guilt for the past and shame for the present washed over him until he was drowning in a mixture of emotions he could no longer control. He had to get out of there, get as far away as possible from that place. What had happened there tonight – what had been said and done – was more than he could cope with.

Without another word being spoken, he had turned and made for the door and, a few seconds later, she had watched his tall figure stride out across the pavement to where the Mercedes was parked. He got in and drove off without a backward glance.

And now he had gone and she was alone. The horror of the scene that had just taken place was relived in her head as Anna sat quite still and stared ahead of her. Then the tears came. She made no attempt to stem their flow. She was not even sure why she was crying. She had obtained her heart's desire, hadn't she? She had got even with her father.

The shrill ring of the telephone brought her abruptly back to reality. She let it ring for some time, having neither the strength nor the desire to answer it, but its persistent noise forced her eventually to reach for the receiver.

'Anna – it's Karl!'

'Karl …' She had almost forgotten his existence.

'I saw him leave,' he said. 'Are you all right?'

She wiped a hand across her soaking face and her voice was thick with emotion as she attempted to assure him, 'Yes. Yes, I'm all right.'

'He didn't harm you? He didn't use violence?'

'No. No. There was no violence.'

There was a sigh of relief at the other end. 'Look you're

going to have to get out of there – and fast. For all we know he could come back – could send some bully-boys to get these photographs. You must get out of West Berlin – get back to London right away.'

What he was saying made sense. 'What will *you* do?' she asked, genuinely perturbed at having involved him in this.

'Oh, don't worry about me. I've got plenty of friends I can stay with for the next day or so, until the Rutherford circus leaves town.'

'And the photos. What about the photos?'

He was silent for a moment. 'We've got two choices,' he said finally. 'Either I could attempt to get them to the CIA myself through contacts I have at the university, or I can hand them over to Kurt Kessel in East Berlin.'

She did not hesitate. 'Give them to Kurt,' she said. 'He will know what to do with them.' It seemed only right. It had been his idea, after all.

'And you, what will you do tonight – head straight back to London?'

Her brow furrowed. London seemed a million miles away. Berlin – East and West – was the only reality for her right now. 'Probably,' she said, knowing it was not the truth. The decision was being made in her head as she was talking. She would head back through the nearest check-point to that other world her own people referred to as 'behind the Iron Curtain', to see that man the likes of her father would refer to as 'a Commie bastard'. She would go to Kurt.

'I'll drive you to the airport.'

'No – no, please …' she insisted. What she needed most right now was a breathing space.

'Why the hell not?'

'I – I've got to be alone right now … Please try to understand, Karl. After what has just happened, I need time to think.'

There was a moment's silence at the other end as he tried

very hard to understand. It had certainly been a traumatic evening – a traumatic day for her, come to that.

'This has been the most shattering experience of my entire life. I just need time to come to terms with it by myself. Please, Karl, try to understand ...'

There was a sigh at the other end of the line. 'Well, promise me one thing. Promise me you'll telephone as soon as you arrive back in England. Let me know you've landed safely. I've got to see you again soon, Anna – you know that.' He was almost ashamed of the pleading in his voice.

'I promise ... I'll call you, Karl.' There was an audible sigh of relief from the other side. 'And Karl ...'

'Yes.'

'Thank you. Thank you for everything. *Danke – danke schön für alles.*'

'*Bitte,*' he replied in a flat voice. '*Bitte sehr, Liebling* ... Any time.'

She replaced the phone and stared ahead of her, trying to collect her thoughts. She felt sorry for him – heart sorry. She had not meant him to fall in love with her. 'Love ...' she murmured the word under her breath. What exactly was it, this emotion that wreaked havoc with so many people's lives? Some killed for it, some like her mother died because of it, some never experienced it at all. But maybe they were the fortunate ones.

She got up and walked through to the bedroom. Bill Rutherford's discarded shirt still lay on the floor by the bed. She averted her eyes from it as she walked quickly over to the wardrobe and pulled her small travelling case from the top shelf.

It took her less than five minutes to pack and dress. Before taking her leave of the apartment she stood looking around her for the last time. Would she ever come back here? It seemed as if Karl Brandt had been in her life forever instead of the few days it was in reality. But then nothing seemed quite real just now. She glanced at her watch. It was almost ten o'clock. She would not be sorry to see an end to this day.

A stiff, warm breeze was blowing as she emerged on the pavement a few minutes later and made for the nearest taxi rank.

The young taxi-driver raised his eyebrows just a fraction as she sank into the back seat and asked to be taken to the nearest crossing point to the East. She got out at the barrier and paid him. She shivered slightly as she watched him turn the Mercedes and head back towards the lights of the Western half of the city. The formalities at the checkpoint seemed to take for ever and, once across the barrier, she could not ignore the feeling of being a foreigner in a totally alien environment. It was not a feeling she had ever had across the Wall in the West.

The walk through no man's land towards Friedrich Strasse did nothing to lighten her spirits, and she found it hard to believe how much her life had changed in such a short time. It was as if her mother's life had suddenly become transposed for her own, and the men her mother had known, and loved, had suddenly become the most important human beings in her own life – for good or ill.

Kurt Kessel was both delighted and surprised to see her when she arrived at his office. It was already dark and her face looked deathly pale in the dull light from the bulb on the landing outside his door.

It was obvious to her immediately that Karl had not yet been in touch with the photographs and that Kurt knew nothing of what had transpired in the apartment on Kant Strasse that evening, but he listened attentively to all she had to say.

For almost an hour he sat across the desk from her, thoughtfully puffing his pipe as she poured it all out. She held nothing back. It was as if to tell all was to purge herself. She felt somehow defiled by what had occurred. And when at last she finished he rose from his chair and reached for the schnapps bottle to refill their glasses. 'You are a very brave young woman, Anna. Let us drink together to the more peaceful world you may have helped bring about.'

His words of comfort did little to ease the torment she felt within.

It was almost midnight when finally they took their leave of each other in the glowering shadow of the Wall. A soft rain was falling; it seemed symbolic somehow. A closeness had developed between them that she had not experienced with any man since her adopted father's death.

'It was good of you to come to me tonight, Anna,' Kurt said quietly, as she stood in the queue with others returning to the West. 'Your trust means a great deal to me. More than, perhaps, you can ever know.' He held out his right hand to clasp hers. Just how true those words were she could never guess. It was as if his beloved Eva had come back into his life to say one last goodbye. But more than that, what Anna had had to tell him had brought a warm glow to his soul. Rutherford, the man responsible for Eva's death, had been destroyed. He had no doubt about that.

Anna ignored the proffered hand to clasp him to her. The rough stubble of his cheek rubbed into the soft flesh of her own. Over his shoulder she could see two of the border guards looking at them; two gun-carrying, green-uniformed members of the *Volkspolizei* – no older than herself, they spent their lives guarding this man-made barrier that divided one half of the city from the other.

There were tears in her eyes as she pulled herself away. 'I wish you could come to London,' she said impetuously. She felt she still had so much to learn from this man who had listened to her and offered her comfort tonight; there were so many parts of the jigsaw of her past yet to be filled in. 'I wish we could go on being friends – seeing each other often.'

Kurt Kessel gave a weary shake of the head. 'We live in two different worlds, Anna – you in the West, I in the East.

The two great political systems of our age are in conflict and we – the little people – cannot change that.'

She shook her head and cast a despairing glance at the great edifice of the Wall towering above them beyond the barrier. 'You mean you really believe that – that "thing" will outlast us all? Never again will you be able to take a spur-of-the-moment tram-ride to visit your sister Hanna on the other side?'

Kurt gave a strained smile. 'Perhaps I should be grateful to the builders for that.' His younger sister was the last person he would wish to visit should Berlin's most famous landmark ever come tumbling down.

She gave an understanding smile. Hanna Graubaum was a part of her mother's past that she had no particular desire to remain in touch with either. But that did not alter her affection for Hanna's brother, or her revulsion at the great man-made structure that stood between families and friends in this still troubled land. 'There has to be a future without the Wall, Kurt … How can anyone accept it as a normal part of civilized life in the twentieth century? Surely the will of the people can change even great political systems – if it really wants to?'

'You are one of life's optimists, Anna.' He sighed. 'As for myself, I have lived too long, seen too much … The Wall will not come down, and Germany will not be united – not in my lifetime, not in yours. And, if you believe in a God, then you must thank Him for that.'

He reached for a cigarette and Anna's eyes fell on the mutilated fingertips as he struck a match. Like so many others who had suffered at the hands of a powerful, united Germany, he saw the Wall as his protection from that type of thing ever happening again, and she could not blame him for that.

'We will keep in touch, though … They still let letters through, if not people.'

'We will keep in touch.' He gazed at her through the

cigarette smoke. It was as if the years had rolled away and he was gazing once more on *her* face. 'You are so like your mother. So very like her …' She could have been his own daughter. She *should* have been his own daughter. Once more a deep hatred rose in him for the man who had been responsible for his beloved Eva's death. But there was a justice at the heart of things, after all. Rutherford had paid at the hands of his own daughter. The past had not been buried with Eva in the rubble of wartime London; it had returned in the shape of her own child to inflict retribution at last. The thought brought a deep comfort to his soul. He attempted a smile, but the parting was painful and it showed in his eyes as he held out his hand once more. '*Auf Wiedersehen*, dear Anna.'

She clasped his hand in both of hers. There was so much more she wanted to say. 'I will return,' she promised. 'Till then, *Auf Wiedersehen* … dear Kurt.' She turned quickly to make her way through the barrier, embarrassed by the tears that had sprung to her eyes.

Once on the other side, she turned for a last look at the floodlit frontier post dividing what had once been a perfectly ordinary German street. Now it was dividing the world, East from West, people from people. All her life she had wanted to build bridges, sow the seeds of harmony where there was discord. It was what her parents, Owen and Peggy Lloyd-Jones, had taught her. But that cosy world of suburban London where they had once lived seemed on another planet as she made her way back towards the bright lights of the Western Sector.

She found herself wondering what they – Owen and Peggy – would have thought of what had happened in that apartment on the Kant Strasse earlier this evening. She could not bear to imagine. She still found it difficult to cast her mind back to the events of a few hours ago. It all seemed like the most awful nightmare from which she would surely awaken. God only knew what her father must be thinking. He must really hate her.

It was raining more heavily now and a deep melancholy fatigue pervaded her mind and body as she made her way to the nearest hotel and booked in for the night. The Schiller Hotel was not up to much, and the old man on the desk looked as weary as she felt, but she had neither the energy nor the inclination to go any further. Somehow, to stay in sight of the Wall comforted her. She had people she really cared about on the other side; beyond the guns and barbed wire were her grandmother and Kurt.

But what of that other Berliner with whom she had shared these momentous days? What of Karl? What was he doing right now? She experienced a curious mix of emotions when she thought of the young man who had aided her in her quest for revenge. She had no doubt that in doing so he was in some way getting back at his own father, but she also knew that he had acted out of a growing love for her, and she wished with all her heart that she could have responded to that love. He was a good man, an intelligent, sensitive man who cared for her deeply; why then could she not return his love? What was it that made it possible for her to respond with her body, but not her soul?

That question and countless others haunted her as she closed the curtains on the searchlights above the distant barbed wire and made her way to bed. But she still had no answers as the grey fingers of dawn heralded another day. Her mind was too full, her emotions too raw for respite to come, and the city was already awake and about its business before she fell into a troubled sleep.

Chapter Thirty-Two

As his daughter sat drinking coffee in Kurt Kessel's East Berlin office, across the Wall in West Berlin, Bill Rutherford sat sprawled in a chair in his hotel room, a half-empty whisky bottle on the table beside him and a glass in his hand. He finished its contents in one gulp and poured himself another, drinking it down greedily. The amber liquid burned its way to his stomach, bringing a fleeting feeling of well-being, then reality broke in. There was no escaping it.

What had just occurred there in that apartment on Kant Strasse had shocked him to the core. It was more than he could cope with: the facts of Eva's death; learning she had given birth to a child – his child; then not only coming face to face with that child, but attempting to seduce her ... Dear God, she must really hate him to engineer a thing like that!

The fact that his career would now be ruined did not concern him; he could live with that. What did concern him was the degree of hate it must have taken for his own daughter to be party to such a thing. He felt sick to his very core. He had actually begun to fall in love with her. She had been Eva recreated just for him, after all those years of yearning, all those years of not knowing what had really happened to her. What a grotesque parody these past few days had turned out to be.

He sank back in the armchair and closed his eyes in a desperate attempt to blot out the present and its shame.

Suddenly he was back again all those years ago in wartime England. He could feel the cool breeze wafting against his skin as he lay with her on that hilltop on the Sussex Downs. He had felt it then; something deep within him had told him it could not last. Some things in this world were too perfect to go on for ever. He did not deserve to have found such happiness, when that happiness could only be bought at the expense of others: Mary-Jo Marlowe and her family.

But, despite his inner fears, he had not thought it was the end when he had said goodbye to Eva that evening at the door of her apartment. He was being sent away – for a few weeks, perhaps months, at the most, that was all. And so it might have been if the plane taking him back to New York had not crashed only ten minutes from its destination of La Guardia airport.

He could remember little of what actually happened, only the screaming of the man in the seat beside him, as they plummeted earthwards. Maybe he himself was yelling too when they pulled him from the wreckage. Certainly his injuries merited it. But he could remember nothing of that night in August 1940, nor of any night – or day – for the next six weeks. That was how long he had lain unconscious.

His first memories of that period began in the middle of October when, on his regaining consciousness, the doctors agreed to Mary-Jo's request to allow him to be taken to her parents' home in South Carolina to recover.

He had had little say in the matter really. It was as if his life had been taken over and he was powerless to resist. Mary-Jo had visited him almost every day throughout his spell in the coma, sitting by his bed talking to him for hours, even when the prognosis was anything but optimistic. Then later on, when her faith had been rewarded and he was able to sit up and take notice of his surroundings, she had made it clear she was determined to do all she could to help nurse him back to full fitness and health.

Apart from a badly broken left leg and numerous broken ribs on the same side, he had sustained quite severe internal injuries. It was well into the new year before he was able to get up-and-about again, and then only with the help of sticks.

Ed Marlowe, Mary-Jo's father, drove all the way up to

New York from South Carolina to collect him from the hospital, his battered station wagon specially kitted out to allow him to lie comfortably in the back.

Yes, the Marlowes were wonderful, accepting him into their family as they would a son – which indeed, he knew in his heart, was exactly what they expected him to become as soon as his injuries were on the mend. Nothing was ever said outright, but it was as if it had been ordained from a very early age that he and Mary-Jo would get wed. And, as the spring of 1941 gave way to early summer, and he began to talk of resuming his working life again, the faint sound of wedding bells began to get louder in all their ears.

It was then too that he received a visit from his old friend from Columbia University, Jack Douglas. What Jack had to say had made his hair stand on end. He spoke in glowing terms of the work being done there into the splitting of the atom, and was at great pains to assure him that should he wish to get back into scientific research, the future had never looked brighter for the physicist. The race was without doubt on now between them and the Germans as to who could harness the power of the atom first. 'You'll be right at the heart of things, Billy Boy,' he had said. 'Doing far more important work than you could ever do pushing a pen in the State Department.'

'It would mean remaining in the States for the remainder of the war in Europe,' he had replied uncertainly, and Jack had frowned in incomprehension.

'What's so bad about that? Don't tell me you're missing being blitzed to hell by old Goering's Luftwaffe back in London! You're well out of it, Bill, believe me.'

He had smiled and nodded in agreement to keep his old friend happy, but inwardly he was in turmoil. To accept a university job here in the States was to kiss goodbye to any thoughts of ever seeing Eva again, and that was something he had still not come to terms with. The memory of her still burned, an unhealed wound, deep within him. All those

343

weeks of unconsciousness after the accident, the constant vigil of Mary-Jo, and the months of selfless care by her parents, had made any idea of attempting to contact her again almost an impossibility. Betty, Mary-Jo's mother, saw all the mail that came and went in the Marlowe household, and it would have seemed like spitting on all the care and attention they had lavished on him had he resumed his transatlantic love affair, albeit only on paper.

So he had taken the easy way out. Some would say the coward's way, he knew that, for he had never been in love with Mary-Jo as he was with Eva. Never. Never. But he had agreed to marry her.

He could see it now, that scene on the terrace of her parents' home the day in early June 1941 that he received the letter from Jack, in Columbia, saying he had had a word with his superiors and there would be a place waiting for him. All he had to do was apply.

After his crash, Mary-Jo had given up her own post as a grade school teacher in the Bronx to come back to nurse him, and he knew she was eager to get back to New York. But not without him. That much was implicit in every move she made and every word she uttered concerning the future.

She was wearing a full-skirted cotton dress that day — white with red polka-dots and a wide red belt — and she had stood with her hands on her hips looking at him in exasperation.

'Well, Bill Rutherford, what is it going to take to get you to make a decision? You know that with your injuries the Intelligence people are only going to shove you behind a desk in Washington.'

'I know that.' He had had a medical the previous week and had still not received the all-clear.

'And you've said yourself a limp here and there wouldn't make any real difference to work in the laboratory.'

'I know that too.'

'You like New York.'

'It's a great city.'

'And you know I love you …' She had paused, and then taken her courage in both hands. 'And you love me.'

'Yes, I know that too.' He also knew what was coming next and his heart had sunk to the soles of his shoes.

She had come over and placed her arms around his neck to say softly: 'You are a scientific man, Mr Rutherford. What conclusion does all that lead you to?'

'That I should ask you to marry me and we should accept Jack's invitation and go to New York.'

Her eyes had gazed up into his. 'Well?'

What kind of jerk was he that he would let her almost plead with him like this? 'Marry me, Mary-Jo,' he had said. 'Be my wife.' They were the hardest words he had ever spoken.

The wedding bells had finally rung on 8 August 1941, the day the Soviet air force carried out their first raid on Berlin. He had heard the news of it on the radio in their hotel bedroom in Bar Harbor, Maine, just as they were preparing for bed. Mention of the German capital brought memories of Eva flooding back. So much so that when it came to fulfilling his marital duty for the first time half an hour later, he could not do it. Try as he might he could not be a husband to his wife.

The shame of that first night lived with him for a long time. Too long. For although Mary-Jo had the good grace not to mention it, it made lovemaking with her something he thereafter approached with less than enthusiasm and with not a little apprehension.

He had taken up his post at Columbia immediately on their return from honeymoon. They rented a three-roomed apartment not far from Jack's on Morningside Drive. It wasn't much of a place but it was cheap and Mary-Jo did her best to make it seem like home. Fate decreed that they were not to be there for long, however.

In October of that year he was invited to attend a meeting

of top physicists at General Electric's laboratories in Schenectady, and it was there that he met once again the scientist he admired above almost all others, J. Robert Oppenheimer. To his surprise and quite obvious delight, Oppenheimer invited him to join his own team of physicists in the University of California, at Berkeley, where, like their colleagues on other leading campuses throughout the United States, they were working on the problem of separating out uranium for the world's first atomic bomb.

Mary-Jo had been less than delighted when he returned with the news. In fact her eyes flashed real anger as he told her the details over supper on his first evening back home. 'What do you mean you've accepted? How can you possibly have accepted without talking it over with me first?'

He had looked at her in amazement over the tuna salad. 'But, honey, you know what this means to me. To work with Oppie …' He had shaken his head in wonder at her reaction as he searched for the right words. 'Hell, it's been the crock of gold at the end of my scientific rainbow for years!'

His confession only served to intensify her ire. 'Has it never occurred to you that the "Wonderful Wizard of Oz" Oppenheimer works on the other side of the country?'

'Sure, I know that. Berkeley's got a great reputation.'

'It's also in California – on the WEST coast!' She was shouting now as she pushed her chair back and got up from the table. 'We're east coast people, Bill. All our friends – all our relations – are in the EAST.'

He had got up to come round the table in an attempt to pacify her. 'Hell, Mary-Jo, we can make new friends. Plenty of people do. Folks move around the place all the time these days. California's not the ends of the earth. Lots of people would give their eye-teeth to move out there.'

'Then let them!' She had stood, arms folded, with her back to him. 'I'm certainly not one of them.'

'You want me to write and turn it down, is that it?'

She said nothing.

He swung her round to face him, his voice rising. 'You want me to call Oppie and say I can't accept because my wife won't leave New York – is that it?'

They had stared at one another defiantly, then she had shrugged her shoulders and said bitterly, 'Do what you want, darn you. You always do!'

And so he had. They had moved to Berkeley in the middle of October, into a brand new Spanish-style house on Eagle Hill overlooking the university. An L-shaped, white stucco building shaded by tall cypresses, it stood at the top of a steep, winding drive. They named it 'The Eyrie' and indeed it seemed to cling like an eagle's nest to the very edge of the hillside. With its spacious rooms, tiled floors and wood-panelled ceilings, it would have taken a far harder heart than Mary-Jo's not to fall in love with it.

While his wife's initial hostility at moving to California was tempered with the excitement of choosing furniture and furnishings for their new home, his own professional life was every bit as exciting as he had anticipated. He was made aware immediately of the life-and-death race they were now involved in with the Germans to produce the most deadly weapon ever conceived by man.

And when, less than two months later, on 7 December, the American Pacific Fleet was attacked in its home base of Pearl Harbor, Hawaii, by 360 planes of the Japanese air force, and America entered the war, their work at Berkeley became even more imperative.

He had tried very hard while in California both to be a good husband and to live up to Oppenheimer's expectations of him in the laboratory, but somehow Mary-Jo never quite fitted into the role of an academic wife. To his dismay she did not find it easy to make friends with the other wives, and never could take to Oppie's wife Kitty, who claimed not only to be a German princess, but also the niece of the Third Reich's General Keitel. To the patriotic Mary-Jo, this was something that should be kept quiet about, not boasted of.

'Just who does she think it impresses?' she had asked after a particularly trying evening at the Oppenheimers' nearby home. 'Maybe next time they're round here I should claim to be Adolf Hitler's illegitimate child. She'd find it hard to top that!'

He had grinned at the thought. 'Not half as hard as *Der Führer* would have found it achieving such a thing!'

She had smiled in return but the problem remained, and although he said nothing of his misgivings to Mary-Jo, out of the laboratory he himself was less than happy about some of his boss's political views. Both Robert and Kitty were well known for their decidedly left-wing sympathies and past Communist connections. Even as a fervent Oppenheimer disciple, this was something he found hard to stomach. As far as he was concerned, the United States had been built on the principles of freedom and justice for all and he was darned if he could think of a political system that could be fairer than that. What they were practising in the Soviet Union was a travesty of those principles and, despite his professional respect for his boss, he had little time for anyone who could not see that fact.

For a whole year he and Mary-Jo tried to make a go of life on Eagle Hill, but as time wore on he could sense that she was becoming increasingly unhappy. Apart from missing her folks back home, she longed for a baby and he felt in her heart she blamed him for her lack of success in becoming pregnant. They seldom made love, partly because of the long hours he spent working in the lab, and partly because he now knew he was one of those people who could not turn it on in the bedroom to order. It was not that Mary-Jo was an unattractive woman, far from it – he was simply not in love with her, and in that stark and simple fact lay the root of the problem. He was still in love with Eva.

As the months in California ticked by and the war in Europe intensified, his thoughts turned more and more to London and the young woman he had fallen in love with there. How was she coping with life under the bombs? Sometimes he almost resented the fact that in comparison they were having it so easy out there under the Californian sun. He found himself growing more and more short-tempered with Mary-Jo. What right did she have to complain about the life she was leading when Eva had gone through – was still going through – so much?

As the strain of his laboratory work took its toll, so his obsession with Eva's memory grew, until one night in the front parlour of their house on Eagle Hill, Mary-Jo decided she had had enough. She would confront him with his inadequacies. He was either not in love with her or there was another woman, it was as simple as that.

He had been preparing to go back to the lab to finish off an experiment that evening when the fuse blew.

'Go on then – go! Only don't expect me to be sitting here like a good little girl when you get back!'

He had turned at the door, his raincoat over one arm and his hat half-way to his head. 'What did you say?'

'I said, I'm sick of it – that's what I said! I'm sick of sitting here being taken for granted every night while you go off to do whatever it is you do!'

'You know what I do, Mary-Jo.' His voice was eminently reasonable. 'I slave my guts out in that laboratory so that Hitler and his Nazi bastards don't crack this thing before we do.'

'What proof do I have of that? How do I know that night after night you're not out there with some – some cheap floozie who means more to you than I do?'

'Jeez … I don't believe this! I *do not* believe it! You *know* I go to the lab, goddamn it!'

'How can I know? I only have your word for it.'

'Isn't that enough?'

'No, Bill, it's not. Not any more.'

He had stood there, coat and hat in hand, looking at her. 'What do you want me to say? What can I tell you that will make you feel better?'

'The truth. That's all, Bill. The truth. Who is she? Who is she – the woman you think about as you lie there on your own side of the bed at night, praying I will fall asleep first so that you're not made to feel guilty for ignoring me once again? It's not me, I know that … Is it Darlene?'

Her mention of a colleague's wife who didn't even appeal to him brought a mirthless laugh and shake of the head. 'No, it's not Darlene.'

'Who is it then? Tell me, for God's sake – haven't I suffered enough? Don't I have a right to know?'

'Yes, yes, Mary-Jo, you do.' He had stood there, his fingers toying with the felt brim of the hat in his hands. They said confession was good for the soul, didn't they? Maybe the time had come to ease the burden that had been weighing down on his for the past two years. 'Her name's Eva,' he said finally. 'And she's no threat to you, Mary-Jo. No threat at all.'

His wife's face drained, and she seemed visibly to shrink before his eyes. It was as if the mention of the name had knocked the fight right out of her. Now it was she who was on the defensive. Her voice was so faint it was barely audible as she whispered, 'Are – are you seeing a lot of her?' She held her breath, dreading his answer.

'I'm seeing nothing of her at all. She's a German-Jew, living in London.'

'That's crazy.'

He had nodded, a bitter smile twisting his lips, as he turned to go. 'About as crazy as this whole goddamned world right now.'

Chapter Thirty-Three

Bill Rutherford arrived in Los Alamos on Monday 29 March 1943. It was not at all what he had expected to find. Neither the place nor the countryside around it was like anything he had ever encountered before. Once a school for boys, the Spanish-style buildings and motley collection of log cabins that were now to house America's headquarters for research into the atomic bomb stood at a height of over 7,000 feet, on the flat tableland that forms part of the Pajarito plateau of the Jemez Mountains of New Mexico.

It was a lonely land, inhabited mainly by the birds and animals which haunted its scented pinewoods and reddish-purple cliffs and canyons; the Indians who had once hunted there had long since abandoned their dwellings for the lower ground. Only their holy places remained, and as Bill drove across the deserted plateau towards the United States government's most top-secret place that spring afternoon, the fragrance of the pine trees and mountain flowers drifted in on the wind that blew through the open car window and he felt a strange tingle in the marrow of his bones. It was as if this was indeed a sacred place and the Almighty Himself inhabited this land. Momentous things were about to happen here, things that would change the whole meaning of life on this planet. He thanked God for the good fortune that was allowing him to be part of it.

His first stop before setting out for Los Alamos had been thirty-five miles away in Sante Fe, at 109 East Palace Street, where he had been ordered to report. The address turned out to be that of a beautiful old Spanish colonial building, and he parked the car in front of an ornamental wrought-iron gate and got out. There seemed to be no one around so he pushed it open and found himself in an old stone-flagged courtyard. Intrigued, he headed for an open French window to see if there was any sign of life within.

Tentatively he opened the dusty fly-screen door behind the glass and stepped inside a small room done out as an office and hesitated a moment before calling, 'Is anybody there?'

Within seconds a pleasant-faced, middle-aged woman appeared and introduced herself as Dorothy McKibben. This was Office 109, he was informed, and he had indeed come to the right place.

The five rooms, it transpired, were rented in the name of a Mr Bradley, which turned out to be the assumed name of Robert Oppenheimer himself, and Dorothy McKibben's job was to make all the new arrivals feel at home as far as it was possible, and to inform them of the different turn their lives had now taken.

They were indeed to be the chosen few; America's most gifted nuclear physicists who, under the leadership of J. Robert Oppenheimer, were to create the world's first atomic bomb. But this exclusive status and the top-secret work it entailed could not be bought cheaply. For a start, she informed him, to the rest of the world this place did not exist. They themselves would not exist as long as they worked on the Manhattan Project, as it had been named. Los Alamos itself would be known simply as 'Site Y' and the scientists who worked there would have no address to give out to loved ones: all their mail must simply be forwarded c/o US Army, PO Box 1663, and only pseudonyms or numbers could be used to identify them.

'How do you think your wife would care to address your mail, Dr Rutherford?' she enquired politely, pen poised above a pad for his reply.

'How about "Stubborn Sonofabitch"?' he replied wryly, and she had smiled in understanding.

'It's not very easy for wives to take to all this secrecy stuff at first, but they get used to it, believe me. Will she be joining you soon?'

He gave a non-committal smile. 'I hope so, ma'am,' he said quietly. 'I sure hope so.' He could have added he should have arrived here on the 15th with Oppie and the rest of his team from Berkeley, but Mary-Jo's overdose had put paid to that. He still did not know to this day if it had been deliberate. She swore it wasn't, but it had delayed his departure by almost a fortnight nevertheless, and left him with a feeling of guilt that no amount of rationalizing could overcome.

'Well, until she does you'll be living on "The Hill", as it's come to be known – that is in Los Alamos itself rather than down here in Santa Fe or on any of the dude ranches in the neighbourhood where so many of the others are boarding. I warn you, though, it's pretty primitive here, but things are improving all the time.'

And primitive it was in the beginning. The site itself was enclosed by a high barbed-wire fence, and constantly patrolled by armed military policemen, which gave those on the inside the distinct feeling of being cooped up in a prison camp rather than the country's top scientific establishment.

The apartments were a three mile drive up a pot-holed, dusty road, and even the senior scientists had to make do with the most basic accommodation. Their small single-room bedsits contained only the most spartan furniture: a single bed, a wooden chair, a small table, a chest of drawers and a built-in closet for their clothes. There was a laundry room of sorts, but it operated on a do-it-yourself principle which was both time-consuming and awkward for men having to work very long hours. Almost all the married ones endeavoured to get their wives out to join them as soon as possible, hoping the married quarters they were providing would be an improvement on their present lot. For his own part, with letters heavily censored, phone-calls tapped, and no more than one visit a month allowed for family, Bill knew that the sooner he succeeded in getting Mary-Jo out, the better chance she had of her mental and physical health improving.

In the beginning he was glad she was not there to see the confusion and mess that was taking place in the vast top-secret complex that was being built. The whole area looked like an enormous building site, with trucks and bulldozers creating a massive dust-storm that never seemed to subside. The hammering and banging seemed interminable, but within three months of his arrival, the complex was almost complete.

It was almost summer, however, before their own apartment was ready, and Bill waited with growing apprehension for the arrival of his wife. It was a far cry from their lovely home on Eagle Hill. The newly-constructed apartment blocks stood at the end of a long, rough, dusty road. Each housed four families but, given the scant privacy their paper-thin walls afforded, they might as well all have been living in the one house. Although a slight improvement on the spartan conditions endured by the single men on The Hill, the furniture was still very basic, with little in the way of modern conveniences such as they had known in California. Bill could well understand Mary-Jo's disappointment when he showed her round it for the first time.

He followed her from room to room, his heart sinking as the high spirits and excitement of her arrival evaporated and the eager anticipation on her face changed into a frown. He knew she was looking forward to their reunion and taking over her new home, and he could see she had had her hair done specially for the occasion. She had on a new print dress, with a pretty matching jacket, and she toyed with the double row of beads around her neck as she pensively explored each room in turn. But still she said nothing, and he could only speculate as to her thoughts. They ended up in the kitchen and finally she spoke: 'And just what in heaven's name is this?' She looked askance at the huge, rather threatening-looking object in front of her, its enormous bulk almost filling the small room.

'They call it a "Black Beauty",' he replied miserably. 'It's a wood-burning stove. It's what the Army supply for you to cook on.'

'Holy Moses!' She let out a low whistle and shook her head. 'So this is what it's come down to, is it? This is what life has to offer when you're reckoned to be married to one of the top scientists in the country?'

He had no answer, for there was none to give. Instead he took her in his arms and hugged her to him. He so much wanted her to be happy, to regain some of the vitality she had possessed before she became his wife. What had happened to that lively girl he had gone through high school with? He knew now he had not done her any favour by marrying her, but it had been expected of him. And maybe that was half his trouble – he had spent so much of his life doing what was expected of him – trying not to let people down, particularly people to whom he felt he owed a debt.

He tried to make up for the miserable housing conditions by taking as much time off as possible and driving her up into the clean fresh air of the Sangre de Cristo Mountains. The Conquistadores who originally conquered the land for the Spanish king named them 'The Blood of Christ' because of their blood-red hues at sundown. Almost nothing had changed in that ancient land in the hundreds of years since then. The small adobe houses that clung to the hillsides, each with its own garden of corn and beans, could just as easily have stepped from the pages of a sixteenth-century history book.

'*Es muy bonito*,' Mary-Jo sighed, as she turned for one last look and they headed for the car after a particularly memorable weekend's camping in the foothills. And with those three Spanish words he knew she was at least making an effort to come to terms with her new surroundings.

In the two years that followed it seemed they had achieved some sort of modus vivendi, for their rows grew fewer and, as his hours grew longer in the laboratory, she would endeavour to fill her time alone, not only by learning the language but also by painting the spectacular scenery around them. She would take off for whole days into the surrounding countryside with her easel and equipment, and the fruits of her labours now graced the whitewashed walls of their home.

She grew her hair long and tied it back, Spanish fashion, at the nape of her neck, and took to wearing items of the exotic jewellery made by local craftsmen. Bill took care to compliment her on her appearance. Pride in her looks was something that had disappeared entirely during earlier bouts of depression and he felt gladdened that she seemed to be making an effort to come to terms with their lot.

The pain of remaining childless, however, was still there, and was deepened by Kitty Oppenheimer's seeming good fortune in the motherhood stakes. The director's wife had arrived at Los Alamos with a two-year-old son, Peter, and had recently given birth to a baby daughter, Toni. Mary-Jo would occasionally visit them in their comparatively luxurious bungalow at 1967 Peach Street, known enviously as 'Bathtub Row' by the other scientists and their families in less high-class accommodation. On the days following these visits a brooding look would come to her face that Bill learned to recognize but could do nothing to prevent.

If she still blamed him for her failure to become pregnant she no longer said so outright, preferring to withdraw into herself and work her frustrations out on the canvases that were now piling up on the floor of the bedroom closet – wall-space having run out long ago. They still made love, but infrequently, and usually only after a night out, when a few Scotches would work wonders in loosening the chains of memory that still bound him to the past and Eva.

But in the days of cold sobriety in between their nights out, he thought often about the German girl he had once loved and those few magic weeks they had spent together in England's capital city. Where was she now? Was she still in that same apartment he had found for her? He hoped with all his heart that she was and that somehow when this terrible war was over he could find some excuse to go back there to London and find her. What exactly would happen when that moment came he could not be sure, for ties of deep loyalty and affection still bound him to his wife. That was simply a bridge he would have to cross when he came to it.

Just how soon it would be until the war was over was still anybody's guess. Much of his time at home was spent listening to the radio for clues in that regard and, thankfully, in Europe at least, things seemed to be going the Allies' way.

Then, on 15 August 1944, the evening news bulletin told of an Allied success that was to be of great consequence to himself and his colleagues on the Manhattan Project. The city of Strasbourg, on the French–German border, had fallen to 'Old Blood and Guts', General George Patton, and his troops.

At the time he first heard the announcement he had thought very little of it, but shortly afterwards Oppenheimer called a meeting of his senior scientists to give them the incredible news. When American soldiers occupied the Physics Institute of Strasbourg University a great many documents were found and four German physicists captured. What came to light amazed the American Military, but amazed the scientists at Los Alamos even more. The Germans, who had always been thought to be ahead of the Allies in atomic research, were at least two years behind. They possessed no factories capable of producing the Uranium 235 or the Plutonium 239 required for the atomic chain reaction so essential in the production of the bomb.

This news staggered Oppenheimer, and Bill no less, but it was also an enormous relief. Many believed that, now it was clear there was no race against the Germans to be the first to produce the A-bomb, there would be no need to actually employ the weapon to end the war.

As their work had progressed, and the once unimaginable

destruction device became a foreseeable reality, many scientists, including Bill, had found their thoughts turning more and more to the ethics of actually using the monster they were in the process of creating. And a great many people on campuses throughout the country, particularly at the University of Chicago, brought these qualms into the open and came out quite strongly against the proposed use of the bomb against the enemy – a scenario that was now being mooted by the War Department.

Despite these ethical reservations, however, the work continued apace at Los Alamos and, in the spring of 1945, a study group within the Manhattan Project that Bill found himself included in was given the awesome task of selecting a target for the first employment of the bomb.

Most of the discussion went on in the director's second-floor office, with Oppenheimer, a tall, gaunt figure in his familiar checked shirt, pacing the room as he talked, smoked and coughed simultaneously. There was very little doubt from the outset that the target was to be Japan, and there seemed something surreal about the whole thing to Bill as he sat looking out of the office window across the blue water of Ashley Pond towards the deeper blue of the mountains, while they discussed the possible deaths of tens of thousands of people. Surely this was the nearest any human beings should get to playing God? If he could have changed places with any one of his colleagues on the outside during those stressful days, he would happily have done so.

After countless hours of discussion and gallons of coffee supplied by Priscilla, Oppie's secretary, a shortlist of possible Japanese target cities was compiled, and they were all well aware that, as they argued the merits of various target sites, USAF pilots at Wendover airfield in Utah were already being trained for the dropping of the bombs. It was not a fact welcomed by any one of them as they wrestled with both their consciences and the logistics of the situation.

Throughout this period, Bill had more sleepless nights

than he had ever had. He was under oath not to divulge details of his work to anyone, even his wife, so he could not lessen the load in any way by discussing things with Mary-Jo. Although she never said so outright, he knew she resented being excluded and had deep feelings herself about the ethics of the situation. Living in the comparative isolation of Los Alamos for so long, and taking such an interest in native Indian culture, had given her a much deeper philosophic bent to her mind, and had made her increasingly sensitive to the wellbeing of her fellow men and women.

It was during this period, in the late spring of 1945, that Bill heard from his old friend Jack Douglas, now at the University of Chicago, that concern there was so strong that a committee had been appointed to discuss and report in detail on 'the social and political consequences of atomic energy'. Knowing it was a subject that was also worrying Bill a great deal, Jack offered to forward a copy of their conclusions to him.

Bill was at breakfast with Mary-Jo on 11 June 1945, when the brown envelope arrived with the Chicago postmark. His wife watched with a concerned look in her eyes as he opened it and read through its contents in silence. His face was pensive.

'Well, what does it say?'

'Listen to this, Mary-Jo,' he said quietly. 'They conclude that: "The military advantages and the saving of American lives achieved by the sudden use of atomic bombs against Japan may be outweighed by the ensuing loss of confidence and by the wave of horror and repulsion sweeping over the rest of the world, and perhaps even dividing public opinion at home … It is proposed that instead of the atomic bombardment of Japan as planned, a demonstration of the new weapon might best be made before the eyes of representatives of all the United Nations in a desert or on a barren island. Then America could say to the world: 'You see what sort of a weapon we had but did not use'."'

He folded the paper and placed it back in its envelope. 'That makes sense to me.'

She nodded as she sipped her coffee. It seemed eminently sensible to her too. Thank God, some of them had the courage to air their consciences at last. 'What are they going to do about it?'

'A copy is already on its way to Stimson, the Secretary for War, I understand.'

'Will it have your official backing?'

'Mine?' He glanced back down at the envelope in his hands. 'It's too late for my signature,' he said at last. Then, aware it sounded too much like an excuse, he sighed. 'Anyway, it wouldn't please them on The Hill.'

'To hell with The Hill – *they* don't have to live with *your* conscience for the rest of their lives.' There was no disguising the emotion behind her words.

Unable to meet her eyes, he got up from the table and walked to the window. A dust storm was blowing outside. 'With the war in Europe now well and truly over and that sonofabitch Hitler dead, the pressure is on for a quick end to hostilities all over the globe.'

'Quick, maybe, but not painless, if you actually use that – that "thing" on people.' She grimaced visibly at the thought. 'Good God, Bill, you don't even know for sure what will happen when – or if – it goes off, do you? None of you does. It could blow the whole of Japan into Kingdom Come! Do you really want that on your conscience for the rest of your days?'

He turned to face her, alarmed at the passion behind her words. 'Hell, Mary-Jo, since when did you become the guardian of my conscience – or the nation's? Since when did either of us, come to that? Don't you think they're weighing all these things up at the War Department right now and are in a much better position to assess them than we are sitting here?'

'Your colleagues in Chicago obviously don't think so.'

He slammed one fist into the other in a gesture of both frustration and irritation, and made for the door. 'It's time I was off!' he said gruffly, heading back towards his study to pick up his briefcase. Trust her, in a couple of seconds, to voice all those very real doubts that he had spent hours trying to dismiss from his own mind!

As he drove into work, the dust brought visibility through the car windscreen down to almost zero. It seemed as if even the weather was conspiring to frustrate them in their atomic tests. He couldn't remember the last time a drop of rain fell – it must have been weeks ago, and always there was the wind, this goddamn wind that blew like a hot desert breath over the settlement from morning till night. It turned every blade of grass to a brittle yellowish-white and withered the plants and leaves on the trees.

Every morning and night he would look out of his bedroom window and scan the skies for any sign of change, but to no avail. Just occasionally the heavens would darken and in the distance he would hear the rumble of thunder and see a faint glimmer of lightning over the Sangre de Cristo Mountains, and he would yell to Mary-Jo, 'It's coming, honey! The rain is on its way!' But it never was, and as the summer wore on and the heat and water-rationing began to get even the most cheerful amongst them down, he began to wish to God it was all over and they could just get out of the place and back to civilization.

A directive from the government required the first bomb to be ready for testing by the middle of July, and the second available for what was termed as 'war purposes' by 10 August. Everyone at Los Alamos knew what that meant, but despite the moral reservations of many on The Hill they were all battling against the odds to make this a possibility.

As the appointed test-time drew nearer, the excitement, even amongst the women and children, mounted. It was impossible not to know that something big was in the offing. The test itself was known by the code-name 'Trinity' and Bill and his colleagues found themselves hazarding the wildest of guesses as to the exact power of the coming explosion, whilst the more faint-hearted amongst them simply prayed that it would go off at all.

While the tension was getting to them all, Bill was not the only one of the team to be especially concerned about the look and behaviour of the director. Oppenheimer's face was now white and drawn and his weight had dropped to 115 pounds – far too little for a man of over six feet in height. A few jokes were going the rounds about 'Fat Man', their nickname for the bomb, making a 'Thin Man' of the Boss, but they all knew it was no joking matter. They had been told that the successful testing of this weapon might save as many as a million American lives by bringing the war against Japan to an immediate end, so there was far more than their professional prestige riding on its success. President Truman was relying on it.

This situation brought forth its own examples of black humour in the form of little ditties, and Bill recited the latest one to Mary-Jo over the breakfast table on the morning of Thursday 12 July:

> 'From this crude lab that spawned a dud
> Their necks to Truman's axe uncurled.
> Lo, the embattled savants stood
> And fired a flop heard around the world.'

'You don't really think it's going to be a flop do you?' She was not sure whether to be concerned or elated.

He had grinned, not very convincingly, and shrugged his shoulders as he poured the syrup over his waffle. 'There'll be one helluva lot of mud on one helluva lot of faces if it is!'

She had given a wry smile as she glanced out of the window at the parched landscape. 'Oh well, it'll make a change from dust, I guess!'

He took a mouthful of waffle, then another, before pushing the remaining half from him.

362

Mary-Jo gave an exasperated sigh. 'Honey, you've got to eat *something*!' It wasn't only the director who was losing weight these days, and she was becoming genuinely concerned at the sight of him as he undressed for bed each night. 'Have you weighed yourself lately?'

He lit a cigarette and took a sip of his coffee. 'Uh huh.'

'And how much have you lost? Be honest now!'

'About twelve pounds.'

She sighed and got up from the table to tidy away the waffle plates. 'I wish this "Unholy Trinity" thing was over and done with – or, better still, had never been started at all!'

He said nothing. There was nothing to say. For the past few days he had had to force the food down his throat at Mary-Jo's insistence, and he knew that the feeling akin to nausea that never seemed to leave him would only grow worse as the week came to an end and 'Fat Man', their monstrous creation, was let loose on the world. As for the present he just hoped that everything went according to plan in the days ahead.

It was with some relief that a few days before the first test was due he watched the components for the bomb leave The Hill for the test site. It was to travel along a road named 400 years previously by the Conquistadores the 'Jornada del Muerto' – the Journey of Death – to arrive at its final destination, the Alamogordo bombing range near the New Mexico village of Oscuro, where a tall frame of iron scaffolding had been constructed to house the bomb. The irony of the old Spanish name for the route 'Fat Man' was to travel was not lost on any of those involved, nor was the fact that the last of its components arrived at their destination on Friday 13 July.

'Omens … There seem to be so many omens. It's as if God is trying to tell us something,' Mary-Jo said on the morning of the 15th as she stood at their living-room window and looked out on the torrential thunderstorm that was raging outside.

The water bounced a foot high off the baked-earth roadway and ran in rivers six inches deep down the street. As far as the eye could see the parched earth was awash. Great daggers of lightning lit the black sky over the distant mountains and the rumble of the thunder seemed to shake the very foundations of the building.

She stared outside in a mixture of fascination and horror, before gasping, 'Good God, now it's snowing!'

Bill joined her at the window as the rain turned to hail before their eyes. This was 15 July and they were in the middle of the desert. It was snowing in the desert in high summer. And tomorrow they were to detonate the most awesome device in the history of the human race. Icy fingers ran down his spine. It was indeed as if The Almighty were trying to tell them something.

Chapter Thirty-Four

In the early hours of the morning of Monday 16 July 1945, Bill Rutherford sat alongside his colleagues in the Mess Hall at Base Camp, almost ten miles from Point Zero where, encased in its tower of scaffolding, 'Fat Man', the world's first atomic bomb, was primed for detonation. Two years of intensive work had been brought to fruition, but along with a feeling of satisfaction, there was an all-pervading feeling of dread in the hearts of the men assembled there.

Over the past few days apprehensions had been growing about the result. There was even talk of the explosion igniting the atmosphere. And, to add to the tension, at that very moment on the other side of the world, in the Berlin suburb of Potsdam, the new American President, Harry S. Truman, was meeting with Winston Churchill and Joseph Stalin to discuss the future of the world. The possession of the world's most powerful weapon was to be the ultimate ace up Truman's sleeve in the political bargaining game now taking place. It was imperative that 'Fat Man' fulfilled all their hopes for it.

Right now though it seemed as if even the elements were conspiring against them. The atrocious weather conditions had continued night and day, with no let up in the thunder storms that had been lashing the test site. The greatest fear in the minds of the scientists was of the horrendous consequences should a bolt of lightning strike the weapon before it could be detonated properly.

That was without doubt the thing uppermost in all their minds as throughout the early part of the night Bill sat with Oppenheimer and the other scientists in the Mess Hall, drinking endless cups of coffee and smoking countless cigarettes as they waited for the weather conditions to improve.

They could all see that the director was in a highly nervous state, and this was heightened by the arrival of the Italian Nobel prize-winning physicist Enrico Fermi, who presented them with another alarming scenario that could arise should the wind suddenly change direction after blast-off. The wind and rain would see to it that the test site, including themselves, would be deluged with fall-out. They all knew the consequences of that only too well. Fermi pressed for a postponement until weather conditions improved, but after much heated discussion this was rejected. The President was relying on them to come up with the test – and a successful one at that – to impress Stalin and the Soviets during the conference. The nation's prestige rested on them.

A crucial voice in the decision-making was General Leslie Groves, the Head of the Military at Los Alamos, and it was his idea that Oppenheimer and several of his closest colleagues join him several miles further back, at Station South 10,000, to watch the test from there. Bill guessed it was a move designed to distance the director both physically and mentally from the test site itself, where the tension was at its highest. It was turning out a very long night for them all, and this heated discussion wasn't doing any of them any good, especially Oppenheimer who had to remain on top of his form, for his was the final voice in any crucial decision-making that had to be done if a postponement became inevitable.

Bill joined them in the jeep as it drove off in the darkness towards the bunker. They could not leave their fears behind them, however. The gale-force winds, driving rain and lightning showed no sign of abating and, to add to their worries, dawn was now only a few hours away. It was imperative to test the bomb in darkness in order to observe it properly. A weather update told them that the lightning was intensifying. It could only be a matter of time before it hit the tower containing 'Fat Man', with truly horrendous consequences.

They had been praying for a lull in the storm and a shift in the winds above 20,000 feet to the north-east, so that the fall-out could be guaranteed to miss the areas of population around the site, but it seemed as if The Almighty was not listening.

'What do you reckon, then?' Groves turned to Oppenheimer over their first cup of coffee in S.10,000, as they read the printed hand-out of the weather situation at 4.45 A.M.: 'Winds aloft very light, variable to 40,000, surface calm. Inversion about 17,000 feet. Humidity 12,000 to 18,000 feet above 80 per cent. Conditions holding for the next two hours. Sky now broken, becoming scattered'. A final and irrevocable decision had to be made. Time was rapidly running out on them. 'Fat Man's' fate could no longer hang in the balance.

Oppenheimer's face was drained of colour, the strain showing in a vein that throbbed at his temple as he tensed visibly and drew deeply on his pipe. So much was riding on this – the prestige of the whole nation. 'He goes at five-thirty.'

Groves concurred. The decision was made.

As the minutes ticked by and the tension increased, a few of those in the bunker attempted some feeble jokes about the situation to defuse the charged atmosphere, and it was certainly the case that there was a comic element to the proceedings.

'We look like we're all headed for a day out at the seaside!' someone quipped, and it was true. They all had their faces smeared with anti-sunburn cream and wore dark glasses, specially provided for protection against the coming blast. To add to the incongruity of the situation, big-band music blared out of loudspeakers, to be interrupted occasionally with information from Point Zero as to how the final preparations were going.

Occasionally Bill took a look outside and from time to time he could pick out the silhouettes of men working on top of the scaffolding holding 'Fat Man'. The jagged flashes of light from the electrical storm in the sky outlined the tiny figures making last minute adjustments to the bomb. He could only admire their courage, then the thunder would rumble and they would be lost once more in the darkness and driving rain.

As the time crept nearer to blast-off, conversation ceased as each man became engrossed in his own thoughts. For his part, Bill oscillated between fears that the test would fail, and even greater fears of the outcome should it succeed. There had been nothing like this in the history of mankind. What exactly was about to happen here in the middle of the desert only God could know.

At 5.29 A.M. their reveries were harshly interrupted by the loud wail of a siren over the loudspeakers. It was one minute to blast-off. They knew exactly what to do, for they had been well primed. Their sunglasses in place, they all fell to the ground and averted their eyes from the direction of the blast.

'Minus one minute ... minus one minute fifty-nine seconds ... minus one minute fifty-eight seconds ...' The dull monotone of the countdown filled their ears as their hearts pounded in time to the ticking clock.

At minus forty-five seconds the switch was thrown to introduce the automatic timing mechanism. Sweat appeared on Bill's forehead. Tension was sky high.

'Ten ... nine ... eight ... seven ... six ...'

Someone near him was praying: 'Holy Mary, Mother of God ...'

Bill wished he still had that kind of faith in anything.

'Three ... Two ... One ... ZERO!'

Darkness became day. The desert landscape around them glowed a dazzling white, lit by a searing light so bright it appeared that the whole countryside had melted to become part of the shimmering mass. Its intensity was infinitely brighter than that of the midday sun, and the colours more breathtaking than any rainbow: gold, indigo, violet, silver, blue – it was a spectre of beauty that even poets could not have dreamt of, as all around them everything was touched by the dazzling light.

Then, a few seconds later, the ethereal glow began to dim, and Bill ventured to turn his head in the direction of the blast. What he saw was like nothing he could ever have imagined. The sky was filled with a bright ball of orange flame that was growing steadily in size as it rose from the earth to the heavens. Then the blinding white light turned to gold around the glowing orb, as waves of furiously boiling clouds mounted into the heavens. Like a shimmering umbilical cord, it was connected to the desert by a lengthening stem of whirling dust.

As he continued to stare, a blue haze of ionized air appeared as a halo around it. There was not a single sound as the spectacle unfolded before them in an unearthly, absolute silence. Time was at a standstill. The bowels of the earth had opened and the heavens were split asunder.

Then, 'Good God!' someone screamed, 'they've lost control!' and echoed the fears of many; they watched, transfixed, as the huge blazing ball grew larger and larger, until it appeared to fill the entire sky. Surely it would not stop until it had devoured heaven and earth itself? It was as if they were witnesses to both the birth and the death of the universe.

One by one they staggered to their feet, only to have the ghostly silence shattered by an awesome, eardrum-splitting roar which seemed to rock the earth on its axis. Time and space ceased to exist. In this moment was all eternity.

The air blast that followed knocked the very breath from their bodies, and the young man next to Bill landed on his back, while he himself only just succeeded in keeping on his feet.

On his other side, Robert Oppenheimer was clinging to

one of the metal uprights for support. His face had a haunted look to it and his eyes were glued to the vision in the sky. What they had just witnessed no human being had ever dreamt of. They were in the presence of the Almighty Himself. They were witnesses to the birth of the world: the moment of creation when the Lord said, 'Let there be light', and there was light ...

Totally transfixed, and oblivious to all but the vision of death they had created, Robert Oppenheimer's lips moved silently as the words from the Bhagavad Gita, the sacred book of the Hindus, flashed through his mind: '"If the radiance of a thousand suns were to burst upon the sky, that would be like the splendour of the Mighty One ..."'

He turned to Bill, the tears now running unashamedly down his cheeks: 'I am become Death, the shatterer of worlds.'

Those eight words were to live on in Bill Rutherford's heart.

They returned to Berkeley – he and Mary-Jo – but not until several months after the bomb he had helped perfect had been exploded over Hiroshima and Nagasaki, and the world was witness to the full horror and awesome power of their creation.

Something died in him that summer. Something in his heart turned to stone. It was as if the magnitude of what he had done had numbed his capacity for feeling. He still believed passionately in his country and in his government's right to use their Los Alamos creation as they thought fit, but there was a greater dimension to his fears: What if some other power were to get hold of the device? What if other scientists of a land not as fine as his own were to gain the knowledge ... were to become Death, the shatterer of worlds?

In the first long winter after the war he resolved that somehow, someday, he must do all in his power to make sure that nightmare could never become a reality.

As for Mary-Jo, she was only too glad to see the back of Los Alamos. She longed to return to the comfortable familiarity of her hometown and her folks on the east coast. Her father had suffered a minor stroke just before Christmas and she had used that as the reason for flying back to Greensville and staying on in her parents' home for over three months. It was just after Easter before she returned.

It was not easy to pick up the threads of their life together for, with no children to bind them, more and more they were becoming two separate entities. Mary-Jo still had her language studies and her painting to occupy her time and Bill still had his work, but both knew this was not enough.

But knowing it was quite different from doing something about it. There could be no question of even a trial separation, for the knowledge of that would surely ruin her father's health beyond any hopes of recovery. Instead they went their separate ways within the framework of a marriage that was still based on a deep abiding affection built on a memory bank full of joys and sorrows shared.

It was with a sense of real elation, however, that she received the news at the end of June that she had the perfect excuse for returning to South Carolina for a whole week. Bill had been invited to attend a conference of atomic physicists in London on 26 July and would be out of the country for several days.

Despite his wife's delight, Bill himself had great difficulty dealing with the news of the impending conference. A trip to London was the answer to his prayers, but what would happen when he got there? What if he found he was still in love with Eva and she with him? These questions plagued him in the weeks and then days before he was due to set off.

He arrived in England's capital on the morning of Thursday 25 July 1946. The University had booked him into a good class hotel just off Bedford Square and, as he checked in, an uncontrollable excitement welled within him. In under an hour he could be with her. His dreams were about to become a reality and the knowledge brought him out in a cold sweat.

The midday air was cool with the slight hint of rain as, forty minutes later, he made his way in the direction of her apartment just off Russell Square. London had a depressing feel and look to it, and the bomb craters that seemed to meet his eye everywhere he looked were a graphic reminder of what the city had just gone through. The Allies might have won the war, but the price had been a heavy one. The people seemed happy enough though, and he cheered himself with the thought that Eva too had not been the type to let things get her down.

His concern over the huge extent of the bomb damage increased, however, as he neared the street in which Eva had her apartment. Huge craters gaped where familiar buildings had once stood, with weeds growing tall in the piles of uncleared rubble. Even the British Museum, only a stone's throw from her flat, had not escaped unscathed. His anxiety grew by the minute as he stepped up his pace, eager to quell his fears.

Then, as he turned the corner of her road, he let out a groan – a peculiar animal sound, as if he had been kicked in the gut. It had gone – all of it – the whole north end of the street. The whole block containing her apartment – gone. He took a staggering step backwards as if physically assaulted by the sight.

'Are you all right, mate?' A young, scruffily-dressed man of about his own age paused, a concerned look on his face, as Bill leaned against a nearby lamppost for support.

He nodded, speechless, in return, then jerked his head in the direction of the pile of rubble that had once been Eva's home. He could not bear to turn round and look at it. 'Can you tell me when that happened?' he said at last.

The young man looked round in the direction indicated then shook his head. He hadn't the faintest idea. The whole blooming city was full of such holes. He shook his head. 'I ain't from round here myself, but this lady might know … Hey, Missus, do you know anything about when this lot got it?'

The young mother pushing the pram stopped to look at the two of them, then deciding it was a genuine query, gave a shrug. 'It was quite early on in the war, if I remember rightly. Sometime in '41 I think it was … Yes, that's right, it was just before Margaret Rose here was born.' She nodded down at the small child seated on the front of the pram. 'That's right, she was born in the May, and we passed by there on the way to the hospital; then on the way home a few days later the whole bloody lot had gone. Tragic it was.'

Bill felt as if every drop of blood had drained from his body and a great gaping chasm had opened up in his chest. The pain of that moment was acute and physical as he leant heavily against the lamppost for support. His throat had closed, his mouth gone dry, and his voice grated, 'Survivors … What about survivors?'

'What – out of that lot? You must be joking!'

His eyes glazed over. 'Are you telling me there was nobody – nobody got out alive?'

'Nobody as I heard about anyhow. One of the worst raids of the Blitz it was.' Then seeing the stricken look on his face, her voice softened. 'You didn't have someone in that lot, did you? There was nobody in there that belonged to you?'

He shook his head and the words came out with difficulty. 'No, ma'am, no one that belonged to me.' And it was the truth – it was the cold, sickening truth, for if Eva had 'belonged' to him she might be here right now. He let go of the lamppost and muttered his thanks to the two Londoners before walking blindly back in the direction from which he had come.

The news had knocked him for six. He had expected anything but this. Somehow the thought that she could actually have died in the war had never really been a possibility in his mind. That she could have found someone else, that she could have got married even, yes, he could have bought that — even that she had eventually returned to Germany ... But died. Dear God ...

Throughout the three days he remained in London he knew the meaning of real mental anguish and he continually tortured himself reliving the moments he had shared with her. Once again he would be driving through these same familiar streets, heading for her small apartment, or place of work, and she would get into the car with that heart-stopping toss of her blonde hair. He could hear her voice still: it came to him on every breeze as he paced the bomb-scarred streets, or lay awake in his hotel room at night, endlessly smoking. And the ashes of memory left a bitter taste on his tongue as the words of that young London mother came back to haunt him: 'There was nobody in there that belonged to you?'

He used every minute of his spare time scouring the area around the bombsite that had once been her home to see if anyone could remember anything of the young German woman who had lived there. Most had looked at him as if he had gone crazy: 'German, you say? Come off it, guv, they were up there dropping the bleedin' bombs, not down here copping it!'

Even Arnold Kennedy's little shop had gone, and bind-weed now grew in profusion over the blighted earth where thousands of books had once been stored. Someone told him the old man had perished along with his beloved books, and another that he had escaped and gone back to Ireland. At any rate, the trail had gone cold. And even if he had managed to trace the old Fenian, he might have been none the wiser about Eva's fate. London during the Blitz had been chaos, and the city was still a gaping wound.

After each futile search, he had made his way back to the hotel and headed straight for the bar where he had purchased a bottle of Scotch and taken it up to his room.

And now, all these years later, history was repeating itself.

First one drink then another found its way over his throat … She could be here now if he had had the courage to take her away from all this, if he had not been so hidebound by that misguided sense of responsibility he felt towards Mary-Jo and her family.

'Eva … Eva …' The tears ran down his face, hot and unashamed, as he thought of what he had loved and lost in that city. Her face swam before him and he reached out to touch it, only to have it dissolve in a haze of tears and whisky.

The years had rolled on – long barren years without her. Years in which he had served his time being a good husband to his wife and doing his best by the country he loved. But the ache had remained; an emptiness deep inside him that could not be filled. There was a darkness at the heart of things where the light had gone out of his life never to be lit again.

He thought he had come to terms with life without her – learned to cope with that darkness, with that constant yearning ache – until tonight. He glanced at the date on a copy of *Die Zeit* which lay on the table beside him: *Donnerstag 28 Juli 1966*. It was almost twenty years to the day. Twenty years to the day that the tragedy of that discovery in July 1946 had been brought home to him with a vengeance. His own daughter had accused him of the murder of her mother – of the woman he had loved with all his heart and soul.

His hand shook as he poured one more whisky from the rapidly emptying bottle beside him. 'Anna …' He slurred the name of the child whose existence he had never even guessed at until today as he slurped the pungent, all-forgiving spirit. 'Why, Anna, why …?'

It had not only been his daughter punishing him tonight, it had been The Almighty Himself. The pain of what had transpired in that small apartment on the Kant Strasse cut deep into his soul. He could not live with the pain. Eva … Anna … Their faces floated before him, then merged into one as he reached into the pocket of his jacket for the pills.

Just one, or two at the most, his doctor back in Washington had said. Just one or two if you really feel you can't sleep. He needed sleep now more than he had ever done. The pain was welling within him like some great cancer; it was ready to devour his soul. He shook one into the palm of his hand and looked at it through swimming eyes. One could never be enough, not even two, not tonight. He needed sleep – real sleep – to rid him of this shame – this agony.

Another, then another, then another of the little pink tablets were shaken into his palm, then gulped down with the last of the whisky.

He was barely aware of draining the bottle, or of the glass slipping from his hand on to the carpet.

'Eva …' She was back. She was with him in this room. She was moving towards him, her arms outstretched.

Then suddenly he was no longer there in that lonely hotel room, but walking with her, hand in hand, down a long, sunlit road. They were heading for a light in the sky, and a hill, a green, green hill … Climbing ever upwards into the clouds themselves …

The young captain found him next morning, still slumped in the same chair, his right arm reaching forwards as if to grasp something, or someone. He had a strangely peaceful look to his face, as if death, when it came, had been a liberation; as if he had found on the other side what he had never known in this life.

Lying on the table beside him was a photograph – an old photograph – of a young girl, wearing a pretty summer dress, and carrying a straw hat in her hand. Her long blonde hair was blowing in the breeze and there was a strangely familiar look to the features that smiled out at the young man. The soldier shook his head. He was sure he recognized her from somewhere. In fact, if it weren't for the fact that this picture was at least a generation old, he could swear he had seen her in this very hotel over the past few days …

Chapter Thirty-Five

Anna awoke at eleven in her small room on the third floor of the Schiller Hotel. The feather quilt lay in a heap at the foot of the bed and she was bathed in perspiration. She blinked her eyes in the dull light as she struggled to distinguish the cold reality of the present from the nightmare world from which she had just escaped. Over the past few hours of what had passed for sleep, she had relived her confrontation with her father in grotesque parody, and the experience had left her both drained and depressed to the point of tears.

She washed and dressed quickly and made her way downstairs to the deserted restaurant. She had no appetite, however, and ignored the rolls and assorted cold meats on offer, but ordered herself a pot of coffee which she took to a table by the window.

It was still raining outside. It was a grey, weepy type of day which corresponded perfectly with her mood as she lit a cigarette and took her first sip of the coffee. It tasted bitter on her tongue and she glanced across longingly at the array of bottles behind the bar in the corner of the room. It would be so easy to order one drink, and then another and another, until sweet oblivion left her without a care in the world.

Karl had advised her to leave Berlin as soon as possible, but she knew she could not go without saying a proper goodbye to her grandmother, and she found her spirits lifting at the thought of seeing the old lady again. It was just the boost she needed to lift the deep gloom into which she had descended.

Before setting off for the other side of the Wall, she chose an enormous bunch of red roses from a flower shop on the corner, and filled a basket with a large jar of instant coffee and several other little luxuries she knew were almost impossible to come by on the other side. On the journey across she cheered herself by imagining all the other things she could buy for her once back in London. Didn't Fortnum and Mason's do the most marvellous hampers? She was feeling happier already.

When at last she arrived outside the gaunt apartment block that was her grandmother's home, she was pleasantly surprised to see Rudi Gross coming out of the front door. He recognized her immediately and came across, his hand extended and a genuine smile on his lips. 'Anna, how nice to see you again! You are enjoying your stay in our city, I hope?'

They shook hands and she smiled in return, wondering which half he was referring to. 'Yes – I certainly am. But I'm going back to London this afternoon.'

'*Ach ja* … back to Swinging England! You will return to Berlin, though. For you are half a Berliner yourself, remember.'

How could she ever forget? She stepped into the entrance porch out of the rain and nodded most definitely. 'I will certainly be back. And you must come to London some time, like you promised.'

He gave a quiet smile. 'A gentleman must always keep his promises.' Then he gave a polite bow. 'Give my regards to your grandmother.'

'I will.'

The lift was out of order, so she climbed the stairs to knock tentatively on her grandmother's door.

'*Kommen Sie nur!*'

She pushed open the door to find the old lady still in bed. She had obviously had a bad night, for her face was the colour and texture of parchment as Anna bent to kiss her forehead and clasp the frail body to her own.

'Roses – my favourite flowers!'

'I thought you would like them.' Anna laid the blooms at the foot of the bed and sat down on the edge of the mattress.

'And such things!' Margarete's eyes widened as she gazed at the basket and its contents. 'You shouldn't have …'

'Yes, I should,' Anna replied, as her grandmother sank back against the pillow. 'It is my pleasure.' Then her own smile faded as her grandmother reached across to the small bedside table for her inhaler and took two deep breaths.

Anna reached out a comforting hand. 'You're not well …'

Her grandmother waved the sympathy aside. 'Old lungs get wheezy, and old bones get lazy, my dear, that's all. And I am all the better for seeing you again.' Her voice was little more than a husky whisper as she spoke, but she made a determined smile. Then the smile faded as she glanced down at the overnight case at Anna's feet. 'You are not leaving Berlin already?'

Her granddaughter gave an apologetic sigh. 'I'm afraid so. Duty calls,' she lied.

'Your newspaper – they need you back home?'

Anna nodded. 'I was only here covering the meeting of Defence Chiefs …'

Her voice tailed off and her grandmother intervened. '*Ach ja*, they are meeting in the Western Sector, is that not so? There was something on the radio this morning. Something about that American … The big boss – you know the one who invented the bomb …'

Anna stiffened visibly. 'Rutherford. You mean Rutherford?'

'*Ja*, that is the one.'

'What – what about him?' She could feel her heart beating faster. Surely he hadn't called a Press conference or anything like that? She cursed inwardly for having slept in and not bothered to turn on the radio in her hotel room.

Her grandmother shook her head. 'I don't remember the details – just that the radio announcer seemed to spend a lot of time talking about him, and I thought – that is the one my dear Anna came all the way to interview! It made me so proud!'

She reached over and clasped her granddaughter's hand. 'I'm so very proud of you, Anna. You are all I could have hoped for in a grandchild, and I know your mother would have felt the same.'

Anna balked. Just what *would* her mother have thought if she had known the real reason for her visit? She tried desperately to cast the thought aside as she looked down at the frail fingers in hers. 'It – it means a lot to me that you should feel that way,' she said softly. 'You can't know what finding you again has meant.'

There were tears in her grandmother's eyes. 'Yes, yes, *mein Kind*, I can.'

'Then come with me,' Anna pleaded. 'Come back to London with me. I can arrange it, I'm sure. They say there's no problem in East Germany for older people leaving for the West.'

Her grandmother gave a wry smile. 'That is true. The more of us old ones who go, the less of a burden to the state.'

'Then you'll come?' Anna's hopes rose, only to be dashed by an emphatic shake of the head.

'No, *Liebchen*, this is my home.'

'But you can have so much more in the West,' Anna protested. 'You could live in luxury – not like here ...' She shook her head as she looked round the cold comforts of the spartan room, with its single bed and cheap, utility chest of drawers and wardrobe.

Margarete followed her eyes and knew just what she was thinking. '*Besser was als gar nichts, mein Schatz,*' she said wearily. 'What I have here is not much, but what would I have in your country – in London? I am a Berliner, Anna. I was born in this city and I will die here.'

'Don't – don't talk of dying!' Anna spoke much more harshly than she intended. But the idea was unthinkable. They had only just found each other.

To disguise the tears that had sprung to her eyes she got up and walked to the window to gaze out over the roof-tops in the direction of the Wall, with its no man's land of barbed wire and buried mines. They had driven a gaping wound through the centre of her grandmother's city, just as they had driven a gaping wound through the old lady's heart. 'They' – the politicians – had robbed her of her home and family under one political system, and left her to suffer under another. And yet she would not leave.

Her grandmother watched from the bed. She knew just what her granddaughter was thinking. 'I am an old woman, Anna child. Perhaps just a stubborn old woman – who knows? But these are my people. This is my home. You do not desert a beloved parent or child because they may be disfigured, do you? So I cannot say goodbye to my city. To leave Berlin now would be to turn my back on all my memories, and good and bad, Anna, they are as much a part of me as these creaking old joints.' She glanced down at her arthritic hands, then lay back on her pillow with a deep wheezing sigh as she continued, 'No, child, it is enough for me to know I have found you. To know my beloved Eva is not dead, for you have brought her back to me.'

Anna turned to face her as her grandmother continued softly, 'For as long as you live, child, my Eva will never die.'

Anna returned to the bed to take the old lady's hands in hers. The tears were coursing unashamedly down her cheeks now and Margarete leaned forward to wipe them away. 'I never thought I would live to see those eyes again. Those are Koehn eyes you are blessed with, Anna,' she said softly. 'They are your mother's eyes, and were your grandfather's and great-grandfather's.'

'I wish I could have known them.' Oh God, how she wished that.

'They were good people, Anna. All of them were truly good people, with no bitterness in them. For myself that is not true, for I have hated those who have caused so much pain and suffering. But I know now the harm that such a hate can do to the human heart. It eats away at you, Anna, till

381

there is nothing left but hate, and I thank God that your own heart has never been contaminated by that poison. I thank God that you are your mother's daughter ...'

Margarete lay back on the pillow and looked with love on this child of her own child, and she thanked God that the bitterness she had known would die with her, that this young generation would have no cause to harbour such a cancer within its heart.

Anna remained silent. If only she knew ... If only she knew of the hatred she had felt for so long towards the man who had fathered her. Had that been so very wrong? Then she thought of the needless suffering and death endured by her family. How could anyone remain free from bitterness or hate after all that injustice, all that agony of body and soul? 'You mean if my mother and grandfather had survived that awful war they would not feel bitter about what had happened to them? They would not seek revenge?'

Her grandmother nodded and sighed once more, a deep, heartfelt sigh. 'Bitterness eats into the soul, Anna. It destroys the heart that harbours it far more than the original hurt that has been done. To harbour bitterness and hatred for the past is to defile both the present and the future. An eye for an eye, a tooth for a tooth was never the creed by which anyone in our family lived, no more than I know it would be the creed by which you would choose to live. You are your mother's daughter, Anna, and I am as proud of you as of my own Eva.'

She reached out to clasp her granddaughter to her and Anna closed her eyes to stem the flow of her tears as she held the frail body in her arms. She felt unworthy, tainted by the bitterness she knew had lain within her own heart for so long, so very long ...

Her heart was heavy as she said her final goodbye several minutes later. All the words of comfort she had received from Kurt Kessel were as nothing to her now. She had let her grandmother down. She had let them all down: her mother, her grandfather, her great-grandfather ... In wreaking revenge on her father she had placed herself on a level with those who had perpetrated all those other wrongs in the past. She was no better than any of them. Worse perhaps, for she had perpetrated her wrong on her own flesh and blood: on her own father.

Once outside the apartment block she shivered in the light rain that was still falling and gazed up into the grey sky. Somehow she knew she could not return home to London without reaching out towards the rest of the family she would never know, but whose memory she now knew she had besmirched so badly.

Once across the border, she headed for the nearest taxi and, to the driver's obvious surprise, requested him to take her first to the Putlitzstrasse goods yards, where she knew her grandfather had been transported to the death camps of Theresienstadt and Auschwitz. To stop off there was the least she could do: a small token of respect to a man she would never know, but whom her mother and grandmother had loved.

The yards were situated between the overcrowded working-class district of Wedding to the north, and the industrial area of Moabit to the south and west, and the next twenty minutes did nothing to lift her spirits, for it was a depressing journey through an area light years away from the Ku-damm and other fashionable streets of West Berlin. The cityscape was veined by waterways and inland docks, huge power stations dominated the skyline and, in the warren of grey streets surrounding the factories, the faces were mostly of a much darker hue. This was where the *Gastarbeiter* – the Turkish 'guest workers' – toiled in their hundreds. Scrawled in white chalk on the brick wall opposite to where the taxi pulled up were the words:

> *'Allah ist mächtig, Allah ist gross,*
> *Fünf-meter-sechzig, und arbeitslos!'*

'Allah is mighty, Allah is great, five-metres-sixty and unemployed,' she murmured wryly. Were they to become the Jews of today – the first to lose their jobs when times got hard? But that seemed to be the way of the world. It was always the incomers who suffered most, even if those incomers had been there for hundreds of years: *Der ewige Jude* – the eternal Jew – most of all.

She got out of the taxi and instructed the puzzled driver to keep the meter running once more as she walked slowly along the platform where a generation ago her grandfather had lined up with thousands of others for transportation to the East. But here there was no barking of dogs, or shouts of the uniformed animals who herded other people's mothers and fathers, sons and daughters and grandparents on to the waiting cattle trucks. Now, in 1966, there was no clattering of wheels to be heard, no shunting of lines as the empty trucks rolled up to await their miserable human cargo.

The railway tracks down below her which had once headed on into infinity, towards the East and its camps of death, were now overgrown with tall weeds and rubbish lay strewn amidst the clumps of rye grass. There was a strange silence about the place that hung heavy on her heart. It was as if the sound of a child's laughter, or the song of a bird would never again be heard in that sad, haunted spot. Too many hearts had ached in this place, too many tears had been shed for loved ones never to be seen again, for it ever to be the same.

She could almost see them. She could feel their misery – all those countless thousands who had left this place – torn from their families to suffer and die in those godforsaken camps in the East. Countless thousands whose only sin it was to be of a different faith, whether it be Jewish, Communist, or anything else that those in power chose to disapprove of. And what of those who survived? What of the Margaretes and Kurts of this world? Was their life so much better now, behind that Wall? A deep sadness welled within her for all those still suffering as they were. For no matter what Kurt said, they *were* still suffering behind that Wall, and would go on suffering as long as it continued to stand there, a godless edifice, a last legacy of Nazism, erected in the name of Communism to keep out the evils of Capitalism. She shook her head as she remembered the words of her father: 'Don't you think it's high time all the "isms" in this world became "wasms"?' The wisdom of those words had never seemed more true.

Anna remained there, standing silently by the disused track for several minutes before turning to make her way slowly back to the waiting taxi. She wished she still believed. If ever there had been a time to say a prayer, it was now; a prayer for those like her mother and grandfather who, had history decreed otherwise, she would have known and loved. Their loss had been her loss too, and her grandmother's loss. Her heart ached for the old lady who sat alone in that flat across the Wall, and for the millions of others who had survived the Nazi years, only to find themselves living under another political system which would deny them the freedom she and others in the West took for granted. How different life could – and should – have been for them all.

'*Tegel Flughafen*,' she instructed the driver as she got back into the car. '*Schnell, bitte.*' She was not sorry to be leaving this place.

It was in the airport departure lounge that she learned the news. It stared her in the face from a newspaper hoarding beneath the main newsstand: 'AMERIKANISCHER VERTEI-DIGUNGS-CHEF TOT AUFGEFUNDEN'. 'American Defence Chief found dead!' Anna mouthed the words silently as she stood rooted to the spot staring at the words scrawled on the placard before her.

She could not move. It was as if the last breath had been knocked from her body. Then slowly she was walking forward and taking a newspaper from the stand.

It was the first edition of the evening paper and as she glanced down at the front page there could be no doubt about whom the headlines referred to. Her father's face was staring back at her. It was a recent photograph, taken at the conference that week, and he was smiling. That made it worse, somehow.

As if in a trance, she walked to a nearby seat and sat down heavily. She spread the newspaper on her lap and her eyes swam as she took in the first few sentences: 'Early this morning, General William J. Rutherford, Chief of America's Nuclear Defence Programme was found dead in his hotel room. The cause of death is not yet established, but it is understood that General Rutherford had been suffering from a heart condition for some time ...'

Dear God ... Dear God ... She had had no idea. She could read no further.

Then from somewhere above the din of the departure lounge she was aware of her name being called. There it was again: 'Would Miss Anna Lloyd-Jones, waiting to board Flight LH 256 to London, please report to the reception desk immediately ...'

She stood up, clasping the newspaper to her as the clinical tones of the announcer repeated the message once more.

'I'm Anna Lloyd-Jones.' Her voice was barely audible as she reached the reception desk and addressed the young woman seated behind it.

'Ah, yes ... There's a telephone call for you, madam. The gentleman has called in to check if you were booked on the last two London flights, so it must be important.' She handed Anna the receiver and turned to deal with the next passenger.

'Hello?'

'Anna?' It was Karl's voice on the other end of the line. 'Anna – is that you?'

'Yes, it's me.' Her voice was flat, almost unrecognizable. There was a pause at the other end. 'Have you heard?'

'Yes, I've heard.'

'He's dead, Anna. Rutherford's dead.'

'I know.'

'I'm sorry, Anna. Really sorry.'

'So am I, Karl.'

There was a silence as both searched for the right words to say, but none came. Then Karl said quietly, 'I didn't hand over those photos, Anna. There's no point now, is there?'

'No … No, Karl. There's no point …' Her voice choked, and she replaced the receiver in its rest. She could talk no further.

'Is there anything wrong, madam?' The young woman behind the desk looked up curiously as Anna stared down at the silent phone and fought to control her emotions.

Anna nodded. 'Yes, there is something wrong. My father's dead,' she said quietly. 'My father's dead and I killed him. You can't get anything more wrong than that, can you?'

Epilogue

Professor Anna Lloyd-Jones looked up from her desk in her third-floor office within the majestic white walls of the Social Science Faculty of the University of London and glanced at the clock on the shelf opposite. It was almost twelve o'clock – lunchtime. But she still had one more letter to write.

She yawned and stretched her arms. The central heating always made her feel drowsy after a couple of hours seated at her word processor. She had felt quite virtuous coming in at all during the Christmas break, but there seemed little choice; there were so many things on the agenda these days. Who on earth would have believed, even a few weeks ago, that 1990 would see the toppling of the Berlin Wall itself? Twenty-five years ago Kurt Kessel had told her it would never happen – not in their lifetimes – but there it was ... Her fingers reached forward to touch the lump of cement hacked with her own hands from the part nearest the Unter den Linden, and which now stood in place of honour on her desk. Her own personal piece of history. She wished he could have lived to see it.

But Kurt was dead. He had died of a heart attack within weeks of her returning to London after that first fateful trip to Berlin. The news had filled her with a deep sorrow. At heart, she knew him to have been a good man, and his death had been the severing of one more link with her mother's past.

But, with the momentous events of the past few months, all that now seemed part of another era. The world had moved on so dramatically in recent weeks that even attempting to keep pace with day to day happenings was a hard enough task. Who would have believed it back then in 1966? Certainly not Kurt Kessel. Certainly not anyone who knew anything about politics. The Wall, that awful symbol of a world divided, had fallen to the will of the people.

But more than that, one of the greatest injustices of the twentieth century, the denial of democratic rights to Eastern Europe, was about to be rectified, even within the Soviet Union itself. It gave Anna new hope for the world as it entered the last decade of the century. However, it left that other great injustice still to be put right: the bridging of the gap between the affluent nations and the poor. For almost a quarter of a century she had worked towards that goal.

Since returning to academic life in the autumn of 1966, she had succeeded in establishing herself as both a popular teacher and a recognized authority on the Third World, and the conferences she now organized were regarded as the touchstones for much of the work being done in under-developed countries.

She had had no heart to continue in the public domain as a journalist and interviewer after the events of that awful summer in Berlin. In returning to academic life she knew she could at least attempt to do something constructive for those less well-off than herself. Was it some kind of atonement for what had happened in '66? That was something she could never be quite sure about, but she had never regretted the decision. And her perseverence had paid dividends, both personally and professionally – sometimes in the most unexpected ways.

Her eyes returned to the page of white, headed notepaper on the desk in front of her. This was one of those dividends, and one that she had certainly not expected. And it was high time she replied. Hadn't she promised herself she would make the decision before the weekend?

She sighed and picked up the piece of paper. The question was begged and stared her in the face: Would she be willing to accept the honour of the title of Dame of the British Empire to be bestowed upon her by Her Majesty the Queen in her next Birthday Honours List? It was to be a recognition of her years of service to the various charities and government think-tanks emanating from her involvement with Third World poverty programmes.

'Dame Anna Lloyd-Jones ...' She tried the title out for size on her tongue. It was a bitter-sweet decision she must come to. She could just imagine the comment she herself would have made at such a suggestion twenty years ago. But a lot had happened in her life since then; she had come a long way intellectually, and, she hoped, emotionally. She was no longer so quick to judge and condemn; she was much readier to see the other person's point of view, even though she might not agree with it.

In the staff dining-room the other day, someone had asked whatever had become of the intellectual rebels of the Sixties, and quick as a flash the answer had come back – they had all become the university lecturers of today. And, for good or ill, she knew that to be the truth, at least as far as she and many of her friends were concerned. Here they all were, the archetypal *Guardian*-reading, Volvo-driving, claret-drinking members of the Soft Left; most of them, like ageing hippies, still clinging to the last relics of the Sixties, whether they be old Bob Dylan records or membership cards of CND. Had she sold her principles down the river in the process? It was a moot point that even she did not yet have the answer to.

Someone once said that each generation was a secret society unto itself and she now knew that to be true, for the students she had taught in the Eighties were light years removed from those of her own generation. It was sometimes difficult to believe that the self-possessed young of today could get really impassioned about anything. But was that necessarily a bad thing? Too much of any emotion could be as destructive a force as it could be constructive – she had learned that lesson with a vengeance twenty-four years ago when her obsessive desire for revenge had ended in the death of her father.

A knock at the door brought an end to her musing and she glanced across at it in irritation. Who could it be at this time? There were hardly any students left on campus over the Christmas break, and the others weren't yet back for the start of the new term.

She got up to answer it and her expression showed her surprise when, on opening it, she came face to face with one of her American students. 'Jacqui!'

Droplets of melted snow clung to the fringe of dark hair that protruded from beneath the gaily-coloured woollen hat of the young woman on the doorstep, and her grey-blue eyes smiled apologetically as she held out her hand and wished Anna a Happy New Year, adding, 'I do hope you don't mind me barging in on you like this?'

'Not at all, come on in.' She stepped aside to allow her visitor to enter. She had always had a soft spot for the slim, pertly-pretty New Yorker with the soft voice, although her classes were so large these days she never got the chance to know any of her students really well.

Jacqui O'Malley's normally pale skin was flushed a bright pink from the exertion of running up the three flights of stairs and the sharp, biting frost of the air outside. It had not been a white Christmas, but the weather seemed to be making up for it now. She brushed the remaining snow flakes from her coat as she said breathlessly. 'I was just passing and I saw your light on and thought I'd take a chance on finding you here. I've actually just dropped in to say goodbye. I'm leaving for the States this evening.'

Anna was genuinely surprised. Most of her foreign students stayed for at least three semesters. 'I'm sorry to hear that. I didn't realize you were only here for the one term.'

Jacqui shrugged her shoulders and sighed. 'It would have been real nice to stay longer – for the year, say. I had hopes of that in the beginning, but it didn't quite work out that way.'

'It – it wasn't money problems, by any chance?' Anna asked. It wouldn't have been the first time she had managed to help out in that line.

'No, it wasn't that ...' The young woman shifted uncomfortably and avoided her eyes.

'I'm sorry, I didn't mean to pry.'

'Oh, you're not prying – honestly. It isn't money that's the problem ...' Her eyes met Anna's and she decided she might as well be honest. 'It's my mother, actually. I feel bad about leaving her for so long. She hasn't been well, you see, since my dad died.'

'I – I see. I hope she's on the road to recovery very soon.' Anna's voice reflected her concern. She knew just how much family problems could affect a student's work.

Jacqui shook her head. 'There's not much likelihood of that, I'm afraid. She's been in a nursing home for the past twenty-four years.'

'Good God, you must have been just a kid when she was admitted!'

'I was four, actually ... But she'd had nervous problems for years – since long before I was born.' Jacqui gave a wry smile. 'I was a late arrival. Mom was in her forties when I came along. It was ironic, really – from what I've heard she had longed for a baby for over twenty years, then when I eventually came on the scene she couldn't cope – got post-natal depression, and all that. Then when Dad died a few years later, that was the last straw. She finally cracked for good.'

Anna's heart went out to her. What a rotten childhood. She had never even guessed such a tragedy lay behind the calm, smiling exterior of the attractive young woman who had graced her lectures and Tuesday morning tutorials for the past three months. 'Did you see much of each other after she was admitted?'

'Oh sure. The nursing home is only a few blocks from where I now live. And, even during my childhood, my foster parents were really good in that respect; they used to take me to visit her every weekend. My foster-father was an old friend of Daddy's, which made all the difference. They've been like real parents to me – in fact, I call them my Mom and Dad Douglas.'

'And your real mother is missing you too much right now, is that it? You feel guilty about being away from home for so long?'

Jacqui sighed. That was it in a nutshell. 'I guess that's what it boils down to.'

'Parents can have quite a disruptive influence on their children's lives.' The words came from the heart.

'Oh, I don't mind really. I feel so sorry for her locked away in that place – no matter how nice it is, it can never be home. She still talks about him, you know – my father – she still speaks of him as if he were right there beside her. It was kinda spooky at first, but I've got used to it now, I guess. I think what finally did it – pushed her over the brink – was the fact he took his own life right at the peak of his career, when he had everything to live for.'

She paused, shifting from one foot to the other as she wondered how much to say. The last thing she wanted was to burden other people with her family problems. But pride in her dead father's accomplishments overcame her natural reluctance. 'You see, Professor, not only was he at the top of his tree professionally, but the very week before his suicide he had received a letter intimating he'd been nominated for the next Nobel Prize for Physics.' She shook her head in incredulity at the waste of such a life. 'Why would anyone do that, Professor – take their own life with everything to live for?'

Anna gripped the edge of her desk and pulled open a drawer looking for her cigarettes. Despite all the evidence about lung cancer, she still had not given up the habit. She pulled out the packet and offered it across to her visitor.

'No thanks, I don't. But you go right ahead.'

She lit one with a jerky movement, blowing the smoke out in the opposite direction to her visitor. 'What – what did you say your surname was again, Jacqui?'

'It's O'Malley. My full name is Jacqueline Mary O'Malley.' She gave a sheepish smile. 'The Jacqueline is after my Dad's best friend who is now my foster father – his name's Jack – and the Mary is after my mother. Her name's Mary-Jo, actually, but I guess they thought Jacqueline Mary-Josephine was a bit of a mouthful.'

Anna breathed easier. 'Your father – he was Irish, was he?'

'Heavens, no! O'Malley's my married name.' Her smile faded as she continued quietly, 'Jeff and I were divorced last year. That's why I've taken so long to get my degree. I took a few years out to try and make a go of being a wife and mother, but the mother thing didn't happen, and the wife bit … Well, we did our best, but Jeff was convinced I was looking for someone to replace my father and he could never measure up.' She studied her nails, avoiding the sympathetic look from across the room. 'Not that I blame him. I doubt if anyone could ever measure up to Daddy.'

'And your father was?'

'William J. Rutherford.'

'The nuclear physicist.'

Jacqui's dark brows rose in astonishment. 'How did you know that?'

Anna leaned heavily against the desk for support as her worst suspicions were confirmed. 'He was a famous man at one time, you know, Jacqui. But you're too young – much too young – to remember that. I – I interviewed him once, back in the Sixties, for a newspaper I worked on.'

'Really? You mean you actually met my father? Tell me, Professor, what did you think of him?' Her eyes were shining now as she looked expectantly at Anna. 'How did he strike you? Did you get along?'

'He was a very nice man. Very easy to get along with.'

Jacqui gave a satisfied nod. 'I knew you'd say that. Everyone who knew him says that. Daddy Jack claims he was the finest man he ever knew ... I suppose it's not so surprising really that Mom just couldn't face life without him. Although the feminists today would say that's a terrible indictment of the female condition.' She gave an embarrassed smile. 'I don't mean to insult feminists in any way. I mean, I know you're a very keen one yourself.'

Anna raised her eyebrows. 'What makes you say that?'

'Well, the fact you've kept your own name for a start – you don't care to be known by your husband's name.'

Anna smiled. 'I think that arises more out of avoiding confusion, seeing that we're both lecturing in the same establishment, rather than any militant feminist point I want to make.'

Jacqui gave a relieved half-laugh. 'Oh really? I'm glad to hear it ... Anyway, now we're back to the subject of the university, before I go I just wanted to say how much I appreciate all the marvellous lectures you've given over the last three months. I'll never forget them. In fact, I mean to go on now and do my Masters back at Columbia on the Third World's poverty programmes.'

'That's great news, Jacqui. That really is.' Anna smiled across at the young woman she now knew to be her own flesh and blood, her half-sister. Her heart was beating much too fast and the palms of her hands were damp with nervous perspiration. For over twenty years now, since her *Oma* Koehn's death in East Berlin in the spring of '67, she had believed herself to have no known relatives. And now this ... With all her heart she longed to rush up and embrace the young woman beside her, to greet her like the long-lost sister that she now knew her to be, but too much emotion stood between them. The gulf was too wide and too deep for such impulsive reactions. Perhaps the truth would be told one day, but not right now – not like this.

Observing the strained look that had come over the other's

face, Jacqui assumed she must be outstaying her welcome. 'Well, I guess I'd better not take up any more of your time, Professor. I know how busy you are.' She held out her right hand in goodbye. 'It's been a privilege being taught by you, Professor Lloyd-Jones.'

Anna clasped the slim fingers in hers. 'Keep in touch, Jacqui,' she said softly. 'Leave your address and phone number with the departmental secretary, will you? I'm in New York quite a bit these days and I'd like to look you up.'

'That would be great.' Jacqui's eyes lit up in appreciation. 'I'll certainly do that.' Then, impulsively, she leaned over and hugged her mentor. 'Goodbye, Professor. And thanks for everything!'

Thanks for everything ... those last words echoed in Anna's head long after the door closed and she was left alone once more. Thanks for everything ... Thanks for being instrumental in their father's suicide. Thanks for ruining her mother's health. Thanks for blighting her own childhood. Thanks, Professor ... Thanks for everything ...

Her eyes were smarting as she walked to the window and looked out at the steadily falling snow. Over twenty years it had taken to find out she had a sister. Over twenty years of living with the guilt of that fateful trip to Berlin during the long hot summer of '66. It seemed as if every single time she discovered someone who belonged to her, that relationship was doomed from the beginning.

She had not the shadow of a doubt that she would never have considered getting back at her father had she known of Jacqui's existence, but her bitterness had stood in the way of rational thought and she had never bothered to find out. Maybe she had never wanted to know, for to know details of a wife and child back in the States was to rub salt in the wound of the woman and child that should have been recognized as his over here in Europe. The woman and the child that he had walked out on all those years before.

She sat back down at her desk as a sigh shuddered through

her. This was the last thing she had expected when she left her Highgate home for the office this morning. But the past she had spent so many years trying to bury would not lie down. There was to be no respite from the agony of the folly of her youth. And, if she were honest with herself, perhaps it was just as well. Perhaps there was a justice at the heart of things that said we must all pay for our mistakes. Regret is not enough.

Memories crowded in on her in the silence of her room. It was snowing more heavily now, the flakes swirling past her window as the people and places in her life cascaded through her mind. The desk-top calendar was still on December and automatically she reached across and flicked it over to the new month. The first of January 1990. A new year and a new decade had begun, one that should prove to be one of the most momentous this century. She sighed as she leaned back in her chair. If only dispensing with the past was as easy as turning over a new leaf on the calendar. Alas that was not the case. She knew now, more than ever, that you carried it with you – all your emotional baggage – it was the cross you bore for the rest of your life. And, at this moment, her back was as bowed with the weight of that cross as at any time in her life.

The sound of the door opening and a familiar voice roused her from her reverie. The past once more merged into the present at the sight of the overcoated, slightly shambling figure who stood before her, unwinding a snow-caked scarf from around his neck.

'Anna, *Liebling*, have you seen the time? I thought we were going for lunch at 12 o'clock!'

Anna looked up at her husband of sixteen years. Karl Brandt's beard was much greyer than when they had first met all those years ago, but his love for her had remained as steadfast as ever. He was the bedrock of her life, and she was the first to admit it.

And perhaps most important of all, he was the one – the only one – to see behind the successful academic exterior to the vulnerable young woman who still existed beneath. Only he knew the truth of what had really happened during that summer all those years ago, and only he knew the true extent of the price that had been paid. There had been no sweetness in revenge, only an unspoken sorrow that time could not heal.

Her decision to marry Karl had been made in the summer of '74, and it was news of another Berliner from her past that was to bring them together again. She had met Karl for the first time in years, just a few weeks after learning that Rudi Gross had been arrested as an East German agent in the West German capital of Bonn.

The arrest had been made along with that of his superior, Günter Guillaume, one of the West German Chancellor's closest advisers. The scandal, which had forced the resignation of Chancellor Willy Brandt himself, had shaken the West German government to its foundations, but it had shaken no one more than Anna. It seemed incredible that the smiling, personable young man who had confessed to loving her mother as a child, and who had been instrumental in reuniting her with her grandmother, should have been unmasked as an enemy agent. But, then, who exactly was the enemy? Her grandmother and Kurt? Had they been enemies too, for loving their country and refusing to leave it?

It was a strange quirk of fate that Rudi's arrest should have brought Karl Brandt back into her life. Save for the occasional Christmas card, she had lost touch with him over the years, but she could still remember the delight on his face when she walked into the BBC television studios at Shepherd's Bush in early May 1974, to record a programme on the Third World, and found him there to take part in a discussion on the implications of the Guillaume spy scandal on West German politics.

His joy at meeting her again had been immediate and genuine, and when they had gone out to supper later that evening he had given a wry smile as he reached across the table and took her hand, 'We have a saying in Germany, Anna: *Liebe kennt der allein, der ohne Hoffnung liebt* – That man alone knows what love is who loves on when hope is gone … Hope ended for me when you flew out of my life that day they announced your father's death, but it never stopped me loving you. Not for a single second.'

She had raised her brows in surprise. 'You never mentioned it again, Karl.' They had gone on exchanging letters and the occasional phone-call for several months, until their correspondence dwindled to almost a full-stop after several years.

He sighed. 'I guess I felt I had thrown my hat in the ring way back in Berlin that summer; you hadn't picked it up then, so …'

'So it would have been too humiliating to risk another rebuff.'

He grinned sheepishly. 'Something like that.'

'And now?'

'Now I am either too old, or too stupid to care if I risk another rejection or not. I want you to marry me, Anna. I never want to let you go again.'

And she had never regretted her decision to be his wife. It had been an opportunity to rebuild and strengthen a relationship – to construct rather than to destroy. It seemed a natural conclusion, somehow – a consolidation for both of them of a relationship based on mutual respect that had begun as love in his case, and in her own was to deepen into that emotion with the passing of the years. Karl's eventual transfer to a lectureship in the Department of Political Philosophy in London had seen their love for each other continue to grow, and a peculiar peace had come to her in middle-age that she would never have believed she could ever achieve, and in her heart she knew she did not deserve. And now more than ever she was convinced of that.

In her mind's eye she could still see the pain on the face of young Jacqui O'Malley, and the sorrow and bewilderment in her voice as she said, '… the very week before his suicide he had received a letter intimating he had been nominated for the next Nobel Prize in Physics. Why would anyone do that, Professor – take their own life with everything to live for …?'

Why indeed.

'Well, are you going to sit there all day, or are we going for that bar lunch we spoke about?'

Anna gazed down at the headed notepaper lying on the blotter in front of her. 'Just a moment, *Liebchen*, there's something I must do first.'

It was something she should have done immediately the letter arrived. There could be no question about it. How could she possibly have considered herself worthy of such an honour?

It was with a sense of relief that she took up her pen and began to write:

Dear Sir,
    It is with deep regret …